The
Changeling

BOOKS BY KENZABURO OE FROM GROVE PRESS

The Crazy Iris and Other Stories from the Atomic Aftermath
(editor)
Hiroshima Notes
Nip the Buds, Shoot the Kids
A Personal Matter
A Quiet Life
Rouse Up O Young Men of the New Age!
Somersault
Teach Us to Outgrow Our Madness

The Changeling

Kenzaburo Oe

Translated from the Japanese
by Deborah Boliver Boehm

Grove Press
New York

Published simultaneously in Canada
Printed in the United States of America

FIRST EDITION

ISBN-13: 978-0-8021-1936-0

Grove Press
an imprint of Grove/Atlantic, Inc.
841 Broadway
New York, NY 10003

Distributed by Publishers Group West

www.groveatlantic.com

10 11 12 13   10 9 8 7 6 5 4 3 2 1

Contents

Prologue: The Rules of Tagame   1

Chapter One: One Hundred Days of Quarantine (I)   59

Chapter Two: This Fragile Thing Called Man   109

Chapter Three: Terrorism and Gout   165

Chapter Four: One Hundred Days of Quarantine (II)   221

Chapter Five: Trial by Turtle   267

Chapter Six: The Peeping Toms   317

Epilogue: Outside Over There   389

The
Changeling

PROLOGUE

The Rules of Tagame

1

Kogito was lying on the narrow army cot in his study, his ears enveloped in giant headphones, listening intently. The voice on the tape had just said, "So anyway, that's it for today—I'm going to head over to the Other Side now," when Kogito heard a loud thud. There was silence for a moment, then Goro's voice continued: "But don't worry, I'm not going to stop communicating with you. That's why I made a special point of setting up this system with Tagame and the tapes. Well, I know it's probably getting late on *your* side. Good night!"

The recording ended on this rather vague and unsatisfactory note, and Kogito felt a sudden, excruciating sadness that seemed to rip him apart from his ears to the very depths of his eyes. After lying in that shattered state for a while, he put Tagame back on the nearest bookshelf and tried to go to sleep. Thanks in part to the soporific cold medicine he'd taken earlier, he fell into a shallow doze, but then a slight noise wakened him and he saw his wife's face glimmering palely under the fluorescent lights of the study's slanted ceiling.

"Goro committed suicide," she said softly. "I wanted to go out without waking you, but I was worried that Akari would be frightened by the rush of phone calls from the media." That was how Chikashi broke the news about what had happened to her only brother, Goro, who had been Kogito's close friend since high school. For a few moments Kogito just lay there in disbelieving shock—waiting, irrationally, for Tagame to start slowly vibrating, like a mobile phone receiving an incoming call.

"The police have asked Umeko to identify the body, and I'm going to keep her company," Chikashi added, her voice full of barely controlled emotion.

"I'll go along with you till you meet up with Goro's family, and then I'll come back here alone and deal with the telephone," Kogito said, feeling as if he were paralyzed from head to foot. The avalanche of media calls probably wouldn't begin for a few hours, at least.

Chikashi continued to stand silently beneath the fluorescent lights. She watched attentively as Kogito got out of bed and slowly put on the wool shirt and corduroy trousers that were draped over a chair. (It was the dead of winter.) After Kogito had finished pulling a heavy sweater over his head he said, "Well, then," and without thinking he reached out and grabbed Tagame off the bookshelf.

"Wait a minute," said Chikashi, the voice of reason. "What's the point of taking that thing? It's the cassette recorder you use to listen to the tapes Goro sent you, right? That's exactly the sort of absurd behavior that always infuriates you when somebody else does it."

2

Even in his late fifties, Kogito still took the streetcar to the pool, and he had noticed that he was usually the only person on board with an old-fashioned cassette recorder. Once in a while he would see a middle-aged male listening to a tape and moving his lips, from which Kogito deduced that the man must be practicing English conversation. Until recently, the streetcars had been teeming with crowds of youths listening to music on their Walkmans, but now those same kids were all busy chatting on mobile phones or nimbly typing text messages on the tiny keyboards. Kogito actually felt nostalgic for the days when the tinny cacophony of popular music used to leak out of the young people's ubiquitous headphones, even though it had seemed annoying at the time. Nowadays, Kogito concealed his bulky pre-Walkman recorder in the gym bag with his swimming equipment and wore the oversized headphones clamped around his graying head. At times like that, he couldn't help seeing himself as a lonely, isolated symbol of the generation gap, eating modernity's dust.

The old-fashioned cassette recorder had originally been given to Goro, back in the days when he was still working as an actor, as a perk for appearing in a TV commercial for an electronics company. The recording device itself was just a common rectangular parallelepiped, but while the design of the machine was absolutely ordinary, the shape of the large, black, ear-covering headphones bore a curious resemblance to the giant medieval-armored water beetles known as *tagame*—pronounced "taga-may"—that Kogito used to catch in the mountain streams when he was a boy in the forests of Shikoku. As he told Goro, the first time he tried using the headphones he felt as if, after all this time, he suddenly had a couple of those perpetually useless beetles fastened onto both sides of his head, crushing his skull like a vise.

But Goro said coolly, "That just tells me that you were a kid who couldn't catch anything worthwhile like eels or freshwater trout, so you had to be satisfied with those grotesque bugs. I know it's a little late, but in any case, this is a gift from me to the pitiful little boy you used to be. You can call it Tagame or whatever, and maybe it'll cheer that poor kid up, retroactively."

Goro seemed to think, somehow, that the tape recorder alone wasn't a sufficiently grand gift for Kogito, who was not only an old friend but also his younger sister's husband. That was probably why, along with the cassette recorder, he also gave Kogito a very attractive miniature trunk, made of duralumin—an item that demonstrated Goro's genius for assembling interesting little props, whether to enhance his personal lifestyle or to add atmospheric complexity to one of his films. And in that beguiling minitrunk were twenty-five cassette tapes.

Goro presented Kogito with this quadripartite gift (trunk, tape recorder, headphones, tapes) one evening after they had both attended a sneak preview of one of Goro's films at a large movie theater in downtown Tokyo. Afterward, riding home alone on the train, Kogito stuck one of the cassettes, each of which was identified only by a number stamped on a white label, into Tagame—for he had, in fact, already started to call the machine by the nickname Goro had suggested.

As Kogito was fumbling around, trying to insert the head-phone plug into the appropriate jack, he must have inadvert-ently hit the PLAY button, or perhaps there was a feature that automatically started playback when you inserted a tape. In any case, his fellow passengers in the tightly packed train car looked extremely startled when a loud, brassy-sounding female voice suddenly began to emanate from the vicinity of Kogito's lap. "Aaah!" the woman shrieked through the tiny speaker. "Oh my God! I think my uterus is falling out! Oh, no, I'm gonna come! Oh my God! I'm coming! Aaaaaah!"

As Kogito learned later, that tape was one of twenty simi-larly sensational recordings made by illegal electronic surveil-lance. Goro, who had a taste for such things, had been talked into buying the tapes by a colleague at a certain movie studio, and he had been wondering how to dispose of them. Since he seemed to consider loosening Kogito up to be one of his mis-sions in life, Goro mischievously decided to bequeath the col-lection of "blue tapes" to his bookish brother-in-law.

Earlier in his life, Kogito wouldn't have had the slightest interest in such sordid diversions, but at this particular time he threw himself into listening to the illicit recordings nonstop, over a hundred-day period, with a zeal bordering on mania. As it happened, Kogito was dealing with a rough patch in his life, and he had found himself plunged into an abyss of anxiety and depression. When Goro heard about this from Chikashi, he apparently said, "In that case, maybe he needs a little hair of the dog, so to speak. When you're dealing with humanity in its coarsest, most vulgar form—I'm talking about that scumbag journalist—the best antidote is more of the same." And so it was that when Goro presented Kogito with Tagame, he included a number of clandestinely recorded tapes that showcased the sleazier aspects of human behavior. Kogito heard about Goro's prescription from Chikashi, after the fact, but she remained blissfully ignorant of the contents of the tapes.

Kogito's depression had been brought on by a series of vicious ad hominem attacks on him by the "scumbag journalist" Goro had mentioned, who was the star writer for a major newspaper. Needless to say, the highly personal criticisms of Kogito and his work—attacks that had been going on for more than a decade—were presented as the solemn discharge of the journalist's civic and professional duty.

As long as Kogito was busy reading and working on various writing projects, he didn't think much about his widely published enemy's vendetta against him. But late at night when he suddenly found himself wide awake, or when he was out walking around town on some errand or other, the peculiarly abusive words of his nemesis (who was a talented writer, no question about it) kept running through his head like toxic sludge.

Even though the reporter was known for being meticulous in his newspaper work, when he sat down to compose his poison-pen missives to Kogito he would take dirty-looking, mistake-ridden manuscript pages and smudged faxes of galley proofs, cut them up into small pieces, scribble unpleasant "greetings" on those grubby scraps of recycled paper, and then mail them to Kogito's home address along with copies of the journalist's own books and magazine articles, many of which were obsessively devoted to Kogito-bashing.

In spite of himself, Kogito would immediately commit every word of the loathsome tirades to memory, but whenever it looked as if one of his enemy's vitriolic insults might be about to pollute his brain again, all he had to do to calm himself down—whether he was lying in bed in his study, or out and about in Tokyo—was to don his headphones and listen to the honest voices of "vulgar humanity." As Goro put it, "It's really astonishing the way listening to trashy stuff like that can take your mind off whatever's bothering you."

Fifteen years went by, and one day Kogito was packing for an overseas trip. While he was searching for some of the research materials he needed to take with him, his eyes happened to light on the miniature duralumin trunk tucked away in a corner of his study. Over the years he had turned it into a repository for the libelous books and articles he was constantly receiving from his nemesis, the accursed journalist, but it still held those electronic-eavesdropping tapes as well. What if his plane crashed, and Chikashi happened to listen to those steamy tapes while she was putting his posthumous affairs in order? To avoid that potential catastrophe, he tossed the tapes into the trash and then asked Chikashi to find out whether the little brushed-aluminum trunk was something Goro might like to have returned.

Goro apparently said yes, and so it was that the duralumin trunk found its way back to its original owner. But then, after another two or three years had passed, the same elegant container turned up at Kogito's house again while he was abroad, teaching in Boston. This time it was packed with a batch of thirty or so different cassettes—not lurid audio-surveillance tracks this time, but rather tapes of Goro rambling on about various topics. Goro explained to Chikashi that he would be sending new recordings as soon as he got them finished, with the goal of eventually filling the container to its fifty-tape capacity. When Goro mentioned that the contents were nothing urgent, Chikashi replied jokingly that since Kogito was approaching the age where he could soon begin losing his mental acuity, she might suggest that he save the tapes for his dotage.

But when Kogito returned from the United States and saw the new batch of tapes, he was seized by a vague but insistent premonition and immediately popped one of them into Tagame. As Kogito had suspected, the voice that came booming through the headphones belonged to Goro, and it soon became evident that the purpose of the tapes was to tell the story, in no particular chronological order, of the things that happened to Kogito and Goro after they became friends at school in the Shikoku town of Matsuyama—"Mat'chama," in Goro's idiosyncratic pronunciation.

Goro's way of speaking on the tapes wasn't a monologue, exactly. Rather, it was as if he and Kogito were having an extended conversation on the telephone. Because of this, Kogito soon got into the habit of listening to the tapes before he went to sleep in his study. Lying on his side with the headphones on, he would listen to the recordings while a host of thoughts floated languidly through his mind.

As new tapes continued to arrive at regular intervals, Kogito would listen to each one, and then—almost as if they were having a real-time conversation—he would punctuate Goro's recorded remarks from time to time by pressing the PAUSE button and giving voice to his own opinions. That practice quickly turned into a routine, and before long, even though Goro couldn't hear Kogito's responses, communicating by way of Tagame ended up almost entirely replacing their occasional phone chats.

On the night in question, a few hours before he learned that Goro had plunged to his death from the roof of his production company's office building in a posh section of Tokyo, Kogito was indulging in his customary bedtime ritual: lying in bed listening to the latest tape, which had been delivered by courier earlier that evening. While Goro rambled eloquently along, Kogito would stop the tape whenever the impulse struck him, and interpolate—not so much his own views, anymore, but rather his natural, spontaneous conversational responses to whatever Goro might be saying. What Kogito remembered about that evening's session, in retrospect, is that he was suddenly struck with the idea of buying a tape recorder with editing capabilities, which would allow him to cobble together a third tape that incorporated both sides of his lively and occasionally contentious "dialogues" with Goro.

At one point there was a stretch of silence on the tape, and when Goro began talking again his voice sounded very different. It was immediately clear from his blurry diction that he'd had a few drinks during the break and had forgotten to stop the tape. "So anyway, that's it for today—I'm going to head over to the Other Side now," Goro said, quite casually.

After that declaration, there was a sound that Kogito eventually came to think of as the Terrible Thud. It was the sort of dramatic embellishment you would expect from a high-tech filmmaker like Goro, who was known for his skillful use of sound effects and composite recordings. Only later did Kogito realize that the thud was the kind of noise you might hear when a heavy body fell from a high place and crashed onto the unyielding pavement below: *Ka-thunk.*

"But don't worry," Goro went on, "I'm not going to stop communicating with you. That's why I made a special point of setting up this system with Tagame and the tapes. Well, I know it's probably getting late on *your* side. Good night!" he concluded cheerfully, in a voice that bore no trace of intoxication.

Kogito actually thought, more than once, that maybe that portentous announcement ("I'm going to head over to the Other Side now") was the last thing Goro said before he jumped, intentionally prerecorded to serve as his final words, and the remarks that followed the thud, made by a totally sober-sounding Goro, were the first dispatch from the Other Side, using the Tagame cassette recorder as a sort of interdimensional mobile phone. If that was true, then if Kogito just went on listening to the tapes using the same system, shouldn't he be able to hear Goro's voice from the Other Side? And so he continued his bedtime ritual of chatting with Goro almost every night, via the medium of Tagame, running through the collection of tapes in no particular order—except for the final tape, which he put away in the trunk without bothering to rewind.

3

Kogito and Chikashi arrived at Goro's house in the seaside town of Yugawara just as the body was being brought home from the police station, but Kogito managed to avoid seeing his dead friend's face. There was a small private wake, after which Umeko, Goro's widow (who had starred in many of Goro's films), planned to stay up all night watching videos of Goro's movies with anyone who wanted to join her. Kogito explained that he needed to get back to Tokyo to take care of Akari, their son, who had been left at home alone, and it was decided that Chikashi would stay in Yugawara and attend her brother's cremation the following day.

Glancing toward the coffin, Umeko said, "I could hardly recognize Goro's face when I saw it at the police station, but now he's back to looking like his handsome self again. Please take a peek, and pay your respects."

In response to this, Chikashi said to Kogito, in a quiet but powerful voice, "Actually, I think it would be better if you didn't look."

Meeting Umeko's quizzical eyes, Chikashi returned her sister-in-law's gaze with a look of absolute conviction and candor, overlaid with sadness. Umeko clearly understood, and she stood up and went into the room with the coffin, alone.

Kogito, meanwhile, was thinking about how distant he had felt from Chikashi while she was staring at Umeko with that strong, defiant expression. There was absolutely no trace, in Chikashi's utterly direct look, of the genteel social buffers that usually softened her speech and conduct. *This is the way it is, and there's nothing we can do about it,* Chikashi seemed to be trying to tell herself as well, in the midst of her overwhelming grief and sorrow. *It's fine for Umeko to gaze lovingly at the destroyed face of Goro's corpse and imagine, wishfully, that those dead features have been miraculously restored to their original handsome, animated form. As his sister, I'm doing exactly the same thing. But I think seeing Goro's face would just be too much for Kogito to bear.*

As Chikashi perceptively surmised, the prospect of viewing Goro's dead body filled Kogito with dread, but when Umeko voiced her request he automatically started to stand up. He couldn't help thinking that he would never be mature enough to handle something like this, and he was engulfed by feelings of loneliness and isolation. But he was conscious of another motivation for agreeing to view the corpse, as well: he was curious whether there might be a mark stretching along Goro's cheek that would indicate he had been talking into a Tagame-type headset when he jumped. The impact, Kogito theorized, could have left an imprint that would still be visible now, and he had reason to believe that that scenario wasn't merely his own wild conjecture.

Taruto, who was the head of Goro's production company as well as the CEO of his own family-owned company in Shikoku, had taken on the task of transporting Goro's body to Yugawara, and after the wake he showed the family some things he had found on Goro's desk at the office. Along with three different versions of a suicide note, written on a personal computer, there was a drawing done in soft pencil on high-quality, watermarked drawing paper.

The picture, which was drawn in a style reminiscent of an illustrated book of fairy tales from some unspecified foreign country, showed a late-middle-aged man floating through a sky populated with innumerable clouds that resembled French dinner rolls. The man's position reminded Kogito of the way Akari sprawled out on the floor whenever he was composing music, and this added to Kogito's immediate certainty that the picture was a self-portrait of Goro. Furthermore, the man who was wafting through the air was holding a mobile phone that looked very much like a miniature version of Tagame in his left hand, and talking into it. (Hence, Kogito's suspicion that there might have been a headset mark on Goro's dead face.)

The fairy-tale style of the drawing reminded Kogito of something that had happened fifteen years earlier. Goro had written a book of essays having to do with psychoanalysis, which was one of his many interests. In the past he had always de-signed the covers for his own books, but he was already busy directing movies, so he delegated that task to a young artist. Rather than the contents of the book it was the cover Kogito thought of now, as he looked at Goro's "floating man" picture.

Soon after the book was published, Goro and Kogito hap-pened to run into each other, and they started talking about the

cover design. "This drawing style is clearly emulating that of
the popular illustrator whose work is all over the major magazines in America right now," Kogito remarked. "To be sure, this
composition incorporates Japanese people and scenery, but the
basic concept and techniques are obviously borrowed. For a
young artist beginning his career, is this kind of derivativeness
really okay?" Kogito posed this question in what was meant to
be a lighthearted, teasing way, but Goro's reaction was blatantly
aggressive.

"If you want to talk about openly copying foreign artists,
or being directly influenced by their styles, that's something you
did at the start of your career, too, isn't it?" he snapped. "But
because this is visual art, the derivativeness is much more obvious: what you see is what you get. In your case, you basically
cribbed things from literature written in French or English, or
else from translations, and redid them in Japanese. But even
so, you hewed pretty closely to the original form of the foreign
literary style, right?"

"That's exactly right," Kogito agreed, but he was taken
aback by this rather stark assessment. "When you're a young
writer, you do have something original to say, even at the earliest stages. The trick is figuring out how to protect your original
voice while stripping away the veneer of borrowed styles. That's
very difficult and painful to do."

"And you've definitely succeeded in doing that," Goro
conceded. "But in the process, you've lost the relatively large
readership you used to have when you were younger. You're
aware of that dilemma, no doubt. As time goes on, isn't it just
going to get more and more acute? This young artist has a lot
of talent, and it doesn't look as if he's going to let himself get

set in any narrow stylistic ways. On the contrary, I think he'll probably stretch himself in many different directions."

At the time, Kogito was bewildered by Goro's response, which seemed to stem from some sort of festering ill will rather than from simple irritation at Kogito's offhanded comments. Kogito told himself that Goro probably just felt protective toward the young artist's book cover, which he obviously liked very much. The style of the paintings Goro was trying to create on his own, toward the end of his life, was clearly a postmodern variation on American primitivism—a term that could also have described that young artist's work—so it was possible that Goro had taken Kogito's perceived attack on the young artist as a personal affront.

After a while, it occurred to Kogito that Goro's last drawing might have been meant as a farewell bequest to Kogito himself: a self-portrait of Goro floating through space, talking to his old friend and brother-in-law via his Tagame headset, in lieu of a mobile phone.

So anyway, that's it for today—I'm going to head over to the Other Side now. But don't worry, I'm not going to stop communicating with you.

4

Kogito left the house of mourning in Yugawara and headed for the Japan Railways station, planning to board an express train for Tokyo. But the moment he walked into the station he was besieged by an unruly horde of TV reporters and photographers who had obviously been lying in wait, eager to talk to anyone with the slightest connection to the late Goro Hanawa.

Ignoring the shouted questions, Kogito tried to steer clear of the ring of jostling reporters, but then a rapidly revolving TV camera collided with the lower part of the bridge of his nose, barely missing his right eye. The young cameraman looked at Kogito with an insolent half smile; he might just have been covering up his distress and confusion with a façade of arrogance, but Kogito felt that his facial expression was very crass and inappropriate indeed.

After escaping from the mob scene at the train station, Kogito started walking up a long, narrow lane that had been carved out of a hillside of mandarin orange trees and paved with cobblestones. At the top of the slope he found a taxi and climbed in. The driver must have been acquainted with Goro, because he took one look at Kogito and said, "I guess it's really true what they say about crying tears of blood!" It was only then that Kogito realized that half of his face was covered with blood from the deep cut on his nose.

Even so, he felt that rushing to the nearest emergency room and getting the paperwork to prove that he had been injured, as a way of punishing that arrogant cameraman, would have been an overreaction. Besides, the cameraman was just the inadvertent point man for that seething mass of journalists, with their insatiable collective appetite for tragedy and scandal. In the short time since Goro's death, Kogito had gotten a very distinct impression from all the media people, whether they were with television networks, newspapers, or weekly tabloid magazines. That is, he had noticed that they all seemed to share a kind of contemptuous scorn for anyone who had committed suicide. At the root of that contempt seemed to be the feeling that Goro—who had for years been lionized, lauded, and treated like royalty by the media—had somehow betrayed them, almost on a personal level, and as a result the fallen idol could never again be restored to his previous kingly status.

The tsunami of scorn that had been heaped on Goro's dead body was so vast and so powerful that it ultimately extended even to family members such as Kogito, Chikashi, and Umeko, whom the media referred to, coldly, as "parties with ties to Goro." A female reporter, who had always treated Kogito kindly whenever their paths had crossed at meetings of the book review department of the major newspaper where she worked, left a message on his home answering machine seeking comments for an article she was writing, but even in her innocent voice Kogito could hear an undertone of barely camouflaged contempt for Goro: the "false king" whose torch of power had flickered and gone out once and for all when he decided to jump off a roof.

Kogito came to that realization after his train station confrontation with the young cameraman who had inadvertently wounded him—and barely missed putting out his eye. No doubt the TV station was liable for the accident, but the unfortunate cameraman was just one drop of water in the giant wave of disdain, so what would have been the point of taking legal action against him alone?

This is getting a bit ahead of the story, but for about a week after Goro's suicide, Kogito made a point of watching the *Wide News* program early every morning and again in the evening. Since no one else in his household showed the slightest interest in joining him, he would carry the small TV set into his study and put it at the foot of his bed, then listen to the sound through his Tagame headphones.

Kogito had expected that he might have difficulty understanding the speech of the younger generation—that is, the anchors and reporters on the news shows and the actors (male and female) who had appeared in Goro's films. But he even found it hard to follow the remarks of the film directors and screenwriters, not to mention the commentators from the arts and from the larger world beyond, who were more or less his own age. And the harder Kogito concentrated on trying to understand what all these talking heads were saying, the more incomprehensible their babble became.

He even began to wonder whether, by surrounding himself with beloved, familiar books and writing so often about those same books, he had somehow exiled himself to a solitary island with its own peculiar language. As he did his novelist's work he had assumed that he was somehow connected with other people, but in reality he seemed to have no bond whatsoever with the people living on the continent—the mainland, so to speak—of language. That realization filled him with anxiety and frustration. Nonetheless, he continued to be mesmerized by the televised coverage of Goro's death, straining his eyes to see the images on the screen with the volume on the headphones cranked up as high as he could bear. After this had gone on for a week, though, he knew that it was time to give it up cold turkey. Kogito lugged the TV set back to the living room, then collapsed onto the sofa in exhaustion.

"I was wondering why you were wasting your time on that garbage," Chikashi remarked.

The thing is, Kogito thought, his head was still in such a muddle that he couldn't do much of anything else. Besides, the time wasn't completely wasted. Why? Because during that week of watching the TV news every morning and noon, in addition to the sensationalistic "specials" that were broadcast every second or third night, Kogito had gradually come to realize that Goro's suicide was something that couldn't be explained in the glib words of modern television and that, consequently, the world would never understand why his brilliant, talented friend had decided to jump to his death.

There was another aspect of Goro's wretched, tragic death that tormented Kogito. During the past ten years or so, Kogito hadn't seen much of Goro—that is to say, Goro's tremendous success as a director had stolen the time they might otherwise have spent together—but he knew that Goro had been living in the world of shallow, incomprehensible blather of the sort he'd heard on all those TV programs. The upshot of that, Kogito thought, was that Goro had started talking into a tape recorder and sending the tapes for Kogito to listen to via Tagame. Perhaps that was because, at the end of his life, Goro needed a language that would express his true self.

Around the time when Kogito stopped watching the relentless TV coverage of Goro's death, Chikashi began to be tormented every morning by a different kind of blather: the lurid advertisements that were splashed all over the daily newspaper, touting a never-ending stream of articles about Goro in the weekly tabloid magazines. As if hypnotized by the ads, Chikashi would inadvertently end up buying and bringing home those "women's magazine" scandal sheets, even though reading their ghastly articles just compounded the damage and made her feel even worse. The primary topic of those articles was Goro's relations with women.

In fact, just before Goro jumped off the building he had printed out a farewell note in which he said that this radical act was the only way to *"deny with his whole body,"* because words evidently didn't seem sufficient, the gossip-mongering tabloid magazine article about his "relations with women" that was on the verge of hitting newsstands.

Chikashi never talked about it, but Kogito wasn't convinced by the language of the "suicide note" or by any of the articles about the tragedy. He couldn't find any words, anywhere, that could provide a satisfactory explanation of the death of Goro, who had always been such an extraordinary presence in Kogito's life.

Kogito especially disagreed with the articles that tried to blame Goro's suicide on a minor slump in his filmmaking career.

After winning a major award at a certain film festival in Italy, a Japanese comedian-turned-director, who was heading for America to promote his popular, critically acclaimed film, quipped, "When Goro was looking down from the top of that building, maybe my award gave him a teensy little push from behind." When Kogito read that soul-chilling, stomach-turning comment, he could only think: *Good God, is that the sort of person Goro was forced to associate with?*

Gradually, though, both Kogito and Chikashi became oblivious to the incessant deluge of TV and tabloid coverage. They left the answering machine switched on all the time, and although their primary aim was to escape the constant ringing of the telephone, after a while they didn't even bother to check for messages.

And so they muddled slowly along, somehow. Kogito and Chikashi never once spoke about what had happened to Goro, but each knew that the other was obsessing about Goro's death, and even Akari seemed to sense that his parents thought of little else. Still, they went on paying (or pretending to pay) careful attention to their respective tasks. They lived this way for several months, seldom leaving the house.

Meanwhile, Kogito had developed a new habit—an addiction, really—which he was keeping secret from Chikashi. He had surreptitiously resumed the lively dialogues with Tagame that he had been engaging in, off and on, during the three months preceding Goro's suicide, with the army cot in his study as the staging ground. Only now he was doing it on a more serious and a more regular basis than before—that is to say, daily. Since Goro's suicide, Kogito had started making rules about how these midnight conversations with Tagame were to be conducted, and

he was very conscientious about following those arbitrary regu-
lations to the letter.

Rule Number One: Never mention the fact that Goro has
gone to the Other Side. This was easier said than done, of
course, and at the beginning, whenever Kogito was chatting
away with (or at) Tagame, he was unable to erase Goro's suicide from his mind for even a moment. Before too long, though,
new ideas just naturally began to bubble up. For one thing,
Kogito was intensely curious about the Other Side, where Goro
now resided. In terms of space and time, was it completely different from the world on this side? And when you were there,
looking back across the existential divide, would the very fact
of your death on this side be nullified, as if you had never died
at all?

Before Kogito met Goro at Matsuyama High School, he
had been thinking about what certain philosophers had written about the various types of death perception, but there hadn't
been anyone he could talk to about such things. Not long after
he and Goro became friends, he broached the subject. In those
days—and, now that he thought about it, throughout their long
association—their basic style of communication had been infused with jokiness and wordplay, and they tended to aim for
humorous effect even when they were discussing profoundly
serious matters.

Naturally, it was inevitable that young Kogito would always take a position contrary to those expressed in the rather
staid language of the philosophy books he was reading. To wit:
"It goes without saying that someone who is living in this world
wouldn't be able to talk knowledgeably about his own death,
based on firsthand experience. That's because the essence of

intelligent consciousness ceases to be at the same moment that one's actual existence is coming to an end. In other words, for people who are alive and living, death simply doesn't exist, and by the time they experience it directly they're already beyond cognitive understanding." Kogito began by quoting that argument, which he had read somewhere, and then proceeded to outline his own interpretative variation on the theme.

"Let's say there is such a thing as a human soul, and it's alive, along with the body it inhabits. In my village, there's a folk belief that when someone dies—that is, when a person ceases to exist in a physical form—the soul leaves the body and goes up into the air of the valley, spinning around in a spiral movement, like a tornado. (The valley is shaped rather like the inside of a widemouthed jar, and the soul doesn't venture beyond those confines.) At some point the disembodied spirit reverses its corkscrew trajectory and returns to earth, landing at the base of a tree high up on one of the heavily wooded mountainsides that enclose the valley—not just any old tree, but a specific one that has been selected beforehand by karma, or fate. Then, when the moment is right, the old soul will make its way down to the village and find a home in the body of a newborn baby."

Goro responded to this bit of folklore with an esoteric reference that showcased his own precociously sophisticated store of knowledge. "According to Dante," he declared, "the right way for a human being to climb a mountain is by going around to the right, and if you take the left-hand route you could be making a big mistake. When a spirit spirals from your valley up into the forest, which way is it moving: clockwise or counterclockwise?"

Kogito's grandmother hadn't shared that logistical detail, so instead of giving a straightforward answer Kogito ventured a wild surmise, half in jest: "I guess that would depend on how people used to think about birth and death. If they thought it was *bad* when the soul left an old body and went to the root of a tree, and *good* when that same soul entered into the body of a newborn baby, then I guess the spiral would be clockwise in the case of rebirth and counterclockwise for death."

Then he added, "Seriously, though, if the soul is able to detach itself from the body in that way, then the spirit must not be aware that it's dead. So what dies is just the body, and at the moment when the flesh ceases to be alive the spirit goes its own way. In other words, the spirit goes on living forever, divorced from the body's finite sense of time and space. To tell you the truth, I don't really understand it myself, so I'm just groping around for an explanation. But I think that just as there's infinity and also a single instant in time, and just as the entire cosmos can coexist with a single particle, isn't it possible that when we die we simply move into a different dimension of space and time? If that's the case, then maybe the soul could continue existing in a fourth-dimensional state of innocent bliss, without ever noticing that there's such a thing as death."

And now that giddy, carefree existential conversation they had enjoyed on that day in their youth, having more fun fooling around with the high-flown words than with the actual concepts—now that seemingly abstract scenario had really come to pass. And here was Goro's spirit, lively as ever, talking to Kogito through Tagame as if he truly hadn't noticed that his mortal body had already gone up in smoke.

5

Late that night, on the day after Goro took his leap into the next dimension, Kogito finally made it home with the bloodstained handkerchief still pressed against the TV-camera gash between his eyes. He made dinner for Akari, who had been listening to CDs with the answering machine on and the telephone ringer silenced, and then, after washing his injured face (he kept the light in the bathroom turned off, and didn't even glance at himself in the mirror), Kogito trudged up the stairs to his study.

He took Tagame down from the shelf where he had replaced it in the small hours of the previous night, after being scolded by Chikashi. On the train home, Kogito had had an epiphany about the tape he'd been listening to on Tagame, before last night's strange farewell—namely, Goro's reminiscences about the time he explained one of Rimbaud's poems to Kogito. (It was late that day, around 5 or 6 PM, when a package containing the final tape recording was delivered to Kogito's house, though by that time Goro's body was already in police custody, being held as the unidentified corpse of someone who has met an unnatural death.) In retrospect, after what had happened, that monologue seemed to be rife with hidden meanings.

"When we were in Mat'chama, how well do you suppose we really understood French poetry? After that you went off to college and majored in French literature, but you mainly read prose, as I recall. And since I never made a formal study of the language, I can't really judge our abilities," Goro had said in his usual smooth, flowing voice, with no hint that anything out of the ordinary might be going on in his head. "But I remember that you used to copy the poems out of Hideo Kobayashi's translation of Rimbaud onto hundreds of little pieces of paper and stick them on the wall at your mother's house in the mountains. Rimbaud really had a hold on us, didn't he?"

"That's true," Kogito had replied nostalgically, after pressing the STOP button on the tape recorder. "In those days, all we did was fantasize about the mystical meanings and how they applied to us. But I think that as time went by we were able to refine our understanding of Rimbaud based on scholarly research, wouldn't you agree?" Whereupon he pressed the PLAY button again. And that was how, the night before, Kogito had managed to have a long, antic "chat" with his already deceased brother-in-law about Arthur Rimbaud, the French prodigy poet.

And now, at last, Kogito became aware of just how dense and thick-skulled he had been: Goro had clearly been using a verse of Rimbaud's to say his own good-bye. It couldn't have been more obvious, really. For openers, the poem Goro had been focusing on was "Adieu," or "Farewell": the same poem (as translated by Kobayashi) that Kogito had laboriously copied onto scraps of paper when they were teenagers.

And then Kogito remembered—though he wasn't clear about whether it had been a phone conversation or a face-to-face meeting—that he and Goro had shared a long discussion about the French poet on another occasion. At the time it had been many years since either of them had read any Rimbaud, and Kogito got the impression that Goro, who did most of the talking, was conjuring up the lines of poetry from the dim and distant recesses of his memory.

Inspired by that conversation, Kogito had rounded up and read several new translations of Rimbaud's poetry. (By that time, almost every French-Japanese translator had published a Rimbaud translation.) Kogito ended up choosing Hitoshi Usami's recent translation to send to Goro, after checking the Usami version not only against Hideo Kobayashi's seminal translation but also against the original French text.

Among the pile of cassette tapes that Goro had sent, there was one in which Goro responded to Kogito's gift of the Usami translation with a long discourse about Rimbaud. After Kogito had listened to that tape again, he went to the section of a bookcase where he kept the French books he had collected during his student days and took down several works, old and new, pertaining to Rimbaud.

On one shelf, a Pléiade edition of Rimbaud's *Collected Works* stood next to a Mercure de France edition of *Poésies;* the latter (a present to Kogito from Goro when they were still in high school) had been Kogito's first introduction to the French language. For the first time in many years, Kogito opened *Poésies.*

He could still remember how his heart had leapt when Goro handed him that little book with the exotic red letters on the cover. There, in the margins, were the minuscule but clearly legible notations he had made as a seventeen-year-old school-boy, written in hard lead pencil.

The reason some of the notes were in English was because before Goro started teaching him French, the book that Kogito had consulted in the library of Matsuyama's American-run Center for Cultural Information and Education (CIE for short) was the Oxford French-English dictionary. In addition, the pages bore two different kinds of annotations in Japanese. The notes in the angular *katakana* syllabary were used to flag what Kogito perceived as the salient points in Goro's discourses. He used the *katakana* in imitation of, or homage to, the marginal printed musings in a collection of essays by Goro's famous film-director father, which Goro had lent him.

Kogito's own schoolboy thoughts (not shown here) were written in the flowing, cursive *hiragana* syllabary, to differentiate them from his notes on Goro's impromptu lectures, which tended to run along these lines:

> In a letter to his teacher, as well as in the poem itself, Rimbaud wrote that he was about to turn seventeen: that is to say, an age that's filled with daydreams and fanta-sies. But it's said that the poem in question, "Romance," was actually written when Rimbaud was fifteen. In other words, when he wrote the line "One isn't serious at sev-enteen," he was misrepresenting his own age.
>
> Even so, this poem is meant to be read by someone who's exactly the age you are now, Kogito: the same age

I was last year, when I read it for the first time. The great
thing is that this absolute genius, Arthur Rimbaud, offers equal encouragement to ordinary humans like us, too.

Kogito was surprised that a gifted youth like Goro, who
anyone could see was seriously brilliant and abundantly talented, would liken himself—and, with exceptional honesty,
Kogito, as well—to ordinary people.

As Kogito was reading "Adieu" in the Pléiade edition, he
was once again seized by an urgent thought. Before Goro's suicide, when he was holding forth about that poem on one of
his tapes and quoting certain lines from it, he obviously had
the new translation that Kogito had sent open in front of him.
Wasn't Goro assuming that for Kogito, too, the entire poem
would immediately be brought to mind by reciting a few
lines? Kogito didn't have a ready answer for that question,
then or now.

Even with the new translation that he had urged upon
Goro, Kogito didn't feel the same sort of passionate emotional
attachment to Rimbaud's words as when he was young and used
to memorize the poems by writing them out, line by line. Kogito
had sensed a similar kind of divergence in their infrequent
encounters during recent years. Could that be the reason why
Goro had ultimately despaired of Kogito's dependability and had
decided to head off into the realm of the Terrible Thud, alone?

"Autumn already!—But why regret the everlasting sun, if
we are sworn to a search for divine brightness, far from those
who die as seasons turn."

Kogito didn't own a copy of the Usami translation that
Goro was quoting from on the Tagame tape, but as he was

jotting down a quick transcription he remembered that this opening-paragraph stanza was the same one that had first enthralled him, in Kobayashi's translation, when he was a seventeen-year-old high-school student. Goro seemed to have had a strong response to those lines, as well. But wasn't Goro, in choosing to die of his own free will, patterning himself after those who were "sworn to a search for divine brightness"? Wasn't he, somehow, just mimicking "far from those who die as seasons turn"?

Moreover, in the next stanza, there was the image of a dead body swarming with maggots. How did that make Goro feel, on the threshold of his own death? This poem, which was teeming with what Rimbaud called "dreadful imagining"—why did Goro feel compelled to go on about it at such length on the tape? Kogito couldn't help wondering about that. It even occurred to him that Goro might have deliberately chosen to hurl those very specific, very horrific words at Kogito and, by extension, at himself.

"Ha! I have to bury my imagination and my memories! What an end to a splendid career as an artist and storyteller!" And then, in the next stanza: "Well, I shall ask forgiveness for having lived on lies. And that's that. But not one friendly hand! and where can I look for help?"

The topic of lies was a major element in the continuing criticism of Kogito that Goro had recorded on the Tagame tapes. Was Goro giving up on finding "one friendly hand," too? *If that was the case* . . . Kogito couldn't stop voicing this question to himself, even though he was fed up with his own endless, obsessive stewing about it. Anyway, if that was the case, as Goro was preparing to ring down the curtain on the final act of a long friendship (albeit one that had clearly grown distant in recent years), why did he give Kogito the Tagame apparatus for the second time and then follow up by sending a slew of long, fervent monologues, recorded on tape for Kogito's ears only?

As he continued reading the poem, all the way to the final stanza, the passage that filled Kogito with nostalgic yearning was the one he and Goro had been most taken with when they were in high school. It was this line: "And at dawn, armed with glowing patience, we will enter the cities of glory." But what sort of meaning could he and Goro, in their extreme youth and inexperience, have been reading into the phrase "cities of glory"? Again, while they certainly found encouragement and inspiration in the concluding line ("and I will be able now to possess the truth within one body and one soul"), what on earth did that have to do with their everyday schoolboy lives on earth? And if Goro happened to be pondering that passage just before he took the final leap into space, what vision of his own future did he see in those words?

In truth, it was always quite a while after the conclusion of each of his Tagame sessions with Goro before Kogito was able to think about the contents of their "discussion" in this sort of lucid, analytical way. Then on the following night, when he once again hit the PLAY button, the quotidian things that had been occupying Kogito's midday mind would recede into the distance as the strangely live-sounding words poured out of the diminutive speakers, like a real-time, real-space dispatch from the mysterious dimension where Goro now dwelled. Kogito would immediately fall under the spell of Goro's words, and eagerly pressing the STOP button, he would launch into a spirited reply.

Whatever Goro may have said about his reasons for recording the tapes, the fact was that he used them primarily as a
forum for continuous rants about Kogito's myriad flaws, faults,
and shortcomings. When Kogito thought about it later, he realized that it must have been the urgency in his own voice, when
he was lying on his army cot trying to defend himself against
Goro's attacks, that had made Chikashi decide it was time to
have a candid talk about Kogito's growing addiction to the
Tagame ritual.

6

Of course, Kogito was always the one who started the conversations with Tagame, but sometimes, just before he pressed the PLAY button, he had the uncanny feeling that the chunky little tape recorder was actually psyching itself up for the next round of combat. For some reason this made Kogito think about the way the real *tagames*—the large, oddly shaped water beetles that lived in the mountain streams of Shikoku—must have amorously bestirred themselves, almost in slow motion, during mating season. All these years later, that image (which may have been pure conjecture) was perfectly sharp and vivid in Kogito's mind.

Kogito always left the tape cued up at the end of the previous night's conversation, and whenever Kogito picked Tagame up he always felt as if he were answering an incoming call on the ultimate long-distance mobile phone. And the moment Goro's voice began to speak, with its distinctive Kyoto/Matsuyama accent, Kogito was repeatedly struck by the fact that whatever the topic might turn out to be, it always seemed to be uncannily relevant to his current situation.

Another odd thing was that when he started talking to Tagame, Kogito was far more enthusiastic than he had been about any other kind of discussion with Goro during the past twenty years or so. There was something engaging about Goro's relaxed way of talking across the vaporous border that separated the Other Side from the land of the living—despite the fact that his comments often consisted of merciless, searing criticism of Kogito—and even though Kogito was completely aware that Goro was dead, the intensity of their exchanges somehow seemed to overshadow that disturbing fact.

Kogito also felt that he had been forced to take another look at his feelings about his own inevitable death, so naturally there were times when the conversations evoked newly urgent thoughts about what really happens after we die. He could imagine himself, in the not-so-distant future, traveling to the Other Side with an upgraded, afterlife-appropriate version of Tagame and earnestly awaiting a dispatch from this side. When he thought that there might be no answer to his Tagame signals, for all eternity, he felt such a deep sense of loneliness and desolation that his entire being seemed to be disintegrating.

At the same time, it was only natural for him to feel that the impassioned "conversations" he was carrying on with Tagame, all by himself, were nothing but an escapist diversion, a self-deluding mind game. As a novelist who'd grown partial to the literary theories espoused by Mikhail Bakhtin, Kogito had started to take the concept of "playing games" very seriously after crossing the threshold into middle age. Consequently, he knew very well that even if talking with Goro via Tagame was a mere diversion, as long as he was acting on that fantasy stage there was nothing to do but throw himself into the part with all his heart.

Furthermore, Kogito resolved that during the day, while he was separated from Tagame, he wouldn't allow his nocturnal conversations with Goro to seep into his daily experiences. And when he was talking about Goro with Chikashi, or with Umeko, or with Taruto, Kogito made every effort not to recall the conversations with Goro that flowed through Tagame.

In this way, Kogito constructed a barrier between the two types of time—real time and Tagame time—and while he was moving around in one zone he wouldn't permit the other to spill over into it, or vice versa. But whichever zone he happened to be inhabiting, he never denied, at least not to his innermost self, the truth or the reality of what he had experienced in the other realm. From his vantage point on the earthly, conscious side, he firmly believed in the existence of the Other Side, and that belief made the world on this side seem infinitely deeper and richer. Even if his Tagame adventure was nothing but a dream, he still embraced it as a positive experience.

Suppose one of Kogito's friends had said something like: "Okay, so Goro committed suicide by jumping off the roof of a building, and his body, including the brain inside his head, was cremated, but his spirit or soul or whatever you want to call it—anyway, that entity continues to exist somewhere, even now. That's what you believe, right?"

If this hypothetical friend phrased the question in that serious kind of way (and if he was a moody type anyway but was smiling as he asked it) then everything would be fine. In that case Kogito, after pondering the matter for a moment, would probably reply while wearing an opaque, noncommittal expression, since like most people his age he had long since become a master of the poker face and the social smile.

"That's true," he might say, "only with some conditions attached. While I'm listening to his voice on Tagame, Goro's soul—that is to say, by my definition, a spirit furnished with something that's invisible yet is extremely close to having physical form, like what they call an etheric double or an astral body—anyway, yes, I do believe that Goro's soul really exists in that state. It's different than if I were just playing back a tape recording of his voice. What Goro left in place for me is a very special system. To be sure, his soul has made the transition into a space that's different from this space that you and I still inhabit. But it just so happens that Tagame is a conduit between this space and that one. That's how it works."

The hypothetical friend is still skeptical. "But when you and Goro aren't having one of your Tagame talks, what form does he take on the Other Side?" he asks. "Wait, let me rephrase that. When Tagame isn't connecting you to the Goro *beyond* Tagame, how does Goro exist in relation to you?"

"To tell you the truth," Kogito would be forced to admit, "when we aren't talking on Tagame, I really can't think very clearly about Goro."

"So the machine you call Tagame acts as an intermediary and makes Goro's spirit a reality for you. In that case, I guess you can't reduce it to the more general question of whether a person's soul exists after death."

"That's right, although the conversations I have with Goro, through Tagame, have also changed the way I think about my own death. As for the deaths of my mentor, Professor Musumi, who did so much for me when I was at university and afterward as well, and my old friend Takamura, the composer, I now believe that there must be a way to communicate with their departed spirits, too, wherever they may be. I don't happen to have a conduit to Professor Musumi or Takamura, but I like to think that there are people out there who have their own versions of Tagame and are using them to talk to the souls of those two, beyond the grave."

While Kogito was carrying on this sort of imaginary conversation, why didn't he think about the possibility of another Tagame system to keep Goro connected with his sister, Chikashi? (Never mind that Kogito's posthumous conversations with Goro were the direct cause of the tremendous strain on his own relationship with Chikashi.) Perhaps it was because Kogito was conscious that his Tagame chats with Goro were his own private realm. Besides, Chikashi was a remarkably self-reliant person, independent from Kogito and from Goro, as well; not at all the type, Kogito thought, who would be drawn into that kind of fantasy game. And surely Goro must have been thinking along the same lines.

One year, Kogito was invited to speak at Kyushu University. While he was in the Green Room waiting for his lecture to begin, he happened to glance at a timetable and discovered that if he skipped the banquet with the other participants and hopped on the next ferryboat to Shikoku, then transferred to a Japan Railways train, he could be back at his childhood home, deep in the forest, before the night was over. He asked the assistant professor who was looking after him to make the travel arrangements, and the tickets were purchased while Kogito was delivering his lecture.

By the time Kogito made his way to the house where he was born, it was after 11 PM and his mother had already gone to sleep. The next morning, Kogito was up early. When he

peered down the covered passageway that led to an adjoining
bungalow, he could see the silhouette of his naked mother, illuminated by the reflected river-dazzle that leaked into the dark
parlor through the gaps in the wooden rain shutters. Backlit like
that, Kogito's elderly mother looked like a young girl as (with
the help of her sister-in-law) she twined the turban she always
wore in public around her head. At that moment, his mother
didn't seem to belong entirely to this world; it was as if she had
already begun to make the transition over to the Other Side.
Her abnormally large ear, which resembled a fish's dorsal fin,
was hanging down from her emaciated profile, almost as if that
misshapen appendage itself was absorbed in deep meditation.

Later, when they were sitting across from each other at
the breakfast table, Kogito's mother began to speak in the local
Iyo dialect, which tends to feature more exclamatory sentences
than standard Japanese. "I've been praying for a chance to see
you since the beginning of last spring, Kogito!" she began. (It
was already fall.) "And now that you're sitting here, I still half
feel as if it's my fantasy eating breakfast in front of me. It doesn't
help that I can barely hear what you're saying—of course, I've
gotten quite deaf, and on top of that you still don't open your
mouth wide enough when you speak, just like when you were
a child!

"But anyway, right now I feel as if this is half reality and
half fanciful daydream! Besides, lately, no matter what's going
on, I'm never entirely certain that it's really happening! When
I was wishing that I could see you, it almost seemed as though
half of you was already here. At times like that, if I voiced my
opinions to you out loud, the other people in the house would
just laugh indulgently. However, if you happened to be on tele-

vision talking about something and I said to the TV set, 'You're wrong about that, you know,' even my great-grandchild would jump in and try to stop me, saying, 'That's rude to Uncle Kogito.' They think it's amusing when I talk to an invisible person, but isn't the television itself a kind of fantastical illusion? Just because there's no machine attached to my private hallucinations, does that make them any less 'real' than the images on TV? I mean, what's the basis for that kind of thinking?

"Anyway, it seems as if almost everything is already an apparition to me, you know? Everyday life seems like television, and I can't tell whether somebody is really here with me or not. I'm surrounded by apparitions. One day soon I, too, will stop being real, and I'll become nothing more than a phantasm myself! But this valley has always been swarming with specters, so I may not even notice when I make the shift over to the Other Side."

After Kogito finished his breakfast, his younger sister gave him a ride to Matsuyama Airport so he could catch a plane that left before noon. When his sister called Chikashi in Tokyo to report that Kogito's departure had gone according to plan, she added, "As Mother was nodding off after breakfast, she said, 'A little while ago I saw an apparition of Kogito, and we had a nice chat.'"

When he heard this story later, Kogito felt unexpectedly moved by his mother's remark. After committing suicide, Goro hadn't really noticed that he'd left this world and become a spirit on the Other Side, had he? When he thought about it that way, Kogito came to see the fluidity between the two dimensions as a positive thing—especially late at night, after he'd been talking to Goro through the magical medium of Tagame.

7

During Kogito's Tagame sessions with Goro, he noticed that things got livelier, and he was able to enter more spontaneously into the discussion, when Goro began reminiscing about their early student days in Matsuyama. At times like that, Kogito could ignore the Terrible Thud (his private shorthand for Goro's baffling suicide). If he didn't have to worry that the conversation might end up being about the future, he was able to follow the rules he'd set up, to the letter. Conversely, whenever a dialogue concluded with a mention of future plans, the Rules of Tagame could be thrown into disarray.

On one cassette tape, Goro was trying to reconstruct the details of a conversation that had taken place when he and Kogito were both in their twenties. "Remember when we were talking about how, once upon a time, there used to be some truly great writers? And I was wondering whether really major, transcendent writers like that still exist in the world—and if so, are any of them Japanese? That was the gist of the discussion, and we even made a list of candidates. After a bit I revised the question and changed it to this: *I wonder whether, in the near future, we'll get to see a truly great author who writes in Japanese?* You were doubtful, as I recall."

Whereupon Kogito pressed the STOP button and said, "I still am."

"To be perfectly frank," Goro went on, "at that point you weren't thinking of yourself as someone who had the potential to become a truly great writer. I remember you confessed to me, soon after we met, that you had always thought of yourself as an ordinary person who in all likelihood was never going to come up with any extraordinary ideas. But then you told me about how you entered the All-Japan Young Inventors Competition, and that was very entertaining. However, you weren't the one who broached the subject—I had to coax the story out of you—and you told it in a typically self-deprecating way. And so, in an attempt to force you to talk more about that sort of thing, I set a trap."

Kogito pressed the STOP button again and chimed in: "Of course I remember, but I always wondered—what made you do that? You really were tremendously zealous about trying to convince me I wasn't ordinary."

"The first thing I did was to make you realize that Kafka was a truly great writer—a genius," Goro continued. "I also talked about how Kafka's fellow writer Max Brod (himself an up-and-coming author in those days, albeit a rather commonplace one) must have felt when he realized that his then-unknown friend was, unquestionably, a genius. The efforts that Brod made after Kafka's death to bring his late friend's works the recognition they deserved—that's another story entirely.

"Then after you started writing novels, when you fell into your first slump, as they say, I dredged up that subject again. I told you that nowadays (that is, in modern-day Japan), if you can't become a truly great writer, then writing novels and such is simply a waste of your life. At that point you'd been a successful writer for more than a year, and you had already won the Akutagawa Prize, but it looked to me as if you were settling into an overly cozy and comfortable place in the literary world. That's when I told you that I thought you ought to take a break from what you'd been doing thus far and start over again, fresh—shake things up a bit. From then on, if you'd laid low for two or three years and hadn't published any new fiction of your own, the journalists and the literary magazines and the reading public would probably have forgotten all about you. And that, to my way of thinking, is where the process of becoming a truly great writer would begin.

"In those days, you always had plenty of energy for studying and doing research, and whether you were writing a novel or an essay, you seemed to be able to make clever use of a variety of literary styles if you just put your mind to it. But it was because of that very versatility that you were suffering, don't you think? You used to say that even though you were still young, as a writer striving for originality you wanted to come up with your own themes and create your own distinctive prose style, and then combine those two elements. You wanted to make the world recognize you as an author who possessed that kind of originality, but you found those tasks daunting, and as you yourself put it, you tended to lose confidence and chicken out.

"As for me, I came up with an elaborate idea for a literary hoax, which I approached as I would a screenplay, although I

never actually wrote it up. The idea was that the protagonist—
in this case, a writer—would be someone who had hit upon an
original concept at a young age, and he would devote his entire
career to delving ever deeper into that particular notion. (For
today's young writers, finding an overarching theme and creating a coherent body of work seems to be the hardest task of all,
but with my method you wouldn't need to be the literary equivalent of a wandering monk, searching for enlightenment or struggling to find your 'voice.') Anyway, I subjected you to a long
harangue about how this would be the ideal game plan for a versatile type like you, who has the gift of fluent composition and a
serious penchant for research as well. Do you remember?"

Kogito remembered that conversation very well, indeed.
After hitting the STOP button, he leaned back and lost himself
in leisurely reminiscence.

Goro's tongue-in-cheek idea went like this: First, Kogito
would invent a fascinating but completely nonexistent writer.
Next, he would pretend to pay a visit to the urban hermitage
where the aging author supposedly lived as a voluntarily unpublished recluse. (When Goro initially described this fic-
tional personage, Kogito immediately visualized a certain
mid-twentieth-century surrealist poet—at that time, already
an old man.) After pretending to conduct an interview with the
imaginary writer, Kogito would write up their "conversation" as
a powerful article for some literary journal.

The article would probably attract a fair amount of attention. After that, Kogito would introduce some of the nonexistent writer's "never-published prose" in the form of selected
excerpts, all secretly composed by Kogito himself. And then,
even though the publicity-shy author was exceedingly reluctant

to open up, through sheer tenacity Kogito would manage to eke out some more articles in the form of notes on their subsequent "conversations." At some point Kogito would gather these fraudulent materials together and publish them in the form of a grandiosely titled book about the "cloistered writer," which would offer a comprehensive assessment of the phantom's purported oeuvre.

The basic story line would be that both before and after the war this impeccably modern writer, who was always ahead of his time, went on writing in his hideaway, following his private vision. Inevitably, after hearing so much about the elusive author from Kogito, both the media and readers in general would become intensely interested in the make-believe writer's work. Needless to say, for the plan to succeed, Kogito would need to write some exceptionally strong and convincing literary criticism.

Was such a charade really feasible? Goro laid out a concrete plan that showed how it could be made to happen, but Kogito thought that converting the blithe blueprint into a work of art by stringing words together, one by one, would be the difficult part. After all, how many talented young writers, their heads full of revolutionary ideas, have ended up failing or giving up in frustration? Even so, Goro argued, for a voracious reader like Kogito—someone who had extraordinary powers of recollection and whose mind was perpetually awhirl with curious fancies—it should be a piece of cake to introduce the phantom writer's work to a wider audience via literary criticism, once Kogito had managed to whip up some samples.

Moreover, as the plan progressed, Kogito would probably get the urge to try creating some of the hermit author's full-length work, as well. All the preliminary work he had done in the process of perpetrating this complex literary masquerade— composing excerpts, transcribing pseudo-interviews, penning literary criticism—would be invaluable when he actually started writing a novel to be published under the phantom's name, since he would have become intimately familiar with the imaginary master's prose style and essential themes and would have a clear idea of how to develop them further.

So the literary hoax would chug along, and when it came time to publish another book of criticism and interpretation, more and more people would probably join the chorus of commenters on the illusory writer's work. Of course, from the beginning the one who was leading the critical charge would be Kogito, writing under a variety of clever pseudonyms, and in the course of pursuing this plan over a period of twenty years or more, his own reputation as a fiction writer would be en- tirely erased by the faux-journalistic process. After that there would be nothing to do but to keep cranking out the backlist of the mysterious writer, while vicariously enjoying his in- vented protégé's success.

Kogito Choko, as a writer of his own original books, would eventually cease to exist in the public mind, and all that would remain was the great writer whose "rediscovery" he had or- chestrated by easy, leisurely stages. And then after a little more time had passed, when the imaginary master finally "died," his previously unpublished work would be brought forth posthu- mously, like water pouring out of a broken dam. And the re- clusive writer (whom no one had ever laid eyes on) would be remembered as a truly great artist—maybe even a Japanese Kafka.

"We really got into the story of that mythical writer, didn't we, Kogito?" Goro chuckled. "It was just when Borges's work was being introduced in Japanese translation for the first time, and we were thrilled to find someone else who thought the way we did. And then, before long, you dug up English translations of the writers who were persecuted by Stalin: Bulgakov, Bely, and so on. In a way, I almost felt as if we were growing old along with our great imaginary *littérateur!*" Then Goro added something that made Kogito feel that his friend had come dangerously close to crossing the line as far as the Rules of Tagame were concerned.

Rule Number Two: Never, ever speak about plans for the future.

"This is what I want to say to you, Kogito," Goro announced. "Right now you're already older than the phantom writer was when you and he first 'met.' From here on, isn't it time for you to gird your literary loins and try to make one last creative leap, to ensure that you yourself will be remembered as a unique writer, at least? (I won't go so far as to say 'great.') I'm hoping that the words that are pouring out of Tagame right now will somehow prime the pump and get you fired up. In your own past—or rather, in the past we share—surely there's a rich vein of experience that hasn't yet been mined?"

One day during the period when Kogito was indulging in long, intense Tagame dialogues (including the one above) on a nightly basis, Chikashi cornered him and, typically, burst out with a torrent of words that had obviously been germinating in her mind for quite a while.

"After all this time," she began, "when I hear you carrying on in your study every evening into the wee hours, complaining to Goro and then seeming to strain your ears for a response,

I can't help wondering whether this isn't exactly the sort of 'absurdity' you dislike so much. I don't see what good can possibly come of indulging in this sort of charade night after night, and I'm really at my wits' end. Every time I hear you talking so impassionedly to Goro I can sense that you're waiting for a reply, and I know it must be terribly painful for you. I sympathize completely, and I truly do feel sorry for you. It's the same as if by some chance you suddenly died in an accident or something—I think about how puzzled and devastated Akari would be and how sorry I'd feel for him. It isn't that I think you're doing these late-night séances as a way of gearing up for your own journey to the Other Side, but still . . .

"In any case, because your study is right above our bedrooms, it's really hard on us when your voice comes floating down. It's a bit like water dripping slowly through a bamboo strainer, and I think it's probably bothering Akari even more than me. No matter how low you keep your voice, and even when it's obvious that you're just listening to Goro's tapes on your headphones, I don't think it's possible for Akari to simply ignore what's going on. So I'm just wondering whether you might be willing to put an end to your sessions, for us?"

And then while Kogito watched, appalled, Chikashi unexpectedly began to cry. He had no choice but to admit that for these past few months he had been so engrossed in living by the Rules of Tagame that he had forgotten there were rules about living as part of a family, too. On another level, he had been startled by the aside Chikashi had tossed out in the middle of her speech: *It isn't that I think you're doing these late-night séances as a way of gearing up for your own journey to the Other Side, but still* . . .

8

"But I just can't do that!" Kogito wailed. He was alone in his study, lying facedown on his army cot with the sheets pulled tightly over his head, talking to himself. "I know my behavior has been shameful—getting so immersed in Tagame to the point where it's become a kind of crazy obsession. But there's another person involved in this. I can't very well just announce, unilaterally, 'Sorry, pal, it's over.' Think about poor Goro, all alone on the Other Side. How terrible would that be for him?"

Without getting up, Kogito quickly turned over and thrust his head into the darkness next to the bed. Years ago, one of his former college classmates had been admitted to the hospital with leukemia and had thrashed around on the bed so violently that, as the man's wife confided in Kogito, they were afraid he might end up bursting a blood vessel in his head. (And the fact that the doctors had chosen to conceal the true diagnosis from the patient had probably amplified his anxiety.) But maybe that desperate behavior—that sort of secret, private struggle—

was just a reflection of the buttoned-up attitude toward life shared by the men of Kogito's generation.

Kogito got up, switched on the light, and pulled the dur-alumin trunk out from under the bed. He had just remembered something Goro had said on one of the tapes, and now, using his own topical annotations on the labels as a guide, he found the tape in question, popped it into Tagame, and hastily cued up the relevant passage. Then, as if urged on by the slow, whir-ring vibration of the tape recorder, he gave a decisive nod and pressed the PLAY button.

"Of course, you're always like this," Goro's voice began, ragging on Kogito right out of the gate. "But from what I hear these days, true to form, you've been acting like a mouse trapped in a bag. When you get right down to it, you've brought all your suffering on yourself, and now you're floundering around help-lessly. Chikashi's been complaining to me, you know," Goro went on. "She says that same big-shot scumbag journalist has been denouncing you again, in the nastiest, most contemptible way, making a point of saying things like 'Of course I don't read that guy's novels, but I've heard from some young people that he's been putting me in his books, as a villain.' That so-called journalist even published a showy, slanderous book exploiting the fact that you won a major international award. That ven-detta has already been dragging on for twenty-five years now—don't you think it's time for you to let it go?

"Lately you've been in pretty low spirits, and you've brought Chikashi and Akari down as well. There's no way you can say that's a good thing. Even without having to cope with a depressed husband, Chikashi is someone who's experienced more than her share of hard times. When the busybodies say that your family appears to have a pretty cushy life, you should just reply that the pleasant things pass soon enough, as if they'd never happened, but the painful experiences tend to linger on for a long, long time.

"The sort of person who's forever reveling in every little delight with an excessive, borderline-abnormal kind of euphoria, and who does nothing but cling to those lovely airbrushed memories—that, in my opinion, is a thoroughly unhappy and unfortunate person. Chikashi has been through far too much suffering already, but in spite of that she has never turned into the sort of weak person who's always longing to return to happier days. Don't you agree?

"Anyway, I've been thinking about your situation, and I was wondering—how would it be if you took a little breather and left town for a while? You've been toiling away at the novelist's life for all these years, and I really think you could use some quarantine time right about now. I think if you just got away from your novels for a while . . . If you left for good it would be rough on Chikashi and Akari, that's why I say 'for a while.' What I mean is, you need to impose a quarantine on yourself and take a break from the sort of life where you're being confronted by the distressing gutter journalism of this country on a daily basis."

"Give me a minute to check something in the dictionary," Kogito replied. "When you first mentioned this, some time ago, I had a passing familiarity with the word *quarantine,* so I didn't take the time to look it up and find out exactly what it meant. But the word hasn't taken root in my mind to the point where I would actually use it."

After pressing the PAUSE button, Kogito brought out one of his dictionaries and flipped the pages until he found what he was looking for:

quarantine (kwor-ān-teen) *n*. 1. A state, period, or place
of isolation in which people or animals that have arrived
from elsewhere or been exposed to infectious or conta-
gious diseases are placed. *v*. [with object] to put a person or animal in quarantine. 2. *n*. The period of this
isolation. Origin: mid-seventeenth century, from Italian
*quarantin*a, "forty days," from *quaranta,* "forty."

After he had finished reading the definitions, Kogito turned back
to Tagame, making an effort to keep his voice as low as possible
while simultaneously striving to pronounce every word with perfect clarity. "Listen, Goro," he said, before pressing the PLAY button again. "I know you're using this word to try to advance a certain
agenda, and I understand exactly what you're driving at."

"Of course, it doesn't have to be exactly forty days," responded Goro's recorded voice. "You might have a chance to
stay away longer. But what do you think about Berlin as a temporary haven, to put some distance between you and that journalist? (On the bright side, *he* isn't getting any younger, either!)
For me, at least, Berlin is an unforgettable place. If someone
asked me what connection that city might have with your self-
imposed quarantine, I couldn't say exactly, but. . . ."

"Berlin, eh? Now that you mention it, I did receive an
invitation to go there, for considerably longer than forty days!"
Kogito exclaimed, hearing the surprise and excitement in his
own voice, which had grown suddenly loud as he momentarily
forgot about the need to whisper. "I'll check now, but I think
the offer's still good."

Whereupon Kogito stopped the tape and went to his study
to look for the file in question. S. Fischer Verlag, the publisher

who had put out the first German translations of Kogito's early novels, was still doing so, even though sales weren't what they used to be. Every few years—or, more usually, every ten or twelve years—a new translation of one of Kogito's novels would come out in hardcover, but as a rule the subsequent printings would be in paperback. Whenever Kogito gave readings at places such as the Frankfurt Book Fair or cultural associations in Hamburg and Munich, there would be a book signing afterward, where they were always able to sell quite a few of the colorful, beautifully designed paperbacks of his work. And now he had been offered a lectureship at the Berlin Free University to commemorate S. Fischer, the founder of the eponymous publishing house. The course was to begin in the middle of November, so he still had time to accept. The department's offer was generous, and they even said that they would keep the slot open for him through the first half of the term.

By the time he climbed back into bed, Kogito had dug up the most recent fax from a secretary in S. Fischer Verlag's editorial division and learned that he still had three days to let them know whether he wanted to accept the position of guest lecturer at the Free University. To his own amazement, in a matter of a few minutes he had made up his mind to take Goro's rather drastic advice and get out of town for a while.

The tape on which Goro suggested a "quarantine" had been recorded several months earlier, but now his casual suggestion had become a necessity, for a different reason: namely, Kogito's need to pull himself together and get over his addiction to talking to Goro through Tagame. Even after Chikashi's heartfelt complaint earlier that evening, Kogito hadn't been able to leave the tape recorder on the bookshelf for even this one night. And, as it turned out, it was Goro, his Tagame partner, who had dropped the hint that had galvanized him into positive action. Somehow, mixed in with his decision to make a bold move, Kogito felt a resurgence of his old dependence on Goro.

He was just about to ask, "What's going to become of our sessions with Tagame?" But then, without pressing the PLAY button, he answered his own question. Or, to put it more precisely, he consciously crafted a response along the lines of what he thought Goro might have said in real life. *That's for you to decide. But when Chikashi criticized your behavior last night, rather than any annoyance or inconvenience to her and Akari, she was probably more concerned about finding a way to free you from your addiction to our Tagame sessions, don't you think?*

Nevertheless, right up until the night before he was scheduled to leave for wintry Berlin, Kogito was unable to give up his nightly ritual of talking to Goro by way of Tagame—although he did, at least, make every effort to keep his voice low. The thing was, when he told Chikashi the next day about his decision to go into Tagame-free quarantine in Berlin, she naturally interpreted this action as a direct response to her request: a way for Kogito to take a break from his "séances" with Goro. That being the case, no matter how much he lowered his voice Chikashi was probably still aware that the conversations were continuing, but because the end was in sight her silence on the matter seemed to constitute a sort of tacit approval or at least forbearance.

Then one morning, as Kogito's departure date was rapidly approaching, Chikashi (who had been busying herself every evening with packing and repacking his trunk) said: "Last night I felt like going through Goro's letters, and I came across a watercolor painting that he sent from Berlin. Would you like to see it? It's a landscape, on lovely paper. It's actually drawn with colored pencils, then blurred with a wet brush so it ends up looking like a watercolor. The painting seems to have a really buoyant, happy feeling. On the back is written 'This morning is the only day that's been this clear since I've been here,' and on the front, in the lower corner, is Goro's signature."

Kogito looked at the landscape painting, which was on soft, thick, pale-sepia paper with slightly ragged edges, like a pricey wedding invitation. In classic Goro style, the paper had been roughly torn into a rectangular shape. The centerpiece of the composition was a huge tree, seen from above. stout trunk, barren treetops, and a chaotic tangle of leafless branches with attenuated tips, all minutely detailed in such a way as to delineate the subtleties of light and shade amid the homogeneous hues of gray and brown. The only green came from the perennial creepers that snaked around the tree trunk, while patches of deep blue sky thickly sprinkled with fluffy white clouds could be glimpsed through the lacy jumble of bare, thin branches.

"These leafless white-barked trees in the painting, the ones whose skinny branches are draped in something that looks like the hair of a doll made from woolen yarn? I think they're called European white birches, and in the springtime they put forth leaves that are smaller than the leaves of our Japanese white birches. There were some in front of the window of my office at Berkeley," Kogito remarked.

"Goro must have wanted to paint that sky because it was such a gorgeous color," Chikashi said. "I think this was when he went to Berlin the last time, for the film festival. It had been quite a while since he and Katsuko broke up, so he no longer had the contacts from her film-importing business, and even though his movies were very well known over there, most of the attention was probably going to younger directors, so he seems to have been a bit dejected. I remember he told me on the phone that Berlin was cloudy every day, from morning on, and then it got dark around four PM. He said things like 'Berlin in winter isn't a fit place for a human being.' But that makes it seem even more remarkable that this painting is so bright and full of life. He was probably walking around the city when an unusual set of colored pencils in an art-supply store caught his eye, and he just bought them on the spur of the moment. And then when he was looking out his hotel window at the first clear sky since he'd arrived, he suddenly felt like painting it. He didn't have any proper drawing paper, so he must have used the back cover of the film-festival program or something. The thing is, Goro really wasn't the type of person who would make a sketch of the view from his window while he was alone in his hotel room, was he? Remember when he was working at a commercial-art studio, and whenever he reached the final-design stage on one of his posters, he used to send you a telegram at your student lodgings, because he needed you to be there with him? Anyway, he told me, 'There was someone there with me, watching me paint this picture. It was the person who was working as my interpreter/attendant, so no one was likely to gossip about her being in my hotel room. She was a really nice girl, and it's only because she was there that I was able to make that sketch in an easy, relaxed way.' Goro said that when he finished the picture, it seemed quite possible that the young woman might have asked impulsively whether she could have it. As he put it, 'It would have been hard to refuse a request like that, so I took preemptive action: I told her I was going to send it to my younger sister, whom I'd been neglecting for far too long. I knew the address, of course.' That's the explanation Goro gave me, when I thanked him for the gift. But, you know, Goro never had much confidence in his art, even though he sometimes allowed his drawings to be published as illustrations for his writing, and he simply couldn't bring himself to give his paintings to anyone."

"I wonder what became of those watercolor pencils?" Kogito asked, momentarily awestruck by Chikashi's unusual burst of eloquence. "I don't think I've ever seen such beautiful, subtle colors."

"Goro told me that they were too bulky to pack in his trunk, and the pencil leads would probably have gotten broken in transit, so it just seemed easier to give the set to that girl. Apparently she had taken the university entrance exams, but decided to work in an office for a while before starting classes—I gathered that a lot of young people do that, in Germany. That's how she came to be working as an interpreter/attendant, and the film festival assigned her to help Goro get around the city. At the time, I remember thinking that I would rather have had the colored pencils than the drawing, but now, of course, I'm very glad to have this picture."

Kogito enjoyed doing handicraft projects, and he happily set to work on installing Goro's watercolor painting in a suitable frame.

CHAPTER ONE

One Hundred Days
of Quarantine (I)

1

As he began his solitary sojourn in Berlin, Kogito wondered whether it would be even slightly easier to distance himself from Goro—or rather, from Goro's spirit—there than in Tokyo. Kogito knew himself well enough to realize that this was a delicate question.

True, he had left Tagame and the small duralumin trunk stashed in his study at home. But if he started to feel a desperate need to have these things with him, all he had to do was call Chikashi, and she could send them by international mail. (They were already packed in a vinyl box, wrapped in strong paper, and addressed to his lodgings in Berlin, just in case.) The arrival of the sea-mail boxes bearing the books he had shipped from Tokyo to Berlin before his departure had been delayed for some reason, so Kogito was using that emergency process to obtain the German dictionaries and other books that he needed right away. When he stopped to think about it, though, the very act of using Tagame as a means of contacting Goro on the Other

Side was nothing more than an arbitrary rule of the game he and Goro had set up. If Goro felt an urgent desire to get in touch with Kogito from his new dimension, surely he would find a more direct method.

As soon as Kogito had boarded his All-Japan Airlines/Lufthansa flight from Narita to Frankfurt, he put on the headphones that were provided. He jabbed repeatedly at the various switches and buttons on the side of his seat, hoping to find some clue or conduit that would lead him to a new message from Goro. But there was nothing, not even a whisper, and Kogito figured that was probably the way Goro wanted it.

After all, it was Goro who had broached the idea of going into quarantine in order to rescue Kogito from his unhealthy addiction (though Goro was talking about Kogito's obsession with the "scumbag journalist," not about Tagame). But it was Kogito himself, already feeling cornered by Chikashi's request for a moratorium, who had seized on that suggestion and made it a reality by accepting the invitation to live and work in Germany for three months. Surely a brief period of separation at this point wouldn't matter to Goro, who had moved on to eternity.

In any case, after moving his own earthly headquarters to Berlin, Kogito didn't make any further attempt to contact Goro. There was no word from the Other Side, either, but it wasn't long after his arrival that Kogito received some unsolicited information about Goro's time in Berlin.

Due to the unconventional way the campus of the Berlin Free University had come into being, its buildings were scattered around a leafy residential district. In one of those buildings—the assembly hall of the School of Comparative

Culture—a meet-and-greet panel discussion took place one night, with Kogito as the primary participant. The audience included students, faculty members, people from the publishing company that was endowing the commemorative chair, and a media contingent. It was also open to local residents who were interested in Kogito's presence in Berlin.

After the formal meeting was over and most of the crowd had dispersed, Kogito was approached by a stranger who appeared to have some information about Goro's previous sojourn in Berlin—information that might have some bearing on his subsequent life, and death. When he thought about it, now that he was living alone in this foreign place, with no one to shield him from other people the way Chikashi always did in Tokyo, Kogito wasn't able to pick and choose among the potential informants who descended upon him. Because of that, he found himself standing before them unprotected and utterly vulnerable.

The hall was rather small, and it was filled to bursting. After a panel discussion that featured an animated exchange of questions and comments, a crowd gathered around Kogito and the assistant professor of Japanese studies who was acting as his interpreter. Kogito remained standing, leaning against the tall table next to him while he signed paperback copies of the German translations of his books.

From one side of the lectern, a Japanese woman approached and stood very close to him. She was enveloped in a cloud of heavy perfume, and her voice had a distinct Kansai accent (that is, typical of the Kyoto-Osaka-Kobe area). "I'd like to talk to you about Goro and the new generation of German filmmakers," she announced abruptly, and then continued in a pretentious manner, sprinkled with knowing bits of German, evidently in the hopes of forcing Kogito to listen closely to her every word.

"Please don't worry," she said, "I have no interest whatsoever in discussing any dreary tabloid scandals. That's just the revenge of the *Mädchen für alles,* anyway. In case you aren't familiar with that expression, it originally meant 'maid of all work,' but in the latest editions of German-Japanese dictionaries, it's now translated, with impeccable political correctness, as 'factotum' or 'a person who will do anything for you.' In English, they might say 'girl Friday,' though in my mind it implies something a bit more, shall we say, *personal* than that." Kogito had no idea what the woman was referring to, although he would learn the true meaning of the German expression soon enough, and he was shocked by the barely concealed scorn he heard in her voice. (He hadn't had a chance to look at her because he was still busy signing books.)

Meanwhile, the next person in line told Kogito, in English, that the book was a Christmas gift for his mother and asked him to write a specific greeting. But as Kogito started to inscribe the title page his mind went completely blank, and when he asked the student to repeat the request he found himself, inexplicably, speaking French. After those little glitches, he finally got the book signed and handed it back to the student. Then, for the first time, he turned and looked directly at the woman who was standing beside him. He was surprised to see that she was considerably older than she sounded; she looked tired, and she seemed to be surrounded by an aura of impenetrable gloom.

"About that *Mädchen* . . . that girl Friday you mentioned. Was she Goro's interpreter while he was here?" Kogito asked.

"Heavens, no!" the woman exclaimed. "She could barely speak German herself. And she wasn't what you would call a legitimate assistant, either, if you get my drift. That's why I used the term 'girl Friday.'"

The woman appeared to be from the same generation as Kogito, which is to say well into late middle age. Her small face was completely overwhelmed by the unnaturally dark, voluminous mass of deep-black hair that was piled on top of it—hair that seemed to be at odds with her years—and when she closed her mouth there was a conspicuous puffiness around her lips, almost as if she were holding something in her mouth.

Kogito couldn't think of anything to say to keep the conversational ball rolling, but the woman didn't seem to notice. Handing him her business card, she said, "It's great that you have so many fans in Germany, but you seem to be awfully busy today, so I'll say good-bye for now. As I mentioned earlier, I'd like to have a long talk with you about Germany's new generation of filmmakers, so please keep that in mind."

As the woman walked away, Kogito noticed that a television cameraman who had been filming the panel discussion had turned his lens on her retreating back. Petite though she was, she walked with long, bold strides, like a man.

"Are you planning to film this kind of conversation, too?" Kogito asked.

"No," replied a Japanese producer, sticking his head out from behind the cameraman. "It's just B-roll footage, to set the scene. By the way, I didn't mean to eavesdrop, but I was surprised to hear that an expression like '*Mädchen für alles*'—which is what you might call seriously un-PC—is still floating around. Germany's very strong on feminist issues, you know."

Afterward, Kogito somehow managed to leave the woman's card behind on the table where he had been signing his books. The truth is, he was only interested in one of Goro's female acquaintances in Berlin: the "really nice girl" who had been with him when he painted that watercolor of trees in winter.

As for the "scandalous" woman who figured in the Tokyo tabloid story that had catalyzed (if not precipitated) Goro's death, even if she turned out to be the same person who was supposedly getting her revenge for having been treated as a *Mädchen für alles,* Kogito could not have cared less about that sordid bit of ancient history.

2

As it turned out, Kogito wasn't able to free himself from the attentions of the big-haired, heavily scented Japanese woman that easily. The S. Fischer memorial lectureship formally began the following week, with sessions every Monday and Wednesday. Kogito taught from twelve till two, but as he learned from the German assistant professor of comparative literature who came to pick him up at his apartment on the first day of classes, there was a custom called the Academic Fifteen, which required instructors to arrive at their classrooms fifteen minutes late and leave fifteen minutes early. Kogito didn't want to spend the fifteen extra minutes before his lecture killing time in the classroom, so instead he dropped by the department's office to say hello. When he peeped into the pigeonhole that had only just been assigned to him, he found a notecard from the woman whose business card he had "accidentally" lost.

> Someone—a German university student—kindly let me
> know that one of my business cards had been "dropped"

at the meeting hall the other day. I have *never* dropped
one of my business cards in my life.

On the day in question, I clearly remember handing out only two cards: one to that assistant professor and
one to you. I believe in giving people the benefit of the
doubt, so I'm going to assume that you left my card behind inadvertently, due to the sort of absentminded care-
lessness we associate with professors and authors. In any
case, the thing I still want very much to talk to you about
has nothing to do with the *Mädchen für alles* affair that I
impulsively mentioned the other day, or anything like that.
I actually have a very constructive proposal regarding the
future of the German film world.

I have to go to Hannover this afternoon, so I won't
be able to attend your lecture, but I have the telephone
number of the Center for Advanced Research, and I'll be
in touch in the next few days. By the way, I'm hoping the
lecture will be a huge success. Yours, etc.

Kogito wouldn't have gone so far as to call the lecture a huge
success, but it was certainly well attended (indeed, only forty
copies of the English text of his speech had been made, to be
distributed before the talk began, and an additional batch had to
be hastily printed), and after he had finished reading the speech
in English, the explanatory lecture went off without a hitch.

Afterward Kogito headed home on the bus he'd been in-
structed to catch, and as he rode through the city in the deepening dusk, he suddenly remembered the strangely vivid expression
"bean harmonica," a colloquial Japanese nickname for a small
pocket harmonica. That memory was directly related to the un-

usual facial configuration of the woman who had accosted him, and when Kogito thought about it he realized that he had heard the expression on one of Goro's Tagame tapes.

This was while Goro was still alive, during the period when Kogito had started listening to the second batch of tapes—an activity that, in a surprisingly short time, had turned into a nightly ritual. Goro had evidently foreseen that development, because each tape he sent was a seamless continuation of the one before, with no introductory greetings or pleasantries, so that when Kogito pressed the PLAY button Goro's monologue always picked up exactly where it had left off.

Hence, it was entirely natural that listening to Tagame should have turned into an indispensable daily routine. Right after Goro's death, there was a time when Kogito forgot to change the batteries (Tagame was a rather archaic piece of equipment, not designed to be user-friendly, so there was no warning that the batteries were running low), and he was afraid the tape recorder had broken down. After that he had developed a fear of allowing anything to interrupt the conversational system Goro had so painstakingly set up. The thought of how bleak his evenings would be if that happened seemed to hover above Kogito's head like the shadow of a giant bird.

In any event, when he first started listening to Goro's tapes one of the recorded anecdotes that had especially impressed him invoked the bean harmonica. Goro hadn't set out to tell the harmonica story from the outset; he just segued naturally into it from a discussion about teaching people how to act in films.

"When you edited that paperback edition of my father's collected essays, one of your commentaries was on a treatise my father had published somewhere else, about how to coach actors—remember?" Goro began. "You compared it to Kenji Miyazawa's *Outline of the Essential Art of the Peasant,* and as a result you were criticized not only by a group of Miyazawa scholars who believed in the strict 'textual criticism' that was flourishing at the time, but also by a group of film critics who had gotten together to make a new study of my father's written works. They thought your approach was a bit off the wall, as I recall. But although I had reservations about the rather high-flown literary style you chose to use, I did think at the time that there was a visceral, intuitive basis for the parallels you drew.

"The early days of the film industry in this country were really something else, you know? Any time they wanted to invoke a 'Japanese-y' feeling in a scene—which is to say, in pretty much every single scene—the soundtrack would, without fail, be playing some variation on 'Sakura, Sakura.' And when they shot a crowd scene, you could sense that beyond the narrow confines of the set, which was crammed full of extras, there wasn't a soul in sight. That was the sort of thing my father wrote about. And if you want to talk about the origins of the first film actresses, most if not all of them came from that peasant class that Kenji Miyazawa poured so much energy into trying to help. They were probably from the same background as the girls whose parents were so poor that they had no choice but to sell their daughters to the pleasure quarters, or worse. I think my father must have had the same feelings of wanting to do something altruistic for those poor country girls. Both my father and Kenji had the same sort of humanitarian motivations, you know.

"Once the camera was turned on, the actresses would never smile, and when they spoke their lines they barely opened their mouths—those things drove my father crazy. But he always wanted to try to help those camera-shy actresses; that was the feeling he brought to the set. Kenji, of course, tried to introduce the farming class to the magnificence of art and culture, but making that noble ideal a reality was easier said than done. Even Kenji himself probably understood that, ultimately, it was an impossible dream. As for my father, rather than just trying to whitewash those ruddy-complexioned young farmgirls and turn them into pretty, decorative blossoms, I think he was trying to come up with a concrete plan to help them develop their acting skills. As someone who comes from a valley in the middle of a forest, you're probably able to grasp that better than most people. And the plan that my father came up with way back when, in that acting guide, is something that's genuinely useful even today. When I myself was first starting out as an actor, I always kept in mind the advice my father used to give to up-and-coming actors: *When you're speaking your lines, always pitch your voice a note or two lower than your usual speaking voice.*

"Well, of course, I'm from a different generation, and the moviemaking industry is fifty years farther along than it was in my father's day, but when you think about the teaching of acting that's going on today, it's become so simple that I have a feeling my father would be plunged into despair if he heard about it. The way I see it, if you pour all your efforts into the casting process and put together an absolutely perfect cast, then the movie's already as good as made! Beyond that, there's no need for coaching.

"You hear some people talking about the clique of A-list actresses and so on, right? The truth is that some of those same actresses, even while they are just the latest cute new face, floundering around in a fog, often end up winning the 'best newcomer' acting prizes. And that's what wakes them up to the truth about performing. If the director treats them like serious actresses, they'll give him more or less what he wants, and before too long, as time goes by, they'll end up being classified as top-flight, A-list actresses. That's just the way it is. People may call that kind of skillful acting 'great,' but when actresses get put on a pedestal like that they get into a rut, and they just end up giving the same performance over and over. It's really a staggeringly tedious tautology, you know. An actress who has always played pure, virginal roles gets cast against type and throws herself into a really gritty portrayal of a courtesan in the Heian era or some such. In my father's day there were people like that . . . but that's nothing more than another rotation of the same tautology. That type of over-the-top performance—you know, the tragic geisha—is meant to make people cry, but I can never watch that sort of thing without laughing.

"On the other hand, many of the women I've actually met up with in everyday life (and these aren't professional actresses, mind you) have dropped their masks and said to me, at some point, 'This is who I really am,' and I'm just blown away by how formidable their acting skills are. You really have to take off your hat to them.

"And it's not as if I've only run into one or two of these specially talented women in my life so far. In the circles I move in, whether I wanted to or not, I couldn't help meeting women like that, one after the other. It's gotten to the point where I think that sort of encounter is the only reason my life has unfolded as it has. All I can say is that it's been a never-ending parade of trouble, with plenty more where that came from! That seems to be my fate, and I embrace it."

This was typical of Goro's disquisitions; the "harmonica-mouth" saga may have been his main topic on the tape in question, but it was prefaced by this extended free-association ramble. Now that Kogito was in Berlin, far away from Tagame, he was remembering more consciously the way Goro spoke on the tapes, and he realized that quite a few of the recordings had probably been made under the influence of alcohol. When they were younger—in high school, even—he had been with Goro on quite a few occasions when he was drinking. The reason he hadn't picked up on Goro's tipsiness when he was listening to the recordings was because now that they were adults living in Tokyo, they each had their own families and their careers had taken them in different directions. So although they occasionally went out for sushi or Chinese food and had a drink or two with their meals, there had been only a couple of times when they met up at some watering hole for the express purpose of drinking the night away. This probably sounds strange, considering that Chikashi was Goro's only sibling, but although Goro had dropped by once or twice on short notice, in recent years there hadn't been a single time when Kogito and Chikashi invited Goro over to their house and they all stayed up till late at night drinking and talking. The reverse was true, as well: the first time Kogito ever set foot in Goro's house in Yugawara was the day after he died.

When Kogito heard that Goro had consumed a large quantity of brandy before jumping off the building (Umeko had even placed an open bottle of Hennessy VSOP in front of the coffin), it struck him as strange and disturbing. Kogito himself had for many years made it a habit, if not a ritual, to have a night-cap before going to sleep, but he tried to keep the damage to a minimum by limiting his intake. Still, no matter how hard he tried to reform his lifestyle (especially after he turned fifty), that single tumbler of whiskey before bed remained an immutable rite. Nevertheless, when he was listening to the cassettes that were delivered before Goro went to the Other Side, it never occurred to him that Goro's extraordinarily high spirits and emotional openness—to a degree that would have been un-thinkable if they were in the same room—might be due to the liberating influence of alcohol. Also, it was clear that the dis-tinguishing feature of Goro and Kogito's relationship, from start to finish, had always been their tutor-pupil dynamic. (Goro, needless to say, played the role of tutor.) Now, of course, that relationship was on hiatus, but when Kogito thought about his Tagame conversations with Goro, he had a feeling they might not yet be at an end.

As Goro was riffing about coaching actors, he invoked the woman he'd nicknamed "Bean Harmonica." She was, he main-tained, a classic illustration of his theory that even with all the acting training he himself had received over the years, he couldn't hold a candle to the normal, everyday behavior of someone who was naturally endowed with remarkable histrionic gifts.

"There was one woman, especially," he recalled. (He never did mention the woman's name.) "She always tried to conceal it by wearing her hair down over her face, but if you were to lift up her bangs with both hands, you'd see that she had some-thing not often seen among Japanese women: a majestically high forehead. She had very expressive, deep-set eyes, and the space between her splendid nose and her upper lip was very small.

It's hard to describe, but the overall effect was indescribably attractive. However, in a matter of seconds that lovely, smiling face could be transformed into a mask of resentment, bitterness, and discontent. Or else she would start wheedling, trying to talk me into something with tears welling up in her eyes.

"And then, suddenly, she would just clam up. At times like that it looked as if she was holding one of those toylike miniature harmonicas in her charming, oversized mouth, with her lips closed over it so that her mouth was stretched into a rectangle. And with her complicated facial expressions playing around that harmonica mouth—there's no actress, no matter how accomplished, who could ever portray such a roller-coaster range of emotions on screen. I can't even imagine it. The thing is, that acting ability was hereditary: the gift of the mother, passed on to her daughter!"

Now, in Berlin, as he ruminated about what Goro had said on that tape, Kogito gradually began to discern a thread of logic running through the chaos and confusion. He had initially been reminded, vaguely, of the phrase "bean harmonica" by the facial expression of the woman who accosted him after the panel discussion, and that was what had inspired him to try to recall its context. Goro's powers of observation and description were prodigious, as evidenced by the nicknames he bestowed on various people. If the friend he called "Bean Harmonica" was the same person as Goro's "nice young girl," then wasn't it within the realm of possibility that the big-haired woman might be her mother? If that was true, then Kogito had seen the parental version of the pouty, stormy-faced expression Goro had described. Given that peculiar facial structure, and assuming it was shared by a biologically related mother and daughter, it wasn't difficult to visualize the daughter's face based on that of the mother.

But if (Kogito's flight of conjecture continued) Goro's "nice young girl in Berlin," his interpreter/assistant, really was the aggressive woman's daughter, why would a mother betray her own offspring by saying such disloyal and harshly critical things to a stranger? That question added a new riddle to Kogito's list of unsolved mysteries.

3

As he gradually became used to his days (and especially his nights) of quarantine, Kogito made frequent phone calls to Tokyo, as if to compensate for being deprived of his Tagame sessions with Goro. On the occasions when he phoned the unfailingly helpful assistant professors or the department secretary at the university, the telephone would start to ring in the German way: *puu-tz* . . . silence . . . *puu-tz* . . . silence. In contrast, when he placed an international call to Tokyo, he would hear the familiar Japanese ring—although he knew that what was actually echoing through the living room was probably a few bars of Mozart's chamber music, which Chikashi had installed as a customized ring. And then a quiet, sorrowful voice would answer the phone: "Yes?"

Although they weren't really able to engage the gears of conversation, Kogito and his son would always imbibe each other's "vibrations" over the phone line for a couple of wordless minutes. Then Akari would either hand the phone to his mother or else say, "Mama isn't here," in that same melancholy tone of voice, and then lapse into silence.

Chikashi, on the other hand, was usually upbeat and voluble on the international phone line. Sometimes she and Kogito even talked about literature—something that rarely happened when they were face-to-face in Tokyo. One day, after winding up a conversation about various practical matters, Chikashi asked a question that she seemed, characteristically, to have been carefully composing in her mind: "When you were still young, during the time when you were mainly reading literature in translations, there were times when you talked so fast that I couldn't quite catch the pronunciation, even though you were speaking Japanese. Still, the content of your talks was always very interesting and enjoyable. It seemed to sparkle, and you used to use some really quaint, fanciful expressions. Then after you came back from your long stay in Mexico City, you began to read things in their original languages rather than in Japanese translation, and the feeling of the words you used in conversation seemed to change as a result. I sometimes think that your words took on a new depth after that.

"However, I didn't hear as much of the curious, quixotic strangeness and interesting flavor that I used to notice before when you talked. And wasn't it the same with the words you were using in your novels? Maybe it was a matter of maturity, but your words just didn't seem to sparkle like they used to. And somehow, while I was thinking that way, I stopped reading your novels altogether. So I can't really speak about the novels you've written over the past fifteen years or so, but I can't help wondering whether there might be a connection between the change in your style and the fact that you started reading for-

eign books in the original languages. I realize that the usual thing
you hear from the very same people who read books in the original is that those are much more entertaining than when they're
translated into Japanese, so what I'm saying probably contra-
dicts the conventional wisdom."

"That may very well be true," Kogito said. "It was when I
was in my late forties that sales of my books started to slow down,
and that was right about the time that I cut way back on reading
work in Japanese translation. Just as you say, the sparkling appeal of my prose, such as it was, probably did fade a bit. For me,
the attraction of reading work in translation—something entirely
separate from the pleasure of reading it in the original—is that
there's something incredibly lucid and straightforward about it.
I often find myself marveling at translations, being surprised at
various things (*Oh, is that how they translated this part? Can they
really get away with taking such liberties?*) and also thinking that
I myself could never use Japanese in such a way. Some of the
young, prodigiously talented translators, in particular—they show
a strength and authority that's almost uncanny."

That day's phone conversation ended on this note, but after
an interval of several days Chikashi, who had been putting in
order the incoming gifts of books and magazines, called to report on the presentation copies of books that had arrived from
various friends during Kogito's absence and various other matters. Afterward she ventured, "This is picking up where we left
off, but some of the prose by young people who are translating
new works from French into Japanese is extraordinarily interesting, don't you think?" she asked.

"Well, yes, I would agree with that," Kogito responded. "At
the other end of the spectrum, leaving aside the groups at the

West Coast American universities who have been directly influenced by Foucault, English writing can be a bit of a slog—
rather like a local train that stops at every station. In particular,
what's being written by scholars in England . . . in fact, I think
the reason my style lost its sparkle might have something to do
with having read too many Cambridge University Press research
monographs about everyone from Blake to Dante."

Ignoring Kogito's typically self-mocking digression, Chikashi
said, "Anyway, the passage I'm finding interesting right now may
not be important at all, but it really struck a chord with me. It's
from a Japanese translation of a French book called *René Char
in His Poetry,* which was written by a French-literature scholar
who seems to be quite well known and accomplished in the
field. It's a gigantic book, and I have to admit that I can't understand the interpretation of Char's surrealist poems and so on,
at all, but anyway, I've just faxed you the section I mentioned."

Chikashi's fax was a page from that book—a monumen-
tal work of biographical literary criticism in which the author
makes reference to everyone from Wittgenstein to the Marquis
de Sade—underlined here and there with what Kogito recognized, even on the blurry fax paper, as one of the no. 2 pencils
Chikashi used to render preliminary sketches for her watercolor
paintings.

The rambling section begins with a discussion of René
Char's difficult relationship with his mother, which the critic
describes as "more Baudelairean than Oedipal." A brief digression about Char's three favorite pursuits ("writing, fighting, and
making love") is followed by a metaphorical passage comparing the poet's mother to a she-bear. It goes on to say that there
comes a time when a man must reject the part of himself that

was licked by the mother bear; that is, he must throw away the rules he learned at his mother's knee.

In the phone call that followed the fax, Chikashi explained the thoughts this passage had awakened in her, and Kogito found himself borne along on the same wave. Chikashi was particularly excited by the nuances of one particular phrase—"the time is ripe to think about throwing away the part that was licked by the mother bear"—in the lines she'd faxed to Kogito in Berlin. "Licked," of course, referred not only to maternal affection but also to the sterner aspects of child raising. (Indeed, people in medieval Europe used to believe that bear cubs were born as eyeless, formless lumps of flesh and had to be literally licked into shape by their mothers.)

"When I first read this phrase, I thought it said everything there is to say about Goro," Chikashi declared. "He grew up being constantly 'licked' by the mother bear we called Mama. There's a saying that someone's being smothered with affection, right? Well, when Goro was a child, from my point of view as his younger sister, he really did appear to be suffocating under the weight of our mother's affection. Even so, I wasn't jealous; I thought it was perfectly appropriate for him to receive special treatment and extra care. He was a remarkably beautiful child, and he was so talented at drawing pictures that a publisher in Kyoto once asked him to design the cover for a book. This was during World War Two, but as you know he was even chosen for the special science academy that was created by the government.

"Supplies were tight during wartime, but our mother somehow managed to get her hands on a collection of art supplies that a professional painter would have envied. She also made up a reading list featuring science books aimed at children and got hold of all sorts of unusual things for Goro to read. But she had a severe side as well, and sometimes when Goro didn't seem to be taking her efforts seriously enough, she could be quite frightening. It's true; he really did grow up being 'licked by the bear,' in every sense of the phrase.

"Remember when Goro got to know some psychologists who specialized in Freud and Lacan? He allowed himself to fall meekly under their influence in a way so unlike him that it struck me, watching from the side, as really strange . . . almost creepy. While that was happening, Goro was so completely spellbound that he used to talk about those psychologists really ingenuously, with such total trust and naïveté, and he wrote later in one of his books that they had helped him to finally get free of his mother. For me, though, I never thought he could escape so easily. I know I'm an ignorant person, and I realize it's a childish kind of skepticism, but I can't help wondering whether psychology can really be effective on fully formed adults. I mean, look at Goro; he was a sophisticated intellectual who'd been around the block a few times, wasn't he?

"To be honest, I always thought that at some point the whole psychology thing would turn around and bite him. I'm not saying that he died the way he did as a direct reaction to all that psychiatric mumbo jumbo. But when it comes to the tangled complexities of Goro's psychological state, I can't help thinking sometimes that I really would like to see those meddlesome psychologists take some responsibility for what happened in the end."

4

Although Akari was singularly uncommunicative when Kogito phoned home from his Berlin apartment, he was perfectly comfortable with putting his thoughts down on paper and sending them to his father by fax. When Chikashi began drawing illustrations for Kogito's essays, Goro had remarked, "She's only just begun, but already she has her own style." Remembering that, Kogito thought: *If only he could see Akari's drawings*. For example, next to a picture, drawn with marking pen, that showed Akari and his mother climbing the ramp to a giant jet airplane, Akari wrote, "I think I will go to hear the Berlin Philharmonic. Schwalbe and Yasunaga are very good first violins. I will bring Chikashi to Berlin with me." However, Chikashi nixed that plan because she was concerned that Akari might have one of his epileptic seizures if they traveled to a northern European city in the dead of winter.

Kogito glued Akari's faxed drawing to a piece of thick, heavy paper and kept it on the table in his apartment's kitchen. Akari was good at math, and he had written in the fax number by himself. While Kogito was looking at that number, which was for the machine at the Center for Advanced Research, he noticed something. Akari had not only memorized the long number, including 0014930, the international dialing code for Berlin —that sort of thing was his forte—but also incorporated the number into the picture he drew with markers. That, surely, was because when Goro had been in Berlin for the film festival, he had called unexpectedly and had left that number so Kogito could call him back.

Kogito had forgotten Goro's callback number in Berlin, and Akari saved the day by quietly reading the number off one of his sheets of five-line music paper, where he had jotted it in the margin. He had been sprawled on the floor nearby, composing music, and had apparently been listening when Kogito repeated the number into the mouthpiece. Kogito and Chikashi had both praised Akari to the skies for this feat, and he clearly hadn't forgotten. On top of that, he was probably delighted anew by the pleasingly symmetrical fact that the first half of his father's current fax number was the same as that of the number Goro had left several years earlier.

And then Kogito remembered that a young woman had been at the hotel with Goro on the day in question. After that, all sorts of details came flooding back. Goro had called from Berlin with an unusual request: "You know that story about how you met one of your more, um, enthusiastic fans in Nagasaki? There's someone I'd like you to share it with. And please tell it in English, just the way you told it to O'Brian, years ago. He helped you to improve it so it would sound more like the Queen's English, right? So tell it just like that. Chikashi said that the

corrections O'Brian wrote down on some index cards and sent
to you were very amusing. See if you can dig up those cards,
and then call me back. There's a speakerphone switch on this
telephone, so we'll be able to hear you all over the room."

When Kogito asked, "And why do you want me to do that,
pray tell?" Goro responded cheerfully, "There's someone here;
she's Japanese, but she was raised overseas, and now she's acting as my German interpreter. She speaks very good Japanese,
as well. But when she told me that she was only able to laugh
at a joke or a funny story if she heard it in her first foreign language, English, that really blew me away. I mean, I'd never heard
of such a thing. So I figured that she would enjoy that story
about your adventures in Nagasaki, and you've already put it
into English. You even have those cards with O'Brian's notes
about how to improve the wording."

Abruptly, Goro segued into a treatise about the weather.
"They say it's going to snow today for the first time this year,
but in the places where the thin branches of the bare black trees
are intricately interlaced, you can already see some light snow
beginning to accumulate, weighing down the trees," he said.
"Sometimes the forward-tilting trees will be pressed back by a
slight current of air, and in that instant of contrapuntal tension
the throngs of trees seem to be perfectly still. I've been watching them a lot, and for some reason it's put me in a very good
mood, so I just felt like asking you for an unreasonable favor.
Call me when you're ready—I'll be waiting!"

Kogito had fond memories of that conversation with Goro,
who seemed to be unusually high-spirited and loquacious. He
was obviously enjoying the outrageous spontaneity of asking for

an elaborate favor over an international phone line, and having a young woman next to him, listening in, must have added to his pleasure.

O'Brian was a famous English—or, more precisely, Irish—actor who had costarred with Goro in *Lord Jim,* in 1965. When O'Brian happened to come to Japan for a visit, Goro threw a small party for him at the house he shared with his then wife, Katsuko (the only daughter of the owner of a company that imported Western films), and he asked Kogito to come and keep the Englishman company.

While Kogito was chatting with O'Brian, the anecdote the Englishman seemed to find most entertaining was about something that had happened not long before the party, when Kogito was in Nagasaki. He had been invited by the chairman of a left-wing publisher's labor union to give a lecture to a gathering there, but whether it was publishers, newspapers, or broadcasting stations, the hard-core union organizers had very little use for so-called progressive novelists—at least not for those who didn't officially belong to the Communist Party or to the extreme-radical minor factions. And on this day, sure enough, that was the sort of treatment that Kogito received: minimal, almost grudging hospitality.

Because of the inconvenient scheduling of nonstop flights, Kogito arrived in the morning, but the "finger-flute" (that is to say, finger-whistling) concert and Kogito's literary lecture weren't scheduled until evening. As expected, after being given a dubious-looking box lunch he was peremptorily shuttled off to the union's lodging house.

Kogito had hardly finished eating the greasy fare when severe cramps and diarrhea set in. He ventured out onto a lively thoroughfare to buy some medicine, but there were no pharmacies to be found. As he was wandering around, he ventured down a narrow alley that looked more like a dimly lit path leading into a mountain vale than a byway in the middle of a city. There he found a small apothecary shop, crammed into a storefront no more than six feet wide.

When Kogito pushed open the old-fashioned glass door and entered the shop, the fortyish woman who was sitting in a cramped space with her back to the medicine-laden shelves turned her round, pale face in his direction. "Oh!" she exclaimed, stifling a shriek of surprise.

Paying no attention to this odd response, Kogito asked for some paregoric, but when he tried to pay for his purchase, the proprietor, who was still seated, gazed up at him, flushed and perspiring. "Oh, my goodness," she said, in a low voice that was almost a moan. "Sometimes you really do get what you wish for!"

Then, abruptly, she launched into a remarkably spirited account of her life story. She explained that she had attended the pharmaceutical studies department of a university in Kyoto and was a passionate fan of Kogito's work who owned a hardcover copy of every book he had ever published. She had taken over this family-owned pharmacy after her father's sudden death. The shop was near a red-light district, and it had stayed in business for many years by specializing in contraceptive devices and remedies for sexually transmitted diseases. After the Anti-Prostitution Law was passed there had been some lean times, and it had looked for a while as if the pharmacy might have to close its doors, but she always clung to the belief that as long as she could hunker down and stay in business, someday she would have a chance to meet Kogito Choko.

Kogito was a little concerned about a disreputable-looking middle-aged man who was loitering outside on the curb next to the gutter with a kimono-clad woman in tow, so he tried to take his leave as quickly as possible, but the female proprietor reached under the counter, took out a carton containing a six-pack of larger-than-usual bottles of some sort of energy drink, plunked it down on the counter, and said, "Please try this—I'll give you a special VIP discount."

"Actually, I don't really drink that sort of health potion," Kogito responded.

"Oh, no!" the pharmacist protested. "This isn't your simple, garden-variety health drink. It contains garlic, and Korean ginseng, and even ground-up seahorses. See what's written on the bottle? DRINK IT NOW! GET IT UP! DO IT TWICE! I'll let you have a six-pack for only two dollars, so why don't you take a couple of cartons home with you?"

As the woman slapped a second six-pack down on the counter, the shady-looking man who had been hanging around outside barged into the pharmacy with his female consort and shouldered his way to the counter. "If you're having a sale, I'll buy some," he said gruffly. "Two cartons, please!" The timing seemed suspicious, and Kogito couldn't help wondering whether the man's appearance might be part of a prearranged charade.

"Coming right up," said the proprietor. "The special price for one box is thirty dollars, so your total will be sixty dollars. I'm sure you're familiar with this amazing product. You know their slogan: DRINK IT NOW! GET IT UP! DO IT TWICE! Your lucky missus is going to be in seventh heaven! Thank you for your business."

That's all there was to the story, but O'Brian showed his marvelous character by not only laughing uproariously but also helping Kogito, afterward, to make his laborious telling of the anecdote much tighter and more forceful. When the Irish actor was on the airplane, heading home to London, he spent a good deal of time reworking the English translation of the advertising slogan (DRINK IT NOW! GET IT UP! DO IT TWICE!). He even gave his notes to a crew member on the flight, which was returning to Narita, with instructions to deliver them to Kogito. O'Brian suggested a way of making the slogan "a bit more lewd," and Kogito obligingly changed the words to GET IT UP! GET IT ON! SHAG ALL NIGHT!

By the time Kogito had located the card bearing the English-language version of the anecdote it was already midnight in Tokyo, but it was still late afternoon in Berlin. While he was telling the story over the telephone, he couldn't help noticing the contrast between the youthful freshness of the girl's laughter— she was clearly excited about the first snow—and the mature rumble of Goro's satisfied-sounding laughter, as the two merry voices intermingled.

Kogito was pleased to realize that a memory that had seemed to be extinguished was actually very clear, especially since it was a recollection that seemed to be infused with (these were the first words that sprang to mind) a sort of crystalline brightness. In Goro's twilight years, which had come far too soon, that kind of delight was rather rare.

While Kogito was living in Berlin, he always had Saturdays and Sundays free. There were no classes, no lunches with his colleagues at the Center for Advanced Research, no academic presentations. Kogito had very little desire to stroll around the noisy, teeming streets, so he usually passed the time by lying on his bed and reading a book, or reminiscing about various things having to do with Goro. While his mind was meandering dreamily through his memories, it sometimes headed off in a distinctly R-rated direction.

One such reminiscence dated back to a time when Goro, who was still married to Katsuko, was frequently going overseas for film roles. Goro was just back from America when he turned up one evening in a taxi to visit Kogito, who had himself only recently returned from a teaching stint at the University of California at Berkeley. Goro rarely took taxis—he preferred to tool around in his sleek, luminous Bentley—and the reason he deliberately used one on this night was because he was planning to drink a large quantity of whiskey in the hopes of routing the depression that was plaguing him.

Throughout the evening, Goro held forth while sipping continuously from a glass filled (and refilled many times over) with Old Parr whiskey, neat, from a bottle Kogito had received from his publisher as a holiday gift. Chikashi kept them company until shortly after 10 PM, then excused herself and went to bed. After that it was just Goro and Kogito, one-on-one. Maybe Goro had been restraining himself while Chikashi was present, but from then on, even though he seemed to be growing increasingly melancholy, he kept up an antic, eloquent stream of anecdotes.

The previous year, Goro had spent six months acting in a Hollywood film that was made with the intention of justifying the western side of the Boxer Rebellion, and he had just returned from attending the movie's premieres in Los Angeles and New York. He had been given a major role as a military officer attached to the Japanese embassy in Beijing (then known as Peking)—there was even a scene where he cradled the lead actress in his arms and helped her to escape while bullets were ricocheting off the walls and the unpaved road around them. The review in Los Angeles's leading newspaper singled Goro out for special notice, rhapsodizing about his "glamorous charm" and remarking that he had an unusually charismatic presence for an Asian actor. Kogito happened to read that article, and he clipped it out and sent it to Goro's then wife, Katsuko.

But when Goro returned home and looked at the Japanese reviews, he discovered that most of them completely ignored his performance. One anonymous weekly-magazine film reviewer focused on a scene in which Katsuko had a walk-on part as a married woman, splendidly dressed in kimono, who attends a Christmas party for the employees of all the foreign embassies in Peking. The review concluded with the snide remark, "This is the reason Goro Hanawa passed his audition," implying that Katsuko's family-business connections had been a factor.

As Goro slid ever deeper into drunkenness, Kogito started talking about Yukichi Fukuzawa's trademark word, *enbo,* meaning resentment, bitterness, or envy. Kogito quoted liberally from Fukuzawa's seminal treatise, *An Encouragement of Learning,* which he had used as a text in a class he'd taught at Berkeley. In Japan, he explained to his increasingly bleary-eyed brother-in-law, there was only one reason why Goro, as a Japanese actor who was successful abroad as well, would be slighted or even looked upon with disdain. That reason was pure *enbo:* bitter, envious resentment.

According to Fukuzawa, virtually every word that's used to describe people can be a two-sided coin. For example, depending on your tone, *frugal* can mean admirably thrifty or despicably stingy, while *rough and ready* could imply either courageousness or bellicosity. The exception, he says, is *enbo.* No matter how you look at it, *enbo* is a complete waste of time; there's no way you can put a positive spin on envy, bitterness, and resentment, or turn those emotions into positive human traits.

To which Goro replied, "When it comes to being tormented by the envy and resentment of others, you're in the same boat as I am, with that vindictive journalist making a cottage industry of dragging your name through the mud. Just watch— as soon as you win a big international prize for literature, that 'eminent authority' will rush to press with a book that totally trashes your entire life and work." Goro as prophet: that was exactly what did happen, some years later.

"I really don't worry too much about this kind of stuff," Goro went on. "But getting back to that article that you went to the trouble of cutting out and sending to Katsuko, where the writer singled me out for special praise? Well, the truth is, I've been having some personal problems with that writer. You're lucky you don't have to deal with that sort of thing." Kogito felt disappointed by the way Goro seemed to be changing the subject, as if he wasn't taking Kogito's point seriously, so he was gratified to learn from Chikashi, some time later, that Goro had been enthusiastically sprinkling his conversations with his new favorite word: *enbo*.

It gradually emerged that the film critic who had singled Goro out for such lavish praise in that L.A. newspaper was a fiftyish woman named Amy, who had traveled with Goro's group for part of the time while he and some of the other actors were on a promotional tour for the movie. After the initial interview, whenever Goro had a little free time she would invite him to join her for dinner at some small restaurant near wherever they happened to be staying, to continue the more detailed interviews she said she needed in order to write a longer article about him.

When Goro returned to San Francisco on the day before he was scheduled to go back to Japan, the film critic took him to a cozy restaurant in Chinatown and did a lengthy follow-up interview. After that, as they were wending their way up the steep, narrow road that led back to the hotel, they stopped for breath and somehow fell into a passionate embrace. Goro made no effort whatsoever to hold his hips away so the reporter wouldn't be aware of his arousal; on the contrary (he told Kogito) he was insistently pressing his erection against her abdomen the entire time.

Perhaps it was a response to the rather formal English he had been forced to communicate in during the series of interviews, but something definitely awakened his aggressive-male tendencies. Or maybe it was because he had built up a lot of sexual energy during the ten days he'd been traveling around America to promote the film. Anyway, the upshot was that instead of heading back to her own place, Amy accompanied Goro up to his hotel room.

"Before that," Goro explained to Kogito, "it was obvious that she was very healthy and vital, but she just seemed like a plump, jovial, intellectual sort of woman. Once we got down to doing it, though, she turned out to have an absolutely mind-boggling appetite for sex. I mean, any aperture you could think of—she didn't seem to care whether it was front or rear. All through that night, until morning, she was constantly touching my body somewhere, and when we weren't actually having intercourse she would use every trick imaginable to get my penis to stand at attention again. All she wanted to do was to have sex with me, again and again. And when even the famously indefatigable Goro finally reached the point where there was simply nothing left to ejaculate, she would take my cock in the corner of her mouth and then show me exactly what she wanted me to do with my fingers while she worked on me furiously with her tongue. Then when I somehow managed to come again, she would catch my semen on that tongue of hers, like a chameleon. And when the limo came to pick me up the next morning, she hopped in, too, and she kept on playing with my poor, worn-out penis, all the way to the airport. Then just recently, when I found out that I had gotten an acting job that involved going to Spain for three weeks, to shoot on location, she informed me that she had booked a room in the same Spanish hotel. Frankly, I'm terrified by the prospect of twenty more days of carnal excess, and I think I'm speaking for my penis, too, when I say, 'Enough already!'"

Kogito could feel the amusement breaking through his old friend's subdued mood, but then Goro lapsed into a dark silence and went back to guzzling whiskey with an undisguisedly sorrowful look in his eyes. Kogito couldn't resist offering some unsolicited advice; it was an old habit of his, dating back to their days as schoolboys.

"Why don't you try looking at it this way?" he suggested. "Between your last meeting in America and your departure for Spain there's what, two or three months or so? In that case, when you finally get together again you'll be overflowing with pent-up passion—at least for the first three days. And soon after that, you'll take off for location shooting at special sites around the Spanish countryside, and there will be days when you don't go back to the hotel at all. And then when you do return to the hotel, after being away for a few days, you'll probably be thrilled to be reunited with Amy again, and your reunion will have a kind of nostalgic freshness."

Goro was completely drunk now, and his extreme intoxication was probably part of the reason why his voice suddenly sounded as if he was on the verge of tears. "You may write dark, heavy, gloomy novels," he said, "but when you say something like that it makes me think that you're really a fundamentally optimistic person. You don't really act like it, though. I mean,

even though you married someone totally down-to-earth like
Chikashi, who isn't in the least bit needy or demanding, you
still choose to spend your nights alone on a monastic cot in your
library. Still, I really can't believe that you're a completely solitary, pessimistic guy at heart—especially when you start going
on about thrilling reunions and 'nostalgic freshness'!"

As it happened, Goro's Spanish rendezvous with the
American film journalist turned out unexpectedly well; indeed,
everything transpired in almost exact accordance with the comforting scenario that Kogito had conjured up out of thin air in
an attempt to alleviate Goro's anxieties. According to the story
Goro told Kogito much later, on the day Amy arrived at the hotel
that would be the crew's base of operations, she and Goro ended
up having sex twice while the sun was still high in the sky, and
again late that night, and then one more time the next morning. Afterward Goro broke out in a cold sweat, thinking that
twenty more days of this would be absolute hell, but fortunately
the bacchanal was brought to a halt after only four days when
the Spanish investors whisked the actors away to Madrid.

And then, just as Goro was wondering why they were all
partying in Madrid instead of working on the film, it was announced that the Spanish location shooting had been canceled.
In order to placate one of the backers, who had made his fortune by exporting inexpensive Spanish wine, the producers had
initially promised to shoot at a typical wine-producing location,
but apparently the production side wasn't serious about this
plan, and the majority of the supplies and equipment hadn't
even been shipped.

That was the situation, and it was a mess. As a result, it
was decided that the location shooting would move within the

week to Flores Island, in Indonesia, and Goro spent the better part of his final two days in Spain engaging in genuinely warm, friendly, heartfelt sexual intercourse with the American journalist. In order to catch her plane, which left long before the film crew's flight to Indonesia, Amy had to crawl out of bed while it was still dark, so there was no time for a voracious sexual farewell, and this richly experienced woman of the world said good-bye to Goro with the solemn, dignified air of someone who knows how to control her desires . . . if she really has to.

Goro's obvious exhaustion from shooting a movie in the tropics over a long, hot summer could have been a factor as well, but as he shared this tale of adventure, Kogito got the impression that he was lost in contemplation of some sort of hardship or suffering that Kogito couldn't even begin to imagine. Whatever else might have happened, Kogito thought that Goro's heroic performance on the day the plump, insatiable American woman arrived in Spain from California, when he managed to perform sexually four times in less than twenty-four hours, was a triumph of perseverance and effort. And as he listened to the story, Kogito felt a resurgence of the childish feelings of respect and esteem for his old friend that had first sprouted when they were in high school.

6

In Russia, before the revolution, there was a craze for building vacation villas in Berlin, and one Russian millionaire spent a small fortune erecting an enormous mansion, complete with Greek-style murals on the façade and cylindrical columns supporting the roof. The exterior still retained its original opulence, but the interior of the building had been remodeled and turned into apartments for the faculty of the Center for Advanced Research. Kogito's flat was on the third floor, overlooking a lake.

After the Christmas holidays, and after the birth of the new millennium had been celebrated with a noisy all-day eruption of fireworks that continued until midnight on December 31, 1999, the Free University opened its doors again and Kogito resumed his routine of riding the bus to and from work. The entire journey took no more than thirty minutes. From nearby Hagenplatz (where Kogito always went on foot to buy wine and groceries) he boarded the bus that ran down Königstrasse, and when he got to Rathenauplatz he changed to a bus that originated just before the busy boulevard of Kurfürstendamm, better known as Ku'damm. Even on days when the frozen lake was piled high with snow in the morning, the white stuff always stopped falling by midday, and although there were days when the city streets seemed to have been turned into frozen ice-*bahn*s, traffic always went on running smoothly under perpetually cloudy skies.

One afternoon, after Kogito had finished both his formal lecture and the subsequent Q-and-A session with students known as office hour, he had just stepped out into one of those typically dark, overcast Berlin afternoons, where the sun isn't really shining but doesn't seem quite ready to set, either, when he heard the familiar voice of a Japanese female calling his name.

In short order, the woman caught up with him as he walked down the narrow road, which was piled high on both sides with plowed snow. She looked rather odd, wrapped in a heavy greatcoat that fell nearly to her ankles, but even though Kogito had been approached by a large number of people during his stay in Berlin, he remembered this person immediately, with her cryptic talk of a *Mädchen für alles* and her curiously puffy, oblong harmonica mouth.

"I hope you won't mind if I keep you company while you're riding home on the bus," the woman said. "Though I'm not sure whether I'll be able to say everything I want to in such a short time." Without waiting for a reply she fell into step beside Kogito, so close that their shoulders were almost touching. And then, abruptly, her previously polite way of speaking changed into a style somewhere between inappropriate intimacy and outright intimidation. "Just as I thought, you don't have any sort of assistant or *Mädchen für alles* yourself, do you?" she demanded.

"I've tried telephoning you a number of times at the office, but even when the switchboard forwards the call to your apartment, there's never any answer!"

During all his years in Tokyo, Kogito had hardly ever been subjected to this sort of behavior: having someone lie in wait for him, then brashly invite themselves to keep him company. In Berlin, though, it took a good ten minutes to walk to the bus stop from the Free University's classroom buildings (which, as mentioned before, were in a residential district), and Kogito seldom walked alone on his customary route, which involved trudging down the slope of a wide, shallow former pond that had, at some point, been drained and turned into a park, then climbing up the path on the other side. Most often, he was accosted by students who still had questions about the lecture he'd just given; other times, he was joined by Japanese expatriates who were auditing his class or young journalists from Taiwan who were living in Berlin and sending articles back to publications in Taipei. If he could just manage to get past his instinctive negative reaction to the intrusions, he sometimes ended up feeling that the ensuing conversations weren't entirely meaningless.

As for this vivacious person who was marching along beside him with long strides, kicking up the hem of her ankle-length overcoat: although she was clearly the same person who had first approached him on the night of the panel discussion, on this day she seemed very different from that rather glum, tired-looking Japanese woman, teetering on the brink of late middle age. Indeed, she reminded him of a certain type of local woman he often saw around Berlin, standing on some street corner waiting impatiently for the light to change—extremely energetic and completely self-centered. The things she said when she approached him this time had an aggressive edge that seemed to be in keeping with her costume and even with her way of striding along, like a man.

"You hear this a lot here," she said, after she had finished berating him for not answering his phone every time it rang. "The German people I've been around often say that Japanese people talk too much about personal matters—even the writers and film directors who have given public talks here. I've had my doubts about that, but after hearing your lecture today I found myself thinking they were right. Maybe it's just because you are who you are, but you really do seem to talk an awful lot about your private life."

"As you know, my English pronunciation can be hard to follow, so I've been distributing copies of lectures that I've given in the past at universities in America," Kogito responded. "Then, while reading those lectures aloud to the class, I incorporate additions and digressions, rather like footnotes. When the text is something with a hard context, I add personal notes from time to time in the hopes of softening the lecture a bit."

"I sat in on your lecture today, and I noticed that the text you used was the same speech you gave in Stockholm," the woman said. "That lecture began with some personal reminiscences, right? You started off by talking about the music composed by your disabled son, Akari, and from there you extrapolated into universals. It was very moving, but I suspect that there are some Germans who might feel that it was more than they wanted to know about your personal life. Too much information, as they say."

"No doubt you are entirely correct about that," Kogito said stiffly.

They had reached the basinlike bottom of the slope, and the notoriously frigid Berlin wind was swirling around them. Kogito's head felt feverish from the strain of having been forced to speak English (not his strong point) for two solid hours, and the radical disparity between that cerebral heat and the profound chill that permeated his body left him feeling somehow detached, as if he were suspended in midair between the two extremes. The woman evidently sensed his discomfort and adroitly changed the subject.

"There's a high place over there, where the snow is still piled up because no one steps on it. Down at the bottom, a woman is walking her dog—do you see? And the man she's with is sitting on a big, round boulder? They say that rock was dislodged by a glacier somewhere around Norway, and it ultimately ended up tumbling all the way down to Germany."

"That one rock came all the way from Norway, by itself?"

"That hardly seems likely," the woman retorted. "Surely there must have been others."

When their climb brought them to an overpass above the train tracks, Kogito spotted a tall bus approaching in the far distance, but he couldn't very well say an abrupt good-bye and sprint off to catch it. Office hour had ended around four o'clock, and he knew that this bus ran only three times an hour, so he resigned himself to being trapped in a prolonged conversation with this woman while he waited for the next one to come along.

That was when the woman got down to business. "I wanted to introduce myself again, properly," she began. "Please don't lose *this* one." As she spoke, she thrust a business card in the direction of Kogito's sternum. She evidently expected him to be less than eager to accept it, because she held on to the card for a few extra seconds even after he had it firmly in his hand.

"I think you've probably heard about me from Goro, by my former name," she continued. "The name I'm using now is a combination of my own surname and that of my current husband. He came here from what used to be East Germany, and he's involved in the redevelopment of the East Berlin area. Let's just say he's in the real-estate business. But he's very cultured, and from the beginning he has been very good about allowing me to continue doing my own work, without restrictions.

"One important aspect of my work is still in progress, but perhaps you might have heard something about it from Goro? In any case, there are some very talented people in the new generation of German filmmakers—following in the footsteps of Volker Schlöndorff, the famous director—and the plan was to have some of them work on bringing one of Goro's screenplays to life. And then that heartbreaking thing happened to Goro . . .

"Anyway, as I told you before, that whole thing with the tabloids was the revenge of the *Mädchen für alles*—the girl Friday from hell. All that turmoil and scandal caused poor Goro to suffer so much. Be that as it may (and quite aside from the earlier work that Goro and I did together) I really do feel, after all is said and done, that Goro meant to entrust me with his posthumous request, and I'm determined to make this project happen. He even sent his written declaration of intent, both by fax and in a personal letter. Anyway, there's someone I'd like you to meet, in connection with that project. He is a very distinguished man in film circles, one generation older than the director whose name I mentioned a while ago, Schlöndorff. The current generation of filmmakers values him as a master and a mentor. At present he has stopped making movies and is concentrating his energies on philosophical writing. However, he's still involved in creating a long-form series for serious television. This illustrious person is interested in making a new program, focusing on Goro's life and work. As part of that process, he told me that he is very eager to do a one-hour interview with you while you're in Berlin. The time has been tentatively set for next Sunday morning, and, on the assumption that you would be free then, I went ahead and talked to a professor of Japanese studies at the university. He agreed to come along as your interpreter, so how about it? Will you join us?" Overwhelmed by the torrent of persuasion, Kogito could only nod in silent agreement.

"You will?" The woman looked surprised. "That's great. Thank you very much. So the plan is, we'll stop by your apartment on the day in question and take you directly to the meeting place. It's a famous hotel, right on Potsdam Square, where they'll be holding the Berlin Film Festival starting next week. Come to think of it, Goro showed his films in that festival from time to time, didn't he? That really takes me back. Anyway, your interview will take place in the main hall—as I mentioned just now, the director who will be handling it is very distinguished, so the powers that be are allowing him to use the large hall for filming.

"Unfortunately, the delegation of Japanese movie people won't yet have arrived in Berlin. If our appointment were a few days later, I would have been able to introduce you to some very famous celebrities. That's really a shame—although on second thought perhaps it's just as well, since I've heard that you've been keeping your distance from everyone in the film industry for some time because of your relationship with Goro."

The bus stop was just a square pillar with a sign that read H. On the other side, down the hill, was another, much larger park; Kogito had never been there, but he knew that it was the location of the university's medical school and the renowned Max Planck Institute. As he stood there being buffeted by the icy wind, he had long since given up trying to hold his own against this insistent woman (whose name, according to her business card, was Mrs. Mitsu Azuma-Böme). All he could do was listen in silence to her relentless chatter, which made him think, ruefully, about the old saying: "No matter how bad your aim, if you fire off enough bullets you're bound to hit something eventually."

Contrary to this Azuma-Böme woman's supposition, Kogito had no recollection of ever having heard anything about a plan for a German director to make a film based on one of Goro's original screenplays. He thought it likely that Goro, who was somewhat weak-willed (or, more charitably, softhearted) and hated to say no to anyone, might simply have been unable to summon the energy to resist this woman's blandishments.

The likelihood increased if you considered the possibility (again, this was wild surmise) that Goro might have had some kind of involvement with the woman's daughter and that relationship had become complicated and problematic. What Kogito did remember hearing spoken of as a certainty, while Goro was still alive, was a plan to take the American profits from Goro's most recent hit movie, bank those funds in Los Angeles, and then embark on a new film project there, using local actors and crew.

If that was the case, given that Germany had always warmly embraced Goro's films, with box-office numbers second only to those they racked up in America, it was entirely possible that Goro had thought about setting up a similar project with a German cast and crew.

On top of that—this was something that happened three years earlier, immediately after Goro's last sojourn in Berlin— Kogito remembered hearing that there were some young German film students who wanted to take the movie Goro had made from one of Kogito's novels (*Der stumme Schrei,* in German), dismantle it, and reassemble it as an experimental film. At that time, Goro had also asked Kogito whether he would need to be paid for the right to use the film or whether he might be inclined to let the young scholars use it for free.

This conversation took place on an evening when Goro, Chikashi, and Kogito, along with their assorted offspring, went on a rare group outing to have dinner in Roppongi. On that night, Kogito wasn't able to do anything more than listen to Goro's proposition and promise to think about it later. That was because Chikashi openly criticized the plan, pointing out that it was uncommonly inconsiderate of them not only to ask Kogito, the novelist, to allow his work to be used without any payment for the film rights, but also to give carte blanche for the work of art to be freely taken apart and rearranged. After Chikashi's tongue-lashing, Goro retreated into a timid, cowed silence, but Kogito remembered having the distinct feeling that Goro hadn't come up with that idea on his own.

Under the cloudy Berlin skies, with dusk darkening into evening—it wasn't long past 4 PM, but it already felt like night to Kogito—the tall double-decker bus finally hove into sight, pitching and rolling like a ship at sea. Kogito started to say his polite good-byes to the woman but she winced, and the expression on her small face, enveloped in that cloud of unnaturally black hair, suggested that he had done something terribly rude.

"Don't worry," she said coldly. "I'm not planning to follow you all the way to your apartment. This same bus goes to Potsdam Square. Didn't you know that? Were you afraid that *I* was going to start acting like some crazy *Mädchen für alles* or something? How would you have dealt with that?"

Huffily, Mrs. Azuma-Böme clambered quickly onto the bus and began to ascend the steep, twisting staircase to the second deck. Kogito somehow ended up following her, and they sat down side by side on the right side of the front row. He found it difficult to say anything to the woman, for fear that her present fierce silence might revert at any moment to the equally intense loquacity she had displayed at the bus stop, so he just stared out the window at the grocery stores and other shops that were just beginning to buzz with early-evening activity.

The bus approached Rathenauplatz, and at the point where Kogito could look out over the lively bustle of Ku'damm from his high second-floor seat, he bowed to Mrs. Azuma-Böme and started to descend the stairs alone. She returned his bow with an authoritative nod, bobbing the mass of hair whose inky blackness looked so incongruous on someone her age, and two perfectly straight parallel lines appeared where her lips should have been. Once again, Kogito had the illusion that the woman was holding a small harmonica in her mouth.

As he waited to cross a wide boulevard, heading toward the bus stop where he would transfer to his final conveyance, Kogito looked up at the already black sky, then lowered his eyes to monitor the color progression of the stoplight. That's when it hit him.

"Aha!" he said out loud, more like a sigh than an exclamation, as he put two and two together. (Soliloquizing to himself in public was a habit that always seemed to be resurrected whenever he was living abroad.) But wait—did the "scandal girl" whose photograph had been splashed across the cover of the tabloid magazine really resemble the woman with the harmonica mouth? Everyone said that photo was a deliberate setup staged by the girl and her unsavory boyfriend, who worked for the tabloid publisher, but in any case that was definitely Goro sitting next to her, looking uncommonly depressed.

If, indeed, the girl in the picture (the purported *M. für alles*) had the same harmonica mouth as her mother—two straight, parallel lines—and if Goro had nicknamed her "Bean Harmonica" . . . *Well,* Kogito thought, *my powers of observation regarding women never could hold a candle to Goro's gifts in that area.* Yet Goro's extraordinary perceptiveness had almost never prompted him to avoid (much less run away from) trouble with women.

And that, too, was classic Goro.

CHAPTER TWO

This Fragile Thing
Called Man

1

Kogito taught at the Free University twice a week, and on the other weekdays he went there to eat lunch with his colleagues. But he spent the majority of his time in Berlin by himself, and one of the things he thought about in his solitude was how many times his conversations with Goro had turned, over the years, to the subject of suicide. That topic cropped up frequently in the Tagame talks, as well. Of course, ever since Goro jumped to his death Kogito hadn't had the slightest desire to talk about suicide—indeed, avoiding that subject was one of the cardinal Rules of Tagame. On the other hand, Goro himself had freely discussed that very topic on the tapes.

"From the first time I met you in Mat'chama, I felt that I was destined to play a certain role in your life," Goro said on one recording. "There's no way of saying whether I played that role effectively or not; maybe the 'problem' was all in my mind, and I was just wrestling with myself—doing one-man sumo, as the saying goes. In any case, when our circumstances changed and we weren't seeing each other as often as before, there were people who came along and assumed that role in my stead. Still, it might not have been entirely my imagination that you needed looking out for. I mean, the people who took over that role from me weren't freewheeling yakuza-hipster types like me." (The self-deprecation was typical Goro, and so was the hyperbole.) "You'll probably deny this right off the bat, if only because you have a deep-seated tendency to be contrarian, but the truth is you've really been a very blessed human being. Now that you're within hailing distance of your sixties, isn't it about time to get rid of the *basso ostinato* in your way of living? You know what I mean: the bass notes of your relentless self-mockery."

When Goro started talking about his predestined role in Kogito's life, Kogito always wondered whether Goro was really trying to say that he had been Kogito's tutor and mentor and, apparently, his guardian angel, too. But then he realized that a thought like that was exactly the sort of naïve oversimplification that *deserved* to be subjected to self-ridicule. At that point, he pressed the STOP button and asked, "Now that you and I hardly ever see each other anymore, who do you think has taken your place?"

When Kogito hit the PLAY button again, Goro charged aggressively on, as if he had known exactly how Kogito was going to respond. "I think Professor Musumi has stepped into my shoes, and Takamura, as well. I'm sure you'll know exactly what I mean when I say they aren't yakuza types like me."

Feeling a bit disconcerted, Kogito stopped the tape again and thought about the link that connected Professor Musumi, Takamura, and Goro. They were all people he had known for a long time and been very fond of, but even though he had been Professor Musumi's student at university, there was no way you

could call that distinguished scholar of the French Renaissance
a tutor, although he had certainly been a mentor. As for the composer Takamura, that was a slightly different dynamic as well.

At the same time, Kogito would have liked to say to Goro:
"I know you like to joke about this, but seriously, you aren't a
yakuza type at all. If anything, you're the anti-yakuza. I mean,
gangsters perceive you as such a formidable adversary that a
genuine yakuza boss sent a couple of goons to attack you!"

Maybe Goro was just getting a kick out of using the
Tagame system, but when Kogito pressed the PLAY button again
he noticed that Goro seemed to be in remarkably high spirits
as he picked up where he'd left off. Once again, he was so
nakedly candid that Kogito was momentarily shocked.

"I think what I was doing in Mat'chama was trying to create a barrier to keep you from killing yourself," Goro said. "Of
course, I'm not sure to what extent I was consciously aware of
that, at the time. But when I think back now, that's the only
thing it could have been. That strikes me as very strange, because it's not as if I was some teenage saint, hanging out with
everyone I met in Mat'chama from purely altruistic motives.
Although you couldn't say that I was a totally selfish, self-serving
scoundrel, either, by any means! But in your case, especially—
from the time you were seventeen or eighteen, there were some
things about you that I simply couldn't grasp. You were really a
hard nut to crack, even more than you yourself realized. Maybe
it was in spite of your isolated deep-mountain upbringing, or
maybe it was precisely *because* of that, but you were definitely
a horse of a different color.

"Still, it wasn't until we were both in our thirties that I
started consciously thinking about you as a potential suicide,

and even then, that was only because someone shoved the idea under my nose. That was when you and I were both busy all year round—I had started my own career and you were always reading or writing books—and we only got to hang out once in a blue moon. As you know, there are some bars around Tokyo where certain people in the movie business congregate. (Or, I should say, people who have made a career on the production end of moviemaking.) Anyway, when I used to go to one of those bars I would sometimes run into your friend Takamura, who was there because, as you know, he often composed film scores. This was before he got sick, of course. He would spot me from the entrance and swoop down on my table like a great black bird. And the first thing he always did, after sitting down next to me, was to ask about you.

"'Have you seen Kogito lately? Is he all right?' and so on, without even bothering to lower his voice. And it wasn't the usual sort of small talk about how your work was going or how Akari was getting along. No, he always came right out and said it, without beating around the bush: 'I'm worried that Kogito might commit suicide one of these days.' That's exactly what he said. And he asked me the same questions every time I saw him, so there's no way it could have been a onetime misunderstanding. And after that I finally understood why I, too, had felt a vague compulsion to watch out for you, back when you were seventeen or eighteen—it was because I was afraid you might kill yourself. That explains everything!

"Okay, I know what you're thinking: it's very possible that Takamura would have thought such a thing, but what about Professor Musumi? You probably find it hard to imagine how that distinguished professor could have given me the same idea, right? Of course, there's no reason for someone like me to see a great scholar like that on a regular basis. I did meet him briefly when you and Chikashi had your small wedding, but I hadn't seen him at all since then until we happened to have dinner together in Paris. His wife was there that night, as well."

Kogito pressed the STOP button, took his book of Professor Musumi's *Complete Works* off the shelf, and checked the chronological tables in the back. (Later, he had taken that same volume to Berlin with him, with the intention of donating it to the school of comparative literature before he returned to Tokyo.) Then he turned back to Tagame and replied in great excitement: "That must have been at the time of Professor Musumi's last stay in France! It was the year there was a trash collectors' strike in Paris. I still have a souvenir that he brought back for me; it's a miniature-type painting that shows the entire city of Paris, and here and there you can see smoke rising from the piles of burning trash in the streets. It's sitting on the desk in front of me, here in Seijo."

Goro continued his anecdote. "My former mother-in-law, who as you know was the vice president of a Japanese company that imports films from abroad, was a huge admirer of Professor Musumi's, and she had been hoping to persuade the Musumis to be her guests for dinner at a three-star restaurant in Paris. Professor Musumi happened to hear that I was in Paris at that time, and he apparently said, 'We'll accept the invitation on the condition that Kogito's brother-in-law will be there, too.' I was still quite entangled with my in-laws, and I had heard that my ex-wife was in Tokyo just then, so she wouldn't be there. But anyway, I agreed, and I set out for the restaurant in a suitably humble frame of mind. I was a few minutes late, and it was obvious that the professor had been waiting eagerly for me to show up. The minute I sat down, the first thing he asked me was, 'Do you suppose Kogito might be planning to commit suicide?' My former mother-in-law got a strange look on her face when she heard that, but the professor was totally nonchalant. Then his wife intervened. I have to say that I've never seen a woman of that age who was so incredibly beautiful"—here Goro stopped for a moment, as if searching for a word, and Kogito had a feeling that he was remembering his own mother—"and I don't mean only Japanese women, either. Anyway, Mrs. Musumi said, 'My husband is always worrying about that sort of thing, to the point of being rude. I have to admit that when I first met Kogito I thought there was something a trifle morbid about him, but now I believe that he's turned out to be a very well-grounded person.' After that the vice president—my former mother-in-law—said that she had heard from her daughter that Kogito is kind of a left-winger, politically, but in spite of that he's very amusing. Then Professor Musumi turned his magnificent face to me, with a stately, dignified expression that seemed to say, 'I don't care a fig about that sort of nonsense, do you?' And that's what happened, that night in Paris."

The tape in Tagame kept running after that, but there was only silence. Kogito didn't feel like asking, "And what did you reply?" Even if they had been having an actual, real-time conversation, Goro would probably have shrugged off the question without a word. Because even though you couldn't say that Mrs. Musumi's comment about Kogito's having been "a trifle morbid" was entirely inaccurate, the indisputable fact was that he had actually managed to keep himself alive for a rather long time.

Kogito didn't even think of asking, "And what are *your* thoughts about suicide?" Since Goro had already killed himself by the time Kogito got around to listening to the tape, he felt that to ask a question like that would be a violation of the Rules of Tagame. After an unexplained silence, Goro's voice once again started emanating from the tape recorder, and in his careless way he said something that could have been seen as an infringement of those same unspoken rules. "I know talking about this sort of topic probably makes you feel tired. Of course, in the realm *you* live in, and at your age, people are tired most of the time, anyway! Anyway, let's leave it here for tonight, shall we?"

2

When he jumped off the roof of his office building, Goro left behind two typed notes that he had written on either a word processor or some more versatile microcomputer, Kogito wasn't sure which. Or rather, that was the official announcement made by Taruto, the head of Goro's production company. In actuality, there was also a third note, which was shown only to Kogito and other members of Goro's inner circle. From then on, Kogito frequently found himself thinking about one particular line in that third, unpublished note: "I feel as if I'm starting to fall apart, on every level." No matter how much he pondered those words, Kogito couldn't understand why Goro would talk about himself in those terms.

Goro had been an exceptionally beautiful youth, and even though his hair had started to get a bit thin in both texture and volume by the time he was in his fifties, he was still a fine figure of a man with a charismatic presence. He was also highly proficient in the art of self-presentation and knew how a man at his stage of life should look and carry himself. In the eyes of the world, Goro most certainly didn't appear to be going to pieces, in any way. Kogito could honestly say that there was only one time when he had ever seen Goro falling apart in public, but he didn't recall that incident until he was living alone in Berlin with an abundance of leisure time for dredging up old memories.

On one of the major Japanese television networks there is a popular, long-running late-night program called the *Wide Show* that offers a combination of celebrity chat and cultural news. One night Goro, who was still working as an actor at the time, was one of the guests. Also on the program was a composer who had a wide circle of acquaintances in Parisian society, even though he had spent only a short time studying in Europe. The composer was dressed in a tuxedo that had been custom-made for him in Paris, while Goro was resplendent in a costume of his own design, crafted for him by a Japanese tailor who specialized in occidental garb. It featured a long Mao-collared coat made from lustrous black satin that seemed to have subtle crimson highlights glimmering in its depths, and the two stylishly turned-out men dominated the stage from the moment the program began.

Goro and the composer chatted for a while on camera, both sipping champagne, and before long they were joined by a novelist decked out in his own tux, glass of bubbly already in hand. This author's novels showcased his distinctive views of European literature and customs (particularly the cult of Epicureanism); he was a lively, vivacious conversationalist, but Kogito was acquainted with the man and knew that under the sparkling surface the novelist's true personality was actually rather closed off and curmudgeonly. He was, in reality, a difficult man who always seemed to be seething with resentment about the fact that his talents and insights had never received the kind of treatment they warranted—a "life-sized" response, to use one of his favorite expressions—either in the domestic media or in cultural circles abroad. Eventually, wallowing in his perpetual grievances had caused the man to stagnate as an artist.

On the night in question the novelist was clearly irritated, no doubt because he was having a hard time trying to inject his own "flavor" into a conversation that the composer and the actor were monopolizing with an animated dialogue about Europe. A look of perplexity seemed to be spreading over the face of the well-known host of the *Wide Show,* as well. In an apparent attempt to salvage the mood, a special showing of a short film about Europe was inserted, and after that, Goro (along with the composer and the novelist) reappeared on-screen to join a special live segment featuring a historian and a cultural anthropologist.

But by this time Goro was visibly exhausted, and the alcohol seemed to have suddenly kicked in as well. He launched into a whiny, self-pitying (really, almost feminine) tirade, harping on about how sadly misunderstood and underappreciated he was by the Japanese movie world. As he spoke, his upper body was swaying drunkenly back and forth, and he kept hitting the back of his head on the high-backed chair he was sitting in. At that point Kogito, watching at home, switched off the TV.

Not too long after Goro's embarrassing performance, Kogito learned that his brother-in-law was going through an exceedingly trying time because he and Katsuko were in the process of getting a divorce. But even so, that appearance on the *Wide Show,* when Goro allowed the public to see him in such a shaky and mortifying state, was truly a rarity.

More recently, on the night when Goro was attacked by a pair of yakuza—and, as the proverb says, survived by a one-in-a-million miracle—the TV cameras were at the hospital to record his arrival on a stretcher. (He had already been given emergency first aid to patch up his innumerable knife wounds.) At that time, Goro didn't seem to be falling apart, by any stretch of the imagination. On the contrary, he appeared, at least on camera, to be in a happy, even euphoric mood.

At the time, Kogito happened to be in America—as one publication reported derisively, "her husband's absence left Chikashi free to visit her injured brother"—and he saw the filmed coverage of the yakuza incident in Los Angeles, not on some obscure cable station aimed at the Japanese-speaking market but on a major national network's prime-time early-evening news broadcast. After he returned to Japan, Kogito read an off-the-wall article about the attack, in which one half of a pair of twins—entertainers and pop-culture reviewers who were known for commenting on the news in Japan's distinctive gay patois—made the ludicrous suggestion that the attack might have somehow been staged as a publicity stunt.

To make sure he hadn't misunderstood this shocking allegation, Kogito watched the same entertainer when he appeared on a program targeted at a female audience and was overwhelmed by the dreadful aura of desolation that seemed to be oozing from the man's inner core. It was heartrending to think that Goro had been working in a business populated by such cruel, vicious "elder statesmen," but Kogito's feeling of pity was soon supplanted by a hot rush of anger about the words he had heard and read earlier. And yet in that heartless show-biz world, both after the yakuza attack and all the way through the ensuing trial, Goro was always upbeat—triumphant, even—and he never appeared to be losing his grip on things in the least.

Among the cassette recordings that Goro left behind for Kogito to listen to on Tagame, there was one in which Goro praised a book-length essay titled *This Fragile Thing Called Man,* which Kogito had written when he was young. The gist of the essay was that if we resist the tendency to break—that is, to fall apart—not only will we ourselves remain intact, but we won't hurt other people, and those who were once broken will become whole again. It was, in essence, an evaluation of the direction Kogito had been pursuing in his own way of living in the world. Kogito listened to the tape over and over again, contrasting it with that final, surprisingly self-critical suicide note, in which Goro said that he felt he was falling apart.

The first time Kogito played that particular tape (plucking it at random from among the thirty or so that were delivered all together) was soon after he had begun the ritual of communicating with Goro via Tagame, but Goro's words had a liveliness and power that suggested he was speaking only after having given a considerable amount of concentrated thought to the matter. Ostensibly, he was talking about Kogito's son, Akari, but he approached the subject in a roundabout way.

"When you published *This Fragile Thing Called Man,* my first thought, almost reflexively, was that I'd like to make a film called *The Unbreakable Man,* to explore the other extreme," Goro began. "I told you that directly, and I can still remember how miffed you looked. At some airport—I forget whether it was here or abroad—you happened to see a suitcase with stickers plastered all over it that said FRAGILE, and you came up with the idea of symbolically pasting those stickers on your own back.

I gathered that that experience was your source of inspiration for the essay. But I had a problem with your basic premise that 'breakability,' or whatever you want to call it, is a very common-place attribute of human beings. And I even wondered, at first, 'Is he turning into just another sentimental humanist?' Because the Kogito I knew originally would never have bought into that sort of cheap, popular palaver.

"Anyway, I was thinking about starting my movie by letting the camera reveal how fragile and easily injured we all are—showing the details of the outside of an actual human body, with all its unsightly scars and imperfections, to the point where the audience says, 'Enough, already.' On top of that, I got the idea of having the film tell the story of a protagonist who by some process or another, I'm not sure exactly what, attained a superhuman level of strength and became invulnerable to pain. Sort of a 'brave Lloyd' (as in Harold, of course) for our current era of materialism.

"This goes without saying, but from the earliest days of filmmaking the movie genre has offered portrayals of the 'unbreakable man.' While they're watching the invincible hero, viewers forget how fragile they themselves really are; it's a simple device for engendering catharsis. Of course, there are plenty of breakable people in the supporting roles, getting slashed and killed right and left by the indestructible sword-wielding hero. But they're nothing more than ciphers or symbols on the screen. For example, as a director, if one supporting character gets killed, you don't want to place too much emphasis on his suffering or portray it too sympathetically. If you did that, in the blink of an eye the superhero and the supporting player would end up trading roles. On the other hand, when you show the hero twirling his pistol and then stashing it in the holster, you have to imagine the 'existentially alienated' supporting player, to put it in your terms, lying nearby, mortally wounded.

"Anyway, that was my initial response to that little book of yours, but in the meantime you and Akari, who inspired you to write *This Fragile Thing Called Man,* have been forging ahead with your own lives. And you finally managed to repair Akari, who was born a 'broken thing.' You equipped him so that he could become a functional human being, with his own unique way of living with his obstacles. When I'm listening to music with Akari, I'm always impressed that such a deep and intelligent young man even exists. And he composes those beautiful chords and melodies, music I couldn't even dream of creating. Because of what you've done for him, Akari, who was broken, has been restored. Of course, Chikashi played a big role in that transformation, too, and I admire you both deeply, more than I can say. When Akari was born, I went to the hospital for a visit, and quite aside from the hell you yourself were going through, I really grieved for the dark future ahead of Chikashi. But you were able to put Akari's situation aside when you set forth your insights in *This Fragile Thing Called Man,* and that's what saved it from being sentimental mass-market treacle. I truly believe that. To be honest, though, when you wrote that book, in your younger days, I really don't think you were predicting that Akari would end up as he is today. Yet with no real prospects of success, you all kept struggling valiantly, and eventually Akari was somehow repaired and turned out to be a truly captivating human being. I can't help being profoundly impressed and deeply moved by that.

"I honestly believe that Akari's recovery was a signal from a higher power, far beyond mere humans, that was deciphered on this side. And no, this isn't one of my hyberbolic exaggerations. I know it probably sounds like something out of a science-fiction movie, but I sometimes think that there must be a tremendous flurry of cosmic signals converging on this planet as we approach the end of the millennium. Or maybe it isn't so far-fetched, after all—I mean, there's no question but that the same sort of thing happened around the time of the birth of Jesus Christ! Every time this planet is on the verge of transitioning from one millennium into another, you have to at least admit the possibility that some kind of universal salvation might come to pass, don't you? Of course the signals would be converted into some sort of secret code and beamed down to various locations on the planet. If we could unravel enough of that code, the human race should be able to gather the necessary wisdom to sustain the entire universe.

"Anyway, I think that what you and Chikashi did for Akari is a prime example of a brilliantly successful deciphering of that code. The reason Akari's CD is receiving such an enthusiastic reception all over the world is because he managed to tap into that scrambled cosmic code and translate it into music, and people are responding to that on an unconscious level. I realize there may be some resistance to the expression 'breaking a code,' so let's put it this way instead: You and Chikashi took a mechanism that had fallen apart during its long journey from the cosmos to earth, and you repaired it and made it work—and work perfectly to boot."

Based on the strangers' voices and the other ambient noise that could be heard in the background, Kogito imagined that this tape alone (unlike the others, which had evidently been recorded in Goro's production-company office) had been made in his private room at the hospital. If that was the case, it was probably recorded after the yakuza attack, while Goro was still recovering from the worst of his external wounds. One day around that time, when Chikashi came home after visiting Goro at the hospital, she was distressed because one of the fingers that he needed in order to play his guitar wouldn't move—probably because of some sort of neural-network misfiring caused by the deep cut on his neck from the yakuza attack—and she was concerned that this new complication would make his recovery even more difficult.

So when Goro talked about Akari's birth injury (that is, the broken part) and how it had been perfectly repaired, wasn't he really making an appeal to Kogito on his own behalf, while ostensibly applauding Kogito and Chikashi's tireless efforts to "fix" their son? Goro's injuries weren't life threatening, but some important parts of his body had been damaged ("broken") and there was no guarantee of a full recovery. So it was no wonder that a man like Goro, who was past middle age, would rhapsodize on and on about Akari's miraculous resurrection.

It wasn't just the physical part of Goro that was destroyed by the meaningless, unjust yakuza violence; he was also falling apart mentally as a result of this life-changing incident, while he struggled to figure out how to restore himself to normal. With the "unbreakable man" tape, surely Goro was trying to send Kogito a questioning signal: searching for answers, pleading for help. For Goro was clearly continuing to have a very real reaction to the ongoing pain and terror caused by the yakuza ambush—not to mention the vague feelings of malaise that haunted him long after his external scars had healed. He didn't talk directly about it, but . . .

Kogito had once written a short story about a young Japanese man who was working at a boat harbor on a large river in Uganda. When he was bitten by a hippopotamus—the hippo actually chomped down on the youth's torso, with the head and legs hanging out of opposite sides of the beast's huge mouth—the Japanese expatriate worker who was the model for the character in the story said later that he hadn't been able to do anything except to scream piteously, "Aah, aah!" As Goro put it: "My impression is that those helpless, inarticulate syllables were the exact expression of what he was actually going through."

At the time—this conversation took place at the movie studio where Goro was directing the film version of Kogito's novel *A Quiet Life*—Kogito and Goro had both averted their eyes and lapsed into silence. Obviously, they were remembering Goro's horrific experience of being attacked by yakuza and having his handsome face slashed to ribbons.

3

"The other day I got a phone call from a freelance journalist," Goro said. (This was before the Tagame era, and he and Kogito were talking on the telephone.) "He's a weird, gloomy sort of guy and he's obviously aware of that, so he goes overboard trying to lighten up. Anyway, he said that he wants to research an article based on your old novel about the young right-wing activist who assassinated a politician and then committed suicide in jail. He's even got a charming little working title: 'The Politically Hypocritical and Cowardly Life of Kogito Choko.' His plan is to publish it first in a popular news magazine, and he said that he's already gotten comments about the young Choko from a major critic from the conservative faction and from an international film director, too. You know who I'm talking about, but let's be discreet and call them 'Uto' and 'Mogusa,' in case anyone's listening. Then he said that he especially wanted to talk to me about Kogito's 'numerous character flaws,' as he put it. He even boasted that he's going to corner 'that guy'"(meaning you) and lead you around like a dog on a leash until you have no choice, this time, but to have a direct confrontation with the right wing. What do you think about that?"

"Whatever I might think, you should handle it as you see fit," Kogito replied in a tone of cool indifference. "To these young journalists, the sixties are ancient history, a past long forgotten. I wonder why he's so gung ho about exhuming that old incident?"

A few days later, there was another phone call from Goro. "I decided to go along with that journalist's plan for the time being, so I had him come to the production office," he said. "When we actually met face-to-face, you'll never guess who he reminded me of. Remember back in Mat'chama there was a big, curly-haired guy called Arimatsu, who was always kind of pushy and obnoxious? Well, this reporter looks and acts a lot like him. If that Arimatsu had ended up struggling to make a living as a bottom-feeding journalist, he would probably have turned out just like this guy. Anyway, he acted as if being invited to my office meant that he was already in like Flynn. I don't know why, but he has somehow convinced himself that *I* detest you, too, and so he's confident that he's someone I simply can't do without. Anyway, he made himself right at home in my office, and when I was about to leave for a previously arranged business lunch at a nearby Italian restaurant, he tried to tag along. At that point I realized it was time to put an end to the charade, and I blurted out, 'Okay, Arimatsu, I think that's it for today.' (Like I said, he really reminded me of that guy in Mat'chama.) But, get this, he said: 'Since you're kind enough to call me by that nickname, I think I'd like to use it as my new nom de plume—but what would be a good first name to go with it?' So I said off the top of my head, just trying to get rid of him, 'How

about Arimi?' He said, 'That's perfect!' and then he finally went
away, in an obvious state of exultation."

Not long after that, Kogito heard that Chikashi, too, had
inadvertently encountered "Arimi Arimatsu." At the time, Goro
was in preproduction, organizing the materials for his upcoming film, A Quiet Life, and when Chikashi took Akari's sheet
music for the score to the production office, Arimatsu happened
to be there. Goro didn't introduce Chikashi to him, but as the
conversation went along the journalist apparently deduced that
she was Kogito's wife and promptly tried to muscle in.

He started out by saying something obsequious, like "Of
course, there's no need for *me* to say that Akari's CD is beautiful," as if he was holding back his real opinion. (Kogito suspected
that the man was probably being cautiously ambiguous in stating his true feelings about the CD, for reasons unknown.) Then
he went on to report, with the air of having some sort of hidden
agenda, that a famous Japanese actor-composer, currently headquartered in New York City, had remarked in a published conversation that he really couldn't bear to see the music of a mentally
disabled person being foisted on the world under the banner of
political correctness. (The interviewer was a trendsetting Japanese scholar and culture maven who had burst on the scene with
his Japanized interpretation, dubbed "New Academyism," of the
movement associated with Derrida and Barthes.)

It was hard to tell from the angle of the reporter's body
whether he was addressing his remarks to Goro or to Chikashi,
but Chikashi made no attempt to reply. Goro, unable to stand
by in silence, said, "And what do you think about that?" to which
the journalist answered, in a forceful way, "I don't have any truck
with political correctness or New Academyism or any of that

stuff. I'm just a backward pupil, myself—I'm Ari-*matsu!*" This was a double-edged witticism, replicating the "Sir, yes, *sir!*" cadence of a crisp, military-style response while also evoking a perennially popular cartoon character.

Kogito, who found this very amusing, remarked, "There used to be a character in Fujio Akatsuka's manga who was something like a custodian or janitor in an old-fashioned elementary school, remember? Before his transformation he had supposedly been a pine tree, so no matter what he was talking about, he would always add '*matsu*'—'pine tree'—to the end of the word, as a suffix. That was hilarious. So it sounds as if this journalist must have been using that old joke as part of his own shtick. What a clown."

"No, that's not it," Chikashi said. "Apparently he only started talking like that since adopting the pen name of Arimatsu."

Kogito's smile faded as he recalled the belligerent, confrontational article, written under that very pen name, declaring that if Kogito Choko was going to keep on talking like a progressive, he ought to go ahead and publish *Death of a Political Youth,* which had never been released as a complete book in Japan due to fear of violent right-wing retaliation. (It had, however, been serialized there in a magazine and published overseas.)

Later on that same day, Goro had gone to the sushi restaurant at the Hotel Okura for lunch with his actress-wife, Umeko, and Taruto from his production company, and he invited Chikashi to come along. Something unexpected happened on that outing, although fortunately it didn't turn out as badly as it might have.

The elegant hotel's sushi restaurant was a branch of a venerable *sushiya* on the Ginza; Goro was well known there, and they received the usual warm welcome. The party was given four seats at the right end of the counter, and when they had finished ordering beer and sake and were wiping their hands with the customary hot, damp towels, they heard a commotion behind them. Taruto was in the seat farthest to the left, and the six guests who had been sitting next to him abruptly stood up and moved to a table in the back of the restaurant. Observing this, Chikashi said in all seriousness, "Hmm, I wonder if someone from the imperial family is coming in for lunch."

Then, just as Chikashi and the others were about to pick up the first few morsels of sushi, the sushi maker behind the counter suddenly stood at attention in a most unnatural way, with his back concave and his chest thrust out, while a man who was apparently in charge of all the restaurants on that floor of the hotel poked his head in from the corridor and said to Taruto, "I'm sorry, but would you mind leaving these seats at the counter and moving your party to a table?"

Without giving the stunned Taruto time to ask for an explanation of this unheard-of request, Goro (like the trained actor he was) responded in a sonorous tone that was at least an octave lower than his normal speaking voice. "No, we booked these seats for an hour. We've only been here for a few minutes, so we'll just finish eating our meal here at the counter."

At any rate, the people who filled up the six open seats at the counter were all large, taciturn men wearing sunglasses. Chikashi complained later to Kogito that for someone like her who wasn't drinking beer or sake, it was hard to bear sitting at the counter for so long, and she had inadvertently ended up eating too much. Goro, it seemed, had lingered longer than necessary, just to make a point.

When they left the restaurant, even though there were plenty of conspicuously unoccupied seats inside, they saw a group of men in their prime, all dressed identically in gangsterish black suits and looking surprisingly lithe despite their rugged builds, lined up in the passage with their backs against the wall. Obviously, they were standing guard for some Very Important Yakuza.

Once Chikashi and her companions were finally alone in the elevator, Umeko explained what had happened, with a serious smile that seemed to reflect her tired, somber mood. "In the group that came in after we did and chased away the people who were eating at the counter, did you notice the one in the middle wearing superdark sunglasses? He's the head of a yakuza crime syndicate, and because Goro was so stubborn about refusing their request to take over all the seats at the counter, even though he's in a court case against them right now, I was really expecting to die at any moment."

"So if Goro had agreed to give up our seats, you would have followed?" Chikashi asked.

"After spending an hour and a half eating sushi like it was going out of style, I think I'm going to have to go on a diet for the next week!" Umeko groaned, nimbly evading the question.

Goro had no plans to share this near misadventure—which could so easily have turned into a hostile confrontation—with the media, but an article about the incident turned up in a popular tabloid magazine, bearing the byline of Arimi Arimatsu, as Goro had dubbed him. Presumably the journalist must have overheard some unguarded conversation as he was lurking around the production office. Kogito, who was no stranger to threats from unwholesome organizations, couldn't help wondering whether Arimatsu might have written the story in the hopes of stirring up the yakuza—not the top brass, necessarily, but the feisty, trigger-happy younger members. Because in the same article, the journalist once again leveled the charge that Kogito had conducted his life in such a way as to avoid being physically attacked by the right wing, and he went on to announce that Kogito really ought to try to emulate his courageous brother-in-law, who was willing to risk being slashed again over a matter of principle—even something as seemingly trivial as the seating in a sushi restaurant.

Chikashi shared Kogito's thoughts about this with Goro, and during the same conversation she broached the theory that the people who write that kind of article seem to be actively hoping that something terrible will happen.

To which Goro replied: "You're absolutely right, Arimatsu and his ilk are probably *praying* that something terrible will happen. You know that big-shot journalist who's been denouncing Kogito for all these years? He used to write a so-called humor column for the weekly magazine of a certain newspaper. It was called, tongue in cheek, *For the Gentlefolk of the Right Wing,* and among the other drivel he wrote was a blatantly provocative essay about the increasing dilution of the imperial family's blood by intermarriage with commoners. He actually challenged his right-wing readers, saying something like, 'Are you going to stand by quietly and let this happen?' And then he went on to state the obvious fact that the new crown princess is of common birth, and he even asked the inflammatory question outright: *What are you going to do if she gets pregnant?* If there were some right-wing 'gentlefolk' who took that seriously, isn't it possible that they might stage some sort of heinous terrorist act to prevent the childbirth from taking place? Of course, that isn't something a normal person would dream up, much less encourage, but his type of right-wing journalist—the self-styled 'moral crusader'—really is a breed apart."

4

One day, Kogito got a call from Goro (a rather rare occurrence of late), saying that he wanted to get together to discuss some business having to do with "societal matters," as he put it. Surprisingly, the meeting place Goro suggested wasn't his usual hangout, the little Italian restaurant next to the office building where he worked—the same restaurant that would later be splashed all over the tabloids in surreptitious photographs of Goro's "secret rendezvous."

As it happened, Kogito had a favor to ask of Goro, too. An American film student, whom Kogito had met when he gave a lecture at the University of Chicago as part of its centennial celebration, had come to Tokyo for the express purpose of interviewing Goro Hanawa. When Kogito explained the situation, Goro graciously agreed to the interview (he was always very good about that sort of thing) and that may have been his reason for suggesting a classier meeting place. The location he chose was the coffee lounge on one side of the lobby of the Imperial Hotel, and when Kogito arrived he found his brother-in-law already deep in conversation, displaying his fabulously fluent English, with Oliver, the young man from the University of Chicago. Oliver was actually quite proficient in Japanese, but when Goro initially addressed him in English he probably hadn't had the nerve to respond in Japanese. In any case, Kogito suggested that they switch to Japanese, starting immediately.

It soon emerged that the matter Goro wanted to discuss with Kogito had to do with the video release of his controversial satirical film about the violent world of yakuza protection rackets, which presented a comically unflattering portrait of the modus operandi of Japanese gangsters. The release date was fast approaching, and it looked as if that event might stir up trouble with the yakuza involved in the case that was presently in court—members of the same group as the men who had been sitting at the Hotel Okura's sushi counter. Although the video situation didn't involve the same syndicate that had sent assassins to attack Goro, there was no question but that Japanese-mobster groups, large and small, were working behind the scenes to try to stop the video of Goro's hit film from going on sale. It had gotten to the point where the police department was talking about possibly reinstituting police protection for Goro and Umeko.

Meanwhile, Goro was dealing with a separate lawsuit, which also had something to do with a video release. Kogito remembered having heard about this before, and he was also acquainted with Goro's selfless habit of mentoring, so he knew that Goro had once hired a talented young director and had gone on to produce a film directed by that protégé. This truly was a selflessly altruistic undertaking, especially when Japan's economic slump seemed to be here to stay; independent production companies led by well-known directors were posting red ink across the board, and even the major film studios, with very few exceptions, were finding it difficult to break even.

Goro knew going in that he wouldn't make a profit from showing this small film in theaters, and he counted on the revenue from video sales to repay his production company's investment. Umeko made a special appearance in the film and Goro was in constant attendance on the young director, guiding him through every step of the filmmaking process . . . perhaps more closely than he might have wished. (Kogito suspected that Goro's hands-on participation might have contributed to the litigious young director's complicated mental state, but that type of collaboration was different from the literary student-teacher relationships that he himself was familiar with, so this was just amateur speculation.) In any event, during a discussion of potential earnings from video sales, Taruto had told Goro's apprentice up front that the director's fees would not be shared, but the communication on that point had been purely verbal.

When the video went on sale, the young director filed a lawsuit, claiming that he hadn't received his rightful share of the profits, and the directors' guild threw its weight behind his cause. The court seemed to be leaning toward ruling in favor of Goro's production company, and as a result, Goro found himself isolated from the rest of the movie world.

"And the people who rallied behind that young director when he was suing me, gathering signatures to support him and taking a stand in the media—now they've turned around and are gathering signatures to support *me* in my case against the yakuza who are trying to prevent the video's release," Goro said, shaking his head in disbelief. "I heard this from that journalist,

Arimatsu. It's all the exact same people (directors, actors, actresses, film critics) who were united against me before, only now they're signing petitions on my behalf. Doesn't that seem a trifle inconsistent? But if the logic behind their activism dictates supporting whatever stance they think is right, I see no reason to refuse their support."

As Kogito listened, he understood immediately that Goro, in spite of having become rather cynical with the passage of years, still retained an essential childlike goodness, and because of this he was misinterpreting the information.

"If the heavy hitters in the directors' association are at the center of a movement to prepare a new statement, and if they're collecting signatures, then that has the opposite meaning of the way you're interpreting it," Kogito said. "Arimatsu must have deliberately misled you with the way he relayed the news. From where I stand, it looks as if the petition signers from the directors' association are expecting that one of the many organized crime syndicates who can send out yakuza hit men anytime, anywhere, will threaten you, and cause the video release to be canceled—that is, if you lose your nerve and knuckle under. They're certain that you'll end up canceling the video production, and when that happens they're planning to claim that your self-censorship is jeopardizing the future freedom of expression of the entire film world. It's the same manipulative scenario as Arimatsu's denunciation of me."

Kogito paused and took a sip of coffee. "After all, when you were stabbed by those yakuza, the directors' association didn't lift a finger to organize a protest demonstration. (Even young Oliver, here, along with his colleagues, was trying to put together a sympathy protest on both sides of the Pacific.) And it's just the same, now, too. Those directors and their cohorts aren't thinking even for a moment of staging a direct confrontation with the yakuza for your sake, believe me! You should just go ahead and release the video, as planned. But of course, you and Umeko will need to make sure you have police protection."

Goro nodded. "Is it really true that during all the turmoil surrounding your controversial book *The Death of a Right-Wing Youth,* the literary association and the Pen Club—to say nothing of the police—didn't actually do anything in the way of backup?" he asked. "When that newspaper article came out saying that you talked a good game about telling truth to power, but when push came to shove you were protected by that same power, Chikashi was really indignant. But I gather you said that on the contrary it was actually just as well, since that sort of article could have the effect of calming down the so-called rogue elements of the right wing, if it made them see you as a craven hypocrite rather than as a threat."

"But in your case," Kogito responded, "you were actually stabbed by the yakuza minions, and now you're taking on the puppet masters themselves in court. There's a very concrete and specific danger there, and part of the reason they're so angry is because the cultural impact of a hit movie is so much greater than that of, say, a work of pure literature."

By and by, Oliver, who had been listening intently to what Goro and Kogito were saying but was clearly feeling ill at ease about something, finally jumped into the conversation with an air of determination. (He may have been encouraged by the favorable things Kogito had said earlier about him and his colleagues at the University of Chicago.)

"On my way here, following Kogito's instructions, I took the subway to Hibiya Station, and when I climbed the stairs to the street I noticed a right-wing propaganda truck parked a little ways away," he said. "Even if they had some other reason for sitting in the front seat and watching the hotel's entrance, isn't it possible that they recognized either or both of you when you arrived? And then, even if it wasn't their original purpose for being here, maybe they decided to use this serendipitous opportunity to send Kogito some kind of intimidating message? I have a feeling some of them are in the lobby right now, looking this way. Please don't turn around right now, but there are some men dressed in khaki slacks and colorful sports shirts. They look totally out of place in this high-class hotel, right? I think they just took off their uniform jackets and marched in here in their casual clothes."

"I haven't noticed anyone who looks like a right-winger . . ." Just as Kogito was saying this, four bandy-legged men decked out in zooty black suits appeared in his field of vision. They were descending the stairs from the mezzanine floor in a leisurely yet menacing fashion, and they had an unobstructed view of Goro's table. "I'm actually more concerned about a different type of gentleman—and I use that term loosely."

From the time Oliver began talking, and even after Kogito picked up the conversational thread, Goro was silent, his mind obviously elsewhere. Still without saying a word, he abruptly stood up and turned his imposingly large body to face the crowd of people milling about in the lobby, then made a conspicuous show of removing the long coat he was wearing. After that he just stood there, nattily dressed in a suit worn over a silk shirt and a vest of diagonally woven silk, and beamed a neutral smile around the lobby, directed at nobody in particular. He looked for all the world like an actor taking a curtain call, and his actions seemed designed to attract the attention of every eye in the room.

On the side of the lobby that was screened from the coffee lounge by nothing more than a row of leafy potted plants, a crowd of celebrity spotters immediately began to gather. Whereupon Goro casually leaned across the table, holding his coat under his arm, and said to Kogito and Oliver in a tone that brooked no argument, "Let's go somewhere else where we can have a proper conversation. I still have an hour till my next appointment."

As Goro strode across the lobby toward the exit that led to the Imperial Palace Plaza, nearly everyone in the vast room was staring in his direction, and the atmosphere was not conducive for anyone to step boldly forward and try to block his way—not even the black-suited yakuza bruisers or the young zealots from the right-wing propaganda truck.

Young Oliver from the University of Chicago, obviously thrilled to be sharing an adventure with the famous director, bounded after Goro while Kogito stayed behind to pay the bill. As he was standing at the cash register, a young woman's voice called out from a table where a group of three or four people was sitting. Their backs were turned to the table that Kogito's group had occupied, but they were close enough to have overheard the entire conversation.

"Hey, Choko!" the woman said loudly. "Leaving so soon?"

Sitting right next to her was a big, curly-haired man. Kogito instantly identified him, based on Goro's typically vivid description, as the infamous Arimatsu.

5

When Goro was slashed by the Kansai-based yakuza who had come up to Tokyo on their terrorist errand, Kogito (as has already been mentioned) was in Chicago for the university's centennial celebration, at the invitation of the Asian Studies Department. His lecture ended before noon, and the plan was for a panel discussion, featuring Kogito and the American scholars who had issued the invitation, to begin in the early afternoon.

During the lunch break, Kogito went to the University of Chicago's library to research a point of contention that had come up during the question period following his lecture. While he was there, Oliver and a group of his fellow film students came to tell him that they had just seen a television news report about the attack on Goro. There was something beautiful about the way they were obviously struggling to disguise their alarm and concern, to spare Kogito's feelings, but they still radiated an aura of irrepressible youthful energy.

Kogito asked a few questions, then lapsed into silence, and the students, too, fell silent and formed a protective circle around him. It was as if they wanted to give him time to digest the shocking news. When Kogito left the library stacks and headed into the lobby, the students all began to talk at once, saying that they thought people from the film business and university students in Tokyo must already be planning a protest demonstration, and they wanted to join in (taking into account the substantial time difference), if Kogito could just find out the day and time when it was going to take place. They wanted to organize an intrauniversity meeting right away and hoped to be able to announce a firm plan of action before the day was over.

Kogito respectfully declined to participate, and he tried to explain his position to the disappointed students—noting that he had arrived at this conclusion while he was in a place far from Tokyo, and he hoped very much that he was wrong.

"The Japanese film world is currently dominated by directors of a certain age, who are a generation or so older than Goro, and they probably won't view this incident as a terrorist act against the Japanese film industry," he said. "I suspect that they'll just see it as Goro's personal misfortune. In other words, there isn't likely to be any demonstration of protest or solidarity by film people. As for Japan's university students, at this point I honestly don't think they have the gumption to mount an organized protest against this incident, even if they do see it as a threat to culture and society."

Kogito left Chicago the following day, and while he was on his way back to Japan—stopping on the way to give readings at UCLA and at two universities in the Hawaiian Islands—he happened to get hold of a Japanese newspaper. As he read the coverage of the attack on Goro, he realized that his brutally frank (some might say cynical) prediction had been right on the mark.

Whenever he was at his hotel, Kogito kept a careful eye on the news broadcasts, and he got to see a number of reports about the attack on Goro, with video sent from Japan via overseas feed.

One of those videos showed Goro arriving at the hospital on a stretcher, with his injured head wrapped in gauze that looked rather like a swimming cap—no doubt a temporary measure to cover up the wounds. That way of bandaging is probably common in hospitals today, but on Goro, the trendsetter, the bathing-cap bandage somehow gave the impression of being a chic new Western style that he was introducing to Japan. The entire scene came across as positive, even festive, with Goro going so far as to flash a triumphal V sign at the waiting throng of reporters.

He managed to transform the dynamics of the situation so that it seemed as if this wasn't a passive or defensive mishap but was, rather, brought on by Goro's own expressionistic action. The subliminal suggestion seemed to be that he might conceivably end up taking on the yakuza again, both in art and in life, with his entire being. Kogito understood that right away. The American television-network people seemed to pick up on that message, too—they had made the incident the lead story on this evening's broadcast—but Kogito couldn't help wondering whether the Japanese media would be doing the same. Probably not, he thought sadly. Rather, he suspected, Goro's upbeat reaction would be viewed as a gratuitously over-the-top performance by his colleagues in the worlds of movies and television.

In the following scene, the news camera had captured an exhausted-looking Umeko, lagging slightly behind the media mob that was chasing after Goro's stretcher and accompanied by Chikashi, in the role of her sister-in-law's protector. Kogito could tell that Chikashi was in an extremely dark mood, but her always-serene face showed only grief and gravitas. Watching his wife on the TV screen, Kogito sensed that she was trying to protect her injured brother, and at the same time she obviously felt that there was something unseemly about the overexcited way he was talking and behaving. She looked, too, as if she might be thinking about the fact that the video now being filmed would eventually be broadcast with voiceover reaction by the newscasters, and the emotional tenor of those comments probably wouldn't be supportive of Goro.

Kogito never forgot a talk he'd had with his younger brother, on one of Chu's infrequent visits to Tokyo. This was after Goro's death, and Kogito's brother expressed his deep sympathy about that loss and the yakuza disaster that preceded it. Especially toward Chikashi, the bereaved sister, he demonstrated a fond regard that was close to adoration.

The same Chu who had stared suspiciously at Goro from behind his sister's skirts so many years ago, when Kogito brought his school friend home for a visit, had joined the police force right out of high school and had for many years been the officer in charge of the violent crimes unit in Matsuyama. Chu evidently had no intention of taking the requisite tests for advancing in the police hierarchy (the fact is, Kogito felt that Chu resented his older brother for having graduated from the Tokyo University Department of Literature, which was regarded by the outside world as the virtual equivalent of law school), and his life plan seemed to be to remain a rank-and-file policeman until he retired.

Uncle Chu, as he was called, was loved and respected by everyone in the family. He was a tough, hard-bitten policeman through and through, but while he was talking about the yakuza attack on Goro, his face wore an expression of undisguised horror and anguish.

"The people who utilize yakuza . . . well, that's already a bit of an oversimplification, because the problem is far more complicated than that," he began. "But anyway, the politicians and other people who make use of the yakuza do so through underlings, of course, but sometimes the tables get turned and the higher-ups who were trying to make discreet use of gangsters end up being directly threatened or blackmailed by their own yakuza 'tools.' It's a bit like the old story about the would-be thief who went into some Egyptian tomb to steal a mummy and ended up getting trapped and turned into a mummy himself, you know? Now, this kind of sophisticated terminology may sound strange coming from me, but in any case, there's no need for me to tell you about the sheer rottenness of some of the people at the top of the 'organizational structure' that has yakuza at its base. I know you've met your share of famous politicians!

"This is a separate matter entirely, but the people who are on the periphery of the organizational structure that includes the yakuza—you might call them yakuza subcontractors—but anyway, they're really a motley crew! I'm talking about pimps, touts, drug dealers, leg breakers, that sort of thing. They aren't officially considered yakuza, but they might as well be. As for Goro's world of show business, I really think the people who make movies that glorify and idealize gangsters, or who use organized crime as financial backers for their entertainment projects, are even lower than the lowest yakuza slime. Since Goro staged a direct frontal attack on the yakuza in his own films, I think it would be great to make a movie about him, with Ken Takakura in the leading role. If there were a young director whose talent and courage met with Chikashi's approval, and if she weren't opposed to having Takakura play the part of Goro . . ."

That prompted Kogito to ask Chu about something that was never far from his mind. "I really only ever talked to Goro about his experience with the yakuza attack on the most objective level," he said. "And even then he was just kidding around, making reference to the young Japanese man who got bitten by a hippo in Africa as an example of feeling totally helpless. As for me, I simply didn't have the guts to bring up the topic for a serious discussion. I mean, I've tried to think realistically about what Goro was going through in his own mind, but I don't think I'll ever really understand the most important thing— indeed, I think it's probably going to end without my ever having managed to comprehend the motive behind his suicide. When I say 'end,' I mean that I'm going to die myself before too long, never knowing the answer."

"So are you saying that you think Goro's suicide is somehow tied in with the yakuza attack?" Uncle Chu inquired, in a voice that had something dark and cold swirling around in its depths, behind the usual calm stubbornness. Kogito had the odd feeling that he was seeing something in his brother's facial expression for the first time, but surely that paradoxical tone was natural for a policeman who had spent most of his career in the organized crime division.

Kogito felt as if he was being cross-examined by a professional; that is, by someone very different from the gentle, easygoing Uncle Chu who, as he was greeting Chikashi (whom he hadn't seen in quite some time), had praised her dignified conduct on the same video footage that Kogito had seen on TV in the United States. But he could sense that Chu already had an answer to his own question firmly in mind, so he just nodded receptively and waited for his brother to continue.

"I'm pretty much convinced that being slashed by those yakuza was the direct cause of Goro's suicide," Chu said. "Since the main office of Goro's production company was in Matsuyama, in the course of my official duties I've talked to a police detective there who has researched the background of the case. This is a bit off-topic, but when Goro was gathering material for his yakuza satire, he got to know some of the top brass at the National Police Academy. Later, one of those high-ranking officers was the victim of a terrorist attack by a religious cult, and I heard that while he was recovering in the hospital, Goro sent him a copy of Akari's CD. After that, Goro proposed to the official that they sit down together, as two people who had both been attacked by terrorists, and have a conversation about their experiences, to be published in *Bungei Shunju* magazine. However, the official turned Goro down. Personally, I think that was the right thing to do, but . . . anyway, I heard that the official wrote a letter to a third party, and apparently he said in the letter that he thought Goro was rather naïve but that he was a man of integrity, courage, and strong moral fiber. He also said that Goro was someone who had clearly made up his mind not to give in to violence. I heard this from a very reliable source, and the man who wrote the letter definitely knew what he was talking about, too. He was an extraordinarily strong man himself, both physically and mentally: someone who had his own violent encounter with terrorism when he was the chief executive of the national police but managed to bounce back. He's still working, and he now holds a top job in the Foreign Affairs Ministry or someplace like that. The point is, someone of that caliber called Goro 'a very naïve person' after the yakuza attack.

"I'll have to defer to you, as a graduate of Tokyo University, on the finer points of using foreign words, but even I know that 'naïve' doesn't carry the most positive connotations. On the other hand, we have someone who has himself experienced terrorism calling the victim of a separate terrorist act a man of integrity, courage, and strong moral fiber. I think that's a pretty impressive assessment, and I've never forgotten it to this day. Nevertheless, the fact is that same strong, courageous person ended up snapping and committing suicide over a trifling matter. Even so—and I don't mean to keep flogging the same point over and over—regarding Goro, whatever may have happened in the end, there really isn't any doubt that he was a brave, intrepid, upright man . . . I mean, who better to judge than a career police officer who was himself injured by terrorists? That's what I believe, anyway.

"The things that my colleague in Matsuyama came up with in his investigation were really just those sort of tabloid-level truths. But he gathered together a pile of flimsy rumors and then somehow managed to solidify that squishy mountain of gossip into something that seems as if it might contain a kernel of truth, although it's probably the sort of thing a sharp prosecutor could make mincemeat of in no time. I'm talking on the level of gossip now, but if you look at it objectively, on that tabloid level, what you see from any perspective is an already late-middle-aged man who is talented, accomplished, and successful in his career, getting hopelessly entangled with some slightly disreputable woman. At the beginning it's just supposed to be a lark, but before he knows it he finds himself trapped between the devil and the deep blue sea. That sort of thing happens all the time, right? There are men who get involved with the kind of woman who figured in Goro's tabloid scandal, and even though it's a dreary quagmire that they got into of their own free will, they make no effort to escape and they end up being resigned to their unhappy fate. Someone who is gifted and accomplished, who has a lot of pride and self-respect and who is also a 'very naïve person'—that's exactly the type of man who gets dragged into that sort of situation. But of course this is just the mundane speculation of someone who exists on the level of the weekly tabloids," Chu said half jokingly, then added in all seriousness: "Please tell Chikashi that for a cop like me who's been dealing with violent crimes for a long time, this is the easy, conventional interpretation—especially when you have this kind of spiteful woman's plot and when there's an unsavory man in the mix, as well (in this case, the woman's scheming boyfriend). Because in his suicide note, Goro flatly denied any intimate involvement with the woman in question, and you have to respect that!

"So what I'm left with, Kogito, and it's such a cut-and-dried conclusion that it literally makes me feel sick to my stomach, is that after all is said and done, Goro's suicide was a direct result of having been slashed by the yakuza. Because if he hadn't been subjected to violence by the yakuza, surely he wouldn't have gotten it into his head to perpetrate such a violent act upon himself."

"I haven't allowed myself to think about what you're saying, even in my daydreams, but it all rings completely true," Kogito said. "You've had a lot of direct experience with the terrible specificities of yakuza violence, and the fact that you haven't even touched on that topic in this conversation just makes me feel more acutely aware of its terrible menace."

Uncle Chu had been drinking steadily all this time, and that may have been a factor, but now he got a strangely gleeful look in his eyes—a look Kogito remembered from when they were children and which he found, in the grim context of their discussion, distinctly off-putting.

"The thing is, big brother," Chu said tipsily, "among the huge number of people who have been violently attacked by yakuza, there isn't anyone who's died as a result. Everybody has survived, even the ones who have been repeatedly stabbed or slashed or have been shot in the back by snipers—not a single one has died! I mean, the victims have been subjected to the most extreme sort of terrifying, ghastly violence, and they've still managed to go on living without losing their sanity. To be perfectly frank, I really think that's amazing!"

While they talked, Kogito and Uncle Chu had been drinking red wine from Italy. By this time, the evening was already slipping away. Suddenly Chikashi, who had presumably long since gone to sleep, appeared in the doorway with a fresh bottle of Italian wine in one hand and, in the other, a strong-smelling cheese covered with an inedible rind of grape seeds—a gift from an American cultural theoretician of Italian ancestry who was an acquaintance of Kogito's. Whenever Kogito's brother came up to Tokyo from Shikoku, Chikashi always plied him with the finest food and drink from her domestic stockpile.

Uncle Chu had been talking about Goro in his naturally loud voice, and now he speculatively narrowed his eyes as if he were squinting against a dazzling light, obviously trying to gauge how much of the preceding conversation Chikashi might have overheard.

6

Some time after Kogito read the third suicide note, the one in which Goro said that he felt he was falling apart, he finally asked Chikashi a raw, unusually unguarded question. (Kogito had needed a few days to mull over those baffling words, again and again.)

"You know what Goro said in that note, about feeling as if he was falling apart?" he asked. "Looking at it objectively, I find that really hard to believe. But right after his death, there was some relatively sensible commentary in which someone said that Goro's sense of himself might have been distorted due to presenile depression or melancholia. Do you remember?"

As she nearly always did, Chikashi took a few moments to reflect before answering Kogito's question. "I don't believe Goro chose to die because of some kind of degenerative illness or mental lapse," she said slowly. "I think it was a completely sane and conscious decision for him. Remember a long time ago, in Matsuyama, very late one night, when you and Goro came back to the 'Little Temple,' where he and I were lodging?

I don't have a very clear memory of you on that night, but Goro definitely seemed to be in a bad way—falling apart, as you say—and I wonder whether you were in the same state."

While Kogito was in Berlin, engaging in a solitary marathon of reminiscence about Goro, he recalled this reply of Chikashi's and realized that he hadn't really picked up on the full import of what she'd said. In particular, when Chikashi unexpectedly alluded to that long-ago incident in Matsuyama, he realized that he had filed those memories away as something important to be dealt with at a later date—which could well have been a defense mechanism to postpone stirring up old ghosts. The way Chikashi answered his question was surprisingly clear and forthright; that should have been the end to it, but he couldn't resist the urge to rehash a bit of ancient history that had been on his mind.

"If you want to talk about seeing Goro in a state that could be described as falling apart—close to a breakdown, really—the only instance that comes to mind is one time when I saw him on late-night TV. It might have been because the filming of the program had dragged on for such a long time, but while I was watching I noticed that he was getting very drunk, very rapidly. Looking back on all the time he and I have spent drinking together, I've never seen him so far gone. It's not just the fact that Goro wasn't the type of person who would let other people see him in such a pitiful state, but really, in essence, he simply wasn't the sort of person who would be falling apart in the first place, don't you agree? From what I've heard, your father was exactly the same. Even during his long recovery from tuberculosis, writers such as Shiga Naoya and Nakano

Shigeharu—who were famously tough themselves—took off their hats to him for refusing to go to pieces."

"I'm not sure I really understand the meaning of 'falling apart,'" Chikashi said, after a few moments' reflection. "Is it primarily a state of mind? Or is it when people looking at you from the outside say that you seem to be falling apart and there's no way you can deny it?"

Once again, Kogito stammered out a reply. "But don't they both occur simultaneously? Like when you're forced to admit that comments from outsiders have hit the nail on the head?"

Then Kogito, having once again decided to postpone thinking about the traumatic incident in Matsuyama until another day, remembered a time when he himself was falling apart in front of Chikashi. To make matters worse, there was nothing he could do to control his shameful disintegration. It happened during the time when they were renting the second floor of a big old house in the same neighborhood as their present home but some hundred yards closer to Seijo Gakuen-mae Station.

Akari had been born in June, and several months had passed since then. It was a wildly windy autumn day, and the dried-up leaves of the Chinese parasol tree were rattling on the branches, making an immoderate racket. Kogito was lying face-down on the bed that had come with the furnished house; his head was twisted into a diagonal position, and he was holding the sheets down over his head with all his strength. The fact was, he truly couldn't move.

Chikashi stood beside the tall bed, and in a feeble, sorrowful voice that made her sound like a plaintive adolescent girl, she kept saying, over and over, "What's wrong?" But Kogito

didn't answer. It wasn't that he was shirking human contact or
being rude; he was simply unable to utter a word. He had always been that way, ever since childhood; if he wasn't physically able to get out of bed, he wouldn't be able to speak or
respond to questions, either. He really was falling apart, quite
literally, as he lay there in a stupor listening to the violent sound
of desiccated leaves clattering in the wind-tossed Chinese
parasol trees.

Earlier that day they had gone to the hospital and received
the final prognosis regarding Akari's condition. The report stated
that their son's physical problems would gradually improve
(though never to the point of perfection), but went on to add
that there was no reason to expect that his mental faculties
would ever be normal. Chikashi, too, had been sitting there
when the doctor shared this news, and Kogito understood keenly
how hard it must be for her to sympathize with his present predicament: this unseemly catatonic collapse brought on by sorrow and despair. But much as he wanted to, he was truly unable
to move a muscle.

In any case, on the day many years later when Chikashi
left the living room and started working on an illustration project
at the kitchen table, Kogito, finding himself alone, had started
to think about the incident in Matsuyama, which seemed to
have made an even stronger impression on Chikashi than the
day he fell into a paralytic depression after hearing the doctor's
verdict regarding Akari's bleak prospects for the future. That
incident in Matsuyama was evidently etched in Chikashi's
memory as an experience Kogito and Goro had shared, even
though Goro was clearly the focal point of her recollections.
Kogito felt as if he'd been backed into a corner and compelled

to revisit that important and disturbing memory, which was usually banished to the deepest recesses of his mind.

Whenever he thought about Goro's falling apart, those images were always directly connected to Kogito's consciousness of his own disintegration, so why hadn't he immediately recalled that incident in Matsuyama? Was it because he had been consciously suppressing that schoolboy memory even while he was thinking obsessively about that one mystifying line in the third suicide note Goro left behind? When that explanation occurred to him, Kogito felt an unpleasant sense of escalating discomfort, as if he were being steadily beaten with a blunt sword.

He lay down on the living room couch, but rather than starting to read a book, as he usually did, he concentrated on trying to avoid attracting Chikashi's peripheral attention. She, meanwhile, was busy at the kitchen table with her sketchbook open, putting the finishing touches on her most recent drawing. Akari was firmly planted in front of his collection of new CDs, which were kept against the wall on one side of the short flight of steps that led to the kitchen. Kogito didn't want his son to notice him, either. There was something he needed to ponder undisturbed.

For a long time, it had been Kogito and Chikashi's habit not to indulge in arguments—matrimonial spats, in common parlance. On Chikashi's part, she would always offer either some sort of reasonable, carefully thought-out proposal or else an expression of opinion. As for Kogito (the listener, in these cases), he would usually approve the proposal or express sympathy with the opinion, and that would be the end of the discussion. The proposal would be implemented; the opinion would be accepted. If something was clearly vetoed by Kogito, that, too, would signal the end of the matter. Kogito invariably expressed his vetoes by silence, and even if Chikashi wasn't satisfied with that outcome, she never pursued the argument beyond that point. If Kogito had a strongly negative reaction to whatever Chikashi had suggested, his silence might last a day or two, or even more.

On one hand, in all the time they had been married Kogito could recall only two or three times when Chikashi had apologized and said that she was mistaken about something. On the other, it was not at all unusual for him to end up tacitly withdrawing his earlier objections, not by saying outright, "Okay, you win," but by essentially giving up the argument and retreating into his shell. (This was a separate issue from the exhausting of the argument and the subsequent reconciliation.) In any event, that was the way Kogito and Chikashi had managed to muddle through thirty-plus years of living together.

In recent years, though, Kogito had privately noticed a change in Chikashi's behavior. It had begun just after she started to paint watercolor illustrations to accompany Kogito's essays about the family's everyday life with Akari. Chikashi spent several days on each watercolor painting, starting with extended observation of the subject, and she became so absorbed in her work—especially when she reached the stage of adding the finishing touches—that she wouldn't even look up when Kogito called her name. If he had some urgent business and called out to her several times, she would eventually answer in a terse, abrupt way, like a man. Kogito had never seen that side of Chikashi before, and he eventually realized that her intensity about her creative work was probably a genetic predisposition.

It wouldn't be an exaggeration to say that Goro and Chikashi's father was the man who founded Japan's tradition of sociosatirical film comedies. During the long period while he was recuperating from tuberculosis, he wrote three volumes of collected essays, which were strong on morality and logic but were also overflowing with witty, open-minded observations. During the time before Japan started producing motion pictures, he had been a painter. Taking all this into account, Kogito had thought at first that it was Goro, the child-prodigy artist and polymath, who had inherited his father's myriad talents. But before long he began to notice that Goro had actually been more profoundly influenced by his mother.

There was a time when Goro himself, hoping to control these maternally transmitted tendencies, became deeply involved (too deeply, some said) with psychology. At that time, even when he read Goro's published chronicle of his conversations with scholars of Freud and Lacan (a book that, to put it uncharitably, was a half-baked treatise, rushed into print), Kogito couldn't help feeling that there was something fishy about the so-called psychology experts who were reverently showcased in Goro's account. At one point, a young editor of Kogito's acquaintance had the nerve to say cattily, "Isn't it possible that you're just jealous of Goro's new friends?"

Meanwhile, the manager of a certain pharmaceutical company in the Kansai area came to visit the Choko household and happened to see a watercolor painting that Chikashi had made as a birthday card for Akari. As a result, she was commissioned to do a series of illustrations for some essays of Kogito's that were being published in a commercial magazine whose primary audience was medical doctors. From then on Chikashi's artistic style began to blossom so rapidly that Kogito soon became convinced that it might be Chikashi, not Goro, who had truly inherited their father's talent for painting.

As for Goro, after the siblings began to lodge in a temple compound in Matsuyama immediately after the war (they nick-named their digs the "Little Temple"), he accepted the younger but stalwart and dependable Chikashi as another mother, in a way, and depended on her for everything. He didn't seem to have any expectations that Chikashi would turn out to be an artist but, as has already been mentioned, he did comment fa-vorably that she had always had her own distinctive style from an early age.

With Goro's own drawings, his first principle was to re-spect the "real details" of a given subject, and there were times when the balance of the entire composition ended up being destroyed as a result. At the same time, Kogito felt that the two siblings were similar in the way they shied away from the usual academic, textbook ways of making a picture, without ever re-sorting to the easy clichés of art naïf.

On another day, some time later, Kogito was on his way back to the living room from getting a drink of water in the kitchen when he stopped for a moment to watch Chikashi working on a new watercolor painting at the kitchen table. For inspiration, Chikashi had chosen a photograph from among the many that her father took with his Leica, during a period stretch-ing from before the war until it was about half over. This photo-graph (and the painting Chikashi was making) showed her as a young girl, hanging upside down from the strong yet supple Y-shaped crotch of a large oak tree—it looked like either a garden-variety evergreen oak or a Japanese emperor oak—with her older brother standing off to one side. Goro was wearing a flat-collared, khaki-colored school uniform, and his hair was cropped close to his head. As he stood next to the tree watching his sister's acrobatic antics, he wore a complicated expression that combined good-natured cheerfulness with a certain measure of reserve—an expression often seen on his grown-up face, as well.

"In my experience, whenever I try to write something about the various types of oak trees, I almost always get it wrong," Kogito remarked in a light, playful way. "Someplace like California is ideal, because you can actually see the different varieties of oaks—not just the distinctions among their trunks and branches and bark, but even the way the lumber is used. I've gotten letters that say things like 'In this country, if you say "oak," the image that's evoked in a reader's mind is likely to be rather vague and indistinct, and then you sometimes write about houses that use oak in the interior finishing, but in fact the wood of the oak tree isn't used in that way in Japan.'"

"I happen to have a very clear memory of this particular tree," Chikashi replied, with the abruptness that was a normal part of her artist-at-work persona. But on this day, it wasn't as if Chikashi was working on a terribly important picture. Rather, there seemed to be something she needed to think through, and painting a picture helped her to concentrate on that task. While Kogito was still standing behind her, peering over her shoulder, Chikashi (without lifting her eyes from her sketchbook) finally gave voice to the matter she had presumably been thinking about all along.

"Do you remember what Uncle Chu said the other day about the conclusion he had reached regarding the reasons behind Goro's suicide, based on his own experience as a policeman? When I think about my own experience of living with Goro and with our mother, I have to agree. I don't think it has anything to do with the sort of tripe they're publishing in the tabloid magazine that's put out by the publishing house you've been most closely involved with"—and for that very reason, Kogito had terminated the association—"saying that Goro killed himself because he was worn out after having been played for a fool by an 'evil woman.' In one of the notes he left behind, Goro wrote that he had never been involved with the woman in question and that he was going to die to prove that fact to his wife, Umeko, and to the media—and for that other woman's sake, as well. Uncle Chu told me that he believed that, too. However naïve or gullible that way of thinking or of dying may have been (and especially for a man who was past sixty, it really was almost unbelievably naïve), I myself get angry at that kind of terrible innocence or gullibility, but I still want to believe that note. No, what I mean is, I *do* believe it, with all my heart. Whatever anyone may say about 'evil women' or 'good women,' the fact is that the only woman in Goro's life who could ever profoundly influence his life was our mother. I really wonder how Goro could have rashly committed suicide knowing that he was abandoning our mother at a time when her Alzheimer's was progressing at a rapid rate . . . Remember Chu was talking about some police official who had the reports from the time when Goro was receiving threats from a crime syndicate, and didn't that person say that Goro was a man of integrity, courage, and strong moral fiber? But I think Goro died because even a strong, brave person can reach a point where he just feels irreparably crushed by the weight of everything that's accumulated during the course of his life.

"As for the straw that broke the camel's back, I really don't know what it was. But I'm certain it was during that long night when you and Goro came back in a really messed-up state that he first began to change. I've never asked you this before, but what really happened that weekend? If you don't write down whatever you know—without telling any lies or concealing the truth with embellishments—then I'll never be able to understand what happened. At this point, of course, neither you nor I have very many years left, and it seems to me that just as we want to live the rest of our lives honestly, without resorting to lies, you would want to write that way, too . . . for the rest of your days.

"It's a little bit like what Akari said to his grandmother in Shikoku, during her final illness: 'Please cheer up and die!' Only in your case, I'm asking you to be brave and write only the truth, until the very end."

And then Chikashi turned her head and gave Kogito an intensely searching look.

CHAPTER THREE

Terrorism and Gout

1

For the past decade and a half, Kogito had been dealing with a foot problem that cropped up periodically: a condition he described to the outside world as "gout." In fact, he really did have a genuine attack of gout during his late thirties, when his uric-acid level became elevated; he was put on a regimen of medication, and after that the level never rose above 6 or 7 mg/dcl. Nonetheless, every few years Kogito would be forced to venture out into the world walking with a cane and dragging his left leg behind him. When friends and people from the media asked what had happened, he would just quip that he was having a wee bout of gout, and to his perpetual surprise that explanation was readily accepted by everyone he met.

In truth, though, the second, third, and fourth attacks of "gout" were not due to the usual medical cause (that is, uric-acid accumulation), at all. The real reason was simply too bizarre to share. Every so often, three men would show up to punish him, and their mode of operation was always the same. First, they would seize Kogito in some deserted public place and overcome his resistance (which was only token in any case, since he didn't want to make matters worse by struggling). Next, they would remove his left shoe and, in their quest for accuracy, his left sock, as well. Then, taking careful aim, they would drop a rusty miniature cannonball onto the second joint of his big toe. It was this "surgical treatment" that triggered the pseudogout.

This had happened a total of three times, and as a result the first and second joints of the big toe of Kogito's left foot had been crushed to the point of permanent deformity. In time, it got so bad that his mangled foot would no longer fit into ready-made leather shoes. Fortunately, this was during a time of national prosperity, and the gluttonous overindulgence that went with financial solvency had produced a rapid rise in the number of people suffering from gout. So when Kogito reached the point of needing specially fitted shoes, all he had to do was go to the shoemaker's and explain that the bones of his foot had become abnormal due to gout, and they immediately understood. He fed the same tale to members of his family; only Chikashi knew the true source of Kogito's affliction, but he didn't share the complete backstory even with her.

Kogito first heard about the attack on Goro while he was overseas, and even while he was listening to the news reports explaining that it was a yakuza crime, he couldn't help wondering, as feelings of pent-up anger and impotent frustration coursed through his body, whether his regular tormentors had turned their violent attentions to Goro this time. When he learned that Goro's attack was a retaliatory act of terrorism by gangsters, he still felt angry, of course, but contradictory though it may seem, he also felt a deep sense of relief that his first surmise had been mistaken.

So why did Kogito allow himself to be repeatedly assaulted and afflicted with faux gout by a bunch of thugs, without reporting them to the police? Because from the very first attack, Kogito already had a pretty good idea of where the men had come from and what their motivation might be. That was why, after that first encounter, he made up his mind not to make an issue of the incident. At that time, the ruffians' methods were laughably primitive, and if they hadn't made a point of inflicting severe pain on his foot he would almost have seen the attack as a sort of warped children's game. And of course he never dreamed it would happen again.

But the men were a strangely tenacious bunch, and they seemed to have a sincere, simple-hearted confidence in the basic righteousness of what they were doing. At any rate, after a series of three attacks, the structure of Kogito's left foot ended up being so badly mangled that it was beginning to look as if he might have to give up his one outside interest, swimming, for fear of attracting unwelcome attention from the other people at the pool.

The first time the men turned up, Kogito sensed that they might have had an inkling about his genuine gout and had chosen their weapon accordingly. He also felt certain that the motive for the violent attack was the content of a medium-length book of his that had been published a month or so earlier. It was a novel that took place the summer of the year Japan surrendered to the Allies. Written in the form of an account of the extraordinary circumstances surrounding the death of Kogito's father as told through the eyes of the son (i.e., Kogito), the narrative derived dramatic tension and contrapuntal balance from the distorted denigration of the boy's story by his cynical, sharp-tongued mother.

Kogito wrote that book one summer while staying at his mountain cabin in the resort town of North Karuizawa. While he was struggling desperately to get past a particularly difficult patch in the second half of the book, a simple but effective solution occurred to him and he was subsequently able to overcome the obstacles. The idea came to him one day on the narrow road through a grove of trees that he took from his mountain cabin to the shopping area, in front of the now-defunct train station for the So-Kei Line, when he went to buy food. And from then on, forever, every time he passed that spot he remembered his liberating epiphany. He finished the manuscript in a rush of enthusiasm, and it was after that, around the time the initial installment of the story appeared in a magazine, that he had the first attack of gout. He was drinking a fair amount in those days, and that may have been a contributing factor.

Kogito wrote about the background of the story—including his Karuizawa breakthrough and the subsequent attack of gout—in the arts-and-literature column of a major newspaper, and it seemed likely that whoever sent the attackers had read both the book and that column, and had showed them to the hooligans as well.

In the first attack, one of the men grabbed Kogito from behind and pinned back his arms, then gagged him with a flimsy hand towel. The second thug immobilized both of Kogito's thighs, while the third, after removing only the left shoe and sock, surveyed the aftereffects of Kogito's genuine gout—a dark, swollen mass that covered the bones of the foot—with the air of a medical examiner. (There might have been other cocon-spirators, as well, watching this operation from nearby.) Kogito found himself looking down at his own unsightly feet with a kind of detached disgust, as if they were alien entities that didn't belong to him at all.

The third man took an iron sphere out of a battered leather Boston bag; it was smaller than the ball used in the shot-put event, and Kogito recognized it as ammunition for the small cannons that had been acquired by the leader of an insurrection in his village, during the early years of the Meiji era. Kogito had heard about the balls from his grandmother, who had some-how ended up with a sizable stockpile. While the third man was holding the grapefruit-sized ball at chest level and taking aim at Kogito's vulnerable left foot, the second assailant (the one who was keeping the victim's left leg rigidly in place) solemnly cautioned his cohort about the importance of dropping the ball right on the "sweet spot." And the dialect he spoke in—an ac-cent redolent of the deep forests of Shikoku—instantly trans-ported Kogito back to his childhood.

Then, suddenly, he realized that the unthinkable was about to happen. Feelings of fear and loathing bubbled up fu-riously inside him as he watched helplessly, and at the moment of impact he gave a loud scream and passed out. Humans know instinctively that they will lose consciousness when they are subjected to more physical suffering than they can bear—or at least bear in a conscious state—and that knowledge gives them the optimistic certainty that they'll be able to avoid experienc-ing the pain by being insensate when it occurs. Kogito had believed in the existence of this automatic shutoff valve since childhood, but this was the first time he had actually experienced it.

When he came to, he was sitting on the bare ground in the garden of his house in Tokyo, with his back propped against the trunk of a large mountain camellia tree and both legs stretched in front of him. This was before Chikashi started cultivating roses, and she had planted a great many mountain wildflowers, with the result that this section of the garden didn't look unlike a vacant lot densely overgrown with weeds— although you could still tell that Chikashi's additions differed from the weedlike plume poppies that Kunio Yanagida (who once lived nearby) mentioned as a feature of the local vegetation of this long-standing residential district.

The bony parts of Kogito's left foot felt as if they were filled with live embers, and the skin that covered them was so swollen that it resembled the gelatinous covering of pickled pigs' feet. The throbbing pain seemed to be keeping time with the pulsing of blood to the site of the injury. Remembering that he had been attacked, Kogito took a closer look at his left foot, which was so grotesquely dark and disfigured that he almost laughed out loud.

Kogito tried to cheer himself up by theorizing that the pain in his crushed foot, like the echo that reverberates through a mountain valley, would be more intense at first (that is, now) and then would gradually diminish. With the "normal" gout he'd experienced before, the opposite had occurred: at the first stage all he had felt was a delicate itchiness, but that mild sensation had gradually blossomed into full-blown, excruciating pain. When he compared what he was experiencing now with that earlier agony, it seemed, according to this theory, as if his present discomfort should continue subsiding second by second until it hit zero.

The back of Kogito's head was leaning against a fork in the thick trunk of the mountain camellia (a trunk that he had discovered on another occasion was just the right size for him to encircle with his arms), so if he moved his head slightly he could look up at the bell-shaped canopy of luxuriant, low-hanging foliage that surrounded him. The stout branches, which resembled the legs of a baby elephant, were firmly supporting the canopy, and that sight prompted another rush of nostalgia. When he was a child in the forests of Shikoku, he often used to climb into the mountains and gaze dreamily up at the leafy tree umbrellas from underneath. Assuming that the man who had been holding Kogito immobile from behind was the same one who had picked up his body (while he was still unconscious and oblivious to the unbearable pain) and carried him to a place where he could look up at the glossy foliage of the mountain camellia—and since his assailants were speaking the same dialect Kogito grew up with—it could even have been one of his childhood playmates who had left him here.

Presently Kogito saw Chikashi and Akari coming into the garden from the street through a low wicket door that stood open on one side of the main gate. The mere thought of trying to shout loud enough to attract their attention caused the pulsating pain in his foot to flare up again. As he watched, Chikashi headed toward the front door with her head bent down, like someone nursing a great sorrow. But Akari, who was unusually sensitive to the world around him, stopped in midstep, looked around, and spotted his father slumped down on the ground in a completely unexpected place.

"Hey, look over there. I wonder what happened? He's sitting under a tree!" Akari called out to Chikashi.

Chikashi turned around and walked back toward her son, whose entire face was wreathed in smiles. Her own perpetually tranquil, sorrowful-looking face wore a look of surprise, and Kogito adjusted his own pained expression to convey the message, *Don't worry, it's nothing serious.* Chikashi brushed past Akari, who was threading his way unsteadily through the clumps of wild plants, and approached her husband alone. She didn't seem to notice the apparent recurrence of his gout, and he decided to tell her that he had gone to check out the cesspool and had tripped on the concrete cover and fallen down.

This turned out to be a satisfactory way of dealing with the incident, and that was why it was never reported to the police and didn't even show up as a minuscule item in the "police blotter" section of the newspapers. As for the subsequent bouts of violence at the hands of the same ruffians, which occurred every few years, Kogito ended up explaining the resulting injuries in much the same way. He even began to feel a silent complicity with the men who shared his secret.

The second attack occurred three years after the first. Once the initial injury had healed and the pain had become manageable, Kogito had become quite sanguine; he even began to think of his surrealistic encounter with the hoodlums as an amusingly bizarre adventure. But when he actually felt the pain again, it was so unimaginably acute that he realized it could only be fully experienced in the moment. Even so, he didn't feel inclined to file a police report this time, either, because he still felt that the decision he'd made after the first attack was the right one.

The basis for that decision was Kogito's feeling that this wasn't a matter that should be resolved through the intervention of the outside world. And that intuition was bound up with the fact that Kogito had felt, from the first, a fleeting sense of nostalgia—even fondness—toward the men who had brutalized him. Clearly, those feelings were evoked by the way they talked. When Kogito analyzed his rush of homesickness, later on, he figured out that it had two elements. One was geographical: that is, the men spoke the same way as the people from the remote area in Shikoku where Kogito had grown up. The other element was a temporal nostalgia that dated back to forty years earlier.

Kogito had been going back to his native province to visit his mother nearly every year, so he knew that the region's distinctive accent and tempo of speech, and its characteristic tone of voice, were gradually disappearing from the forests where he'd spent his boyhood. However, Kogito had no memory of ever having seen the three men before, and they hadn't made the slightest attempt to disguise themselves or cover their faces. Even making allowances for the ravages of time—that is, even if he made an effort to picture the faces of the men (all of whom were past their prime) as they might have looked in their youth—Kogito still couldn't recognize them at all. Nevertheless, the short, rapid-fire phrases they barked at one another during the vicious assaults on Kogito's left foot were inextricably intertwined with his childhood home, a time and place he still remembered with great fondness.

2

While Kogito was living alone in Berlin, with an overabundance of free time on his hands, his thoughts kept returning to the long-ago past . . . He remembered the seventh year after the end of the war, when the seventeen-year-old Kogito was spending every afternoon in the library of the CIE in Matsuyama, studying for his university entrance exams. One day, out of the blue, a man who had been a disciple of Kogito's dead father suddenly turned up, accompanied by a group of much younger men.

The high-school students were sitting in a reading corner on the east side of the library, perusing collections of questions from sample exams, while Kogito gazed absentmindedly out the window, watching the leaves of the Japanese chinquapin doing their wild dance in the wind. After a time he noticed that the eyes of all the students who were sitting at desks facing the other way were riveted on the entrance behind his back.

Kogito turned around, too. His eyes were bedazzled from staring outside into the bright light, but an image registered dimly on his retina: a group of men, standing motionless outside on the landing. Kogito could see clearly enough to be disturbed by one of the men's eyes, which reminded him of the embers that nestled, glowing redly, amid the ashes of the straw fires that could be seen here and there this time of year around the forest valley where he grew up, deep in the mountains. And then Kogito became aware that the eerie, burning eye was staring right at him. The man apparently noticed Kogito's head movement, because he responded with the slightest of nods, whereupon Kogito gathered up the rough paper that he used for physics calculations and his cheap unfinished-wood pencils (bought at the school-supply stand), and stuffed them into his school briefcase.

He picked up the lovely-smelling, hardcover, English-language edition of *The Adventures of Huckleberry Finn* that had been open beside him—and which was the reason for his earlier absentminded reverie—and went to replace it on the open-access bookshelves on the west side of the library. As he started to walk back toward the group of men, Kogito became aware of a Japanese staff member, who was dressed in black slacks and a white shirt, and appeared to be a nisei (that is, a first-generation American of Japanese ancestry). He was standing on the other side of the glass partition beyond the bookshelves, keeping a wary eye on the intruders—who did look conspicuously out of place.

In the middle of the group of interlopers stood a one-armed man, still staring straight at Kogito. Though he seemed to be listing slightly to one side, the man's posture was resolute and determined. His open-necked white shirt was tucked into the waistband of his well-worn trousers and held in place by a belt, which created a sunburst of wrinkles. There was no excess flesh on his deeply sunburned face, and one of his eyes (but only one) was darkly bloodshot. Nonetheless, he seemed to be radiating a strong light in Kogito's direction. Kogito realized that the initial impression he'd gotten, of embers glowing deep amid the ashes of carbonized straw, was due to this man's single bloodshot eye.

The one-armed man and his younger companions greeted Kogito silently, with polite nods and bows, as he approached. Together, they descended the stairs from the library. Even when Kogito stopped at the reception desk on the first floor to open his bag for inspection, the one-armed man remained standing next to Kogito, withdrawing just a foot or so, while the younger men kept their distance. During this interlude the young men maintained a defiant attitude that came across as simultaneously pious and uncouth, and when the Japanese staff member in the black pants and white shirt pointed questioningly at the assorted baggage they were carrying, they banded together and refused so aggressively to submit to inspection that he shrank back and didn't press them further.

When they left the Center the older man fell into step with Kogito, but because he was walking next to the man's armless side, Kogito came to feel, illusorily, as if his companion's upper body were leaning on him. The Center was built in a district called Horinouchi, on a site that had once been a military parade ground. From there they walked along the road that led to town, and when they came to the bank of the moat (which surrounded a distant castle, barely visible through the trees), Kogito led the group around to the left, to a place where there were some benches arrayed under a row of cherry trees in full bloom. The men appeared utterly oblivious to the glorious display of cherry blossoms.

In the center of the expanse of flat, grassless ground that surrounded the three benches, there were the messy remains of a bonfire, with dirty, half-burned pieces of wood scattered about. Kogito sat down on a bench facing the moat, and the older man sat down too, leaving a small space between them, with his left side—the one that had an empty sleeve tucked into the belt—next to Kogito, who was still feeling slightly uneasy about the whole encounter. He couldn't help wondering, idly, what would happen if the man thought he might have to defend himself. Which side would the one-armed man turn toward Kogito?

Facing them on the left side, between the canal and the street where the tramcars ran, was a bank building that had escaped the flames of the Allied air raids, bathed in the pale light of the late-afternoon sun. Abruptly, the hitherto-silent one-armed man began to speak in a spirited, exclamatory way, with the same sweetly nostalgic deep-forest accent that Kogito would hear from the men who attacked him, twenty years later.

"It's me, Daio! You know, they used to call me Gishi-Gishi! You remember, don't you, Kogito? I'm sure having me suddenly turn up wanting to talk to you must be a big nuisance," the man went on, "especially when you're in the middle of studying for your entrance exams. Still, I'm really happy to see that you brought us right away to a place overlooking the spot where your father went down in a blaze of glory! It's a great relief to me to know that you haven't forgotten about that day, or about us!"

Now that Daio had introduced himself, Kogito did remember him as one of the men who used to come to the house for meetings with his father, toward the end of the war. What he actually remembered more clearly than the man himself was

the name, "Daio." Kogito's mother and father had singled Daio
out from the other followers for special treatment, and the nickname they had bestowed on him, "Gishi-Gishi," was proof of
that. Kogito had heard the explanation from his younger sister:
apparently the surname "Daio" was also a proper noun meaning a kind of medicinal rhubarb that grew wild among the ruins
of a garden of medicinal plants on the outskirts of the village,
and the country folks' nickname for that plant was "*gishi-gishi.*"

"For the next five days or so, I'm planning to stay at an inn
at Dogo Hot Springs," Daio went on. "I really want to tell you
about the ideas I've been formulating during the past seven
years, so please come visit me there! Of course, I haven't had
direct access to your father's wisdom, as I used to, but we've
been working really hard and encouraging each other all along.
We've planted new fields and rice paddies, and we repaired the
training hall and built an annex, too, so the old place in the
country is twice as big as it used to be. We have enough space
to stage drills with a large number of warriors. We're totally self-
sufficient when it comes to food, and we even make our own
doburoku—you know, home-brewed sake! I've brought some for
you to try, along with various local delicacies. Since your father's
blood is flowing through your veins, I'm sure you can't say that
you've never tried drinking sake, even once?

"Anyway, at our training camp we still follow the fundamental tenets that were the basis of your father's philosophy.
We don't bother much with money, and we make a point of
having almost no need of it. Of course this trip is an exception,
leaving our rural hideout and paying to stay in lodgings provided
by this consumeristic society! But that's just for me; everyone
else is bunking at various temples and shrines in the area. The

reason I took a proper room at an inn is so I could have a place to entertain you. These guys will be coming to my room in the evenings, too, because I want to talk to all of you together. I'm sure there must be some jobs for temporary laborers around Matsuyama, so these lucky stiffs will get to work to pay for my room at the inn!"

On the evening of that day, Kogito did, indeed, pay a visit to Daio's inn at the Dogo Hot Springs resort. Even now, he could still summon up a clear image of himself and the taciturn young men, sitting around that little room listening to Daio's fervent oratory. The truth is, whenever he remembered that scene, it was always with a painful stab of regret because of the way things turned out.

The dimly lit room was about eight and a half feet by eleven and a third feet, with a thick electric cord leading directly from the ceiling to the blown-glass globe that encased a 40-watt bulb. When Kogito recalled that scene, his memory camera seemed to be looking down from an even higher vantage point than that light fixture, like a cinematographer's crane shot. The assorted empty plates, dishes, and bowls from Daio's and Kogito's dinner were stacked up on a small, low table against the wall. A giant bottle of home-brewed sake, holding nearly four pints, had been placed directly on the tatami-matted floor, surrounded by five cups, and the host and his guests were all sitting on their haunches with their knees almost touching the bottle.

There they were: Kogito (the seventeen-year-old schoolboy), Daio, and his followers. Daio had already consumed a fair amount of *doburoku* all by himself, but Kogito had been drinking coarse, cheap green tea all along, as had the young acolytes. Rather than a feast or a party, the gathering was more like a seminar, with Daio at the podium. The lecturer alone reeked of sake, and the potent fumes filled the dismal little room.

Daio began his monologue by saying that Choko Sensei— that is, Kogito's father—had been mistaken in the philosophical theory he espoused during the last stages of the war, and after having lived through that painful experience Daio and his supporters had come up with a new ideology that (they believed) corrected the flaws in the original. Daio held a thin paperback book on his knee—like his audience, he sat on his heels, with his lower legs bent backward under him—and he frequently opened the book to check various points. Kogito couldn't see the title on the Japanese paper cover, and he didn't have the nerve to ask the author's name.

Later, Kogito ended up spending many hours searching for a copy of that book, starting at an old-book shop in Matsuyama's busy shopping district. All he had to go on was his memory of some of the phrases Daio had read aloud, when he wasn't reciting snatches of the Chinese poetry that was quoted in the text. Kogito tried to find that poetry in books written by authors who were involved with right-wing politics, but his quest was fruitless. He realized only much later that he had been wasting his time looking in the wrong places.

It was only natural that Kogito would have assumed that the book Daio relied on so heavily was something that had originated in the right-wing movement. Not only that, but he wondered where Daio had gotten his own copy. After the death of Kogito's father, in anticipation of a possible visit from members of the occupying army, his disciples had dug a giant hole, built a fire, and burned Choko Sensei's large collection of books about ultranationalist ideology. Once all the books had been burned (though in due time Kogito became aware that not all of them had gone up in flames), if Daio had wanted to find prose and poetry that expressed the right-wing philosophy, he would have had no choice but to read books from the other end of the political spectrum—books in which left-wing thinkers and scholars quoted ultranationalist literature in a critical context. And so it was that Kogito discovered, long afterward, that when Daio was chanting those Chinese poems with the traditional sing-song intonation, he was reading from one of those left-wing books of criticism and not from the original text.

The means are unimportant; anything will do.
But if we orchestrate justice, clear and bright,
And if all our thoughts are straight and true,
The emperor's glory will rise like the sun . . .

Daio explained that night that these were the first lines of what was considered at the time an epoch-making historical poem and that at one time, according to one of the defendants on trial for the so-called 2•26 Incident, that quotation was the symbol and the battle cry of their uprising. (The 2•26 Incident was an attempted coup d'état by the radical, ultranationalist Kodaha faction of the Imperial Japanese Army, which transpired between February 26 and 29, 1936. Several leading politicians were killed, and the center of Tokyo was briefly held by the insurgents before the coup was suppressed.) Daio was repudiating the basic ideology expressed in this poem, along with the way of thinking and the course of action—all of which comprised the nucleus of Choko Sensei's "mistaken" theory. Yet in spite of that disavowal, Daio kept reciting those

lines over and over, in a low voice that was full of genuine
emotion.

There were any number of things that Kogito found difficult to understand that night, so what is written about Daio's
treatises in this narrative from here on incorporates Kogito's
adult knowledge, based on extensive reading that illuminated
the complex, murky ideology and movements of right-wing zealots and soldiers.

"Choko Sensei, too, was originally opposed to the 'defeatism' of the commissioned officers who took part in the 2•26
Incident," Daio said. "Why 'defeatism'? Because they themselves had no intention of drawing up an aggressive plan for
taking over the government after the uprising. Anyway, Choko
Sensei denounced that stance as extreme weakness. In fact, he
was very critical of the incident overall, saying that in the end
they decided to go down fighting against the Tokyo municipal
police force—which, in the long run, was exactly the same as
if they hadn't done anything at all.

"However, the irony is (and you know the whole story,
Kogito, since you saw it happen) that Choko Sensei himself
launched a so-called insurrection without having a proper plan
in place. And as a result, he was shot to death by the police of
this little one-horse town. Why did he choose that path to certain doom? We've been asking ourselves that question, over and
over, for the past seven years, and we've finally reached a conclusion that makes sense to us. We think he was trying to write
the final chapter, to put an end to the pattern of defeatism that
had continued from Inoue Nissho (a radical Nichiren Buddhist
priest and founder of the far-right terrorist organization known
as the League of Blood, as you surely know) to the officers of

the 2•26 Incident. By so doing, he was trying to make it possible for the people who came after him to move toward a different path. Seriously, Kogito, I really believe that's what your
father had in mind. And when you think about it that way, then
the road we're trying to follow right now is the path that Choko
Sensei planned for us all along!"

Daio continued his seminar the next evening. This time
Goro was in attendance, as well, but he made it clear from the
start that he was mainly there for the crab and the home-brewed
sake. Picking up where he had left off the previous night, Daio
explained that he and his colleagues often found themselves
reminiscing about the event that took the life of their beloved
leader—Kogito's father—on the day after the war ended. And
the conclusion they had reached was that, contrary to appear-
ances, the young warriors hadn't really been led into battle by
Choko Sensei. That is to say, it looked like a group insurrection,
but in truth their leader seemed to have his own self-destructive
agenda. Perhaps it was the kamikaze action of a terminally ill man
who didn't have long to live in any case. As Daio put it, reverently, "Sensei's existence was like a star, sparkling high above our
heads. And then that star exploded, all by itself."

Choko Sensei's behavior was in essence a reflection of the
theories behind the League of Blood and the 2•26 Incident,
whose leaders believed in practicing terrorism for its own sake
and assumed that the people who come after will take care of
the rest. You'd think such a brilliant man would have been able
to move beyond that, but he ended up clinging to those anti-
quated attitudes and he wasn't able to take it to the next level.

That's what Daio said, adding that Choko Sensei had for-
merly been a disciple of Kita Ikki and was intimately familiar

with the *General Rules for Japanese Reconstruction,* and had
presumably studied a more stable plan for the future, quite apart
from the rather naïve and unrealistic optimism of Nissho and
his officers, and their ilk.

"Moreover," Daio continued, "Sensei must surely have
learned the obvious lessons from those earlier, disastrous incidents and come up with his own plan. Yet in spite of that
he was moved by the ardent aspirations of his young disciples,
and even when he was so desperately ill, he honored us by
riding in our wretched, manure-scented chariot, like a Shinto
god in a palanquin, even though that pitiful, slipshod plan of
action was the best we could come up with." (This seeming
inconsistency—first blaming his mentor, then himself, for the
same catastrophe—was typical of Daio's sake-fueled rhetoric.)

Goro's presence was undoubtedly a factor, but more than
the specious points of Daio's somewhat incoherent argument,
the thing that made Kogito blush was the grandiloquent phrase
"honored us by riding in our wretched chariot," which seemed
to imply that Kogito's father was some sort of exalted saintly
being.

Ridicule was Kogito's mother's natural form of expression,
and she had a field day with the events that took place on the
day after the war ended. When her husband set out to lead the
fatal bank robbery, she jeered at him for having to ride in a
makeshift "tank"—a clumsily converted, foul-smelling wooden
box that had originally been filled with herring fertilizer from
Hokkaido, with rough, round slices of a log for wheels—and
she made fun of Kogito, too, for tagging along on the ill-fated
mission. "You seemed awfully keyed up about escorting that
ragtag band, led by your terminally ill father in his fertilizer box,

as if it was some kind of noble undertaking," she said later, after it was all over.

When Kogito wrote a novel about the incident, incorporating his mother's harsh criticisms, it gave him the opportunity to flip his own perspective and reach a completely different conclusion. It was just after the medium-length book was published that the trio of hooligans showed up again. Three years had passed since their first attack, so Kogito's injuries had healed. At that point, the bones in his foot hadn't yet morphed into permanent deformity, but then along came the assailants to drop a miniature cannonball on his foot yet again.

There was no doubt about it. Whoever had sent the posse of thugs was watching every move Kogito made—or, more precisely, monitoring every word he wrote.

3

At the time of Daio's sudden appearance in Matsuyama, Kogito had already started hanging out with Goro on a regular basis. The event that precipitated their friendship was minor, but memorable.

Kogito had transferred to Matsuyama High School at the beginning of the second year of a three-year high-school program, and one of the elective courses he signed up for was Classical Japanese. At the first meeting of the class, the instructor went around the room asking the students, one at a time, why they had chosen to take this particular course. The teacher was tremendously tall, with a disproportionately tiny head, and his style of dress was rather flamboyant for those subdued postwar times—he even wore a waistcoat, which was quite unusual. His question seemed to imply that it wasn't a very popular class, although Kogito hadn't heard anything to that effect before signing up.

Kogito remembered that from the time he was a child, long before that deadly "insurrection," his father used to entertain him with excerpts from works of classical Japanese. So when it was his turn to explain why he had chosen this class, Kogito replied, "It's because I find the minute little details of the way language is used in classical Japanese very interesting."

For some reason, this innocuous answer threw the teacher into a tizzy. "How dare you be impertinent with me!" he snapped. "If that's true, then you'd better give me an example of what you find so interesting!"

Goro was in the same class, and he later rebuked Kogito with a virtuous expression that seemed to suggest that Goro had momentarily forgotten that he, too, was a student who frequently provoked the ire of his teachers (or maybe it was for that very reason). "Your problem," Goro said loftily, "is that you don't look suitably dejected and you keep on talking back. That just makes the enemy even angrier."

Goro had a point. Instead of meekly giving in to the teacher's intimidation, Kogito had recited the lines the way he had learned them—that is, from hearing them repeated two or three times by Choko Sensei, as was his custom, while enjoying his evening drink of sake—and that was what had made the already angry teacher almost apoplectic.

As an example, Kogito stammered out the story of the eagle who carried off a human infant. When she dropped this hefty morsel into her treetop nest, as food for her own baby, the hungry chick was surprised by the tiny human's cry. Because of that he didn't even peck at the human baby, much less eat it alive.

"What?" the teacher spluttered indignantly. "Which ancient book did you find that foolishness in? How was it phrased in classical Japanese?"

Kogito was getting a bit fed up with this volatile, aggressive teacher, who had all but grabbed Kogito's lapels in his fervor to extract an answer, but he replied politely, quoting to the best of his recollection, "That young bird looking up / Surprised and afraid / Didn't peck at the baby."

"Don't give me that sloppy nonsense," the teacher fumed. "Just answer my first question: what was the title of the old book you read that story in?"

Kogito really didn't know how to answer that question, and he felt distinctly uneasy about the situation he had gotten himself into. The truth was, he had never actually seen those words on the page. He just happened to have memorized them when his cheerful, slightly tipsy father had crooned the lines, as though they were a song.

His father had offered a commentary, too: "When the eagle's offspring saw the strange thing that its parent had unceremoniously dumped into the nest, it was surprised and frightened, and the classical Japanese word for 'looking up' somehow suggests the quizzical curve of the young bird's neck. When the original author recited this line over and over, the expression just naturally ripened, you know. Even if they aren't particularly well educated, people who are good at storytelling always have the characteristic of being able to polish their words and make them better."

Kogito was terribly afraid that the relentless teacher might end up saying, "All right, if you aren't lying, then bring that book to school and prove it." But Choko Sensei's entire collection of books had been burned, for reasons Kogito would rather not have to explain. And that book his father had spoken of—he called it *A Compendium of Supernatural Parables*—did it really exist?

The female students had started to giggle at Kogito's unintentionally cheeky replies, and the teacher, wearing an expression of undisguised contempt, moved on to questioning the next student. After that, right up until the end of the school year, the teacher made a point of completely ignoring Kogito. And among his schoolmates, only Goro—who had been kept back a grade for reasons having to do with his transfer from Kyoto—took Kogito aside and said, "Hey, I think your father sounds like a pretty interesting guy."

So they became friends, and some months later they ended up going together to Daio's inn at Dogo Hot Springs to eat dinner, with a heaping side dish of political proselytization. Daio started off by explaining how his group had arrived at their conclusions, but something about his way of speaking gave the impression that his remarks had been delivered many times and had been polished to a high gloss in the process. Indeed, there was something patently artificial about his fluency.

Kogito's mother was never swayed by persuasive sweet talk from strangers, much less from her own husband. Kogito felt now as if he had discovered the reason why she gave Daio the nickname "Gishi-Gishi," which seemed affectionate enough but was also subtly mocking and not entirely respectful. He was too slick, too clownish, too much of a con man for her down-to-earth tastes.

Kogito's mother often said that the people who dwelt in the forests of Shikoku could be divided into two types. The first type never told a lie, no matter what. The second type told lies

just for fun, even if they didn't stand to profit from the false-
hoods. "Your father was basically a careful, prudent man," she
told Kogito, "but he let himself be played for a fool by people
from outside the village who flattered him with lies. I mean,
even if it wears a sage's beard and puts on pompous airs, a
papier-mâché *daruma* doll is still a toy, isn't it?"

The climax of the two-day seminar at the inn was Daio's
dramatic recounting of the death of Kogito's father at the end
of the abortive bank robbery. Since Kogito had been present
as well and knew exactly what had happened, this was probably more for the benefit of Goro, who had attended only the
second meeting, and for Daio's young colleagues.

Daio threw himself into an impassioned description of the
violent scene that transpired at the bank, telling how when the
police began firing their rifles, he had used his own body to try
to shield Choko Sensei, who was riding in the "tank" made from
a fertilizer box. But then Daio himself was hit in the top of the
shoulder by a bullet and collapsed. He was clearly aware that
an eyewitness to the event was listening to his retelling of it now
and comparing that version with what had really happened, so
even though he may have exaggerated a bit, for effect, he didn't
say anything that was blatantly untrue. And if he had, who was
to say that wasn't a simple trick of memory?

For a while after the war ended, Daio disappeared from
village life, but Kogito ran into him from time to time on the
roads around the valley or on the banks of the river. It would
have been natural to assume that Daio had lost his arm due to
injuries sustained in the bank raid, but Kogito had a vague
memory of an earlier day, while the war was still going on. They
were in his huge stone-and-plaster house, in the dirt-floored

room that had been turned into his father's study, complete with his prized Takara-brand barber's chair. Daio was taking books off the shelf and tidying up the mail, and at that time, to the best of Kogito's recollection, he was already missing his left arm. That defect was surely the only reason why the otherwise healthy Daio, who was in his late twenties when the war broke out, wasn't drafted into the army. The rest of the young men who started coming to visit Kogito's father when Japan was on the brink of defeat were all soldiers on active duty who had taken a furlough.

The ill-omened "insurrection" took place the day after the war ended. A group of officers from the regiment stationed in Matsuyama had arrived late the night before and had camped out on the second floor of the farmhouse. The next morning, they loaded Kogito's father into his wooden cart and lifted that, in turn, onto a flatbed truck. Then, just like in the old stories of farmers' insurrections, they set off downriver. Destination: Matsuyama.

That morning, Daio had gathered up the recycled-cloth diapers and various other necessities for his terminally ill leader, wrapped everything in a large square of fabric, and hoisted the bundle onto his shoulders. Early though it was, the officers were already drunk and obnoxious, and they vigorously pushed Daio aside whenever he got in their way. The question was, did he still have his left arm at that time? Kogito thought not, but he wasn't 100 percent certain.

After they arrived in front of the regional bank building in Matsuyama, which was on the streetcar route facing the Horinouchi district where the CIE now stands, the conspirators unloaded Kogito's father from the truck. For a moment

he stood there motionless in his wooden "chariot," looking like
a small bronze statue. Then, pushing the wagon ahead of them,
the officers charged through the stone-pillared entrance to the
bank. Kogito was watching from atop the rear platform of the
truck, which was now empty.

Immediately, there was the sound of gunfire from inside
the building, and a group of armed policemen appeared on the
road that ran alongside the bank and rushed inside. Kogito was
seized with fear; unable to restrain himself, he dashed across
the street, almost getting flattened by an approaching streetcar
in the process. But he wasn't able to run very far. The next thing
he knew he was slipping and sliding down the bank of the moat,
through the lush summer grass . . .

And then—these were the words his mother always used
in telling the story—when it was all over, a soaking wet Kogito
crawled up the muddy embankment looking exactly like a
drowned rat. He stood above the moat, blinking, with his nose,
too, twitching like a rat's, and he gazed over at the bank building where the wooden cart that had carried his father into battle
now stood once again in front of the bank, with the murdered
man slumped inside it. But could it really be true that Kogito
was still in that sodden state when his mother (who had been
brought from her home in the car of the village police officers
who had gone to notify her) arrived on the scene? It was at least
a two-hour ride from their village in the mountain valley to the
center of Matsuyama.

In any case, Kogito returned home the next morning, accompanied by his mother. This memory was indisputably correct, so there was no question but that she had showed up at

the site of the uprising, even though she must have arrived there rather late. At that time, in addition to his fatally injured father, there was another member of the group who was shot in the shoulder and seriously wounded. If that person was Daio, why had Kogito and his mother never again spoken about that, even once?

It wasn't until after Kogito had graduated from college that he finally came across a book that, he thought, might have been the one Daio had used in his "seminars." The book was by Maruyama Masao, the political theorist and historian, and it included a number of writings that chronicled the evolution of Japanese nationalism during and after World War II—in particular, the changes in small regional right-wing groups that were under pressure from the occupying army for five or six years. That book (which had just been published at the time of the Dogo Hot Springs soirees) also contained excerpts from the same Chinese-style poem Daio had quoted.

The author said that there were members of some wartime right-wing groups who felt such despair over the breakdown of their value system when Japan lost the war that they committed suicide, and he even gave the real names of the leaders of those groups. As it happened, two of the names rang a bell for Kogito.

In the spring of the year he was ten, Kogito was told to put his father's incoming correspondence—which had suddenly become voluminous—into order. He would study each envelope and painstakingly decipher the name and address (these were usually calligraphed with a bamboo brush and fresh-ground *sumi* ink), and then enter the names in a logbook. Among those names, he still remembered two that had struck him as odd, each in its own way. Probably pen names, he remembered thinking.

Other groups simply replaced their Fascist identities with "democratic" window dressing and then continued exactly as before, with their ultranationalistic organizations intact. Still others dispersed and were pursuing nonpolitical social and economic activity on a regional basis; about them, Maruyama wrote: "As a general rule, reflecting the Japanese right wing's propensity for building a country on the 'agriculture first' principle, many of these former political activists joined a movement that advocated reclamation of land and increase in food production."

If you figured that during the seven years after Kogito's father was cruelly killed inside the bank in Matsuyama, Daio had survived by building a training hall in the woods and cultivating new land, then he and the group of which he was the leader must fall into the "agriculture first" category. And then Daio had come looking for Kogito at the CIE library where he was studying for his entrance exams, with the intention of somehow using his late master's son to advance the dubious goals of his own nascent movement.

After the incident (not witnessed by Kogito) that Goro got caught up in—never mind that it was part of an intrigue designed to culminate in a symbolic kamikaze mission by Daio and his followers—did Daio decide, for some reason, to abandon that radical plan of action and to apply himself, along with his colleagues, to protecting their farm and training camp?

When he was attacked with the miniature cannonball, what Kogito wanted most to avoid, deep down, was what would have come afterward. If he had complained to the authorities, he would have had to meet up again at the police station or in court with Daio and his colleagues, who had been pursuing their back-to-the-land venture all these years, conducting all their business (including terrorist attacks on novelists) in that dying deep-forest dialect. The truth was, he didn't want them to be arrested or punished.

At the time of the first attack, when Kogito caught an echo of the provincial dialect he had grown up with in the speech of the three ruffians—a dialect that was all but lost to the new generation—his intuition told him that the men must be preserving the old accent by living continuously in an insular group. So it was only natural that hearing that accent would trigger images of Daio in his subconscious.

Getting back to the second time Kogito was attacked: it was right after he had written a novella called *His Majesty Himself Will Wipe Away My Tears*. As has already been mentioned, that work contained an account of his father's doomed insurrection at the bank in Matsuyama, the day after the war ended. Goro had at one time planned to turn the novella into a film.

While he was writing the book, Kogito kept remembering that eventful ten-day interval when he was seventeen, starting with his reunion with Daio and concluding with the traumatic events at the training camp. He often thought about the ideas Daio had shared on the second night of the "seminar," which Goro had attended, as well. However, Kogito didn't write a single word about Daio's myriad plans, theories, and rationalizations in the novel.

It is undeniably true that, while listening to all of Daio's pontifications, the seventeen-year-old Kogito had serious doubts about many aspects of the man's presentation of self. But even taking into account those questions and hesitations, Kogito could still have found a way to bring Daio into the story if he had wanted to. The underlying psychological reason for Kogito's not having written about Daio was probably because he was afraid of creating trouble for his mother, who still lived near the training camp. If you had asked Kogito for an explanation at the time, he wouldn't have been able to express it in so many words, but surely some sort of protective self-censorship was at work. That was probably part of the reason he didn't report the attacks on his foot to the police, as well.

4

When Daio came looking for Kogito at the CIE library, it seems likely that he was still at the stage of feeling his way toward a plan of action, with nothing very specific in mind. But how had Daio found out that the surviving child of his fallen leader had transferred to high school in Matsuyama and was making frequent use of the library that had been created by the occupying army? He happened to read a small article in the local newspaper about some special recognition Kogito had received from the Americans, and that's what gave him the idea that he might be able to establish contact with the United States armed forces through Kogito. He probably came to Matsuyama, in the beginning, with just that sort of vague, inchoate desire, and nothing more.

When Daio lured Kogito away from the library and they sat talking on the edge of the canal, under the riotously blooming cherry blossoms—not that Daio and his cohorts showed the slightest interest in that wondrous sight—a brief silence ensued after the preliminary small talk related earlier. At that point, as

if exhibiting an important clue, Daio produced a clipping from
the local newspaper. When Kogito made no response, Daio
seemed disappointed, but then the expression around his eyes
suddenly brightened. Turning his sunburned peasant face to
his companions, he said grandly, like an oracle sharing a divine
revelation: "See, this is just what you'd expect from the son of
Choko Sensei—he's not the kind of person who gets all excited
about this sort of thing."

The article in question had been published ten days or so
earlier, in the soft-news section of the morning paper that was
headquartered in a building west of the moat embankment
where Kogito and his companions were now sitting. According
to the article, at the end of the previous school term, one Japanese high-school student had been awarded a commendation
from the Bureau of American Cultural Information and Education. While commuting to the Matsuyama CIE library to
study for his college entrance exams, the story explained, this
second-year student also managed to finish reading an entire
book in English.

The American woman who was head of the department
happened to hear from some of her Japanese employees that
this high-school student was reading a certain English-language
book with exceptional comprehension. The book was volume 1
of a two-volume edition of *The Adventures of Huckleberry Finn*,
by Mark Twain. This book wasn't really aimed at children in
the first place, and the dialogue, which contained a great deal
of African-American dialect from the southern United States,
was particularly difficult. However, when the officials tested
him on certain pages chosen at random, the young boy fluently
translated the indicated pages into Japanese, thus (according

to the article) earning the admiration of the Japanese-speaking American officers who were supervising the project.

Kogito had unwittingly prepared for this challenge by reading over and over, one line at a time, the Iwanami paperback books of the Japanese translation of *Huckleberry Finn* (which his mother had obtained during the last days of the war in exchange for rice), to the point where you could say he knew them by heart. Soon after transferring to Matsuyama, Kogito began to read the splendid English-language volume that he found in the open-access stacks of the CIE's library, applying the Japanese translation of *Huckleberry Finn* that he had all but memorized. Whether or not he brought any extraordinary facility with English to bear on the project is debatable, but the fact is that he spent an entire year in careful reading. Apparently, some of the staff noticed him toiling away and were impressed. The upshot was that the article appeared, relating the whole story in detail, and that was what brought Daio and his followers to the Matsuyama CIE.

When Kogito showed no inclination to discuss this topic, Daio launched into a long, tedious monologue about how, in accordance with Choko Sensei's dying wishes, he had taken over the management of the training camp. They had cultivated new land in the surrounding area and had enlarged the buildings, but because the original training camp had been created by their leader, Choko Sensei, after inheriting the property all they did was finish the construction in accordance with their late leader's vision of a rough-hewn hideaway.

As Kogito listened to this account, he remembered that long before the end of the war—and before a stream of total strangers, including many young soldiers in uniform, started

showing up at the family's rustic, rambling dwelling—there had
been some periods when his father would disappear from the
mountain valley for days at a time. His mother never told Kogito
where his father had gone, and she didn't appear to take any
particular notice of her husband's absences. When people came
to the house on business, hoping to meet with Kogito's father,
they would be sent away without any clear explanation of his
whereabouts. Kogito remembered the baffled looks on the faces
of those visitors, but around that same time, he heard a story in
the village that seemed to have some bearing on where his father had gone.

It was the oft-repeated tale of "another village," which had
taken on the patina of folklore. First (the story went) Kogito's
grandfather had come up with the idea of immigrating to Brazil and persuaded a number of villagers to join him. When the
growing international trend toward anti-Japanese sentiment
turned that stratagem into an impossible dream, Kogito's grandfather and his followers decided, as an alternative, to create
"another village" not far away.

It so happened that a plan was in progress to extend the
railroad to the next town. The village they were living in was
going to be cut off from the route, so his grandfather bought
up a large quantity of land around a deserted village where some
therapeutic hot-spring spas had been operating until around the
middle of the Meiji era. People said that because Kogito's great-
grandfather had given meritorious service (including fratricide)
in the suppression of a local insurrection, the prefectural governor made a secret agreement with Kogito's grandfather, prom-
ising that the new train line would include a station close to
the new settlement, which everyone called simply "another vil-

lage." However, the prospective settlers' hopes were dashed when the actual train route (and a new prefectural road as well) ended up being farther away from "another village" than the original blueprint had specified, and the dreams of creating a new village came to naught. As a result of the serial failures of his grand schemes—first the abortive group immigration to Brazil, then the abandonment of "another village"—Kogito's grandfather lost both his wealth and his popularity, and he ended up being remembered around those parts not as a hero but as the punch line of a rather sad joke.

When Kogito began attending a nationalized wartime elementary school, he used to ride into Matsuyama from his village, and every time the bus reached a place just before the tunnel where a wide panorama opened up, he always thought about his grandfather's vision of "another village" and what might have been. Wasn't it possible that the training camp Daio kept talking about, which had originally belonged to Kogito's father, had been built on the land originally intended for "another village," at the site of the deserted hot-spring village? And as for Choko Sensei's ill-fated "insurrection" on the day after the war ended—wasn't it possible that there was something more to that story than what Kogito had believed as a young boy?

In other words, maybe the preposterous military operation his father and his followers had claimed to envision—robbing a bank to get the necessary funds, then somehow sending a bombing mission from the Yoshidahama Naval Air Base to Ouchiyama in order to spoil the imperial proclamation of the end of the war, because they couldn't deal with the prospect of quiet surrender—maybe that was just them, talking big. Kogito now felt that it was more likely that they (including his father) had wanted to rob the bank to get funds to fix up the retreat in the depths of the forest, so they could go into hiding and bide their time. Indeed, Daio and his followers had built a training camp in that location and had been leading a self-sufficient life there ever since.

In any case, as we know, by the time the conversation by the moat was at an end Kogito had agreed to visit Daio's inn that night. That might have been, in part, because he was intrigued by the concept of self-sufficient living off the grid of civilization.

So off Kogito went to the inn, that first night, and as he was getting ready to take his leave, Daio said that since the next day was Saturday and classes ended at noon, he'd like to talk to him again sometime in the afternoon. Kogito saw no reason to refuse. The only complication was that there was a record concert scheduled to begin at 5 PM at the Matsuyama CIE. Originally, Kogito's only concern regarding the special event had been the inconvenience. The reading corner where the high-school students were cramming for their exams would be closed at 4 PM, the desks and chairs tidied up, and the partition that separated it from the meeting room cleared away. That would disrupt Kogito's usual Saturday schedule, which was to study at the library until 5:30, then walk home to his lodgings along the big street where the streetcars ran, and continue studying in his room after dinner.

However, this record concert was to feature chamber music by Mozart and Beethoven, in performances recorded on LPs belonging to the Americans who ran the center; this was a departure from the usual CIE concerts, which tended to be heavy on works by Copland, Gershwin, and Grofé. When Kogito talked to Goro after seeing the program announcement on the bulletin board in the library, Goro—who had often declared that he didn't give a toss for the usual concerts of pieces by modern American composers; "movie music," he called it, noting that unfortunately there were no movies attached—said he would like to go. There was a limit to how many people could be admitted to the CIE record concerts, which were popular with the townspeople, and even the students who practically lived at the CIE library couldn't get in without a ticket. It wasn't easy to get hold of one, either; reservations were required, and a casual would-be attendee had no hope of dropping by and scooping up a ticket on the night in question.

Kogito knew this, and the reason he had mentioned the chamber-music program to Goro in the first place was because he had been given three tickets to the concert in question as a bonus gift along with his main prize, a copy of the *Concise Oxford English Dictionary,* in an official ceremony before the newspaper article about him was printed.

Kogito's several conversations with Daio (in the afternoon and evening of the first day, and again the following day) had been rather disjointed and desultory in nature. When four o'clock rolled around on that Saturday afternoon, Kogito stole a glance at his old Omega watch (the only thing he had inherited from his father) and explained that he had an appointment with a friend—namely, Goro. After saying his good-byes, Kogito left the inn, and Daio and his colleagues tagged along, presumably just to see him off at the tram stop. But when Kogito boarded the streetcar, they climbed on, too. Noticing Kogito's perplexity, Daio declared in a perfectly calm, matter-of-fact voice, "These guys want to do some sightseeing around Matsuyama, and they'd like to see how our friend Kogito lives. To tell the truth, so would I!"

So that was how Kogito happened to have Daio and his young followers in tow when he approached the entrance to the CIE. On the east side of the building, where some large trees had been cleared away to reveal a fine view of the verdant Horinouchi district, they saw a group of men engaged in a shoot-around in an empty lot where a basketball net had been installed. And there, in the midst of the action, was Goro! Scrambling for the ball, dribbling, trying to get a shot off: Goro stood out from the rest of the players with his height, his splendid physique, and his shirtless, suntanned torso. He was brimming with youthful vigor, yet there was something cool and laid-back about him, too.

As they were watching, Kogito noticed that every time the ball ended up in Goro's hands, the people around him seemed to be working as a team to protect his shot. The other players on the makeshift court were all Japanese employees of the CIE. Watching from the sidelines was a young American man dressed in a linen ice-cream suit (his name, Kogito knew, was Peter), along with an older student who was never far from Goro's side. That student was what is colloquially known as a *ronin* or masterless samurai; that is, he had failed his college entrance exams on the first try and was waiting to take them again. Recently, when Kogito had received the award for reading *The Adventures of Huckleberry Finn* in English, Peter was the Japanese-speaking American officer who came from the military base to attend the ceremony.

Kogito wasn't particularly surprised to find Peter there, but he was amazed to see that the Japanese staff members (who tended to be unfriendly toward the local residents who used the facilities, sometimes to the point of outright discrimination) had included Goro in their basketball-practice group. Goro hardly ever came to the Center, yet he already appeared to be part of the in-group. To make matters worse, Kogito had an embarrassing memory of something that had happened to him in this little "sports corner," as it was euphemistically called.

In the fall of the previous year, while Kogito was still getting used to the routine of studying for his entrance exams at the CIE library, he became obsessed with the fact that ever since he'd moved from his village to the provincial city, his skin had been getting very little direct exposure to the sun, and he felt certain that that wasn't good for his health. So one day Kogito trotted down to the primitive sports corner, shed his shirt, and started doing bare-chested calisthenics. Seconds later, a Japanese staff member sneaked up on him, stealthy as a ninja—actually running on tiptoe to conceal the sound of his footsteps—and scolded him severely. Kogito had the feeling that someone was watching this spectacle from a window on the second floor, and sure enough, when he looked up he saw an American officer, no taller than the average Japanese, looking down on the mortifying scene. Now that he thought about it, that American was Peter.

Meanwhile, back in the present, several groups of the local intelligentsia and their female companions had already gathered by the front entrance and in the driveway to wait for the record concert to begin. In spite of this growing audience, the Japanese staff members were still allowing Goro to go on playing basketball, naked from the waist up. Clearly, Kogito thought ruefully, there was a double standard at work.

The basketball shoot-around continued for a while after
Kogito and his companions had stopped at courtside to watch.
Then the Japanese staff members discussed the situation in
loud, exhibitionistic English (of course) and decided to call a
halt to the game. They returned the ball to Peter; someone else
was apparently in charge of the physical-education facilities,
but perhaps today's use of the court had been arranged through
Peter. In any case, he took the leather ball, which was a truly
precious commodity in those days, and dashed toward the east-
side entrance of the building. Goro alone lingered at the base
of the pole from which the net was suspended, obviously reluctant to leave.

As Peter was about to go into the building, he looked back
and saw Goro moping around under the basket. Shouting something in English (Kogito had no idea what it meant), Peter threw
a Hail Mary–type pass toward the court. Goro leapt into the air,
caught the ball, did a balletic half turn, dribbled for three or four
steps, and took his shot. The ball clanged off the backboard and
dropped into the hoop. Goro caught the ball as it fell through
the knotted-string net, dribbled briskly down the court until he
was in three-point range, then turned and let fly a perfect shot:
nothing but net. Then, holding the ball at his side, he headed
toward where Peter was waiting.

After taking the ball, Peter pointed at the shiny film of
sweat on Goro's chest and shoulders, and appeared to be saying something. Not long after that, as Goro was sauntering back
toward the court, a thick towel was thrown from the second-
floor window by someone who looked unmistakably like an
American soldier. Nonchalantly catching the towel in midair,
Goro began wiping the perspiration off his upper body.

When Goro finally made his way to where Kogito and his companions were standing, he didn't show any surprise at seeing them there. His buddy, the masterless samurai, handed Goro a long-sleeved jersey shirt, and Goro put it on over his bare skin. Kogito had heard the story behind that shirt: it was part of an ice-hockey uniform and had been a gift from a college-student friend of Goro's when he was living Kyoto.

The masterless samurai didn't look too happy when Goro tossed him the damp, crumpled towel, but he dutifully trudged toward the east entrance to the building to return it. That was when Kogito produced the two extra tickets to the record concert and handed them to Goro, who was smiling broadly at him, obviously exhilarated by his workout. Neither Goro nor his crony, who came running back a moment later, offered a word of thanks.

Daio had been standing silently by Kogito's side, but now he gestured for his followers to step back. Stretching his mouth into an ingratiating smile, he addressed Goro in an almost absurdly humble, forelock-tugging manner.

"You must be Goro!" he began, in his usual overly enthusiastic tone. "Kogito's pal, the son of the famous film director! After the record concert is over, I'd like to invite you to come to my inn with Kogito. If you stay for the concert, you'll miss your dinner at your lodgings, won't you? So come and join us for some simple mountain food—or maybe I should say 'simple mountain-and-river food'!" Here Daio proffered another affable smile. "Whatever you want to call it, we brought lots of boiled Japanese mitten crab and home-brewed sake with us from the country. We didn't really have a proper party last night, but maybe if he has a friend along, Kogito here will loosen up a bit. Anyway, please stop by later and have a drink and as much crab as you can eat!"

Later, at the concert, another curious thing happened. Peter's seat was next to the giant loudspeaker that was used to broadcast the commentary, but he sent one of the Japanese staff members over to where Goro was sitting with his two friends. The man was carrying a small, custom-bound book, and he showed one bookmarked page to Goro. "This is a book by William Blake," the man announced in a theatrically hushed tone. "Peter was saying that he thinks you look like this child with the wings."

Sitting up very straight, Goro held the proffered book at arm's length and stared intently at the illustration, but he made no reply. Kogito was peering at the book from the next seat over, so he couldn't see the winged infant's face very clearly, but he did notice that the young man who was holding the little seraph above his head looked quite a bit like Peter. While the audience was waiting for the concert to begin, Peter was sitting in a chair made from metal tubing—something not often seen in those days—and his heart-shaped face, with its large, widely spaced eyes, was perpetually turned toward Goro.

Much later, when Kogito got hold of the Trianon Press edition of Blake's *Songs of Innocence and Experience* and looked at the illustration again, he wasn't able to see any trace of Peter's features in the face of the beautiful young man who was holding the winged infant aloft. However, when Kogito scrutinized the angelic-looking infant, with its abundant hair swirling above a wide forehead, its well-defined chin, and a nose and mouth that clearly showed both a headstrong nature

and a sense of humor, he saw, this time around, an undeniable resemblance to Goro. To put it more precisely, based on
old photos and on what he'd heard from Chikashi, he could
imagine that the little seraph bore a marked resemblance to
Goro as a child, when his unclouded beauty caused him to
be loved by everyone he met.

5

After the record concert ended, the intelligentsia assembled in a separate room to drink coffee, but the schoolboys were not invited to join them. This seemed perfectly natural, and besides, the truth was that Kogito felt strangely apprehensive about the prospect of encountering Peter again. So Kogito, Goro, and the masterless samurai left the CIE building and walked along the gravel road in the darkness, mingling with the rest of the postconcert crowd. Kogito knew that Goro had decided to take Daio up on his invitation, but he hadn't yet figured out how to say a tactful good-bye to Goro's silent sidekick, who was still tagging along with them.

When they finally got to the stop for the streetcar line that traversed the wide bridge over the moat, Kogito's problem was solved by a Daio ex machina: the one-armed man suddenly loomed up out of the darkness looking unusually clean and tidy, as if he had just climbed out of the bath. (Kogito deduced that he had paid a visit to Dogo Hot Springs' famous public bathhouse.) Totally ignoring the third member of their party, Daio hailed Goro and Kogito by name, and the masterless samurai, taking the hint, faded into the night without a word.

"I wasn't worried about Kogito, but I thought Goro might hesitate to take us up on the invitation, so I came to meet you," Daio explained. "Since you're able to talk about culture and music and that sort of thing, I think you're plenty grown-up in your heads. Again, I don't know about Kogito, but I'm sure Goro doesn't mind taking a sip or two of sake once in a while. As for the food, it may seem barbaric to you city folk, but river crab is more delicious than you might think. The inn says they can only serve as much rice as our ration coupons will buy, but we've made up for that in other ways. This feast is our way of saying thanks for all the times that Kogito's mother treated us to sake and meals, free of charge, at Choko Sensei's house. If it could be arranged sometime," Daio added, as if it were a casual afterthought, "I'd like to give that American officer a taste of our countrified cuisine, as well!"

Once again on this night, all through the meal and the ensuing seminar, Kogito didn't drink a drop of home-brewed sake. Goro, however, fell immediately into a party mood, and after fearlessly draining his first teacup full of *doburoku,* he held it out to be refilled from the three-pint-plus bottle. He even remarked that this sake was better than the expensive stuff he had sampled one night in Kyoto, when a female editor who was an admirer of his father's work had taken them to a high-class drinking spot frequented by poets and writers. As for the crab, Goro applied himself to devouring it with such guileless enthusiasm that for a time he didn't even acknowledge the questions that were addressed to him.

The night before, Kogito had noticed a red leather trunk leaning against the wall and had recognized it as something that had once been in his father's study. After a while Daio cleared away the empty platter that had held the mitten crabs and placed the trunk in the center of the gathering. Using the hand of his one outstretched arm, he unfastened the clasp, which snapped open with a loud click. Then, with his hand still resting on the lid of the trunk, he turned his oily, darkly gleaming face toward Goro and Kogito.

"We like to call this trunk our portable armory, but there's something in here that ought to bring back memories for you, Kogito," he said. While Daio was rummaging single-handedly through the truck, sitting in front of it with his knees in the air, Kogito was so engulfed in embarrassment at the prospect of the shameful secret that was about to be revealed to Goro that he felt as if he were suspended in midair.

Sure enough, what Daio finally fished out of the trunk— Kogito recognized it right away, with heart-sinking certainty— was the short sword that one of the employees of Kogito's family, who had been sent to the front during the Russo-Japanese War, had brought back as a souvenir. (Such instruments were commonly known as "burdock swords," in reference to the vaguely sword-shaped root vegetable.) That dull-colored, rusty old weapon had hung by the ten-year-old Kogito's side as he marched off to the ill-starred battle at the bank, behind the wooden cart that carried his father, who was clad in his usual bloody diapers. Goro would probably laugh himself sick over that pathetic image, if he knew.

But the sword wasn't Daio's main quarry. What he finally pulled out, after much time and effort (the object in question had obviously gotten tangled up with the other contents of the trunk and had to be dislodged) was a fish spear. Made from rubber, bamboo, and thick wire, and resembling a large, attenuated insect, it was the weapon Kogito had used ages ago when he dove under the water in search of eels.

Nowadays the banks of the Kame River are surrounded by a concrete wall, but when Kogito was a child, the bamboo grove that grew along the river had created a natural embankment. It was just as Goro said teasingly, many years later, when he presented Kogito with the Tagame system: although not entirely friendless, Kogito was a bit of an outsider who didn't play that much with other children. The person who cut a stalk of bamboo and made a rubber speargun for Kogito was the patriarch of a Korean family who had been brought in to do the job of carrying lumber out of the forest. Kogito's mother took care of feeding the three families of imported workers, and they became quite close. But Kogito ended up being a laughingstock yet again, because the pointed tip of the wire that was inserted into the hollowed-out bamboo as a power source for the rubber hadn't been properly worn down and polished. Now that Kogito thought about it, it was Daio who had gone to a blacksmith's shop, some distance from the village, and gotten the metalworker to exchange the original mechanism for a thicker wire attached to a small harpoon with a curved hook on the end.

Kogito found a pair of old swimming goggles and tried to repair them, but they still let in some water. Undaunted, he put them on and dove under the place where the current was flowing around the rocks. Truth be told, he wasn't really interested in catching eels; he just wanted to make a token attempt to play at the challenging water games that all the younger children were so good at. Before long, in the long cleft of a rock that separated the rapids from the deeper water, he found a tiny eel, not much larger than a finger, spewing clean water into the murkier river around it. The eel looked back at Kogito with its inky eyes, and he noticed that the pupils seemed to be incongruously far away from the creature's eyelids.

After lifting his head out of the water again and again to snatch a breath of air, Kogito finally managed to get the little harpoon on the end of his spear close to the eel's gills. He unfastened the clasp to release the power. Bull's-eye! The impaled eel struggled frantically for a few seconds, causing the spear to shake and sway, and then it was suddenly still.

Kogito raised his body so that he was kneeling in the rushing water, and when he looked down at the dead baby eel hanging from his spear end like a piece of garbage, he didn't feel like a triumphant hunter at all; he just felt utterly wretched, contrite, and ashamed. That was the bamboo speargun's first and last adventure on the river, and Kogito had no idea how it had ended up in the ragtag "armory" belonging to Daio's paramilitary training camp. (He didn't think about this until many years later, but that same trunk might very well have contained a rusty cannonball or two, left over from some local insurrection.)

Goro grabbed the speargun and was having a grand time, playfully pulling back the elastic cord and then letting it go with a loud snap, while Daio anxiously cautioned him not to aim it at anyone. After a while, when Daio had already asked him twice to stop fooling around with the speargun, Goro gave it back, acting as if he had been planning to toss it aside in any case. Then, in a voice that was shrill and blurred from all the *doburoku* he had drunk, he said dismissively, "That really isn't much of a weapon, is it?"

Daio's face turned suddenly serious. "Oh, really?" he said frostily. "Suppose you make a little hole in an entry door or a wooden wall, and the light from inside is leaking out. If somebody comes snooping around, it's only human nature for them to put their eye up to the illuminated hole to see what's going on inside, right? And suppose that in the same hole there's the tip of a spear, narrow enough so it doesn't block all the light, and suppose all the energy in the rubber band has been stored up and is ready to spring. How about that, huh?"

"You call that stupid thing a weapon?" Goro scoffed. "What a joke."

"Hey, right now we're just a humble resistance movement, hoping to make life difficult for the occupying army," Daio said defensively. "If we could get our hands on some more sophisticated weapons, we wouldn't have to resort to this 'stupid' kind of guerrilla fighting, you know!" The leader of the humble resistance movement spoke with naked candor, and by the time he finished, Kogito had put two and two together: Daio, he realized, had been paying court to Goro because he saw him as a possible conduit to augmenting the contents of the rebels' armory.

As for Goro, while he never extinguished the dreamy, drunken smile he had worn all evening, he didn't say anything in response, either, and his body language didn't offer any clue to his feelings one way or another. Still, it was clear that Daio had figured out exactly what he wanted, and he even went so far as to ask Goro whether he could somehow contrive to become friendlier with that nice Japanese-speaking American officer.

While this subtle maneuvering was taking place, another showstopping delicacy was served: dumplings made from glutinous rice, pork, and lots of garlic, decoratively wrapped in bamboo leaves. This was a Korean-influenced dish that had been adopted by the people of Kogito's village during the time when his mother was cooking for the Korean workers and their families. As the boys agreed when they were comparing candid notes on the way home at the end of the evening, it was the single most thrilling dish they had enjoyed during the seven years of privation and turmoil that had followed the end of the war.

Toward the end of the party, Daio had suddenly launched into a discourse about the origin of Kogito's unusual given name. Needless to say, the name had been inspired by the famous catchphrase of the Western philosopher Descartes, but there was more to it than that. Kogito's village had a long-standing business connection with Osaka, which was the closest big city. Many local students commuted to a school there called Kaitokudo, where they studied neo-Confucianism, but the school's academic tradition also incorporated the classically influenced ideas of Ito Jinsai, the seventeenth-century Confucian scholar.

"As you may have heard," Daio said, "the father-in-law of our former teacher, Choko Sensei, was unsuccessful, first with his plan for immigrating to Brazil and then with his dream of creating 'another village.' Anyway, when he was a boy, that man—Kogito's grandfather—studied *The Analects* of Confucius at Kaitokudo, and then when he was a teenager he learned about 'Cogito, ergo sum,' in French, from Nakae Chomin, the famous Meiji era prodemocracy philosopher and human-rights activist from Tosa, who studied in France. Of course there's no *co* in Japanese orthography, so they had to write it 'Kogito,' but that's just the sort of weird, erudite name you'd expect from the Choko household, don't you think?"

Goro laughed uproariously at that, to the point where Kogito started to feel something very close to loathing toward his friend and the buffoonish Daio, who had insisted on telling the embarrassing story.

Later that night, though, Kogito and Goro patched up their differences, as boys will, and they talked excitedly about every-thing that had transpired, all the way home.

CHAPTER FOUR

One Hundred Days
of Quarantine (II)

CHAPTER FOUR

of Quarantine (1)

1

As he embarked on the second half of his stay in Berlin, Kogito couldn't help feeling that this sojourn, more than any of his other extended trips abroad, had a pleasing sense of stability. When he thought back on his travel experiences, they seemed, in retrospect, surpassingly strange—especially the adventures he'd had when he was young, traveling on a shoestring budget and deliberately setting out for destinations where he didn't know a soul, places that were far off the beaten track and not designed for the comfort of tourists.

The reason his life in Berlin felt so settled was because the Berlin Free University and the Institute of Advanced Research had made him feel completely welcome, and despite the fact that he had waited till the last minute to make his decision about coming, every aspect of his stay had been flawlessly arranged in advance. Another element in his "settledness" was the undeniable fact that he seemed to have lost the bountiful vitality that had spurred him to push the experiential envelope as a young traveler, and that realization made him feel quite forlorn.

It was on a Sunday morning, with the Berlin Film Festival due to begin in the middle of the coming week, that Kogito went to a hotel in Potsdam Square. And there, for the first time on this trip, he had the disturbing feeling (deeply familiar from many other trips abroad) that the ground was shifting under his feet.

Earlier that morning, he had been standing on the curb in front of his rococo apartment building, waiting in vain for Iga, an assistant professor of Japanese studies at the university, to pick him up. Finally, thirty minutes past the appointed time of 10 AM, he decided to go back inside. Just as he began climbing the stairs to his apartment, he heard the telephone ringing. He didn't get there in time to take the call, but a few minutes later the phone rang again.

When Kogito answered it he heard the rather annoyed-sounding voice of Iga saying that Mrs. Azuma-Böme had been grumbling to him on the phone a moment earlier that Kogito was impossible to get hold of. On the previous day, the woman had evidently proposed a new plan wherein she would first pick up Iga, then Kogito, and that had been agreed on. But when this morning rolled around she informed Iga that she had to deal with a sudden work-related crisis, so she wouldn't be able to join him and Kogito at the filming of today's interview, after all.

Iga said that if he came to pick Kogito up in his car they would both end up being late, so he suggested that they make their separate ways to the hotel by taxi, then share a cab on the way home to avoid the hassle of parking. In spite of the earlier glitches, the revised plan went smoothly, and the two men met in the lobby of the hotel a short time later. Iga immediately went to the festival's reception desk but found the people there singularly unreceptive because, it seemed, no one had bothered to register him or Kogito. Iga protested, to no avail, and he ended up being passed from one functionary to another in a classic red-tape muddle.

Kogito had been standing nearby for nearly an hour, watching this scene unfold, when he was approached by a white-maned man whom he had noticed, moments earlier, majestically descending the staircase from the second floor to the lobby. The man appeared to be some years older than Kogito, and he had an air of amiability and intelligence. He said that he had enjoyed the filming they had done in Frankfurt, ten years ago, and wondered whether Kogito had received the video of that event, which had been mailed to Tokyo.

The man then flung his arm around Kogito's shoulder as if they were the most intimate of friends and began to hustle him toward the staircase. Kogito was concerned about leaving Iga behind but, unable to resist the natural force that was bearing him away, he allowed himself to be led to the entrance of the festival's main hall, on the second floor. From that floor on up, everything seemed already to have been taken over by the organizers of the pending film festival.

Kogito's escort, the friendly older man, wore an official registration badge hanging on a lanyard around his neck, and the person in charge of the entrance pretended not to notice that Kogito lacked a badge of his own. He practiced the same selective myopia on Iga, who had noticed Kogito's departure and came galloping up the stairs behind them. As the two visitors were following their rescuer along a passageway that led to the main meeting hall, they came to a place where a number of men were standing around in front of a large, half-open door, and their little procession ground to a momentary halt. Their guide simply threaded his way through this roadblock without greeting or explanation, then ushered Kogito and Iga inside.

They found themselves in a vast, airy room with a ceiling that was twice as high as normal. People were bustling around on the stage at the front of the room, making preparations for filming. Just inside the entrance, there was a chair piled high with four or five overcoats, and a corresponding number of stagehands was busy installing lighting apparatus and punctuating the hall with small viewing screens. The rest of the filming equipment appeared to be already in place. Even at a flashy event like the film festival there was an air of German practicality, so it seemed natural when a sturdily built young woman wearing khaki-colored jeans came up and handed Kogito (who was still standing near the door) a cup of coffee, a small plastic container of milk, and a packet of sugar. But she didn't say a word, even though Kogito had noticed that most bright young German workers were usually quite fluent in English.

Meanwhile, Iga had been led into the shadow of the main screen by the older man, and they were deep in conversation. As far as Kogito could tell, they were trying to clear up some late-arising point of confusion. Nevertheless, when the older man (who, it emerged, was to be the interviewer-director of the day's filming) returned from his impromptu conference with Iga, he shepherded Kogito with complete naturalness and ease to a pair of chairs that had been placed in front of the screen and sat him down on the right-hand side. On the left side, Iga, still looking somewhat bewildered, was being fitted with a microphone by the sound engineer. When Kogito had been similarly equipped, the director took a seat beside the camera that faced them and gave instructions to the crew member standing next to him.

A monitor had been pushed forward to a place where Kogito and Iga could see it, and it suddenly flickered into life. The scene that began to unfold on the screen was so uncannily convincing that Kogito thought for a moment that he was having some sort of Kurosawa-era samurai-film hallucination, complete with Japanese actors.

The terrain is a rather wide, low basin or hollow, with a thick, flourishing forest of Japanese cedar trees closing in on it from either side. On the near flank, a military camp has been set up, and in the midst of a welter of spears and colorful pole-mounted banners stands a group of samurai warriors, encased in ornate medieval-style armor from head to toe. On either side of the foot soldiers are rows of mounted horsemen. Everyone is obviously on high alert, and the tension is palpable.

The camera pulls back, and on this side, some distance from the samurai encampment, a huge throng of half-naked farmers comes into view, seen from behind. There are too many of them to count, and because of the camera's angle they seem to swarm into the scene, entirely filling the frame. The farmers continue to advance, like a tidal wave. On the other side, the samurai forces surge forward to meet their adversaries. Just as the two hard-charging factions are about to collide, the scene changes to something completely different.

Now we're looking at a contemporary sports broadcast of a rowdy, exciting rugby match between an English and a German team. In this scene, too, the forces on the near flank are on the offensive, gradually gathering strength as the focus of the battle moves into the opposing territory. The game rages fiercely as the opponents stage a bold counterattack. Then, climactically, one player on the near wing fields a spectacular pass and starts charging down the right side of the opposing team's territory. It's virtually a one-man race, and it looks as if no one can stop him.

The scene changes again, and we're back on the Japanese battleground. The army of farmers has already taken occupation of the terrain surrounding the cedar grove where the samurai forces have dug in. At the head of the mass of farmers is a rough-hewn box with wooden wheels, and atop this makeshift chariot, like a threadbare Roman centurion, stands a man whose disproportionately large, egg-shaped head is wrapped in layers of dirty, patched cloth. The wooden cart, with its odd-looking passenger, is pushed forward and then swallowed up as the multitude of rebellious farmers surges into battle. Thousands of bamboo spears are hoisted into the air, and the farmers raise a mighty battle cry in unison. And . . . fade out.

After the monitor had gone dark, the cameraman began filming. The director of the interview turned toward Kogito and asked a question in German, with a smile that was almost shy, and Iga began to translate the query into Japanese. Then he paused and, without trying to hide his perplexity, asked Kogito a question of his own.

"Of course, it's up to you to answer the question as you see fit," Iga said, "but I'm getting the feeling that the subject matter now on the table is very different from what the director originally proposed. How shall we handle this? Rather than answering the question right away, would you like to have them turn off the cameras for a while and then start over after we've agreed on some ground rules?"

Kogito had no idea what was going on, but he could see that the camera was still rolling, the sound-recording technicians were looking intently in his direction, and the young woman in khaki-colored jeans was opening a notebook, apparently to chronicle the proceedings. In that highly charged atmosphere, it would have been extremely awkward to ask the director (who was not only kindly-looking but clearly highly intelligent, as well) to call the operation to a temporary halt. Quicker than thought, Kogito rejected that idea. "Just translate the questions," he told Iga. "I'll answer them as we go along."

So the interview recommenced, and the first question was about the film-in-progress that was being made from one of Kogito's long novels, which had been published in German translation as *Der stumme Schrei*. They had just watched all the completed scenes.

"We would like to hear your reaction to the film so far, as the original author," the director said in German, as Iga translated. "Also, we would appreciate hearing your comments about the acclaimed Japanese film director Goro Hanawa, who was so generous with his advice and encouragement at the beginning, during the screenplay-conversion stage of the project, while the young filmmakers were persevering in the face of enormous financial difficulties. We know that you had a long-standing friendship with Mr. Hanawa, who so tragically committed suicide, and on top of that, you were his brother-in-law, as well."

Kogito replied: "The Japanese title of my book, *Rugby Match 1860,* is a metaphor that ties together two events. One is the peasant uprising that occurred in the important year of 1860—a year that also saw the second opening of Japan to the West—and the other is the civilian movement to oppose the

signing of the Japan-U.S. Security Treaty, a hundred years later
in 1960. I see that the filmmakers have made the bold choice
to render the metaphors with literal imagery, and I think it
would be interesting to continue in the same vein. If it was Goro
who proposed to the young German filmmakers that it be done
this way, then I can definitely see traces of his trademark humorous yet coruscating satire, and I marvel at the young filmmakers' skill in making that a reality on the screen.

"In case you don't know the background, the clan authorities, under the feudal system, condemned the leader of the first
peasants' revolt to death by beheading. The peasant activists
managed to retrieve the head of their leader, which had been
preserved in brine, and after reattaching the pickled head to their
leader's dead body, they went off to mount another attack, this
time on the castle town downriver. That trope, like the rugby
match, is something that I wrote as a metaphor in the novel, but
this film seems to be transforming everything into literal images.

"Anyway, the leader, restored to a semblance of life, is once
again riding in the box with wooden wheels, being propelled
along the road by his followers. This is a reference to something
that really did happen just after Japan lost the war; it's an incident that is important to me as both a member of my family
and, personally, as an individual. I wrote about it in a novel
called *His Majesty Himself Will Wipe Away My Tears*, and elsewhere, as well.

"The last thing I would like to point out is that the scenes
of the mountain valley depicted in these video excerpts have
succeeded brilliantly in capturing the essential atmospherics
of the terrain around the area where I grew up. There's an essay
by an architect friend of mine, in which he analyzes the topo-

logical characteristics of my novels. What I saw just now on the screen gave me the feeling that the architect's superb structural logic had somehow been transformed into visual images. I remember hearing about an extensive field-research trip that Goro went on, accompanied by my wife—as you mentioned earlier, she is Goro's younger sister—that included a visit to the house where I was born and raised. (This happened about twenty years ago, while I was living and teaching in Mexico City.) This film has made excellent use of that research and brought it vividly to life. In all likelihood, the filmmakers based their production design on the particulars that Goro gave them in his informal lectures, but to transform those details into film in such a vivid way and with such a high degree of integrity—well, I have to say, these young German filmmakers have really earned my respect."

When Kogito had finished speaking, the interview director, making no attempt to disguise the tension he felt about having a hidden agenda, broached the crucial question.

"May I assume that you, as the author, have a strong desire to see this film project completed?" he ventured. "The team that's working on it noticed a problem in the contract with the original author—that is, with you. Your agent pointed out the same thing, and then the funding for the project dried up, so production unavoidably ground to a halt for an extended period of time. Is there any chance that you might have the inclination to offer these young artists the assistance that would make it possible to overcome these obstacles?"

After translating the second question up to this point, Iga asked the director a question of his own, this time in English rather than German, so that Kogito would be able to understand as well: "When you say 'inclination' and 'assistance,' what exactly are you hoping to obtain?"

"Well, it's like this," the director replied. "First, contractually, there's the option itself; these young artists haven't officially acquired the film rights to the original novel, and we were wondering whether you might consider letting them have those rights without paying a fee? Second, it has been reported that the estate of Goro Hanawa, the director, may be worth as much as five million deutsche marks—that's nearly nine million U.S. dollars. If that's true, could we possibly ask you to try to persuade the bereaved family to invest in this film?"

After first translating that question for Kogito, Iga quickly added a postscript of his own in Japanese. "Speaking as a third-party observer," he said in a low voice, "I really don't think this is the sort of thing that you should have to deal with during the filming of an interview. It's extremely self-serving on their part, in my opinion. What's more, I can't help suspecting that the ulterior motive for setting up this so-called interview was so they could push the conversation in this direction, and then if you agreed to their terms they would have proof of it on film. So what do you think—shall we call a halt to this charade right now? On the other hand, to look at the situation in a more positive way, if you want to help them finish a production that's run aground, and if you'd like to actively offer them support for that purpose—look, I agree that it's a worthy project, and the part that's already finished is, as you pointed out, really very fine work. So if that's what you want, I'll be happy to translate your response, whatever it may be."

Kogito chose to proceed with the interview. First, though, he gave his word, in reply to the director's leading question, that he would let the young German filmmakers have the rights to his novel for free, provided the rest of the production was consistent with the samples that were already in the can. After having seen the video playback of the scenes, he felt certain that both the screenplay and the staging had Goro's distinctive fingerprints all over them. Why? Because they corresponded exactly with the ideas and interpretations that Goro had talked about on some of the tapes he made for Tagame, before he went to the Other Side.

Kogito found himself seriously regretting not having brought Tagame with him to Berlin, because he would have liked to compare Goro's recorded remarks with the film he had just seen. Of course, he had no right whatsoever to speak about the use of Goro's estate, nor did he have any intention of meddling in the bereaved family's financial affairs, and he made that perfectly clear to everyone on hand.

After the interview was over, the white-haired director quickly reverted to his original kindly, genteel mien. As he was escorting Kogito and Iga out of the hotel, he said that Kogito's filmed remarks would provide encouragement and inspiration for the young artists who were trying to rebuild the German film industry—a goal that the country's chancellor himself had endorsed in a video message he'd sent for the opening of the film festival. The director added that it was especially good that they had filmed Kogito's gratifyingly specific comments right there in what would be the central venue for the upcoming festival.

On the way home in the taxi, Iga said, as if to confirm the director's remarks, "The reason Germany's New Cinema is getting off the ground now is because they have that director leading them. It's only natural that you would want to come to their

rescue when they're struggling financially. But do you suppose
Goro realized that he would end up becoming so deeply involved
with the young German filmmakers? It just seems odd that they
went ahead and started work on the film version of your novel
without making sure they had the rights sewn up. Or is it possible that they didn't make their plan clear to Goro, and he
unwittingly got dragged into their plan to go ahead and make
part of the film and then present it as a fait accompli?"

"Mrs. Azuma-Böme seems to have been helping them out
quite a bit, as well, but I wonder whether she was unaware of
what was really going on," Kogito mused. "Or, on the contrary,
maybe she knew exactly what was going on, and was trying to
make them finish it so it would be, as you say, a fait accompli?"

"Hmm, that's hard to say. One thing I do know for certain
is that she really loves film. I've often seen her at showings of
the young artists' experimental work at the Berlin Film Festival and elsewhere. But would she really go so far as to participate in a legally dubious scheme during the production stage?
She started out as an actress, you know, and they say that when
Goro was being promoted as a 'new face' at the beginning of
his acting career, she costarred with him as a senior actress.
I've heard her bragging about that, more than once."

"She told me that she met Goro again when he came here
for the Berlin Film Festival, and they probably realized that they
had some sort of history," Kogito said. "But what about Mrs.
Azuma-Böme's daughter? What's the connection there?"

"Oh, did you hear the way the mother bad-mouths her own
daughter?" Iga laughed. "I think that rather than being opposed
to the girl's involvement with Goro, the mother was just generally critical of her daughter. I know the girl helped Goro out on

one of his trips to Berlin, in a variety of ways. Naturally, there were lots of people who were interested in meeting Goro while he was here, and I heard that some of them were complaining that the girl was monopolizing his time. Apparently the mother felt responsible for her daughter's behavior, and that was the beginning of the friction between the two of them. After that terrible thing happened to Goro, a horde of tabloid-magazine reporters came here looking for background, and apparently they really got on the wrong side of Mrs. Azuma-Böme. I've even heard that her grievances against the reporters might eventually end up in court," Iga said.

"But why do you think the relationship between the mother and daughter degenerated so radically?"

"Apparently the mother said, 'Don't try to be too helpful, because then you'll be no better than a *Mädchen für alles,* and if you do that he'll get bored with you right away,' and I gather that her daughter asked a German friend of hers, who explained about that term's derogatory meaning. And the girl's feelings were so deeply hurt that she wasn't able to forgive her mother for saying such a thing. Anyway, that's what I heard. The daughter was brought up in Tokyo by her father, Mrs. Azuma-Böme's ex-husband, but after the mother got married again, to a German, the girl came to live with them in Berlin. That's why she can barely speak a word of German."

"You certainly know a lot about this," Kogito said.

"That's because I happen to know the German woman who told the girl what that phrase meant; in fact, she actually came to me afterward to make sure she had explained it correctly in English. After she told the girl, she started to worry that she might have gotten it wrong."

"How did you explain the nuances of that phrase, I wonder?"

"Well, my wife was born in Berlin, but she says she never heard that expression used around her house, even once," Iga said. "Mrs. Azuma-Böme's present husband is a successful businessman, quite a bit older than she is, so it's possible that he learned about 'Mädchen für alles' while growing up in an old-fashioned household. Anyway, the same mutual friend was saying that when that terrible thing happened to Goro, Azuma-Böme's daughter went around saying that he had been murdered by yakuza. She kept insisting that he'd been killed because he had agreed to do a project for NHK, an investigative documentary that was supposedly going to expose the truth about yakuza control of the waste-incineration industry." Iga hadn't really answered Kogito's questions about the semantics of Mädchen für alles, but he decided not to pursue the matter any further.

The strange thing was that Kogito never heard from Azuma-Böme after that, nor did he ever hear anything further about her daughter, the mysterious girl Friday. The only result of Kogito's visit to the Berlin Film Festival was the video he left behind, in which he made an outright gift of the film rights to one of his novels to some young German filmmakers without even knowing the name of their group.

2

Kogito's "quarantine" in Berlin lasted for a hundred days, so it actually ended up being more than twice as long as the forty days mentioned in the dictionary definition, based on the word's Italian etymology. When he traveled from Tokyo to Berlin, Kogito had almost no ill effects from the time difference, but he knew that the return trip would be a different story. Sure enough, he ended up suffering horrendous jet lag for ten full days.

During that time, Kogito was searching for a way to get a firm grip on reality once again—he had made a conscious point of not putting fresh batteries into Tagame—and he would sometimes lie on the army cot in his study and daydream about telephoning one friend or another. That's when the stark reality would hit him. Goro's criticism, on the Tagame tapes, that Kogito didn't have any intimate younger colleagues was true. Professor Musumi, Takamura, and some more relaxed, easygoing friends as well—practically everyone Kogito might have felt like calling up was dead!

Not only that, but he couldn't seem to find a book that would soothe his head, which always seemed to be throbbing hotly from jet lag and sleep deprivation. There was a pile of packages at the door of his study, and while he was unwrapping them he would idly browse through the books. He might, for example, be enticed by the style of a Japanese translation of Proust, and that might put him into a mood of leisurely remembrance of all things past. When that happened, Kogito found himself thinking with newfound serenity about his own death as an event that wasn't too far off. He couldn't bear to think that he would still be hanging around for another fifteen or twenty long years after this, and rather than *Time Regained* (the title of the final volume of Proust's magnum opus), the phrase "Death Regained" popped into his overheated head.

"That's it!" Kogito exclaimed out loud. "'Death' is 'Time'!" In his deliriously befuddled state, wild thoughts that would probably have been rejected if he were fully awake now struck him as profoundly persuasive epiphanies. He even felt as if his own death was something that had already taken place, some time ago. It seemed as if things that had occurred in the recent past were rapidly receding into the mists of time, and even Goro's death seemed to have happened a hundred years before, or more. And then he saw himself, too, as someone long dead, dwelling on the Other Side along with Goro, who seemed to have died ages ago. And if Kogito was indeed a shade, then it didn't seem unnatural for him to be half dozing and nodding off all the time.

When he was "thinking" along these lines, Kogito (who was absolutely certain that his epic jet lag would prevent him from ever falling asleep) was actually sleeping, and what seemed to be conscious, waking thoughts were in fact dreams that were visiting him in his shallow sleep. The next day, like those premonitions that come to us in dreams, thoughts such as "Death is Time," too, would inevitably fade into obscurity. But before long the harmonic overtones of that thought might end up reverberating in some new dream . . . if he was lucky enough to fall asleep.

3

Kogito had convinced himself that his quarantine in Berlin had two main goals: first, to return to the way things were before he embarked on the Tagame dialogues with Goro, and second, to discipline himself until he was sure that he was capable of giving them up for good. Gradually, that plan began to produce results, and at certain times (sitting in his office before he went off to give his lecture was always a time of particular tranquillity) he would find himself almost able to rearrange reality by convincing himself that the communication he and Goro had exchanged after Goro's defection to the Other Side was nothing more than a self-conscious game.

Yet he never thought it was meaningless just because it was a game. It was only through the form of a game that he could achieve the necessary deepening of consciousness, and it was clear that he had reached that level by way of the Tagame ritual.

Since entering his forties, Kogito had often poked fun at himself as a "late-blooming structuralist," but he managed to figure out the unique role of a game, in contrast with, say, a ritual, by reexamining some of the arguments that had already begun to be abandoned by the clever, trendsetting cultural anthropologists. Kogito realized that, as if to prove that the Tagame dialogues with Goro were just a game, he had invented any number of rules for that diversion and had followed them scrupulously. Goro, too, had seemed to respond to the conversation as a fellow player who was honoring the rules. (Of course, that could have been because Kogito was careful never to make any moves that might cause Goro to overstep those rules.)

Even so, the communication he exchanged with Goro by means of Tagame had the element of unpredictable dynamism that's found in any conversation, in varying degrees, and thus it had the effect of stimulating Kogito and pushing him forward toward new perspectives and ways of looking at things that had never occurred to him before. At the same time, Kogito felt confident that, apart from the occasional slip, he and Goro were respecting the rules of the game—in particular, the rule that no matter how impassioned the conversation might get, neither of them would ever again propose that they work on something together in real time, in the real world. (This actually fell under Rule Number Two: *Never speak about the future.*)

Thus when Kogito was in his apartment in Berlin, continually reviewing the conversations he'd had with Goro, he was still able to make a clear distinction between the messages that had come to him through Tagame (especially the ones that had been recorded close to the date when Goro suddenly and unexpectedly went off to the Other Side) and any discussions they might have had on the telephone, which of course predated Tagame and were not subject to its rules.

"Chikashi was saying that when you turn sixty-four, Akari will be thirty-six," Goro had said in one of their telephone talks, toward the end. "So if you add up both your ages, that's a hundred years! According to the mystical beliefs of your pathetic schoolboy days in Mat'chama, by the time you get to be a hundred years old, you should be a genuine, card-carrying Man of Wisdom. And then there's the hundred years (give or take a few decades) that you yourself have already lived . . . I'm not sure how this should be calculated, but if you include the previous fifty years and the fifty years after that, for a total of two hundred years, you could come up with a perfect vision of human life. The way I'm thinking now, if you put together the years that you and Akari have lived individually—that is, sixty-four plus thirty-six—then I figure you've already lived for a hundred years. See what I mean?"

"It's certainly true that Akari and I have collaborated on being alive for close to a hundred years," Kogito acknowledged, "and I do get the feeling sometimes that I'm a centenarian already. When 1999 rolls around, I expect I'll feel it even more acutely. Whether the feeling will strike on my birthday, or on Akari's, that's another matter . . ."

"Wait a minute," Goro interrupted. "You two have different birthdays? When I was talking to Chikashi the other day I somehow got the impression that you and Akari were born on the same day. As you know, Chikashi isn't what you would call arrogant, by any means, but she is a person of strong convictions, and her confident personality sets her apart from the typical modest, self-effacing stereotype of Japanese women. Anyhow, I guess she's somehow become convinced that she gave birth to you and Akari on the same day—in other words, that both of you are her children! That's probably because she's truly a maternal type. When she and I were living in those lodgings in the temple compound in Mat'chama, she gave me more motherly support than I ever got from my real mother."

At this point Kogito was on the verge of saying glibly, "I know that your mother plays a major role in your personal psychology, whether positive or negative, but what does that have to do with this?" but he swallowed his words. A moment later, he thought of saying: "It must have been kind of uncomfortable for you, having two supermoms on your back!" but he managed to suppress that comment as well.

While Kogito was busy biting his tongue, Goro used the resulting silence to shift the focus to a proposal that had clearly been on his mind before he called. "When you used to talk about becoming a sage, back in Mat'chama, I didn't want to cross-question you, but what I was imagining vaguely went something like this. You would become a wise old man, so wise that not only would you have a vision of the hundred years you had actually lived and the fifty years before your birth, but you could also see ahead for fifty years to come, for a total of two hundred years. In other words, you would be so wise that you could predict the future, just by studying and thinking about what had gone before. But then, what about me? When you're a hundred, I'll be a hundred and one, and even if I'm still alive, I can't imagine that I'll still be working. Anyway, there was something disarming about your way of thinking that you were going to live to be a hundred. That was when I first started to think that rather than becoming a scholar, as I had originally predicted, you might end up being a person who did something creative.

"Remember when you wrote *Rugby Match 1860* as a magazine serial, and I phoned you from Venice? In those days it was ridiculously expensive to make a long-distance phone call through the hotel switchboard, and I remember my wife wasn't too happy about the extravagance. At that time I hadn't yet read your novel, but I was talking to a reporter who was in Venice to cover the film festival, and he had just read the final installment in a magazine and was very excited about it. That was how I came to hear the details of the plot—in spite of the fact that, as you're always quick to point out, I'm not very good at reducing things to a summarized version, whether it's a novel or a movie. I have to tell you that it was a huge relief to hear over the international phone line that *Rugby Match* had nothing to do with your plan for becoming a Man of Wisdom. At that time, even though I was appearing in movies overseas, I wasn't exactly the toast of the town here in Japan, and I was still just a half-baked actor, struggling to find my path. Naïve as it may sound, I only had one great wish: that I could somehow be a party, through my work, to your plan for living to be a hundred. Actually, I did try to take that idea of yours and turn it into something concrete. I once drew up a plan for a TV series that would have followed the path of modernization since the Meiji era, as my way of trying to make a stab at your vision of the Man of Wisdom. That didn't pan out, but I've continued to think about the idea of showing this country's last hundred and fifty years in a cinematic way, using your house in the forest as a setting. I've also thought of showing that historical time line by starting at some point in the future and going back a hundred and fifty years into the past. Of course, that's assuming you would collaborate with me on the screenplay. Even if that ultimately proved to be impossible, we could still have the fun of brainstorming together. And now that I've been making films for twelve years, I'm conscious that I've reached the end of this particular chapter of my career. Then when I heard from Chikashi about your new way of thinking about making it to your hundredth birthday, that reignited the spark and inspired me all over again. Until now I've always made light of that, saying that you had plenty of time until you hit a hundred, because when you were younger it really did seem as if you had forever ahead of you. Of course, you've been partial to doing magic tricks with numbers ever since our days in Mat'chama, so you got me this time with a bit of mathematical sleight of hand, so to speak. But, really, to think that your age and Akari's add up to a hundred this year! To be honest, that really knocked me for a loop. I can't wait to hear what you think about all this."

"So you mean that's why you're calling me now, from Venice?"

"Exactly," Goro said with such complete candor that Kogito felt as if he, too, had been knocked off his feet. "Up until now," Goro went on, "it isn't as if I haven't wondered why you were so fixated on making it to a hundred or why you even thought about something like becoming a Man of Wisdom in the first place. But I don't think you'll live the forty or so years between now and your hundredth birthday in a random, haphazard way. As Chikashi always says, you simply don't have the gift of being idle for long periods of time.

"I've been thinking, too, about your life's work and the philosophy you've constructed, with the goal of reaching your hundredth year on earth, and I think that the day will eventually come when you'll try to find a way to start to write about

THAT while you're still at an age where you can work. Truth be told, you can't go on avoiding the necessity of chronicling that experience forever. It's very much the same for me. And you can't possibly reach a final conclusion if you push me aside, since you don't know everything that happened.

"I guess what I'm trying to say is that if you reach a point where you want to tackle THAT, as the crowning accomplishment of your life as a novelist, I won't let you do it all by yourself."

4

Kogito's apartment, in one of Berlin's poshest residential districts, was as quiet and peaceful a place as you could imagine: a place where no one ever came to call, where he prepared his own meals and washed them down with wine from Spain and Italy. It was while he was getting ready to confront the inexorably approaching Berlin winter, which was a formidable thing in itself—"*Das Ding an sich,*" in local parlance—that Kogito often found himself remembering that "Man of Wisdom" phone call from Goro, which was one of the last talks they ever had. (This was after his obsession with the Tagame dialogues had begun to recede into the background.)

At other times, as he gazed out at the darkening sky through the overlapping tangles of bare black branches on one of the many winter days when it had been threatening to snow since morning, Kogito was reminded of a conversation he'd had with his composer friend, Takamura, as they looked out a hospital window at a gray Tokyo sky that also held the promise, or the threat, of snow.

On that winter's day, Kogito had gone to visit Takamura
at the hospital in Akasaka and had heard from his friend, firsthand, about the increasingly dire prognosis. Kogito had known
since two years earlier that cancerous cells had been found in
his friend's kidneys during an annual physical examination. It
wasn't as if Kogito had been in denial about the lethal implica-
tions of that discovery, but he had been clinging all along to
the hope that Takamura (this man on whom he had depended
since they were young and who could only be described as a
genius) would somehow find a way to overcome this crisis.

Takamura showed Kogito a notebook filled with delicate
lines that were reminiscent of botanical drawings—the same
spidery script the renowned composer used for writing his
musical scores. At the top of the page were the heart-wrenching
words "Abridged Composition Plan for the Remainder of My
Life." Takamura's conversation with Kogito on this day seemed
to be a way of adding figurative footnotes to the plan set forth
in that notebook.

The patient's condition was very grave and (as he explained
to Kogito) when he considered the dreadful side effects of the
anticancer drug therapy and the physical stamina that would
be required to endure that treatment, Takamura had realized
the necessity of scaling down the work plan he had been following till now. He had asked Kogito to write an opera libretto,
and he said now that if the text couldn't be completed over the
next six months or so, he would have to abandon the entire opera
project.

"I imagine you've probably heard about this already,"
Takamura said, "but there's a libretto that was written by a
young American novelist. However, because the idea is to co-

ordinate his work with the nucleus that you're going to create, if your work can't be finished in time, I won't be able to keep the opera on this list. Is there any chance you might be able to finish by spring?"

And Kogito had to answer, with the deepest regret, "No, no chance at all."

"That's what I thought, somehow—since we've been talking all along, I just got the feeling that was how it would turn out. And I gather that in this case, rather than starting to write something from scratch, it's more a matter of your needing to dig up things that have been deeply buried for a long time and can't easily be unearthed."

Even if Takamura hadn't been a rather diminutive man, his head would still have been disproportionately large for his body, but his essential power and symmetry were evident in every move he made. He was wearing pajamas made from broadcloth shirting patterned with tiny polka dots, and his oversized head, which was bald as a result of radiation therapy, was covered with a woolen cap. He held Kogito captive with his deep, motionless eyes until Kogito, unable to bear the intensity of that gaze, had to look away.

"I had actually started to give up on this project," Takamura said, "but then an American reporter came to visit me yesterday, and he told me that he had heard about the idea for an opera from Goro. So I thought, wishfully, that if you had reached the stage of talking to Goro about the opera, maybe it was on the way to being finished, and I began to feel cautiously hopeful again."

"When I started to think about writing a story about that experience (the one we refer to as 'THAT'), I told Goro right away,"

Kogito explained. "After all, he was there, too. And Goro said, 'The fact that you're going to write a libretto about our shared adventure—well, I guess that means it won't be long until I'll have to think about making it into a movie.'"

"I imagine the two of you must have talked about that incident quite often over the years," Takamura ventured.

"No, not really. Of course, it's something that happened ages ago, when Goro was eighteen and I was a year younger, and several decades have passed since then. Maybe it's because we've never really talked it through, but I don't think the big picture of the incident is completely clear yet, either for Goro or for me. This may sound as if I'm being evasive and making excuses, but I really don't feel that I have a firm handle on the story at this point."

"According to the newspaper reporter, Goro told him about a terrifying memory from his boyhood, but he told it in a *very short* form," Takamura said. "The reason he put special emphasis on 'very short' is because apparently the film that Goro wants to make would be exceptionally *long*. The reporter said he couldn't tell whether Goro was really serious or not, but I gather he was talking about making a film that would last for ten hours or more. I won't say it would be impossible to make a film of that length, but the result would have a very different feel from the usual style of Goro's movies, don't you think?"

"Actually, there's a big difference between the films Goro made when he was a student and the commercially successful movies that he's been making over the past decade or so," Kogito said. "I remember one of his early student films where two young men were in a room, and one was practicing a meandering, serpentine piece on the violin, while the other just sat there, listening intently. That went on for thirty minutes."

For the first time that day, Takamura showed a trace of the devastatingly incisive smile that often used to appear on his face before he was attacked by illness. "What was he practicing?" he asked.

"Bach's Unaccompanied Partita No. 1," Kogito replied. "Once in a long while the boy who wasn't playing the violin would say something to the other one, but he didn't seem to expect an answer."

"Now that you mention it, Goro's ex-wife, Katsuko, was talking about that short film, too," Takamura said. "She said that when her mother (who subsidized the production costs) asked Goro what sort of thing he was planning to make next, he replied nonchalantly, 'I'm going to make a film using the same techniques, only ten or fifteen times longer.' Even after she and Goro broke up, Katsuko was always saying that if he ever decided to give up making movies with one eye on the box office, she would get her mother to shell out the money again and she herself would be the producer. She even said that she wanted to have me write the score, and she was talking like that right up until she collapsed with a stroke."

"Do you suppose Goro talked to that reporter about his own ideas, or maybe even shared part of the synopsis?" Kogito asked.

Takamura shook his outsized head, which was snugly covered by the extra-large cap. In his eyes and around his mouth, as well, Kogito could discern faint vestiges of the familiar perspicacious smile. "I wanted to ask that question, too, even though I knew it was probably just a pipe dream that would never come to fruition," he said. "If Goro was the only person you had talked to in detail about the story for the opera, the next step before that would have to be for Goro to gather everything together in a notebook. I have a fantasy where I steal a peek at those notes, over Goro's shoulder, and realize it's the libretto I've been hoping for . . ."

Kogito's heart lurched as he returned his old friend's gaze.

"But the newspaper reporter didn't seem to have been able to ferret out much information, either," Takamura went on. "Sometimes you can find a breakthrough solution to this kind of dilemma in a dream, but it occurs to me that lately I seem to have ended up in a state where I'm half dreaming all the time, even when I'm wide-awake." This sort of naked, self-revealing talk wasn't at all like the Takamura whom Kogito knew so well, and he had to lower his eyes again in discomfort as his friend continued:

"Even if my disease progresses at a slower rate than the doctors are projecting, who's to say which of us is responsible if this opera doesn't get finished, you or I? So what I'd like to say to you today is that I have just one vision about this piece, which I'm assuming I'll never see completed. After I die . . . well, if you could at least *begin* it while I'm still alive, I wouldn't have any complaints. But anyway, after I'm gone, I just hope that you'll eventually get around to finishing the story. That's all. As for Goro, I hope the same thing will happen with his idea for a ten-hour-plus film. I'd like to think that your novel and his film are each one vertex of a triangle, of which the third point would eventually turn out to be my opera. I envision a scene wherein the two of you, through your respective work, are getting stimulation from the galvanizing plasma of imagination, and even though my flesh and spirit have vanished, my opera will somehow come into being by spontaneous combustion, thus becoming the third side of the creative triangle. You may be disturbed by my imprecise use of words, but . . .

"Speaking of word use, do you remember when you explained to me, quite some time ago, about Origuchi's theory about finding repose for the restless souls of the dead? If your novel and Goro's film are two sides of a triangle, then if you can channel my spirit and conjure up my opera to become the third side, wouldn't that put my soul to rest, in Origuchi's terms? You know the Dutch term *orgel*, meaning 'music box,' of course. Well, let's postulate that after I'm gone my soul will live on, appropriately enough, in the form of a music box. Suppose you and Goro—that is, your two sides of the triangle—are feeding off and inspiring each other, and gradually so much static electricity builds up that the music box representing the third side suddenly starts to ring out with an original operatic aria . . . I don't want to get all sentimental on you, but I feel that would be your gift to the repose of my soul."

In his palatial digs in Berlin, Kogito realized that Takamura, who had talked for so long that the weariness was starting to show in his eyes, had been feeling sorry not for himself but for the people he was going to leave behind. Because of that, he had made a special effort to leave Kogito with some words of encouragement and inspiration.

5

On one of the cassette tapes he made for Tagame, Goro talked about his plan for that superlong film. This was another bit of evidence that made Kogito suspect that there might be a link between Goro's preparation of the Tagame tapes and his plan for jumping off the roof of a building—albeit not a simple, straightforward connection.

"These days," Goro said (this was in the mid-nineties), "now that so many households have a VCR, there are young people who watch the same movie ten or twenty times, if not more. But the question is, can you be properly receptive to a film as a work of art when you're watching it over and over in your living room or bedroom? Is that kind of casual viewing really fair to the work of art? To put it in terms of your field, there are libraries where you can borrow books, but people generally keep quite a few volumes on their bookshelves, as a permanent collection. Nevertheless, even if you're profoundly interested in a particular author or a specific book, you probably wouldn't read the same work over and over during a span of a few days or weeks. Of course, it's not uncommon to go back and reread a certain book after some time has passed. But even a masterpiece like *The Magic Mountain*—you aren't likely to read it more than five or six times in one lifetime, are you?

"As for movies, they have these so-called revival theaters, where they show nothing but classic films, and people—myself included—can end up going to see the same film repeatedly over a long period of time. Like Hitchcock's *Balkan Express,* which you and I once went to see at a revival theater on the outskirts of Paris, remember? But nowadays the younger movie buffs and aspiring filmmakers will just watch the same movie over and over on video, back-to-back. When it comes to the details of a given scene, they can spout any number of perceptive-sounding things, but I've never really learned anything productive from that kind of discussion.

"In the case of films, if somebody watches the same film any number of times over a short period of time, even if he's the dullest-witted person on earth, he'll end up being able to see every facet of a scene, in extreme detail. I've met people like that, and they can go on and on, in the most pompous way imaginable, about all the nuances of the way the actor is portraying the character at the center of a given scene or whatever. It really gets ridiculous sometimes.

"I know I'm repeating myself, but is that really a legitimate way to approach the experience of watching a movie? I mean, can't you say that one work of art, flowing along for a little under two hours, should give you the experience of living those two hours one instant at a time? Maybe on the second viewing you'll catch some things you missed the first time, but does that really deepen your receptivity or your perceptions? From the second viewing on, isn't our hypothetical viewer really watching what you might call a meta-movie of the film he saw the first time? In which case, unlike the strong emotional effect you get from seeing a new film, isn't it just a separate, diluted experience? That is to say, a secondary, meta-movie experience? That's why I'd like to make movies that you don't need to watch over and over again. I want to make films that you can totally 'get' after just one viewing with fresh eyes. But I won't do anything painfully obvious like using a lot of extreme close-ups to signal to the viewer when there's something they need to notice." (Goro pronounced "close-up" in perfect English, instead of using the phoneticized Japanese loanword *kurosu-appu*.) "The guiding principle is to film the entire scene in a single take. That way, you give the people who are watching the movie enough time to get a firm sense of the details of the scene.

"Needless to say, the films that I've presented to the public thus far don't meet this criterion. They're films made up of discrete sections or vignettes. Someday, when people watch the films that I plan to make from here on out, they'll be able to take them in as a seamless, natural whole, so there won't be any need to watch them twice. What's more, through the overall experience of seeing a film just once, the viewer's way of looking at the world will end up being transformed."

On another topic, Kogito had never met the Los Angeles–based newspaper reporter who went to visit Takamura in the hospital and told him that Goro's idea for a superlong movie appeared to have something to do with the opera libretto that Kogito was planning to try to write eventually, when the moment was right. However, he knew that Goro trusted the man and gave him preferential treatment.

Kogito remembered being impressed when he read the journalist's account of the yakuza attack on Goro in the Los Angeles newspaper. (This was while Kogito was stopping over in California, after his visit to the University of Chicago.) The article reported that late one night, when Goro came home and parked his beloved Bentley in the garage, he was attacked from behind by two armed men as he was taking his baggage out of the back seat. While one of the men pinned both of Goro's arms behind him and the other was slashing his cheeks with some sort of knife or sharp-bladed tool, Goro *didn't resist at all*. (The reporter emphasized that fact.)

But then, a few moments later, Goro began to struggle with almost superhuman strength, managing to free himself and send both thugs flying. On top of that, he actually tackled one of the fleeing gangsters and tried to hang on to him. The hapless hit man, trying desperately to escape any way he could, ended up ineffectually waving his lethal weapon in the air as he fled.

The reporter went on to explain, with great empathy, why Goro suddenly began to fight back after having submitted passively while he was immobilized by one gangster and the other attacker carved up his face from behind: it was because one of the hit men had started to slash the upholstery of Goro's luxury car with the same sharp blade he'd used on Goro's face. That made Goro so angry that he went on a rampage, undaunted by his massive bleeding, with such fury that the two gangsters were unable to subdue him. Their reaction was to panic and try to escape the madman's wrath.

Kogito understood very well the motive for the anger that had transformed Goro from passive victim into invincible super-hero. To put it simply, Goro was goaded into action by the injustice of seeing a beautiful, classy object like his Bentley being gratuitously vandalized by a couple of low-class thugs.

Back in the days when Goro hadn't yet had any major movie roles—at the time, he and Katsuko were living at a hotel in Paris and depending on her rich parents to pay their living expenses—the moment he got his hands on his first paycheck for acting in a foreign film, he immediately invested in a Jaguar. A year later, when he returned to Tokyo, Goro had the Jag shipped home, and he always took very good care of it. After that, as the years passed and he became wealthy through his spectacular career as a film director, his Bentley seemed to be the corporeal manifestation of that success, and there was no other material object in Goro's life at that time (and quite possibly no spiritual entity, either) that he cared as much about.

Kogito had for a long time sensed a kind of nihilism behind Goro's lavish lifestyle. "Nihilism" may seem like an extreme term, but that diagnosis seemed to be corroborated by the fact that Goro didn't put up any resistance to the thugs' initial attack on his face and body; indeed, he responded with complete passivity. Kogito had noticed that aspect of Goro's character from the time they were boys, and it had caused him a great deal of sympathetic concern. There was, in Goro, an element of willingness to fling himself into the sort of danger that had the potential to destroy him. Kogito couldn't go so far as to say that Goro was somehow intrigued by the potentialities of self-destruction (or oblivion), but he had seen evidence that his friend wouldn't necessarily go out of his way to avoid a perilous situation if it sidled seductively up to him.

Back in their schooldays, Kogito remembered, there was more than one teacher who picked up on this behavioral trait, which they saw as brazen insolence, and took a strong dislike to Goro as a result. One teacher in particular came to mind. He was the director of the physical education class that Kogito and Goro both attended, a giant of a man who had been sent to the Asia Olympics as a wrestler before the war. His deeply tanned face had the eerie luster of a bronze idol.

When the swimming pool opened for use every year, this instructor would stand at a platform with a grove of poplar trees behind him and explain the rules. One cardinal regulation was that when anyone walked on the pool deck, he was required to be barefoot. In spite of this, Goro would invariably show up wearing rubber-soled sandals because, he explained, the rough finish of the concrete surface that bordered the pool hurt the soles of his feet, and he hated that. On top of that, Goro would blatantly saunter right in front of the teacher, apparently oblivious to the loud *slap-slap* sound his sandals were making, whereupon he would immediately be dragged out of the line of students and yelled at (and often struck) by the irate instructor. Due to the large number of pupils and the relatively small size of the pool, each student was only allowed to go swimming three or four times each summer, but on every one of those occasions Goro would show up wearing the forbidden sandals and would be routinely smacked around by the apoplectic phys-ed teacher.

Kogito felt the same sort of apprehension and uneasiness about Goro's relationships with women. Before Goro's first marriage, and during the time between his divorce from Katsuko and his remarriage to Umeko, Kogito happened to meet a number of Goro's female companions, usually by chance, and he got the sense that there was an alarming pall of gloom hovering over all of them. Whoever the girl might be, Kogito always got the feeling that the relationship was headed for disaster—or, if it didn't quite reach such an extreme point, at least for some sort of trouble or unpleasantness. But Goro had a pattern of forming attachments with difficult young women from complicated backgrounds whose appeal, at least from Kogito's point of view, was not immediately evident.

In any case, when he heard that Goro had been attacked by gangsters, the first thought that popped into Kogito's head was that Goro might have been targeted because he had gotten mixed up with some yakuza moll.

6

While Kogito was talking to Takamura in the Akasaka hospital room, it had started to snow. When he emerged from the university hospital's front entrance, the almost horizontal snowfall, which was blowing directly into his face and upper body, suddenly ramped up to blizzard level. By the time Kogito had managed to flag down a taxi and was headed for home, the roadways were completely blanketed in white.

The next day the storm continued, and it was so dark that the entire day seemed to be one long, endless night. Kogito was gazing out at the incessantly falling snow while listening to an FM radio station with Akari (who seemed to share his father's indistinct yet substantial feeling of foreboding), when the classical-music disc jockey announced the death of the composer Takamura Tohru.

It was just about a year later, on another night in the depths of winter, when Chikashi came to the army cot in Kogito's study to waken him with the news that Goro had thrown himself off the top of a building. So now, when Kogito thought about Takamura's three-sided creative triangle, he realized that the only side left standing was his own.

In the twenty-fifth year since Kogito had been continuously writing novels (a career he had embarked upon during his early twenties), he had become aware of the advent of a major turning point. That revelation wasn't catalyzed by looking toward the future; rather, it was an insight that had gradually been illuminated by examining the past.

At that time, if Kogito had folded the page of his life-to-date in half, it would have been divided almost equally between the years before and after he'd become a novelist. In Kogito's twenty-plus years as a novelist—excluding the first few years, during which he hadn't been consciously thinking about "how to write"—he had always perceived the two major questions of "how to write" and "what to write" as a pair of intertwined vines, and writing his novels had been a matter of somehow finding a way to unravel those tangled vines.

Before long, his consciousness of "writing" became hideously hypertrophied, and it began to interfere with his ability to begin a new writing project. As he was struggling to find a way out of this predicament, looking for some way to go on writing, Kogito came up with a desperate contrivance. He wouldn't be able to get a solid sense of "how to write" until he actually began. Therefore, he had to start writing immediately, cranking out a very rough draft the minute he had even a vague idea of the direction he wanted to go in. If he didn't do that, he would never be able to embark on writing another novel at all.

If, as a next step, he examined what he had already drafted, one section at a time, that would help him to establish "how to write." When he focused on what he had already written, line by line, the search for "what to write" would no longer be like casting a net over the surface of dark water. By following this simple formula Kogito was able to begin to write novels once again, and that was the crucial turning point.

When he was asked by Takamura to write the novel that would serve as raw material for an opera, Kogito made a decision. This time, he would start out by making sure that he had a clear idea of "how to write." Why? Because this time "what to write" was clearly determined from the outset. He knew he was going to try to write about something that had actually happened to him when he was seventeen.

In his life since then, there had been very few days when he didn't think about THAT, if only in passing. In particular, around the time when he graduated from college and married Goro's younger sister, the only time he wasn't remembering THAT was when he was concentrating on something else, and even then it was an underlying current in all his thoughts. Somehow, though, Kogito had managed to make it this far without ever putting THAT in a novel.

That had been a conscious decision. Moreover, the idea was always rattling around in Kogito's head that at some point, after having gotten all his ducks in a row, he would write about the incident honestly and straightforwardly, with full frontal candor. He realized that he probably wouldn't be able to end his life as a novelist without ever having written about THAT. Indeed, when he thought about it that way, he could almost convince himself that he had become a novelist for the primary purpose of writing about the occurrences of that profoundly disturbing "lost weekend."

Goro's provocative comment—"The reason I became a film director is so that, someday, I could make a long, drawn-out film about that occurrence, in its entirety"—had aroused a powerful sympathetic response in Kogito. And then when Takamura asked Kogito to write up the saga so he could use it as material for his opera, Kogito had finally been inspired to begin. *If not now,* he asked himself, *when?* At that point, Kogito even phoned Goro; they got together for the first time in a long while and Kogito announced his resolution. Goro wasn't the type to rush recklessly into a project, but when he said that he, too, was ready to start working on a film about THAT, Kogito believed that he had truly made a commitment, on the spot, to doing just that.

And now, more than a year later, Kogito had a fresh epiphany: he realized that the first batch of thirty tapes that Goro had recorded for Tagame had been delivered shortly after Takamura died. While waiting for Kogito to write the novel that would become the libretto for Takamura's opera, Goro had already begun to do the preliminary work for his movie, as if he felt there might not be enough time remaining for him to approach the task in a leisurely way.

Maybe Goro even felt as though he needed to take Takamura's place, and he had used Tagame as a vehicle for doing his inherited duty of encouraging Kogito to get on with his writing, just as Takamura had done until the end. But now Goro, too, had gone over to the Other Side. While Kogito was living in Berlin, after having gone cold turkey on his Tagame addiction, he finally grasped the full extent of his lonely isolation: all his closest friends were gone.

During the last week of his solitary quarantine in Berlin, Kogito finished up his lectures at the Free University and finding himself with some time to spare, he went to the concert house in the former East Berlin to hear Verdi's *Quattro Pezzi Sacri*. When the orchestra played there wasn't the slightest bit of wasted reverberation or distortion of musical details, even at the maximum level of sound—that is, with all the instruments in action. The imposing building that housed the concert hall was utilitarian as well as gorgeous, and it was the perfect vessel for that magnificent saturation of sound.

And when the chorus sang at maximum intensity, it revealed the glory of the human voice, far surpassing any sound an orchestra could create, and the structure of the music, which seemed to reflect the totality of the universe, reached its fullest fruition in that superb space. But it wasn't all serious and cosmic; there were passages that evoked a lighter kind of sublimity, arranged so sweetly and prettily that it occurred to Kogito that if the children of the gods had musical toys, they might sound like this. That's the sort of thing he was thinking, utterly transported by his passion for the music, and he found himself wishing he could write sentences that were as powerful and transporting as the words that were now being sung, but needless to say he thought that was surely beyond his natural capacity.

Of course, since Takamura was already dead there would be no chance of atonement for the unwritten libretto, but Kogito realized that he needed, on the deepest level, to face up to the fact that both Takamura and Goro were gone. Maybe if he did that before his own death (which couldn't be that far away), he would be able to confront the task of writing about THAT head-on, with no tricks or excuses. And if he did that (he fantasized as the music soared around him), maybe he would somehow be able to conjure up the sort of words that a person can produce only once in a lifetime and write something truly great.

Of course, he was drunk on the music of Verdi . . .

CHAPTER FIVE

Trial by Turtle

1

While he was flying from Berlin to Frankfurt, and then from there to Narita Airport in Tokyo, the problem Kogito kept pondering was this: *When he was back once again at the house in Seijo Gakuen, and the time came to climb into his army cot and go to sleep, what would he do about Tagame, which had been left on its own for the past hundred days?* In retrospect, he realized that his decision to leave Tagame behind in Tokyo had been an impulse born of desperation, but the separation had been unquestionably effective. Whether or not he would be able to continue to leave Tagame stashed on its side on a shelf near his bed once he was back in the same room was an entirely different matter.

Wasn't it possible that the reason Kogito had been able to survive for a hundred days without Tagame was because he always knew that the minute he got back to Tokyo he would be able to resume his conversations with Goro right away? On this day, too, when he boarded a small jet at Berlin's Tegel Airport and again as he transferred to a colossal jumbo jet at Frankfurt

International Airport, his heart swelled with emotion at the thought of being reunited with his midnight companion. His innocent enthusiasm was almost childlike, and as if to prove that self-diagnosis he even bought a six-pack of batteries that happened to catch his eye at one of the airport kiosks, on the transparent pretext of needing to dispose of the deutsche mark coins that were jingling in his pocket.

Furthermore, he had managed to cook up a perfectly plausible rationalization for resuming his sessions with Tagame. Of course, he missed Goro and longed to be in touch with him again, but beyond that he felt a strong need to respond to Goro's recorded criticism of him on the tapes. When Goro was still on this side, their relationship had consisted largely of a freewheeling exchange of criticism. But wouldn't it be a conscious dereliction of duty to choose not to listen to the outspoken advice that Goro had left behind—counsel for Kogito as he was now, and as he would be?

From the time Kogito's first short story was published in the college newspaper, Goro had never praised his friend's work without also expressing some reservations. This pattern continued, without variation, right up until Goro went over to the Other Side. As for Kogito, he made a point of seeing all of Goro's movies when they were first released, and while he appreciated that there was no other director in Japan who could create such films, when Goro appeared on TV to promote his latest project and offered simple explanations of the cinematic grammar of his films, Kogito felt that with each new work the explanations (and, by implication, the films themselves) were becoming more popular and more conventional. He mentioned that concern directly to Goro, and it wasn't long before Goro simply stopped asking for Kogito's reactions to his current work.

Around that time, Kogito found himself thinking more than once that the dynamic of their reciprocal relationship, at least from his perspective, was something like this: Goro's films were incomparably interesting and enjoyable—nothing else that was being produced in Japan at the time even came close—but Kogito couldn't help wondering whether Goro shouldn't be making his own personal, idiosyncratic films instead of the crowd-pleasing entertainments he was turning out. Goro's view, meanwhile, was that Kogito just kept perpetuating the same tiresome flaws in his novels, over and over, and this gave rise to Goro's persistent dissatisfaction with Kogito's work. As always, Goro was much more straightforward than Kogito. This was certainly true of the things he said on the Tagame tapes.

"Right now, who do you think is reading your novels? True, from the time you were an up-and-coming author until you reached a certain age, you've never had an enormous readership, but for someone who writes pure literature you were always in your own special category, as a writer. These days, by doing your usual thing, you're still managing to sell just enough books to make a decent living. Isn't that about right? Maybe it's because you're able to get along this way, but you seem singularly unconcerned about what sort of reader is choosing your books today or who might buy them in the future. You don't seem to be making any efforts to acquire new readers, either. I'll tell you right now, nobody could get away with taking such a laid-back approach with a movie. Take me, for instance; I'm not attached to a big movie studio—though these days most of those companies are awash in a sea of red ink, too—and if a filmmaker (even me!) puts out two flops in a row, it will be next to impossible to get funding for the next project. Chikashi and I were talking about this, and she told me that you said, 'Oh, that probably wouldn't happen to Goro,' but when it comes to this sort of thing you're totally out of touch with the times. What I'm making here isn't Tora-san, you know," Goro went on, making wry reference to an immensely popular series of formulaic, feel-good films about a hapless, sweet-natured vagabond. "The audience is continually changing, and figuring out how to attract new viewers is a truly urgent problem. But that doesn't mean I'm going to sell out. I only pick a subject or a theme that interests me, and I will only film it in my own distinctive style; those are my basic, nonnegotiable requirements, and I refuse to compromise on either one.

"As for you, Kogito—when I think about it, it's rather surprising, but in all these years that you've been churning out novels, there isn't a shred of evidence that you've ever thought about the potential reader when you were choosing either the subject or the way of writing. After you finish the first draft, you rack up endless strings of ten-hour days, rewriting the original within an inch of its life, so it's no wonder your sentences end up being diabolically difficult to read. Of course, the writing is being refined and polished as you go along, but at some point it becomes like an artificial piece of music, with no trace of natural breath. And then there's the trademark impenetrable-prose style that you're so pleased with, whether you want to call it alienation, or dissimilation, or whatever. If readers are being bombarded with radically unfamiliar images and esoteric allusions and convoluted sentences on every page, most of them aren't going to end up wanting to buy another book by the au-

thor in question, unless they're total masochists. This is a bit
of your personal argot as well, but what you call *travailler*—
meaning toiling and agonizing over a work of art—is something
the writer does, not something the reader should be forced to
do. And on top of that, there's your insufferable propensity for
self-reference! Now, I won't go so far as to echo one criticism
that you often receive, which is that if someone hasn't read all
your previous books they won't be able to understand your new
work because of your habit of incessantly referring to what
you've written before. That's just the way you are, but at least
you write the allusive sections in such a way that they can be
understood without prior knowledge of your oeuvre. You're very
conscientious about that.

"Even so, you never let the reader forget that the writer
who's composing this new work, and who also wrote all the
books that came before, is this person called Kogito Choko.
Why do you always have to make such a big fuss about yourself and insert yourself into the story under some contrived
pseudonym? I mean, at the very most you're just another novelist, aren't you?

"In one of your books, when the main character was in
elementary school he wrote a composition in which he said that
all the things his younger brother had experienced in life were
carried in that brother's pocket, so to speak. You found a sentence in Latin that expressed that metaphorical conceit, and
you had the other brother repeat it ad nauseam, remember?"

Kogito remembered. It was a quotation from Cicero that
he had come across in a book by an Italian writer: *Omnia mea
mecum porto*—literally, "I carry all my things with me," but
usually translated as "My wisdom is my greatest treasure."

"Getting back to my main point," Goro went on, "what you need to understand is that when the book you're working on right now is published, and potential readers wander into a bookstore hoping to find an interesting-looking novel, most of those readers aren't going to be specifically searching for the latest offering from Kogito Choko. Assuming there are any people out there who have read all your books and are sitting around eagerly counting the days till the next one comes out, they're probably pretty few and far between. That's what you don't seem to grasp. Or even if you understand it intellectually, you can't seem to escape from your ancient habits. Maybe it's just too late to teach an old dog new tricks!"

As he sat in business class on the jumbo jet, heading back to Tokyo from Berlin, Kogito was reminded of a time when Chikashi told him about a conversation she'd had with Goro, in which Goro (a rarity for him) had actually praised one of Kogito's novels. The book in question was the paradoxically titled *Looking Ahead to Years Gone By,* which told the story of Goro's opposition to their marriage—and which, incidentally, was the book that catalyzed Chikashi's decision to stop reading her husband's novels.

"Goro was saying that he thought the end of that novel was really beautiful, especially the scene where two sisters pull the drowned body of their brother, Gii, up onto an island and are waiting for the police to come," Chikashi said. "And on the periphery of that solemn yet oddly pleasant scene, a young woman who looks like me is playfully gathering wild grasses with Akari, who's still a small child. Goro said that if he shot that scene very carefully, he thought he could create an image that would express the deep meaning of the tableau. He was saying that the last sentence of the book was very novelistic, and so it wasn't something he could translate into a filmed image, but that as an example of the power of words it was really impressive. That's what he said."

The night he heard this, Kogito stretched out on his army cot with a copy of *Looking Ahead to Years Gone By* and reread the passage in question.

> Listen, Brother Gii: I'm going to write you a great many letters about what happened in the past, as if we were still experiencing those moments together, over and over again. Starting now, I will keep on writing to you from this transient world in which you're no longer present, until the end of my own time on earth. And that, I think, will be my task from now on.

Even after Kogito was back in Tokyo, that would hardly be the time to vow to give up his Tagame dialogues with Goro forever. *For me, now,* he mused, *isn't Goro already like another Brother Gii, as we exchange these messages about the much-missed past?* Kogito struggled unsuccessfully to stifle the sigh that rose in his throat, and an instant later a flight attendant who had been hovering watchfully in the shadows materialized next to his seat.

"Excuse me, sir, is something the matter? That is, I mean— is everything all right?"

The subtle rephrasing gave a fleeting glimpse into the flight attendant's private, interior self in a way that Kogito found very appealing, but she immediately reverted to the protocol set forth in her professional manual.

"How about a drink?" she said brightly. "That'll cheer you up!"

2

The jet was now approaching the eastern tip of Siberia, and as the flight continued Kogito attempted to deconstruct his relationship with Goro from a different perspective. Regarding THAT, the one experience he had never been able to escape from and which he now suspected had been one of the themes that had shaped his life's work—wasn't it possible that Goro, too, had been burdened with the same lingering concern, all along? And could it also be true, then, that Goro was thinking about THAT on some level when he made all his films?

Kogito realized that the experience he had shared with Goro (he couldn't recall exactly when he had taken to referring to it as "THAT," but Goro had soon followed suit) stood with his father's fatal "insurrection" on the day after the war ended as one of the principal incidents of his life. But THAT wasn't terribly important for Goro—or was it? Kogito had been wondering about that from early on.

The first cause of his uncertainty was a three-volume set from Iwanami Bunko, which he still had in his library today.

He had bought the books when they were first published; according to the colophon, that was the summer of the ninth year after the war ended, so it would have been two years after the incident in question. At the time Goro hadn't shown any particular interest in the Iwanami paperback books that Kogito had lent him, but nearly forty years later Kogito learned (via Tagame) that Goro *did* remember something about those books, when the topic came up during one of Goro's tapes.

Kogito was surprised, and pleased, by Goro's animated response on that tape. When Kogito thought about it, he realized that during the two years after THAT, he and Goro had only once spoken to each other face-to-face. Goro had gone to live with his mother, who had remarried and moved to Ashiya, and when he did come back to Matsuyama it always seemed to be when Kogito was away in Tokyo, where he was attending a huge "cram school" that specialized in helping students prepare for the rigorous college entrance exams. Considering the circumstances, it's likely that Kogito sent off the Iwanami paperbacks on a childish impulse, hoping Goro would corroborate his memory of the nightmarish event the two of them had shared. And when Goro threw cold water on Kogito's youthful enthusiasm by making a show of his utter lack of interest in the books, that (Kogito realized now) was just a charade.

"Your reading habits always were a bit peculiar," was how Goro raised the subject on Tagame, as if it were an ordinary reminiscence. "I remember when you were counting the days until the publication of the Iwanami paperback translation of some classic of German literature, remember? It was the year you entered Tokyo University, after a year as a 'masterless samurai.'"

Kogito pressed Tagame's PAUSE button and answered with
a mixture of surprise and nostalgia, "The book was Grimmelshausen's *Adventures of a Simpleton*."

"As I recall," Goro went on, "you were taking a course in
the history of German literature as part of your liberal arts curriculum, and you said that you wanted to read a certain German baroque novel because the contents had some special
significance. That was the year my mother became convinced
that you had lots of free time, and she asked you to go to some
secondhand bookstores in Tokyo and try to find copies of the
prewar Iwanami paperback of *The Best of Man'yo Poetry*, as well
as some Winnie-the-Pooh books (those were for Chikashi). You
did manage to find a copy of *The House at Pooh Corner*, as I
recall, and you sent it to Ashiya. The correspondence that ensued was the beginning of your relationship with Chikashi. But
more than that, you were concerned with the story of Simplicius
Simplicissimus, which was scheduled for publication in the fall.
I remember one day you came to the commercial design studio
where I was working as an assistant to my stepfather's younger
brother, who was an artist, and you were talking about it then.
You said there was a certain episode that you wanted to read
very carefully, and when the book finally came out, we talked a
bit more about it, and you lent me the book. It was interesting
in its own weird way, I have to say.

"If I remember correctly, the governor of Hanau and his
retinue decide to make a fool of Simplicius by convincing him
that he has gone to heaven, or maybe hell, and has been turned
into a calf, so they dress him in calfskin and 'asses' ears,' whatever that means. Trying to be a good sport, Simplicius goes
along with the joke and pretends to be a calf, whereupon he

ends up becoming the official court jester. But deep down inside, Simplicius was a rebel at heart."

At that point Kogito pressed the PAUSE button again, went to the bookcase, and took down three volumes, so old that the paraffin-paper covers had begun to turn black from decay. He read a passage aloud: "I was thinking secretly, 'Just you wait, Your Excellency! I'll get you for this. I'm like a sword that's been forged in the fires of hell. Let's take our time and see who wins this bewitch-off.'"

"Mikhail Bakhtin also made a point of emphasizing the toughness and fortitude of the fool, didn't he?" Goro said when the tape resumed. "You had already been focusing on that concept before you ever took Professor Musumi's class on Rabelais. No doubt that's because at the core of your character, there's a definite jocular streak. I mean, when I saw O'Brian again in London the last time, he was saying that he'd never met an Asian with a better sense of humor than yours. But he was complaining that when he reads your novels in English translation, you're so relentlessly serious and so bloody earnest. I really don't think you're 'relentlessly serious,' but anyway, I explained to him that when you speak English you're freed from the repressive shackles of Japanese, and that's why you're able to clown around with impunity."

After that evening's session with Tagame, Kogito continued skimming through *The Adventures of a Simpleton* and was reminded of how surprised he had been, as a college student, to discover that there were significant discrepancies between what he had imagined while listening to lectures about German literary history and what he had actually read in the translation. During the university lectures that dealt with German baroque

novels, Kogito's interest had been aroused by the way in which
the young man was changed into a fool, and then a jester, by
the machinations of his superior officers, who conspired to
deprive him of his powers of reason.

The story begins with a rite wherein the unworldly young
Simplicius is marched off to "Hell" by servants of the governor
who are dressed up as evil minions of Satan. There, he is plied
with large quantities of Spanish wine (the implication seems
to be that it's the cheapest sort of plonk). On top of that he's
severely tortured and spews out bodily wastes from every imaginable orifice, but in the end, he is welcomed to "Heaven." The
lecture seemed to give the impression that, after these weird
tribulations, Simplicius subsequently wakes up in a goose pen
and finds himself inexplicably dressed in the pelts of calves.
Kogito took this to mean that Simplicius's body was shoved into
a freshly harvested calfskin, still warm and drenched in fat and
blood.

That inevitably reminded him of the outrage that had been
perpetrated by the sadistic young disciples at the training camp,
during the ordeal known as THAT. As will be related later, Kogito
and Goro had been sitting on a tall, wobbly platform when a
freshly skinned calf's pelt, about the size of a tatami mat, had
been thrown over them from behind. Enveloped in the thick,
heavy, wet membrane, it was impossible to breathe; they were
overcome by fright and deprived of the use of their arms, and
all they could do was to kick out impotently with their legs.
It was only after Goro (having seemingly lost the strength to
struggle anymore) had collapsed onto Kogito's chest that the
loathsome calfskin was finally pulled off them. Surrounded by
the drunken laughter of the young disciples, Kogito wiped away

the blood, grease, and tears, then stole a glance at Goro, who was sitting next to him, so still that Kogito wondered whether he might have fainted. Then, slowly, Goro's eyes (looking exactly like those of a sulky child) popped open.

As it turned out, the lecture had only touched on the high points, and when Kogito actually read Grimmelshausen's text he discovered that when Simplicius opened his eyes after having been made a fool of, he was not, in fact, wrapped up in a raw, bloody, freshly harvested calfskin. He was, rather, dressed in conventional garments made from processed cowhides: that is to say, leather. Even so, when Goro read the words "clothes of calfskin," surely he would have been reminded of that nightmarish ordeal and the unbearable stench.

That was the kernel of the bafflement Kogito felt when Goro returned the book with a casual, noncommittal comment. "This is a fairly entertaining book," he had said, "but I don't see why you were waiting so eagerly to read it." Kogito (who was then nineteen) didn't have the courage to confront Goro and say: "You seem to have no problem remembering the mundane details of our daily life in Matsuyama, so how is it possible that you would have forgotten something as momentous as THAT?"

Having pursued his memories of himself and Goro to that point, Kogito pushed the call button over his head, even though he knew that the beverage service had already ended. He was hoping that the stewardess who answered the call wouldn't be the same one to whom he'd said, "No, thanks," earlier, when she offered him a drink. Kogito, who hadn't drunk anything more potent than wine the entire time he was in Berlin, suddenly felt the need for a glass of whiskey—the stronger, the better.

3

On this day, Kogito took the airport bus from Narita and arrived at his house in Seijo Gakuen, via Shinjuku, before evening. By Berlin time, it was still early morning, so his circadian rhythms were in complete disarray. During the long hours that followed, as he alternated between trying to grab some sleep and jumping up again in insomniac frustration, Kogito found himself looking for ways to pass the time. Fortuitously, an unusual package was delivered that night, and Kogito became totally engrossed in dealing with it. The return address was a town close to his boyhood home in Shikoku, and someone had paid extra to specify the exact time of delivery. When Kogito opened the box, he understood why: it contained a live turtle.

There was a letter attached to the package, signed with a name Kogito didn't recognize. The prose style was that of someone fairly young, but even though the characters were rendered with a fountain pen rather than a brush, it was obvious that the writer had studied calligraphy.

In the dead of winter, someone we have loved and re-
spected for a long time—someone you know, as well—
passed away. This turtle was caught by our late teacher
on the last of the night-fishing expeditions that he en-
joyed so much, using three sweetfish as bait. Our teacher
was saying that he wanted to send this turtle to you when
you returned from Berlin, and we've been keeping it alive
in a fish tank. (Your travel schedule was posted on your
fan club's Internet site, so we knew when to send it.) Our
teacher had read in the newspaper that you liked to pre-
pare and cook your own turtles, and he was very im-
pressed. Please honor his dying wish, which was for you
to cook this turtle by yourself. The truth is, the day we
sent you this turtle was also the day we disbanded the
training camp where we all learned so much under our
teacher's guidance.

The letter ended with a spine-chilling sentence in the Iyo dialect Kogito had grown up with: *I don't think we'll be bothering*
you again after this . . .

He knew it was purely psychosomatic, but as he read those
words Kogito felt a distinct sensation of discomfort, like a cold
jolt of electricity, shooting through the second joint of the big
toe of his left foot. It stirred him up, somehow, as if a challenge
had been issued. Kogito had a pattern of exhibiting stranger-
than-usual behavior whenever he returned from abroad in a
state of sleep deprivation and in the unpleasant thrall of the
time difference—especially on his first night home, when he
was still in a state of keyed-up excitement. On this occasion,
he was consciously trying to control these impulses, but as

midnight (Japan time) approached he was seized by an irresistible urge to cook the turtle.

The amphibian had arrived in a box that someone had made by cutting lengths of thick plywood and nailing them firmly together. The box was about twenty-four inches long, sixteen inches wide, and eight inches tall, but while some sturdy-looking aquatic plants (the likes of which Kogito had never seen before) were peeking out through the tiny cracks between the boards, the box was soundly constructed and no water was leaking from the bottom. Judging from the weight of the box, it was immediately apparent that this was no ordinary creature.

Kogito finally managed to pry off the tightly nailed lid, and when he pushed aside the thick aquatic plants, whose leaves resembled gecko fingers, he saw the bluish-black shell of the turtle, which was hunkered down on the floor of the box. The creature was at least fourteen inches long and ten inches wide; Kogito had never seen such a large turtle outside of an aquarium, and the word that sprang to mind—rather than the genteel, recreational "cooking"—was "processing," with its connotations of manual labor and sustained effort. Kogito had an awful premonition that turning this monster of a turtle into soup was not going to be an easy task.

The turtle was wedged into the bottom of the box, unable to stretch out its neck because of the narrowness of the space, but its short, thick, stumpy head was plainly visible. Kogito's first task was to try to move the box to the corner of the kitchen, but when he tilted the box, the turtle planted its stout legs and began to raise a ruckus, scrabbling loudly at the boards with its claws.

Kogito realized that he needed to warn Chikashi that he was about to charge into combat against a formidable opponent, so it might be better if she didn't come into the kitchen that night. (She was still awake, reading a book in her bedroom.) After completing that errand—Chikashi had looked a bit bewildered, but he didn't take the time to explain what was going on—Kogito hurried back to the kitchen and hoisted the heavy box, with the gigantic turtle inside, into the sink. Then he got out the heavy artillery: a large, pointed carving knife and a Chinese knife that had some heft to it. The idea was to use these weapons to subdue the turtle but, from the beginning, things didn't go as planned.

The wooden box was just slightly too large to fit into the bottom of the stainless-steel sink, and it kept listing uncontrollably to one side while the turtle stood with its head jammed into the suddenly shallow corner of the box. When Kogito tried to return the turtle's body to a horizontal position, a two-handed maneuver, he couldn't help marveling at how heavy it felt. The creature's tough, three-pronged claws—Kogito was reminded that the Latin word for turtle, reflecting this conformation, was *trionyx* —were scraping frantically at the bottom of the box, and Kogito could feel the unexpectedly powerful vibrations in both his hands.

Clearly, this was not an opponent to be taken lightly. Kogito looked at the turtle, which had fallen back onto the bottom board with a loud clunk, and once again he got a sense of its youth. As nearly as he could tell, looking down from above, there wasn't a single scar on its shell or on the pale yellow border that surrounded it.

As a boy, Kogito had once seen a turtle nearly as big as his head in a shallow pool in the valley, standing very still and blending in perfectly with the vegetal slime. He had been frustrated because there was no way to catch that prize specimen, but from what he could see by peering down from atop a rock, its body was covered with innumerable scars, and the shell itself looked quite old and worn-out. In terms of surface area, this turtle was several times the size of that one. Its whole body had a young, virile look to it, and the shell had the deep blue-gray luster of polished steel.

Kogito gazed wonderingly at the turtle, his mind overflowing with questions. *How on earth had this turtle managed to live so long, and grow so large, without getting a single injury—indeed, with its body as good as new? Was it because it was secretly living in a deep, tranquil pool in the depths of the forest, where humans never ventured? And then did a flood come along and carry it off to a populated area, where it ended up being enticed one night, against its wiser instincts, by three juicy sweetfish dangling in the water?*

Kogito picked up the heavy box in his arms and put it down on a more level surface, between the refrigerator and the back door. When he lifted the far side of the box, the edge of the turtle's shell slipped down until it reached the corner on the side closest to Kogito. A moment later it began to move forward, scrabbling the three-pronged claws of its forefeet on the board. Not wanting to let this chance slip by, Kogito summoned up all his strength and, in a flash, brought the sharp blade of the carving knife down on the neck of the slow-moving turtle. But the turtle, showing the tough resiliency concealed beneath the soft, loose skin of its neck, swiftly withdrew its head into its shell.

Almost immediately, the stumpy head emerged again and the turtle tried to move forward. On one side of its neck, a crescent-shaped wound the size of a fingernail paring was filling with jet-black blood. Now the turtle, which had hitherto been silent, began to make the sharp *shu-shu* sound of labored breathing. The animal was unmistakably angry, but it wasn't being terribly cautious. Indeed, its wounded neck was still stretched out, full-length.

After making a quick visual assessment of the marginal space inside the box in relation to the size of the knife, Kogito attacked the vulnerable, exposed neck again with renewed vigor, but the turtle's neck seemed to be equipped with a preternatural elasticity that caused the carving knife to bounce harmlessly off. With its head pulled only halfway into the shell, the turtle suddenly rushed forward to the edge of the box and then, digging its claws into one side panel, desperately tried to clamber out. Kogito was still holding the knife in one hand, and he had no choice but to hit the turtle on both sides of its neck with the blade in order to push it back to its original position. As he continued this new line of attack, the knife made deep grooves in the turtle's neck, but that wasn't enough to subdue the still-vital head before it retreated into the shell. Now the turtle began snorting loudly before once again poking its head out of the shell, almost as if it were throwing down the gauntlet.

The all-out war between Kogito and the turtle raged on, but for the entire first half, even though Kogito was staging a well-armed, one-sided attack against a defenseless opponent, he still felt as if he was fighting a losing battle. *It's never been like this before,* he thought. Kogito had killed and cooked any number of turtles that had been sent to him by his brother-in-law (the husband of his younger sister, Asa). On those occasions, the initial step of cutting off the turtle's head hadn't been easy, by any means, but it had never been as difficult as this. He had always used the same method: he held the shell immobile on a large cutting board with one hand, then forced the turtle's head out of hiding and sliced it off cleanly with a knife.

When he thought back on his previous successes with that procedure, Kogito understood why he was having such a hard time now. It was really quite simple. When the turtle was resting on a cutting board, there was no obstacle on the other side of the cutting board, nor was there anything on the near side to restrict the wrist-to-elbow movement of the arm that was attacking the neck. The hand that was holding the knife could move freely. Plus, Kogito's sight line was at a diagonal angle to the turtle's neck, so his aim was true.

This turtle, however, was ensconced in a deep wooden box. When Kogito tried to bring the knife down on its neck, the tip tended to run into the edge of the box, and Kogito's wrist movement was restricted by the edge of the box on the near side. Moreover, he was looking down at the turtle's neck from almost directly overhead, so it was difficult to gauge the depth of the box based on his aerial view.

Because he was unable to increase the velocity of the knife on the downward swing, Kogito had to depend on the force of the collision between the heaviness and mass of the knife and the turtle's neck. Therefore, he changed over to the heavy Chinese knife, in accordance with the basic principle he had learned in a physics classroom, several eons ago: mv^2.

When he performed a trial run, the Chinese knife did seem to add to the power of his arm when he brought the blade down on the bottom of the box, and he was able to make substantial grooves in the wood. But when it came to attacking the turtle's neck, it was even harder to measure space and trajectory with the eye because the knife took up so much room and was so heavy. After repeated failures, Kogito had only managed to lop off the tip of the beast's little nose (which was already too small in proportion to the gigantic body), so that it looked like a horizontal cross section of a thick stalk of new-mown grass. And all the while, in the face of Kogito's frenetic onslaught, the turtle kept stubbornly sticking its head out of the shell and making that angry, distressed *shu-shu* sound.

At last Kogito, totally exhausted from his efforts, flopped down on the floor next to the wooden box, where he could hear the turtle breathing unevenly through its truncated snout. The torrent of knife blows didn't appear to have had any significant effect, but the thin blood-tinged layer of water that covered the bottom of the box was proof that at least some of those blows had hit their mark. Without bothering to wash his scarlet hands—his long-sleeved jersey shirt, too, was covered with livid splotches of the turtle's blood—Kogito stood up and left the kitchen, planning to continue his intermission on the sofa in the living room.

To his surprise, he found Chikashi sitting on a chair in the dining room, wearing her pajamas and looking, with her makeup all scrubbed off, like a young girl. She gazed up at him with a fearful expression on her face. "If it's such a struggle, why don't you just turn the poor thing loose in the stream?" she asked. "Remember, that's what you did with the last batch of turtles that Asa sent—you and Akari took them down to the stream and let them go."

"It's much too late for that!" Kogito replied, unable to suppress the wild excitement in his voice. "Anyway, what would be the point of throwing an injured creature into that mucky ditch?"

Without further discussion, Chikashi beat a hasty retreat to her bedroom and Kogito lay down on the couch, breathing in ragged gasps. During the past day, since his return from Berlin, he had been focused on unpacking and on returning a backlog of phone calls, and there hadn't been time to have a real conversation with Chikashi. And now they'd had this disastrous exchange about the fate of the turtle . . . Almost from the moment he began this task, Kogito had been plagued by gradually deepening feelings of regret, but he was a strong proponent of the idea that once you've started something there's no turning back. Thus he had no choice but to persevere until he attained his final goal: homemade turtle soup.

Kogito caught a whiff of his own rank body odor; he positively reeked of fishy-smelling turtle blood. Suppose he gave up right now, without achieving his goal, and let the turtle, with its nonfatal injuries and crudely bobbed nose, take up residence in the kitchen? Surely Chikashi would find a way of feeding it, and every time Kogito poked his head into the general vicinity, it would recognize its tormentor and make that menacing *shu-shu* sound. Would that be a tolerable life, for anyone?

When Kogito returned to work a short while later, he decided to abandon his attempts to sever the turtle's head with a single vertical blow. To put it in Western-movie terms, instead of confronting his adversary with a pistol, he proceeded to blast away with a shotgun, using the Chinese knife to hack away at the part of the shell that was right next to the turtle's neck. Before long he had managed to open a large, bloody wound, and when the turtle was no longer able to withdraw into its shell,

Kogito finally managed to cut off its head. Then it was just a matter of executing the usual dismemberment procedure, but every time Kogito tried to cut off one of the turtle's four legs, the now-headless torso (or, more precisely, the legs themselves) seemed to be putting up a powerful and tenacious resistance.

After he had finally managed to remove all four legs, Kogito pulled back the shell. When he touched the short, thick, pudgy, triangular tail, he was startled to see a crooked, bone-hard penis, as large as an adult human's ring finger, protruding from underneath. When the dirty work was finally done, the bottom of the box was flooded with a pool of blood more than an inch deep. By the time Kogito had finished hosing out the box and wiping up all the blood that had splattered around the kitchen, it was nearly 3 AM.

He took a portion of the huge mass of turtle meat and put it in the refrigerator, to be fried up later. Then he tossed the rest of the meat, along with the soft part of the shell and all the bones, into a giant stew pot. Kogito's legs felt heavy and numb after the long battle, but he stood stoically next to the boiling pot, periodically skimming off the fatty scum with a ladle. After he had splashed in some sake and added some thinly sliced ginger and salt, he realized that he had made enough soup to feed an army, and he felt rather foolish. He himself had no desire even to taste the soup, and he felt as though he wouldn't be able to recommend it very enthusiastically to Chikashi and Akari, either.

After a few minutes of lying sleepless and agitated on the army cot in his study (he could smell the nauseatingly fishy aroma of turtle soup all the way up there), Kogito got up again, put on his stinky, blood-soaked clothes, and headed back down

to the kitchen. With difficulty, he managed to empty the contents of the immense stew pot into the garbage can. He threw
away all the meat that he had stashed in the refrigerator, as well.

It was getting toward daybreak, but the air was still dark
and a severe cold snap was in progress. When he lugged the
heavy garbage can outside the kitchen door, Kogito had the
feeling, in his jet-lagged, sleep-deprived delirium, that some
demonic archenemies were sneering derisively down on him
from the squalid, stagnant sky, having tricked him into reveal-
ing the barbaric violence that lurked in his secret heart. He
seemed to hear the sound of the turtle breathing roughly
through its nose, and he could almost hear his cosmic nem-
eses saying: *If a turtle king like that doesn't have a spirit that
lives on after death, then you probably don't have an immortal
soul, either.*

4

Kogito felt ashamed of himself for having frightened Chikashi (and, possibly, Akari) with his manic marathon of butchery in the kitchen from midnight till dawn on the day he returned home from Berlin. From the following day on, his head felt perpetually feverish due to the sleep deprivation caused by jet lag, and even when he stumbled down to the living room after a short, fitful sleep, he busied himself with sorting through the mail and didn't talk at all to Chikashi about what had happened during his absence. Of course, they had stayed in close touch by fax while he was away, and he had kept her posted, in detail, about what was going on in Berlin.

As for Akari, he seemed intent on shutting his father out. He listened constantly to his CDs or to his favorite classical-music FM station with the volume turned down low, and generally behaved as if Kogito were still away from home. Even so, he kept glancing in Kogito's direction, as if he wanted to show him that he was also listening to the CDs his father had brought back from Berlin as gifts. Kogito didn't mention this to Chikashi or Akari, but—partly because it seemed like the one small favor he could do for them at this point—he had been resisting the temptation to put the batteries into Tagame, even though the little tape player seemed to be waiting for him, almost sentiently, in his study.

And so the days went by, and the thing that gave Kogito the greatest pleasure as he struggled to overcome his jet lag was going up to his study and gazing at the shelves full of books that had a clear and profound connection with his life so far. In order to escape from the censorious eyes of Chikashi and Akari, who were both giving him the silent treatment, Kogito would sink into the armchair he used for reading and writing and spend hours on end surveying his bookshelves. Without leaving his comfortable chair, he could see a volume of Frida Kahlo's collected works (interwoven with a critical biography) on one of the highest shelves. While he was thinking about the reproduction of a certain painting in that book, he got the feeling that the image in question was a perfect metaphor for the bond he felt with his books. Indeed, it became a sort of febrile vision, which he could see with perfect clarity.

He pictured himself sitting there in front of his bevy of books, with a red heart beating inside his skull. From one pulsating valve of this cerebral heart, a Medusa-profusion of small blood vessels came snaking out of his head toward the bookshelves. If he looked closely at those blood vessels, one by one, he could see that each of them was connected to a particular volume on the shelf. He felt a deep sense of relief in knowing that he was connected with all those books through the medium of blood vessels, but that sense of reassurance went hand in hand with a sorrowful feeling of loss. Or maybe that whole fantasy was just one of the dreams that played out in Kogito's overheated head when he fell into one of his brief, intermittent sleeps.

In any case, sometime later, when he was indisputably awake, Kogito was leafing through the aforementioned book of Frida Kahlo's work, and he noticed that the actual painting was different from the recollection that had given birth to his comforting metaphor of head-as-heart. He had been visualizing a painting in which Kahlo is lying in a Detroit hospital bed after a miscarriage, with arteries stretching from inside her chest— that is, from her heart—to various items arrayed around her bed: an orchid, a pelvic bone, a female abdomen on a pedestal, an enormous fetus, a snail, and an autoclave. But when he actually looked at *Henry Ford Hospital,* he realized that while the various objects were indeed hovering above the bed, as he had remembered, they weren't attached to Kahlo's heart. Rather, it was her hand (resting on the sheet next to her abdomen) that was clutching the bundle of cords leading to that portentous assortment of artifacts. Perhaps because the bed was stained with blood from Kahlo's gynecological hemorrhaging, Kogito's mind had somehow made the leap to imagining that Kahlo's blood vessels were stretching from her heart to the symbolic objects outside her body. Or maybe he had conflated *Henry Ford Hospital* with the self-portrait *Two Fridas,* in which the artist is standing in front of a screen aswarm with a scrum of clouds, and the respective hearts of the two magnificent Fridas are clearly joined by a common blood vessel. In Kogito's mind, the blood vessel outside Kahlo's body had somehow gotten scrambled with the red cords that were connected to the various articles in the previous painting.

The reason Kogito felt so immensely relieved to be back in his study in Tokyo was because the books he'd had around him in the Berlin apartment that had been his home until recently weren't what he thought of as *real* books. Usually when he was abroad (as long as he was working in cities where you could buy books in French and English), he had no trouble adding to his library, and before long the bookcases in his temporary digs would be filled to overflowing. But in Berlin, although he went and checked out the imported-book stores listed in the visitors' handbook he'd been given at the Center for Advanced Research, he didn't find the selection of books in French and English particularly appealing. Needless to say, since he didn't read German, he didn't buy any books in that language, either. So during the hundred-day quarantine, he never achieved the familiar, soothing illusion of being safely ensconced in a fortress made of books. Now, though, the metaphorical heart that lived inside his skull was once again connected by invisible blood vessels to the books that were among his oldest friends.

Perhaps the feeling of loss—even downfall—that accompanied his sense of relief was due to the constant awareness that he was growing old and irrelevant, and that he would live out the remainder of his days without ever being able to liberate the heart inside his skull from this vast collection of beloved, familiar books, which were an anchor but also, at times, an albatross.

When Kogito had finished sorting through most of the mail, he moved on to organizing the assorted gifts of books and magazines, which he had unwrapped earlier. He read a number of chapters in these books and also read the major essays and roundtable discussions in a variety of general-interest magazines and literary magazines. At some point he discovered that he was having trouble following not only the treatment of the subject matter but also the style of writing and talking about things.

This most recent sojourn abroad had been relatively short, but Kogito had spent it, from beginning to end, as either a teacher or a researcher. What those hundred days had revealed was that he had grown undeniably distant from Japan's insular world of literature and criticism; that conclusion was impossible to ignore. But, curiously, the sadness he felt about that seemed to have the same root as the sensations of comfort and relief he had been feeling earlier.

Ah, that sense of distance . . . He had a notion that while they were all still running on the same track, so to speak, the younger generation had banded together and taken the lead, and he was lagging a full lap behind them. Thus, in order to be able to relax once again among the books in his longtime home in Tokyo, he would give up trying to catch up with the young literati who were so far ahead and would instead concentrate on giving tender nurture to the things that arose spontaneously in him. To be sure, there was a measure of sadness there, too, but it was hard to distinguish it from an agreeably cozy feeling of quiet enjoyment. Kogito felt as though he would be able to live out the days to come, alone and marooned amid the faint glimmer of twilight, as tranquilly as someone already dead.

But one night, as he was lying on the army cot in his study, Kogito's arm suddenly began to move slowly in the darkness, and even though he changed the angle of that appendage any number of times, it still kept on advancing and retreating. His arm, making no effort to disguise its objective, was reaching out and searching for Tagame, which was ensconced on a nearby shelf among the books. Even while this was happening, Kogito knew very well that Tagame was as he had left it, stripped of its batteries. Moreover, he was conscious of the fact that he had no intention of getting out of bed to search for the batteries and cassette tapes.

And yet the reason he was involuntarily making his arm move like a feeler, as if he were a large insect hunting for a smaller quarry, was because after a hundred days of solitary, silent quarantine, he simply longed to hear Goro's voice. He wanted, too, to go through the motions of whining and weeping a bit, as a kind of play-acting catharsis. This impulse (most unusual for him) stemmed from a recent epiphany about life and death.

Goro, he wanted to say, *if (as I've recently concluded) the approach of death really isn't a matter of very great consequence, then why did you have to pour so much energy—emotional, physical, and spiritual—into throwing yourself off a roof in the prime of life? I know you were upset and stressed out and drunk on brandy, but still!*

Along with the emotional mélange of mortal misery mixed with philosophical acceptance, Kogito was simply feeling the urge to indulge in a bit of posthumous pseudo-pleading with Goro, crying quietly all the while. Because his sleep was shallow, the next time he woke up he was still awash in those same disconsolate feelings, but even in the midst of such intense anguish he felt rather proud of himself for not breaking down and putting fresh batteries into Tagame.

5

On one of a blurry series of days like that, Chikashi came and stood in front of the sofa where Kogito was reading a book. She was holding a thin briefcase made of toffee-colored leather (or perhaps it was more of a reddish amber), which he recognized immediately as something Goro used to carry. Kogito had been lying down, but now he sat up and made a space for Chikashi next to him. Once again, he got the feeling that his time in Berlin had been an actual quarantine for a real disease, because he could tell that Chikashi had something she wanted to talk about but had been postponing it out of consideration for the recuperating patient.

"The night you came back from Germany, you didn't seem like the person I've known all these years, and to tell the truth, I was shocked," Chikashi said. "I imagine that you must have been thinking about a lot of things while you were away, so I put it down to that. Still, there haven't been any late-night murmurs coming from your study, and even though he doesn't say anything, Akari seems to be very relieved about that. Umeko told me that she found some of Goro's writings when she was putting his things in order, and she seemed to think that I ought to take a look at them, so she sent them along. That night when you were all covered with blood after your wrestling match with the turtle, I decided that showing you something like this would be like throwing oil on a bonfire. I was frightened, so I held back.

"Then for the past week or so, you've been at the opposite end of the spectrum—almost too quiet and kind of depressed, and I ended up realizing that if this was something Goro wanted you to read, it really wasn't my place to withhold it. These pages are in the form of a screenplay, but they look like some sort of reminiscence or memoir. I don't know whether he was seriously planning to make this into a movie or not."

Kogito felt an overpowering attraction to the briefcase that was balanced on Chikashi's knees, but the reply he gave was somewhat anticlimactic. "During the ten-plus years that Goro was making movies, he wrote a ton of screenplays that never got produced, though I doubt if they would all fit into that brief-case," he said. "But when he was making a film, he had the habit of publishing the written materials at the same time the movie was released, sort of like a simulcast."

"He left behind lots of other notebooks besides these, you know," Chikashi said. "Umeko wanted to keep the ones where he made notes about her acting scenes, for sentimental reasons, and Taruto is taking care of all the preparatory documentation for the two court cases. There are also a bunch of memos with material for a TV documentary Goro was planning, and I gather those are going to be donated to a new museum celebrating both Goro's work and the films our father made, as well. As soon as the formalities have been completed to release the money from the American box-office profits, work on the museum should begin in earnest. As you know, producing Goro's movies was just a sideline for Taruto, and his main company has already prepared the site for the museum in Matsuyama. They've purchased the land behind it, as well, as a buffer zone. Anyway, when Umeko finally reached the point where Goro's office was more or less in order, she brought this over and asked me to give it to you. She said that she thought it must have been something of special importance to Goro.

"Before you left for Berlin, I . . . well, Akari felt the same way, but in any case, you kindly implemented the change we requested, and now I gather that you've pulled yourself together to the point where you're ready to start writing about what happened to you and Goro in Matsuyama. If you're truly serious about chronicling that incident, the screenplay and storyboards that Goro left behind in his favorite briefcase should be helpful. The whole thing isn't in any particular sequence, and all the details haven't been worked out, either, but I still think you might find it useful."

Kogito was a bit nonplussed to hear that Chikashi had such a clear vision of the novel he was supposed to begin working on next. As a way of temporarily nudging the conversation in another direction, he asked: "When Goro was getting ready to make a film, did he ever storyboard the finished parts when the screenplay was still at the stage where there was nothing but bits and pieces?"

"That doesn't seem like Goro, does it?" Chikashi replied. "I had the same feeling, so I asked Umeko about it. She said that when it came to filmmaking, Goro was a pro through and through, and he wouldn't begin storyboarding until the cast had been completely decided and the production had reached the point of starting principal photography. It could be that Goro wanted to make this movie, but he thought it was impossible given the current circumstances, so maybe he put together this sort of detailed treatment as a substitute for actually making the movie. That's what I was thinking, anyway. It's also possible that he had already decided to take his life when he made those tapes and sent them to you, and perhaps he made the screenplay and the storyboards in the same spirit—as a way of recording his own memories to share with you." So saying, Chikashi stood up and placed the briefcase in front of Kogito with such a formal gesture that he might have been a guest in his own house.

That night after dinner, Chikashi and Akari went off to their separate rooms after they had finished watching a classical-music program on NHK television. Kogito remained alone in the living room, gazing at the briefcase lying on the steel-framed, glass-topped table that stood in front of the sofa. Even though his mind was totally focused on the briefcase, he couldn't quite bring himself to reach out and touch it.

Since Chikashi had made such a point of asking him to look at the contents—speaking in an uncharacteristically stiff way, like a stranger—Kogito knew that he had to open the briefcase tonight and at least take a cursory glance at what was inside. If he had trundled off to bed without doing at least that much, he knew Chikashi would be very annoyed to discover the briefcase lying on the table the next morning, untouched. She had been supersensitive ever since the overwrought coverage of her brother's suicide in the weekly tabloids, and even now, if Kogito made even the most innocent, harmless little comment about Goro, Chikashi would act as if he had personally attacked her and wounded her self-esteem.

Kogito's feeling of trepidation about reading whatever the briefcase might hold was growing stronger by the minute. He had already gone over every detail of THAT—the traumatic experience he and Goro had shared—in his head so many times that he had lost count. There were parts of that chain of events that he didn't have a firm grasp of, and he had never had the courage to ask Goro about them directly. But what if the missing bits were in here, graphically told, and with storyboard illustrations to boot? Wasn't it possible that they might include some accusations or a denunciation of Kogito's behavior on that day? And the other night, when it looked as if he might lose control and start pleading with Goro through Tagame— maybe he'd been in the throes of some sort of inchoate premonition that Goro was about to accuse him of something and had wanted to issue a preemptive apology or explanation in self-defense.

Slowly, Kogito got up from the sofa and picked up the briefcase. While he had been staring at it, mesmerized and magnetized, he had realized that as a thing in itself it really was exceptionally attractive in both color and form. When he opened the front flap, which was the same width as the body of the briefcase, he spied a piece of paper with the texture of parchment pasted on the underside. And then he saw that Goro had written something, copied out from one of his books of French literature (with the italicized portions conscientiously replicated), and the memories came rushing back. Straining his eyes to read the words, Kogito was so deeply moved by what he saw that he let out an involuntary "Ah!"

Je ne t'envoie pas d'histoires, quoique j'en aie déjà trois, ça coûte tant! *Enfin voilà! Au revoir, tu verras ça,* which one translation renders as: "I am not sending you any stories, although I already have three. *It costs too much!* That's all for now! Goodbye to you. You'll see it [the book] later."

Those lines were from a letter from Rimbaud to Ernest Delahaye, circa May 1873; Kogito remembered that they had read it together when Goro was giving him informal lessons in French poetry in Matsuyama. Even for a student of Goro's linguistic gifts, to say nothing of a complete beginner like Kogito, the italicized portion had been especially difficult. At the time, Kogito had consulted the postscript that followed this passage, and he contended that Rimbaud was simply saying that because the price of stamps had risen, he wouldn't send the three stories he had already written for a projected book. But Goro disagreed, translating the lines more abstractly as "Reading this is going to cost you a lot in the end, you know." In a more recent translation, which Kogito had on hand, the passage went like this: "I am not sending you any stories, although I already have three. *It costs too much!* That's all for now! Farewell, and you'll see it later on."

Kogito sat very still for a while, with the briefcase resting on his knees. Then, as if he were attempting some sort of precision handiwork that would go awry if he didn't take the time to do it in the proper order, he slowly took the contents out of the briefcase and placed them on the table. There was a jumble of papers of various sorts; the pile included pages torn from sketchbooks, a loose-leaf notebook with the cardboard cover still attached, and a goodly quantity of small pieces of the motley sort of paper, in miscellaneous colors, sizes, shapes, and tex-

tures, that Goro had delighted in since childhood—all held together by rubber bands. Then there were programs from film
premieres and concerts, which had wide margins with plenty of
space for scribbling. Perhaps because they had been crammed
tightly into a thin briefcase, when Kogito emptied the papers out
into a mountainous heap the faint, nostalgic aroma of Goro's
distinctive imported cigarettes wafted up to his nose.

On this night, Kogito simply extracted the papers from
the briefcase and left it at that. He didn't have the energy to
start sorting through them, or reading. But when he saw the
storyboards, which were drawn on paper that had been divided
into four or six frames, the highly visual sketches had a charm
that was so quintessentially Goro-esque that his hand involuntarily reached out for them. Even without reading the screenplay that was attached to the sketches with beautifully colored
paper clips (though in terms of Goro's intent, it could have been
the other way around: he might have thought he was attaching
the sketches to the screenplay, as decorative incidentals) he
could see that its narrative was endowed with a uniquely engaging visual texture that seduced his skimming eye.

Kogito left the huge pile of papers next to the briefcase,
thinking that when Chikashi came downstairs, his good inten-
tions would be immediately evident: he had decided to answer
Goro's call to action, and leaving the papers out showed, im-
plicitly, that he knew what had to be done and was ready, at
long last, to do it. Still, now that he found himself face-to-face
with Goro's posthumous manuscript, he felt like an inexperi-
enced, intimidated greenhorn, and he had major butterflies
in his stomach at the mere thought of how he was going to
deal with it. As he so often did these days, he felt as if he were

somehow suspended in limbo, and he was bedeviled by a nag-
ging worry that (compared with the ultraworldly Goro) he hadn't
yet accumulated a sufficiently rich store of life experiences to
tackle this challenge. Surely that quote from Rimbaud's letter—
the secret code that had struck such a resonant chord for both
of them—had been written down as a warning from Goro as
he passed the baton of his unfinished work to Kogito. Realizing Goro's intent, Kogito was seized once again by a complicated sort of stage fright, and part of him wanted very much to
chicken out.

6

The following day Kogito started reading Goro's screenplay and storyboards, and despite his initial qualms he soon became totally engrossed. Technically speaking, even from the point of view of a novelist, he found Goro's cinematic approach to telling the story uncommonly interesting and exciting. He even had the feeling that he was discovering a whole new side of Goro's character—not just as a director but as a human being. This may sound like a contradiction, but at the same time he also had keen flashes of realization that Goro was always exactly this kind of person, from the first day they met. Kogito knew that even when Goro opposed his marriage to Chikashi, that was absolutely predictable behavior, and because he knew that extreme reaction was just part of Goro's nature, Kogito never had any feelings of being hurt, betrayed, or disillusioned.

Even during the twelve years while Goro was racking up spectacular successes in the film industry, one after another, Kogito never revised his essential perception of his old friend. Rather, he recognized that the potential for such exceptional accomplishments was there all along, in the facets of Goro's character he had observed during their schoolboy days. Whenever Kogito happened to meet up with people he and Goro had known in high school, he was always surprised when they would say, with an unmistakable undertone of jealousy, "Who knew Goro had that kind of talent?"

Kogito knew. Indeed, from the time the eighteen-year-old Goro transferred to Matsuyama High School and they became friends, Kogito believed that his new friend was so talented that he would end up eclipsing even his famous father. (At that point, Kogito had only read Goro's father's essays—he hadn't yet seen any of the elder Hanawa's satirical samurai films—but that didn't stop him from making expansive predictions.) Just on the basis of what he had already seen of Goro's artistic gifts, Kogito expected him to expand his creative dominion far beyond the sphere of moviemaking.

As Kogito read his way through Goro's screenplay and storyboards, he was impressed anew by the extraordinary scope of Goro's natural talents, but he also marveled at the artistic and directorial skills that Goro had acquired, and polished by daily practice, during his short but fully realized career as a maker of films. Take, for example, the character in Goro's screenplay, called Leader, who was obviously modeled after Daio. No matter which sketch Kogito looked at, he could see no physical resemblance to the Daio he remembered in the way that personage was portrayed in the storyboards. Those sketches did, however, remind Kogito vividly of a comedian who had played the role of a small-business owner in Goro's enormously successful comedy about tax evasion—a character who, memorably, began to weep copious crocodile tears when he was about to be busted for evading his taxes.

Nonetheless, in the screenplay excerpt that was attached to the storyboard in question with a colored paper clip, the stage directions for that scene offered a portrait of Daio as Goro had observed him during the two-week series of events known forever after as THAT—a portrait that was rendered with dazzling accuracy, in a way that matched Kogito's recollections exactly.

> *The Leader is a bitter-faced man with a stubborn look around his mouth and eyes. Whatever he tackles, he will stick with it to the end. Confident in his own dogma, he strives to fulfill his single-minded goals. Never giving up, never vacillating, he'll try again and again, and then he'll rally his forces and try one more time. But it's hard to tell whether the Leader is really serious about pursuing those goals or whether he's just joking around. Isn't it possible that from the beginning he never really intended to carry out his radical, far-fetched plan? Nonetheless, he's the kind of guy who, when confronted with an unscalable wall, shouts, "Charge!" and runs into it head-on, with his foolish, faithful disciples close behind.*
>
> *The Leader has worked out an idea based on a refinement of Choko Sensei's reactionary nationalistic ideology, and this is the motivation for his actions. His theories seem to make sense when you first hear them, yet while the logic behind his motivations seems sincere and serious-minded enough, there's also a sense that everything he says might be nothing more than a frivolous cock-and-bull story or a*

bad joke. He comes across as complex and conflicted: part volatile buffoon, part serious guerrilla. You get the feeling that somewhere along the way he might say, "Sorry, folks, just kidding!" and abandon the entire plan (or fantasy). But if that ludicrous-sounding plan ever did become a reality, it could turn out to be a terrible, bloody, irrevocable thing . . . And if that happened, and people on both sides lost their lives, what sort of expression would the Leader wear as he faced up to what he'd done? (That is, assuming he survived the surreal skirmish with the American military forces.) The dodgy, dangerous jester's face that he showed to the world before his plan came to fruition would be supplanted, after the event, by a mask of tragedy. Or else it could be the other way around. (That will probably be a key point to consider, directorially.) The following scene is a true representation of Daio's plan of action, as told to Kogito and Goro.

LEADER: The peace treaty has already been signed and sealed, and it'll go into effect this April twenty-eighth [1952] at 10:30 PM. So what does that mean? It means that during the entire period of Allied occupation there hasn't been a single incident of armed resistance by Japanese directed at American camps, and time is running out for us to take a stand. There is one famous photograph that will endure forever as a symbol of the entire period of military occupation since Japan lost the war, and as a foreshadowing of the future relationship between America and Japan. It was taken on September twenty-seventh, 1945, at the American embassy. The emperor of Japan stands perfectly erect, wearing Western-style

civilian clothes (formal black suit, white shirt, narrow tie);
beside him is Field Marshal Douglas MacArthur, dressed
in his casual-duty uniform of khaki-colored shirt and trousers, no necktie, both hands on his hips. That photograph's subliminal message is stamped on the collective
psyche of the Japanese people, as strong and clear as the
maker's mark on a samurai sword: *The emperor will never
again be restored to godly status.*

Kogito, too, had a lucid memory of Daio giving this erudite burst of political analysis in the midst of a party. Just as
Goro suggested in the character sketch of the Leader in his
screenplay, the real-life Daio's behavior was a mixture of seriousness and frivolity. You could never let down your guard
around him, and whenever he spoke, no sooner had the words
left his mouth than the listener would begin to doubt their sincerity or veracity. This unsettling ambiguity was in evidence as
the tipsy Daio irreverently imitated the pose in the photograph,
showing them exactly how the emperor was standing and what
sort of expression was on his face. Kogito's amusement was
mixed with abhorrence, but Goro just laughed uproariously. Of
course, he, too, was already drunk on *doburoku* and feeling no
pain.

Naturally Daio, as the heir to Choko Sensei's ideological
mantle, couldn't be expected to stand by quietly while this ig-
nominious situation—the Occupation—came to an end. During the three weeks that remained before the peace treaty took
effect, Daio and his cohorts started gearing up for their armed
attack on the American military base, perhaps hoping to rewrite
the last page of the history of the occupied era, with what they

saw as its shameful theme of passivity and defeatism. What they needed was to get close to the American camp without being stopped by the Japanese police, so they organized an attack party from among the most outstanding disciples, who would be disguised as innocuous members of the local populace. But the soldiers who were stationed at the main gate of the American army base would immediately fight back, and in order to ensure that a violent street fight would break out the minute the attackers showed up, Daio and his ragtag band would charge the gate, brandishing their authentic-looking weapons. To make the MPs perceive them as seriously armed, it would be ideal if Daio's group could attack with the same kind of armaments that the American soldiers were carrying. So what they needed, the screenplay showed, was to get their hands on ten rifles from the military base's armory for the ten members of the attack party to use.

PETER: Even if we're just talking hypothetically, there's no way you're going to be able to steal ten automatic rifles from the camp.

LEADER: But weren't you saying that there were piles of old, broken weapons that were used in the Korean War, just lying around out in the open?

PETER: Yes, there are, but an amateur wouldn't be able to repair rifles that were damaged in combat.

LEADER: But Peter, that's the whole point—there wouldn't be any need to repair them. They don't need to be in working order; they just need to look like American army rifles. If

the soldiers in the camp see ten Japanese warriors charging at them with those rifles, they're going to think it's a
genuine enemy attack, and that's good enough for us.

PETER: But if that's how it looks to the guards at the gate,
you'll all be mowed down in a matter of seconds.

LEADER: Well, why not? I mean, if we didn't know that was
going to happen, why would we charge into battle against
an army camp filled with thousands of soldiers in the first
place? Anyway, from the moment we came up with this
strategy, we knew it was doomed. Like it says in the an-
them of the Imperial Japanese Navy—you know, the song
the kamikaze pilots used to sing before they took off on
their one-way missions?—"I will not die peacefully at
home."

PETER: What if people realize you aren't serious—that you're
just a bunch of suicidal wankers playing at war games?

LEADER: (suddenly taking off his *yukata* and standing there
in an Etchu *fundoshi,* a traditional style of loincloth underwear wrapped in such a way that it ends up with a rectangular panel hanging down in front): In that case, we'll
strip down to our loincloths and back away, doing a colorful folk dance!

The first half of this true-to-life exchange actually took
place at the party Kogito and Goro attended at Daio's inn at
Dogo Hot Springs, after the record concert. The latter half transpired at a subsequent party, which took place at that same inn
on the following evening (Kogito had forgotten all about it), after

Daio had run into Peter somewhere and had invited him to join the festivities. Kogito was surprised by the powers of observation that Goro had possessed as a teenager, but he was equally amazed that, as an adult, Goro was able to combine these disparate conversations into a single scene—especially since (as Kogito recalled) Goro had been busy drinking himself more or less senseless on *doburoku* and had appeared to be nothing more than a thoughtless, innocent young boy, awash in merriment.

Anyway, after the three-day sequence of soirees, and after Daio and his gang had returned to their camp, Kogito had started to feel intensely guilty about all the time he and Goro had wasted in the company of the paramilitary madmen. So Kogito, not wanting to backslide into the habit of staying out late and partying with Goro, very quickly reverted to his previous pattern of going to the CIE library every day after school with a group of his more studious friends, who, like him, were madly cramming for their college entrance exams.

One day, toward the end of library hours, the Japanese CIE employee who had shown Kogito and Goro the book of Blake's illustrations at the record concert made a special trip to the reading corner. Calling Kogito aside, he told him that Peter was waiting for him down at the basketball practice area. This functionary was haughty and unapproachable at the best of times, and Kogito could tell that he was extra-miffed at being asked to run an errand for an American. The fact that the object of the errand was a lowly Japanese high-school student only intensified his obvious displeasure.

When Kogito arrived, Peter was standing under the basketball backboard, hanging his head and looking rather down in the dumps. The American was holding the ball in front of his chest, with his right arm bent, and the cherry blossoms, which had just begun to fall, were floating down and landing on the ball. Kogito could see the line made by the border between the fair skin at the nape of Peter's neck and the red, sunburned part above it. As Kogito came closer Peter raised his head and looked at him with a quizzical expression.

Kogito sensed right away that Peter had been hoping Goro would show up, too. That intuition was confirmed when Peter asked, point-blank: "So your friend Goro isn't with you today?"

Kogito didn't reply, and Peter, undaunted, forged ahead alone. "Speaking of Goro," he said, "he was telling me that after you're finished studying, you Matsuyama high-school students like to jump in the Dogo Hot Springs baths all together to refresh yourselves. Is that true?"

"Dogo may be a hot springs, technically, but the bathhouse is public, so apparently there's some question about the hygiene . . . In any case, I've heard that it's off-limits for GIs," Kogito replied.

"Oh, is that so? I hadn't heard. Okay, here's another idea. At the end of this week—Saturday or Sunday are both good for me—I'll be able to borrow a car. Would you like to go for a drive? Just you and me and Goro . . . Mister Daio was saying at the inn the other night that he'd like us to come and take a look at his martial-arts camp, or whatever he calls it."

Peter lapsed into silence, but his blue eyes were glittering like those of some evil bird, and Kogito couldn't help wondering why his cheeks suddenly looked so flushed. He answered Peter's question with the same careful choice of words he had employed earlier.

"I'm sure Goro would be delighted to go for a drive," he said formally. "Daio also invited us to visit his training camp, and he asked me to repeat his invitation to you if I had a chance. I'll let you know either today or the day after—you're here on alternate days, right? Anyway, I'll talk it over with Goro and get back to you with an answer."

"Actually, I'll be here every day this week," Peter said. "So when you see Goro, tell him he can stop by and visit me, okay?"

Just then a mixed group of Japanese employees and American women came up to the basketball court, making a big, noisy show of catching the falling cherry blossoms that were wafting about on the breeze. Holding the ball straight out in front of his chest with both hands, Peter stepped forward to face them. Turning briefly back to Kogito, he said dismissively, "If I'm not around the day after tomorrow or whenever, leave your answer on the secretary's desk. You can write the letter in Japanese, if you like."

Then, evidently losing interest in Kogito, Peter began to dribble energetically around the court, all by himself. He took a shot at the basket from a goodly distance away and missed. Undaunted, he grabbed the rebound off the backboard, and then, twisting his body, he tossed a high-arching ball into the center of the little crowd of Japanese and Americans, and everybody cheered as if he had done something heroic.

Wearing a sour scowl, Kogito went back to the library. But despite his bad mood, before returning to the reading corner, he peered through the plate-glass wall that separated the library from the office to make sure he knew exactly where to find the secretary's desk.

CHAPTER SIX

The Peeping Toms

1

The following day Kogito discussed Peter's invitation with Goro on their high-school lunch break, and then he returned to the CIE and delivered the answer: YES. The thirty-something secretary took the envelope while coolly looking Kogito up and down, but she didn't say a word. All she did was to snort, with vague disdain: "Uh-huh." (She was the first Japanese person he had ever met who responded with American-style informality . . . or rudeness.)

But not long after Kogito had taken out his textbooks to begin studying for the university entrance exams, Peter came to the reading corner to fetch him. The American led the way to his own office, paying no attention to the snippy, stuck-up secretary, and told Kogito he could use the telephone there to call Daio at the training camp. Like Peter, Daio was in fine spirits; he even said that if they were really serious about paying a visit, he would come to the CIE to discuss the particulars. (That wasn't necessary, as it turned out.)

Goro's screenplay, with the attached storyboards, paints
a detailed picture of that weekend jaunt. They set out early
Saturday afternoon in a pale green, banged-up Cadillac with
Peter at the wheel, Goro riding shotgun, and Kogito ensconced
in the back seat. In the first scene, the Cadillac is pulling out
of the parking area behind the library building. Goro was a car
buff even as a high-school student, and he seems to have remembered this drive as an extraordinary outing during a time
in Japan, just before the peace treaty took effect, when a glamorous American automobile was a very unusual sight.

Matsuyama still bore the fresh scars of the Allied air raids,
but before long they found themselves on the streets of a neigh-
boring town that hadn't been burned at all. The Cadillac was
so wide that it seemed to take up the entire two-lane road, and
the old-fashioned houses appeared to be crowding in from both
sides. Of course, it would have been impossible to re-create the
entire scene of devastation around Matsuyama exactly as it was
before the postwar restoration, but even now there were places
along the highway that would be suitable as period-movie locations. The storyboards were drawn with an obvious passion
for that sort of tableau: the medieval-looking towns, the charred
ruins, the incongruous green Cadillac hogging the narrow road.

After passing through the densely populated areas with
their rows of old-style houses jammed together along the street,
the road began a long ascent through a pastoral landscape of
fields and rice paddies dotted with houses, temples, and shrines.
On the storyboard, the blossoms of the Yoshino cherry trees are
already falling, but the double-flowered cherries are still in full
bloom, and they line the route in glorious profusion. Gradually
the Cadillac wends its way through hillside villages surrounded

by deep green, bushy-treed tangerine groves (with none of the present-day vinyl greenhouses or other such blots on the landscape). At last the Caddy comes upon the entrance to a deep tunnel, near the summit of a low ridge of mountains. Just beyond the tunnel, Daio and his young followers are parked in a small truck, waiting. Following the truck's lead, the gigantic American car (which is so broad that it brushes against the grass on both sides of the road) plunges ahead, oblivious to the clatter as its low-hanging undercarriage jounces along the rough, bumpy road. After briefly climbing a gentle slope, with a large, deep valley on the right side and a thick forest on the left, the road begins its descent.

Looking at the screenplay and the storyboards, Kogito found it odd that Goro had lavished so much detail on his portrayal of the poorly maintained washboard road the Cadillac had traveled, while not providing so much as a sketch of the plants that grew alongside, but Kogito was able to supply those details from memory as he looked at the illustrations. Not only had he grown up in a deeply wooded valley, but he was the type of person who liked to spend time wandering about in the forest, botany books in hand. Because of that, he not only remembered what an unusual experience that drive had been; he also had a clear recollection of the trees and shrubs, thick and leafy with new growth, and the cherry trees that hadn't yet shed their blossoms.

The area they were driving through wasn't too far from the mountain-valley village where Kogito had grown up, but there was something alien about the lay of the land and the aspect of the other villages they passed. Of course, Kogito was sensitive to that sort of thing, having been brought up in such an insular environment. When he used to go on nature walks with his class from the nationalized elementary school, their route often took them upstream along the tributary of the river that ran through his valley and crossed the small mountain. No sooner had the basin below come into view than he would be filled with feelings of awestruck dread, as if he were hopelessly lost in some strange foreign country, even though they were still, technically, within the boundaries of his village. He always half expected a pack of horned demons, brandishing wooden sticks over their heads like swords, to come charging out from the depths of the fields and paddies that were surrounded by quiet groves of trees, and force him to run for his life. Even at seventeen, those childish fears were still vivid in Kogito's mind.

According to Kogito's recollections of the trip to Daio's training camp, right after emerging from the tunnel not far from Kogito's village, the little caravan turned off the highway that would have led them into the village and went down a slope on the north side of a beautiful stand of trees that seemed to be awash in the fresh green leaves of spring. Continuing along, they descended into a dark, ancient-looking forest of Japanese cypress trees. As they approached the mountain stream, which was churning with whitewater rapids, there were places where the shoulder of the road had caved in. Behind the wheel of the Cadillac, Peter was visibly nervous.

After they had safely navigated that hazard, they emerged onto a road that ran along a big river, which was quite wide but didn't contain much water. Its high banks were stabilized by the thickets of shrubbery that grew on both sides. The sky, peeking through the steep walls of cedar forest that bordered the road on both sides, was a deep, intense blue.

Next they passed some long, narrow cultivated fields that lay on a level plain between the river and the road, but the land appeared to have been abandoned. The same was true of the fields and storage shacks that could be seen higher up, where patches of farmland had been cleared on the forested side of the mountain. As far as the eye could see, there wasn't a single private dwelling, or perhaps the houses had been swallowed up by the vegetation when the people who used to live here had gone away for some reason, and now those houses were entombed beneath the tall thickets and wild cascades of ivy that had begun to engulf the old trees, as well, as time went by. That's what the seventeen-year-old Kogito was daydreaming about as they rode along through the mutable scenery.

The unpaved road began to head uphill again, and as they gained altitude the river vanished into the deep valley below. On the opposite shore, surrounded by cedar trees, a wide slope opened up, and at the top were several roofs that looked as if they might belong to warehouses or granaries. As the road swooped down toward the river from a broad clearing, a rickety-looking bridge suspended from steel cables came into view immediately ahead. On the side of the road that faced a small mountain, there was a three-story building that looked like an abandoned inn. Nearby stood a miniature shrine to the local tutelary god, surrounded by its own little forest of dark-leafed deciduous trees.

Daio and his disciples stopped the truck in the wide clearing and signaled to Peter to park the Cadillac behind them. Then the group trudged down a steep hill, crossed the wobbly suspension bridge, and climbed up a slope that was covered with fresh green grass.

Goro's storyboards included a sketch of the entire group standing on a road at the top of the slope, between the main building of the training camp and a large outbuilding. In the screenplay, corresponding to that sketch, the following dialogue appeared:

PETER: That tree with a single red flower is a camellia, and the one next to it, with no flowers but lots of buds, is a dogwood. This is so strange—we have the exact same trees in the garden of my house in America.

KOGITO: My mother grows lots of different kinds of flowering trees. I think my father probably brought these from our house in the village.

LEADER: Choko Sensei used these flowering trees as a way to lure the local maidens over here for a visit. It worked out pretty well for us, too!

KOGITO (*ignoring Daio's little joke*): The one with amber-colored shoots is a pomegranate. And see the one next to it, with the yellow buds? My mother always calls that an ornamental pomegranate. I've heard people saying spitefully that our house is the only place that grows that useless kind of pomegranate. I guess they think it's a waste of space because it isn't actually edible.

PETER: You certainly know a lot about plants, Kogito!

GORO (*jocularly, but with a critical undertone*): Kogito's an odd duck, for sure. He remembers everything he's ever read, whether it's a dictionary or an illustrated book about

plants. Before long you're probably planning to turn into
an encyclopedia yourself, eh, Kogito?

PETER (*laughing*): An Encyclopedia Boy!

Back in the present day, Kogito remembered something.
One day, before they embarked on the Tagame ritual, Goro had
telephoned Kogito and said: "Hey, quick question. What was
the name of that flowering tree in the forest where you grew
up? If you saw it in early spring when the new leaves are coming out you'd know the name right away, but at the moment it
escapes me. It isn't something common like a peach or a plum,
though, I'm sure of that."

Feeling nostalgic for a peaceable time in his village, before he started clashing with his mother, Kogito replied that the
tree in question could have been an edible pomegranate or an
ornamental pomegranate or possibly a dogwood, since while oak
trees did put out showy new leaves in early spring, their flowers were rather plain and unobtrusive. At the time of that phone
call, did Goro get the feeling that Kogito was pretending not to
remember the conversation that took place at Daio's training
camp? Or did Goro just assume that Kogito was shuffling
through his own definitive memories of THAT, trying to help
Goro out by providing the exact names of the plants he would
need to mention in his screenplay?

Reawakened by Goro's screenplay, Kogito's memories of
that springtime scene came flooding back, and he remembered
that the mountain cherries had still been blooming, though only
at the higher elevations, where temperatures were cooler than
in the valley. Peter was standing with his back against an old

cherry tree, its branches laden with fully unfurled double blossoms, that sheltered the meadow in front of the training hall. Kogito was standing beside him, explaining the surrounding vegetation and appearing, at that moment, to be on more intimate terms with Peter than Goro was . . .

Obviously annoyed by this turn of events, Daio gave some orders that were transparently designed to set his plan in motion. Interrupting Kogito's horticultural discourse, he called out to Peter and Goro. "Wouldn't you like to wash off the dust from your long road trip?" he asked, pointing at the building behind them—a bathhouse with mineral-rich water piped in from the nearby hot spring. Then, turning to Kogito (who was no less covered with grime from the journey than the other two), he said: "Come on, I'll show you the room where your father used to spend a lot of his time looking at . . . books."

Peter was enthusiastic about the idea of taking a hot-spring bath, and the young disciples led him and Goro off to the bathhouse, where towels and cotton kimonos were already laid out. Meanwhile, Daio hustled Kogito along a path bordered with round stones, which ended at a two-story building that was contiguous with the bathhouse but had its entrance on the opposite side.

There were no spoken lines in the screenplay regarding what happened next, only directorial explanations of the characters' movements. On the storyboards that were attached to the screenplay with a colored paper clip was a sketch of a scene in which the young American officer and the Japanese schoolboy are naked in the bath.

The bath itself is a small rectangle, set into the ground. Since the Japanese custom is to soap up and rinse off before getting into the bath, there's a Japanese-style washing area with a drain in the floor, next to the bathtub. There, Goro and Peter are washing their bodies before taking turns in the steaming tub, which isn't big enough for two.

After Goro gets out of the bath and returns to the washing area, Peter climbs in and submerges himself in the shallow end of the bath. After a moment, he reaches out from behind and tries to touch Goro's boyish genitals, which are dangling between his thighs. Goro jumps away, and Peter doesn't pursue the matter.

In the next scene the young man and the teenaged boy are perched on a couple of low bath stools, washing each other's backs. Peter's hand (which has been scrubbing Goro's back with a thin towel covered with soap bubbles) suddenly stops in midmotion. Laying down the towel, Peter begins to wash Goro's back all the way down to his loins, massaging the skin with his bare hands, which are covered with foamy lather. Then in one smooth, continuous movement, he tries to stick the palm of one hand in the crevice between Goro's buttocks. Goro leaps decisively to his feet and, still standing, tosses a bucketful of hot water from the bathtub over his body. Some of the water splashes onto Peter, but he just laughs quietly. Goro heads for the dressing room, and after a moment Peter follows.

That's exactly how it happened, Kogito thought as he read the screenplay. He and Daio had been watching from the ceiling cavity above the bathroom, lying on their stomachs in a crawl space about forty inches high atop the sturdy beams of the bathroom's wooden ceiling, each with an eye pressed to his own private peephole. Kogito was led there via a secret passage, accessed through the bottom half of a built-in closet in the room

on the second floor of the building that was back-to-back with
the bathroom.

Earlier, Kogito had been gazing out at the Nepal holly
tree directly beneath the window that faced his father's writing desk, while Daio stood next to the desk paying close attention to a small open area beneath the opulent foliage of
the holly tree. When he got the high sign from the acolytes
who were down there standing watch, Daio squeezed through
the closet into a low-ceilinged space that was above the bathroom, with Kogito close behind. And then Kogito—against his
better judgment, and feeling that he was being coerced into
doing something improper—ended up peering through the
hole Daio pointed out, from which a pale golden light was
emanating. And what Kogito saw through that luminous peephole was the exact same bath scene that Goro described in
his screenplay.

After watching Goro and Peter leave the bathroom, Kogito
heard a noise behind him and turned his head. Daio was scut-
tling toward him, propelling himself along with his one arm bent
at the elbow, as if he were rowing a boat. Then he lay down on
his side on the floor and stretched out his now-free arm to touch
Kogito's buttocks. When Kogito pushed the intrusive arm away,
Daio toppled over, just like that, and lay faceup on the floor as
helpless as an overturned beetle—or cockroach.

Kogito went back into his father's study, alone, and stood
gazing at the rows of volumes that lined the bookshelves.
When Daio eventually came crawling out of the spy space,
his grimy face dripping with sweat from the humidity, he said,
"Your father always used to say, 'If there's a naked body to be
seen, I don't care whether it's male or female.' He only liked

to look, of course; he never actually did anything. What about you, Kogito? Are you planning to live out your days as your father did, without ever letting anyone find out your true nature? That seems like a really dry, boring approach to life. No, I'm joking, I'm joking!"

Kogito was livid. But as a mere high-school student, he didn't feel confident that he had fully understood the meaning of this strange middle-aged man's so-called "joke"—and it wasn't as if Daio had spoken the words with a disagreeable smirk. Since he was there as a guest, Kogito was forced to let the anger fester in his gut.

The next storyboard illustration depicts a training hall of immeasurably vast scale, of the sort often featured in samurai movies; in the films of Goro's father, for example, this sort of capacious wooden-floored room often shows up as subtle parody of that genre. In the center of the room some tatami mats have been spread out, a small oasis in the immense unfurnished space. Clearly, this is the place where that night's makeshift party will take place. With no embellishments beyond those few woven-straw mats, the vast, empty hall seems almost surreal.

In a separate sketch, Peter and Goro are seated in the places of honor, with Kogito nearby. Daio sits at the head of a low table, facing the three guests, with his young followers lined up on either side. A separate sketch shows several extra-large platters, heaped high with Chinese food. This is the only one of Goro's storyboard sketches that is drawn with bright colors.

As he looked at the illustration, the memories that crowded into Kogito's head were couched in the simplest sensory terms: *That was the most delicious Chinese food I had ever eaten in my life, and nothing has topped it since.* There was a stupendous amount of food; Goro's sketch showed only four big platters, but Kogito didn't remember noticing any shortage of delicious things to eat.

One dish was made up of the red shells, legs, and fat claws of crabs, stir-fried with fresh, juicy vegetables; it was essentially the same concoction Daio had brought to the inn at Dogo Hot Springs, made with mitten crabs from the nearby river. On another platter was fried tofu, or soybean curd. (Homemade tofu, prepared at the training camp and peddled in nearby towns and villages, was the commune's only means of generating cash revenue.) Then there was the meat from a whole farm-raised lamb, butchered and roasted, then thinly sliced and fried in a hot wok with heaps of garlic and green onions.

Finally, there were *gyoza* (Chinese pot-sticker dumplings, stuffed with pork or shrimp and vegetables), submerged in savory broth and served in a large cauldron. The individual pots were heated on charcoal braziers placed atop fragments of roofing tile. The lamb dish was always warm, too; no sooner had the fat begun to congeal than the platter would be whisked away and a hot, sizzling substitute rushed out in its place.

Kogito was surprised to see that the person who carried the jumbo-sized, black-patinaed Chinese wok, holding the iron-pipe handles in both hands and getting a faceful of hot steam and garlic fumes—the same man who kept replenishing the supply of *gyoza* in broth, evidently from a big pot that was simmering on a primitive woodstove—was an old friend of his: Okawa.

When Kogito and Daio came downstairs from Choko Sensei's study, both silent after their ambiguous skirmish, they had circled around to the side of the bathroom that faced the main building. An annex to the hall where the party was being laid out housed a kitchen area, and standing at the back door, evidently taking a break, was a man who accosted Kogito.

He had noticed someone lurking there, but it wasn't until Daio had passed by, walking ahead, that the man sprang out like a jack-in-the-box. Kogito recognized Okawa immediately. The big man bowed earnestly, bending nearly in half from his great height. Then, while Kogito was trying to remember whether his old friend had always had such a heartrending look of sadness on his face, Okawa began to speak in an impassioned whisper.

"Please don't be mad at me! I know, I ended up rudely leaving your mother's house after she was so kind to me! I'm truly sorry, so please, please forgive me!" Just then Daio stopped and looked back over his shoulder with a puzzled expression, and Okawa jumped back through the door of the kitchen like a reverse jack-in-the-box, into that aromatic realm of steam and garlic.

Once the party had started, Okawa made frequent trips from the kitchen to the big hall to whisk away dishes that had gotten cold or to refill the giant platters from a boiling pot, but he didn't even glance at any of the guests. His face, with its golden skin stretched tight over high cheekbones, was always staring down, with lowered eyes.

Kogito hadn't seen that face for ages, but he had heard vague rumors that Okawa was at Daio's training camp. Since the camp had been Kogito's father's secret retreat during the wartime years, there was nothing too surprising about that. Okawa was the porter who had carried Choko Sensei's luggage when Kogito's father returned from the Chinese mainland, and he had been in Japan ever since. Before Kogito's house became the favored meeting place not only for soldiers from Kansai and Matsuyama but for other shady-looking strangers, as well, Okawa used to turn up at the house every day to help Kogito's mother with various household chores.

Kogito had a fond memory of one New Year's Day during that period, when the family's close female friends had gathered to share a meal, as was the custom. In the room that was connected to the kitchen by a sunken hearth, Okawa (who was like a member of the family) was sitting by the fire, the whites of his eyes and the surrounding skin tinted a soft, rosy pink from the small amount of sake he had consumed. That gathering included a number of people from other parts of the country who had been evacuated from their homes, so Kogito's mother said, "Why don't we each share a legend from our own region?" Kogito's grandmother, who was still alive at the time, led off, electrifying the atmosphere with her masterful storytelling style.

When it was Okawa's turn, he recited a traditional Chinese tale about a red dragon that swoops down from the hills. A female teacher who was renting a room on the second floor of the house (where Kogito's father holed up in his bedroom after he fell ill) started asking Okawa for details about where he was born. And Okawa, just as he had done with Kogito at

the training camp, pleaded to be let off the hook, saying, "Forgive me, but . . . please don't ask me that!"

Now that Kogito thought back on that day, he could see
that Goro had rendered some aspects of the party (the room,
the people, the food) in considerable detail, but he hadn't attempted to capture the feeling of being in a surreal scene in
some old movie—a feeling that, Kogito realized in retrospect,
had been due to the lighting, or lack thereof. A single spotlight
shone on the center of the room, but beyond that the cavern-
ous room was shrouded in semidarkness.

If you think about the grammar of Goro's filmmaking, that
seems perfectly appropriate. Goro's films are known for being
filled with fanciful notions and whimsical set pieces, but in truth
they are made up entirely of the details of modern life that he
had personally experienced or observed. That may have been
the reason why a film like *Dandelion*, which was essentially a
montage of humorous cinematic sketches, not only succeeded
so spectacularly at the box office but also turned out to have
exceptionally long-lived popularity, particularly among the
European intelligentsia. Kogito had seen evidence of this during his stay in Berlin.

The fact was, even such a consummate observer couldn't
have been expected to retain many impressions of Daio's party
that night. Why? Because Goro, who usually held his liquor
quite well, had gotten exceedingly drunk, to the point of seeming strangely feeble (though not quite "falling apart"). Many
years later, when Kogito turned off the TV set because he could
no longer bear to watch Goro going to pieces on a live chat show,
part of the reason may have been that he was reminded of that
night, when Goro was so tipsy on guerrilla moonshine that he

even started nodding off while still sitting more or less upright at the feast table. Before long he had toppled over onto his back, where he lay insensate, broadcasting unseemly openmouthed snores.

Kogito, who hadn't had so much as a drop of home-brewed *doburoku*, went from trying in vain to prop up the childishly weak and wobbly Goro to simply watching over his drunken friend as he lay there on his back, dead to the world. When he looked up from his labors he noticed Peter watching them with great interest from across the table, all but licking his chops. At that, the phrase "Peeping Tom" suddenly popped into Kogito's mind in connection with the hole in the ceiling of the bathroom. The words filled him with a powerful feeling of disgust, and he called out, in a voice that was almost harsh, "Goro, Goro! Come on, get up. If you can't sit up, you'd better go sleep it off in the other room."

Goro was lying on a tatami mat in the dim light not far from the brightly illuminated center of the room, where the party was going on. Kogito thought Goro was fast asleep, but then he opened his eyes and returned Kogito's gaze with a mocking look. "Goro, why don't you go in the other room and get some rest?" Kogito urged, feeling the anger surging up once again.

"That's right, Goro," Daio chimed in from a few yards away. "There's a little room just down the hall. You can take a rest in there, and then you can take another hot-spring bath or start drinking again or whatever you like. The evening's still young. Right, Peter?"

Peter had been watching Kogito's struggles with a look of amusement, but now he untangled his disproportionately long legs, which had been in the lotus position, and drew them up so both knees were touching his chest. Wearing an expression that reminded Kogito of an arrogant little boy, he ignored Daio's question. A drunken flush had spread over Peter's large face, blending the ruddy portions with the pallid white skin, and there was something childish about the way he moved the compact body that was attached to his oversized head. Indeed, the overall impression he gave was one of almost infantile immaturity. Peter's haughty, scornful attitude was now directed at the sleeping Goro, in spite of the fact that earlier in the evening he had been making Goro pronounce a whole slew of English words (totally unnecessarily, since they were all speaking Japanese) and singing the praises of Goro's "un-Japanese" pronunciation.

Kogito felt the anger boiling up inside him, stronger than ever. Roughly shaking Goro by the shoulders, he somehow managed to force his friend to sit up. Whereupon Goro demanded querulously, with the unfocused look of someone who has just regained consciousness, "So where am I supposed to sleep? Don't you know? You're the one who woke me up!"

Barely glancing at Kogito, who couldn't have answered that question in any case, Goro stood up and tottered away with surprising speed, but the hall was darker than the party room, and he stumbled noisily over the threshold. In a panic, Kogito got up and ran after Goro. Behind him the young disciples, who had been decorously silent throughout the meal, holding back on the sake and sitting with their knees folded under them, suddenly burst into raucous laughter.

Goro made his way to the end of the hall, where he went into the lavatory (it was really just a hole-in-the-floor toilet). He had left the sliding wooden door open, so Kogito closed it after him. Kogito was waiting nearby, gazing out into the courtyard and wondering how to find the room where Goro could lie down for a while, when two men emerged from between the outdoor washbasin and a thicket of the plumy, scarlet-berried shrub known as heavenly bamboo. Kogito was momentarily startled, but when one of the men turned his face toward Kogito, in the faint light from the lavatory window he saw that it was Okawa, looking even sallower than usual.

"You'd better go home to your mother's house tonight and take your friend with you!" Okawa said urgently, whispering just as he had the first time they'd talked, outside the kitchen. "That's what you ought to do, Kogito! This fellow here will give you a lift to your village, in a three-wheeled truck!"

Goro, his face noticeably pale even in the darkness, finally emerged from the lavatory, where he had evidently spent the entire time throwing up. Someone had brought Goro's shirt and trousers and laid them out on the open verandah in front of the washbasin, and his shoes, with Kogito's next to them, were neatly arranged on a stepping-stone. After he had changed out of the cotton *yukata*, Goro's intoxication seemed to be wearing off, and there was no need to explain to him what was about to happen.

Following the young man who had set off ahead of them without a word (Okawa had quickly disappeared), they descended the grassy slope, where each leaf of grass seemed to be reflecting the moonlight. Then Kogito, Goro, and their silent savior crossed the suspension bridge and climbed the hill to the empty lot beside the road where their three-wheeled getaway truck was waiting.

3

These are the things Kogito remembered about that journey: the way the moon glittered fiercely on the surface of the river below, which was like the bottom of a deep abyss, as they were crossing the rickety suspension bridge; the way he and Goro perched precariously, not on the luggage platform itself but behind it on two shallow metal-planking seats, anchored with screws, that flanked the driver's seat; the way the scrawny, sun-blackened neck of the taciturn young driver was thrown closer to them every time he cranked the handlebars sharply to the left or to the right; and the odd shyness Kogito felt about try-ing to start a conversation with the unusually silent Goro, who was sitting on the other side of the driver, as he watched his newly docile, seemingly sober friend's profile floating in the moonlight.

When he looked back on it now, Kogito realized that he must have been feeling exhilarated at the thought that he was now heading for his childhood home with Goro all to himself— although at the same time he imagined that Peter must probably be storming around the training camp demanding to know where the hell Goro had gone, and he was also a bit worried that Daio and some of his henchmen might jump into the other small truck and give chase. Of course, this was all extreme conjecture; imagining the worst that might happen was a toxic by-product of the assorted exasperation, anxiety, and anger Kogito had experienced this day in his stalled-out relations with Goro, Peter, and Daio. In truth, even as his seventeen-year-old self indulged in those florid fantasies, he didn't really think there was any serious danger.

As the little van wove among the overhanging trees that lined the road—trees that seemed to be closing in more aggressively, somehow, than during the daytime—Kogito kept his focus on the surface of the road ahead, unceasingly illuminated by the wobbly headlights as the little truck bounced along. When they finally turned onto the two-lane prefectural road, which was one prong of the three-forked road that ran alongside the tunnel, the mountains were very far away, the valley was infinitely deep, and in the midst of the endless blackness the faint glow of the moon illuminated the slender ribbon of river below.

By and by Goro spoke, in the awed voice of an adolescent who was feeling thunderstruck by the depths of the darkness the little three-wheeled truck was plunging into. "This really is the 'mountain fastness,' isn't it?" he said dreamily. "I knew there was an expression like that, but till now I never knew what it meant."

"We're going to go a lot deeper into the 'fastness' than this," Kogito replied. "This is a high place and the mountains beyond are pretty far away, so you don't get a feeling of confinement, but that isn't the case with my village." Goro didn't reply; Kogito had the feeling that he had never before elicited this kind of silence from his friend, and he felt a small frisson of proprietorial pride at his unprecedented "accomplishment."

After a while it occurred to Kogito that there was something he ought to explain to Goro before they arrived. Spurred on by a sudden sense of urgency, he simply blurted it out.

"Listen," he said, "it's about my mother. On one side of her head, in the place where an ear should be, she has a fold of skin that looks like the kind of flipper you'd expect to see on a fish, or maybe a reptile, so she always wears a cloth wrapped around her head, like a turban. I thought I should warn you, since it's late at night and I'm afraid she might come out with her head uncovered and startle you."

"Don't worry, I won't be startled," Goro said with cool indifference, but he was plainly intrigued by what Kogito had just told him.

"It's not so much a matter of being startled or not . . . rather, if you just react in a natural way I don't think it will hurt her feelings. When she was still in good health, she even used to make jokes about her condition. But if I don't tell you the whole story, it'll be hard to understand."

"So tell me the whole story," Goro said.

There was a sketch in one of the storyboards Goro drew, years later, that showed the way he visualized Kogito's mother while he was listening to the tale: as a woman, well past middle age, with a large snail attached to the left side of her face where an ear would normally be.

Kogito started out by talking about his great-grandfather and how he happened to give Kogito's mother the unambiguous name "Hiré," which means a flipper or fin. From the three-forked road at the tunnel exit, it would take the three-wheeled truck another forty minutes to reach Kogito's house, so there was plenty of time to relate the whole saga, from the beginning.

That great-grandfather died the winter that Kogito's mother, his only grandchild on the paternal side, was seven years old; that's reckoning by the old Japanese system wherein a baby is a year old at birth, so she would have been eight in Western terms. During the uprising that occurred in 1860, the first and only year of the Man'en era—it ended in 1861—Kogito's mother's grandfather, as a duty-bound village official, ended up being forced to kill his own younger brother, who was the leader of the revolt.

He lived an extraordinarily long life, until after the Meiji Restoration of 1868, and when his grandchild (Kogito's mother) was born, the whole village was soon gossiping about her deformed ear, thanks to the garrulous midwife who had delivered the baby. People whispered that the deformity was some sort of curse: divine retribution for her grandfather's having killed his own brother. But her grandfather didn't seem at all perturbed, and he even went so far as to christen her, straightforwardly, Hiré. The young girl never forgot the stories she heard while perched on the knee of this larger-than-life old man (even though she was already past the age where that sort of physicality was considered appropriate). With the Western medicine that was developing, it would have been no problem to tidy up the misshapen appendage, but Hiré herself made the choice to leave her ear the way it was at birth.

Even today, there are a lot of old-fashioned words whose meanings are still passed down in these parts. *Hiré* is one of those words. In addition to its usual flipper-or-fin connotations, it can also mean talent, personal beauty, and the like. In a famous old book called the *Gyokujinsho,* there's a passage that suggests that dull, humdrum, utterly average people often act as if they have some great talent or pretend to be endowed with deep, extraordinary human qualities. As Hiré's grandfather said, "You're a girl with brains and charm. If all the men in the cities and villages around here refuse to marry you because they're uncomfortable with your ear, you'll have to go as far away as necessary to find a man who can see beyond that superficial flaw."

"Maybe your mother just told you that story because she was concerned that *your* ears are so big," Goro teased. "But seriously, your great-grandfather sounds like he must have been an unusually cultured old man."

"My mother grew up hearing stories from old books like the *Gyokujinsho,* but she didn't necessarily remember all the details," Kogito explained. "So afterward I looked up some words in the dictionary."

"You look up a lot of things, don't you, Encyclopedia Boy?" Goro said good-humoredly. "But just from what I've heard so far, there are stories in your family that sound like something Kafka might have written!"

When the three-wheeled truck came to a stop on the private road that curved along the waterway below Kogito's house, the young man who had been driving opened his mouth for the first time that evening. "You know that story you just heard? Well, Kogito exaggerated about his mother's ears," he said to Goro, in a tone that suggested he had given the matter a great deal of thought.

Kogito and Goro jumped off the truck and crossed the stone bridge over the aqueduct. The road was lined by a rock wall that eventually merged with a large wooden structure that doubled as gatekeeper's lodge and passageway through to the estate beyond. (Some of the wood where the building adjoined the wall had rotted out and been replaced with sheets of tin, as a stopgap measure.) A low-wattage electric lightbulb hung in front, barely illuminating the boys' path.

Kogito looked back and saw that the young man was still standing next to the three-wheeled truck. "You can go home now, you know!" he called out in the local dialect.

"I'll leave as soon as you tell me that your mother is still up and you can get into the house and you've no more need of my services, but not before!" was the stubborn reply.

Relying on the light of the moon, Kogito led Goro up the hill along the cobblestoned road that traced a shallow arc toward the main section of the old house. When they passed the compound's so-called driveway, which had fallen into disrepair and was no longer used, the horn of the three-wheeled truck honked three times in a practiced rhythm: *beep-beep-beep.* A moment later, as if in response, a light went on above the large main entrance of the compact one-story bungalow that had been added onto the original structure.

When they finally reached the house and were standing at the entrance, a smaller door next to it opened a crack and a female peeked out. (It took a moment for Kogito to realize that it was his younger sister, Asa, and not his mother.) Asa flung the small door all the way open and thrust out one of her shoulders, which was clad in a yellowish-orange sweater. "Kogito? What are you doing here so late at night?" she grumbled.

"I'm with a friend," Kogito replied. "Don't worry, we've already had dinner."

After his sister had backed away into the house, Kogito ducked through the small door and beckoned Goro to follow him. Goro watched with obvious curiosity as Kogito's sister, in her sweater and skirt and hastily slipped-on wooden clogs, stood waiting for them to catch up in the mud-floored room, which was as wide as the big door and continued all the way to the laundry room. Goro seemed to be dazzled by the brightness of that yellowish-orange sweater (It was almost the color of an unripe persimmon), but he managed a semblance of a polite bow, and Kogito's sister, obviously flustered, lowered her head in return.

"Do you boys want to go to sleep right away?" she asked. "I'll go ahead and spread the futons in the back parlor, but you'll at least pop in and say hello to Mother, won't you? Chu's already asleep."

His sister looked as if she wanted to say something else, but Kogito ignored her and told Goro to climb up on the verandah that connected the bungalow with the section of the huge, rambling main house that was still in use. The two boys walked along the rough-floored hall, and as they passed through the interior of the house Kogito saw a light burning behind some opaque-paper sliding doors on one side, which told him that his mother was still awake. He showed Goro where the lavatory was, and then they went into his own snug tatami-matted room. His sister had quickly slipped past them and had gone into the spacious room next to Kogito's—the back parlor, which looked out on the aqueduct—to lay out their bedding.

Goro sat down in front of Kogito's small student desk and gazed at the pages from Hideo Kobayashi's translation of *The Collected Works of Rimbaud* that Kogito had copied out by hand and tacked up on the facing wall. Kogito was afraid this might turn into an awkward moment. Goro had been teaching him French (though not so frequently now that Kogito had started cramming for his college entrance exams), and the text they'd been using was a copy of the Mercure de France edition of Rimbaud's *Poésies,* which Goro had given him. Goro had previously begun to compile a small collection of Rimbaud's works, including the letters, and at the beginning of his tutoring sessions with Kogito he had said, "From now on, let's agree not to look at any more translations, okay?"

The thing was, Kogito had enjoyed reading Kobayashi's translation of Rimbaud's "Adieu" long before he transferred to Matsuyama High School and met Goro. Goro had two copies of *Poésies,* and as soon as he had given Kogito the extra one, Kogito had ascertained that "Adieu" wasn't included in the contents. So (Kogito was thinking), if Goro had asked him to explain the presence of a forbidden translation on his wall, he would have a perfectly good explanation. But Goro just stared at the end of the first half of what Kogito had written out—"But not one friendly hand! and where can I look for help?"—and then Kogito began to worry that Goro might somehow take that line personally, as an aspersion on their friendship.

However, Kogito knew that his mother was waiting for the requisite visit from her son, so there was no time to fret about imaginary problems. Gesturing vaguely in the direction of the next room, where his sister could he heard vigorously spreading the

futons, Kogito went into the hall on the pretense of checking
on her progress, then headed for his mother's room. (That small
subterfuge seemed easier and less embarrassing than telling
Goro his real destination.)

Kogito's mother was sitting in a narrow space between the
near-side sliding door and the Buddhist household altar, in front
of which her bedding was spread out on the floor. She was
dressed quite formally in a lined kimono, and her head, wrapped
in a turban made from the same cloth as the outside layer of
the kimono, was drooping so weakly from the nape of her neck
that it looked as if she might have nodded off. Kogito remembered how creepy the turbans had always seemed to him as a
child, after he'd learned about his mother's ears.

Now he sat down, straddling the raised seam between the
bedroom's tatami-matted floor and the hall, and said hello. He
left the sliding door open to make it clear that he was just paying his respects, briefly, before returning to join his guest.

"I meant to stop by yesterday; I'm sorry to be so late," Kogito
said.

"The friend who's with you—I assume that's the famous
Goro you've been talking so much about lately? Asa said that
even though he's only in high school, he was reeking of sake! I
gather you got a ride here in the truck from Daio's farm, but
why did you go there in the first place?"

"Only because Daio came to see me the other day, after
reading in the paper that I was studying at the Army of
Occupation's library. One of the American officers there was
interested in Daio's farm and he said he wanted to visit it, so . . ."
Kogito had picked up on his mother's use of the innocuous term
"farm" in lieu of "training camp," and he followed suit by giving

the simplest possible explanation, which also happened to be more or less the truth.

"You shouldn't blame it on someone else," his mother retorted. "If you had just said that you were interested in taking a look at Daio's farm, I wouldn't have forbidden you to go there! But if Daio had an American army officer as a guest, I imagine he went all out with the sake and food. I'll bet he was bragging about his Chinese cook, too. Now that I think about it, I feel sorry for Mr. Okawa, having to work there."

Kogito didn't say anything. He knew that rather than questioning him directly, his mother's style was to ramble along, sharing her own thoughts, and he was waiting to see where that would lead. But his mother made no attempt to pursue the subject of Daio's "farm," and after briefly raising her head to look at Kogito she lowered her face again and said, "Well, then, why don't you and your friend go to sleep now and have a nice long rest. Please ask the young man who was driving the truck to wait for another half hour or so. Tell him we have some rice cakes wrapped in oak leaves, and we'll take them to him shortly, along with some hot green tea."

The last half of this little speech, about the rice cakes, was actually addressed to Kogito's sister, who had come down the hall and was peering into the room over Kogito's back. Kogito couldn't help thinking childishly that if there were extra rice cakes wrapped in oak leaves lying around, he and Goro would happily eat a few. Not wanting his sister to divine his thoughts, he just stood up, wearing a sullen expression, then slipped past her and went back to his own room.

The sliding doors between that room and the large back parlor had been opened, and on the other side of two futons, which were spread out side by side, Goro was waiting. He had already changed into a cotton sleeping kimono. "About that translation on your wall," he began, "I know they say the translator inserted his own emotions into it and got some details wrong and so on, but still, it's really good!"

"I couldn't agree more," Kogito replied, making no attempt to suppress the joy in his voice.

Two years ago, while he was copying out that poem, Kogito had read the first line, "If we are sworn to a search for divine brightness," and had been struck by the feeling that he didn't have a friend he could speak of as "we." Now, he thought, he found that same poem even more moving because he had lately become part of a comradely "we"—and his counterpart was here with him, right now. True, the end of the first section wasn't entirely optimistic, but that did nothing to dampen his happiness. And then Goro, as if to magnify Kogito's delight, said, "In that poem, I feel as if he's talking about our futures. Rimbaud is really something else, isn't he!"

Kogito didn't stop to think about what sort of concrete image Goro might be trying to conjure up when he said "our futures"; his happiness was simply doubled by that heartwarmingly conspiratorial remark. His feelings were best summed up by a word he had come across in his newly acquired *Concise Oxford Dictionary*: he was *flattered*.

"I only copied out the first half, but if you'd like to read the rest of it, I have the *Collected Poems* here," Kogito said, plucking the volume from his bookshelf (it was the edition published by Sogensha) and handing it to Goro. By this time he, too, had changed into a cotton kimono.

Goro quickly jumped into bed, turned on the floor lamp that Kogito's sister had placed between their two futons, and began to read Rimbaud's *Collected Poems*. As Kogito looked at his friend, comfortably stretched out under the quilt with just his head sticking out at an oblique angle, the sight of Goro's perfectly cylindrical neck and sculpturesque jawline filled him with a curious sense of pride.

4

On that night, after settling down under the quilts, Goro mainly talked about his impressions of Hideo Kobayashi's translation of Rimbaud's "Adieu." As Kogito discovered many years later, those same thoughts turned up in the screenplay and storyboards for Goro's final, unproduced film. It appeared that Goro, who disliked the technique of so-called "art" or "avant-garde" films, had tried to write the scene with his usual cinematic grammar—that is, in the same style he used for his commercial films. But the screenplay contained two different versions of the last scene (both of which, based on Kogito's impressions as a reader, were given equal weight in the lineup), and in those scenes, Goro used techniques that would have been inappropriate in a standard mainstream movie. As we'll see later, the fact that both endings seemed to unfold naturally and make perfect contextual sense was typical of Goro's approach to filmmaking.

As a novelist, every time Kogito got bogged down in trying to re-create some past occurrence along a linear time sequence (i.e., this happened, then that happened), he would feel the necessity of changing the focal point of the narrative by jumping around in time and space. Because of that, it was easy for Kogito to understand why, when Goro wrote about that bedtime discussion of Rimbaud, it was in the form of a scene in which he and Kogito were sitting across from each other as adults, recalling that conversation from forty years ago—a scene that never actually took place in real life.

We see present-day Goro talking to present-day Kogito, but we don't need to get any realistic sense of Kogito's actual presence or physical form. We should just get a vague impression of a sort of shadowy effigy, almost like a scarecrow, with its back to us. As another option, without even bringing in the actor who's playing Kogito's character, it might be effective to have this scene show Goro alone late at night, talking at length into a cassette recorder, making the tapes that he will later send to Kogito. (Incidentally, the part of present-day Goro will probably be played by the director himself.)

GORO (*speaking into Tagame's microphone*): That night in the old house in the valley in the forest, I said that I had a feeling that Rimbaud was writing about our futures in "Adieu." You didn't say anything specific in response, as I recall, but I could tell that you knew exactly what I meant. After I'd said something as naïve as that, if you had cynically brushed it aside I would probably have clammed up for the rest of the evening, nursing my wounded feelings. The translation I have with me now isn't the one by Hideo Kobayashi, it's the Chikuma

paperback you recommended, but when I read "Adieu"
again in this newer version, I saw that our lives since then
are proof positive that what I said was right on target.
Indeed, my prediction has come almost heartbreakingly
true. Of course, I knew you were especially fond of the
opening phrase, and I felt the same way. But already, at
that time, I wasn't envisioning a totally glorious scenario
for the future. And that, too, was because I was being
guided by what Rimbaud had written. When you think
about it, I really was adorably earnest, wasn't I? Anyway,
it went like this:

*Autumn. Our boat, risen out of a hanging fog, turns
toward poverty's harbor, the monstrous city, its sky stained
with fire and mud.*

And then he's in the city, and he goes on: *I can see
myself again* . . . remember this part? . . . *my skin corroded
by dirt and disease, hair and armpits crawling with worms,
and worms still larger crawling in my heart, stretched out
among ageless, heartless, unknown figures . . . I could easily
have died there . . .*

I can pretty much guarantee that this prediction of
the future and so on is really and truly accurate, and very
specific to boot, at least for me. I can't claim to be able
to predict your future, but if I think about a vision of my
own imminent fate, it's right on the mark. Bingo! Because
I figure that sooner or later, I'm probably going to end up
taking a fatal dive off of some high place. Of all the avail-
able options, that's the surest way of snuffing it—mainly
because even if you change your mind halfway down,
there's no way to stop. If you film the jumper's descent

and then run the film backward, he'll seem to be floating in air, but of course there's no "rewind" or "freeze-frame" in reality. And by the very nature of the act, it's impossible to have anything like the ambivalent wrist slasher's hesitation marks when you're free-falling through space.

And then my body—rather like the man in the Kafka story who turned into a bug and ended up dying quietly under the sofa. (Do you remember when I told you my interpretation that the insect in question was a cockroach? Only in those days we didn't have a disgusting word like "cockroach," so we called them "oily bugs.") Anyway, what if no one found me—you know, like Kafka's cockroach? I daydream about things like that sometimes when I'm standing on the roof of this office building in the middle of Tokyo, looking down at the alley far below. I mean, suppose my body came crashing down— *ka-thunk!*—amid the mountain of cardboard boxes and other trash that's always piled up down there, and my corpse wasn't discovered for days? If I'm going to end up decaying like that, then I really will have died in exactly the way Rimbaud describes, line by line, crawling maggots and all.

Not only that, but when I come to the following phrase, I naturally think about the movies that I've made: *I was the creator of every feast, every triumph, every drama. I tried to invent new flowers, new planets, new flesh, new languages. I thought I had acquired supernatural powers.*

As for you, Kogito, there are people who relentlessly ridicule you and your work with all the usual stereotypical put-downs. They say that you're a fool who turns up his nose at pop culture and only thinks or cares about old-fashioned belles lettres and so-called "pure art." But I don't think that's the case, at all. And I don't think there's any way that someone who has been writing novels for as long as you have could be unaware that all literature and all art (including your own work) is, basically, au fond, kitsch. If you accept that premise, then the astoundingly popular movies that I make have a deliberate halo of kitschiness around them from the very beginning. But even if I blew my own horn like that—*I was the creator of every feast, every triumph, every drama*—you wouldn't laugh me out of the room, would you? For you, too, as a novelist, surely there must be times when you want to say *I tried to invent new flowers, new planets, new flesh, new languages?* In your recent novels, there do seem to be some elements of supernatural power emerging here and there. Anyway, for people like us who have been friends since we were schoolboys, isn't it all right to acknowledge what we've accomplished so far? After all, this is a private conversation, just between the two of us.

So anyhow, after that, Rimbaud says: *Ha! I have to bury my imagination and my memories! What an end to a splendid career as an artist and storyteller!* And later he adds, *Well, I shall ask forgiveness for having lived on lies. And that's that.*

This passage really hits me where I live. Don't you feel the same way, Kogito? When you think about people who do the kind of work we do—selling the "new flowers" of kitsch and the "new stars" of kitsch by the yard, as it were—we don't have that much time left, and we need to come to terms with that fact and ask forgiveness for having lived on lies. How about Takamura? What was he thinking about at the end, I wonder? Did you try asking him about that sort of thing when you visited him after he was hospitalized with terminal cancer? Surely you wouldn't have told him that his own music was pure art and had no relation whatsoever to kitsch or anything like that, would you? He would have felt disappointed, even betrayed, if you had gotten all deathbed-sentimental and started insisting that his art had nothing kitschy about it.

From the time I first met you, when you were sixteen, I've always told you that you should never tell a lie. I've said it all along: "You shouldn't tell lies, not even to entertain people or give them comfort." I said that again just the other day, remember? But Rimbaud's line about having lived on lies is absolutely true of me, as well. That's right, your exalted mentor is a liar. Anyway, there's something that you and I, together, need to try asking forgiveness for, and then it will be time for us to take our leave.

Needless to say, I'll be heading out by myself this time. And when you get to be our age, if someone makes up his mind to go on alone, there's no way to stop him. Other people can't possibly stop him—I mean, how could they, when the person in question can't even stop himself? And wasn't Rimbaud talking about that kind of departure, the end of this first act, when he said: *But not one friendly hand! and where can I look for help?*

And listen, Kogito, here's the thing. What I'm able to understand of the poem "Adieu" is really just up to this point; that is to say, I only understand the parts of it that have some bearing on my own life so far. That's because I won't be able to perfectly understand the latter half of the poem until after I say my own farewell—at least that's the way I feel now.

You've seen those sequential photographs, taken with a strobe-style flash that goes off every few seconds? I feel as if I'm already starting to see glimpses of the Other Side, like frozen images illuminated by a brief flash of light. And I feel as if once I actually get there, I'll truly be able to understand any and all of the lines in the latter half of the poem. For instance, this kind of passage: *A hard night! Dried blood smokes on my face, and nothing lies behind me but that repulsive little tree!* If you look at it this way, Rimbaud really does seem to be talking about what happened to us: you know, about THAT. It's as if this one line has somehow been layered over my actual memories, and my own past is just a faint pentimento, or palimpsest.

Kogito was shocked by this portion of the screenplay, wherein Goro seemed to be saying that before too long he was planning to jump to his death from a high place—which is exactly what he had done. Moreover, while he was reading that passage, Kogito had a distinct sensation of déjà vu. That feeling led him directly to the drawing Goro had left behind, showing himself reclining lengthwise in midair holding a Tagame clone—and which, Kogito saw now, could almost have been one of the storyboard drawings that corresponded with various scenes in the screenplay. He felt, suddenly, as if he had heard these same words spoken in Goro's voice on one of the Tagame tapes. That realization was so distressing that the blood rushed to his face and he jumped to his feet in agitation.

Of course, the screenplay and storyboards had been delivered to Kogito after Goro's death, by way of Chikashi. But Kogito couldn't help thinking, in a state of consternation verging on panic: *If only I had listened sooner to all the Tagame tapes that were in the small trunk . . . if only I had come across the tape that, even if it wasn't exactly the same as the screenplay, might at least have hinted at Goro's plan . . . and if only I had talked about it to Chikashi and then asked her to discuss the matter with Umeko, surely the women would have taken Goro to the hospital of a famous doctor they had met when Goro was making a movie about dying in hospitals, and then he would have been safely under the care of a physician who specialized in presenile dementia or depression or whatever was ailing him . . . wouldn't he?*

When Kogito took out the little duralumin trunk, his memos about the contents of all the cassette tapes that he had already listened to were on the labels, and by using those notations as clues and constantly fast-forwarding, he managed to run through all the tapes again in half a day. He had to perform this task in the living room, which was the only place where the light was bright enough for him to read the small print on the labels, and when Chikashi saw him wearing the forbidden Tagame headphones, she gave him a look that seemed to say, "Oh, no, not again!" Akari, too, was clearly uneasy about seeing his father so immersed in an unusual project involving large numbers of cassette tapes.

In the end, Kogito wasn't able to find the recording that he'd thought he remembered, albeit in a vague, déjà vu–ish way. Nevertheless, he couldn't help thinking that the very concept of Tagame itself was a signal from Goro, a plea for help, and this ended up reviving the feeling he had, right after it happened, that he himself was somehow to blame for Goro's death.

But on a different level, a phrase from the oft-quoted "Adieu" struck him with new force: *A hard night! Dried blood smokes on my face, and nothing lies behind me but that repulsive little tree!* And he realized that Goro was on to something when he remarked in his screenplay soliloquy: "If you look at it this way, Rimbaud really does seem to be talking about what happened to us: you know, about THAT!"

5

When Goro and Kogito woke up in the big old house in the deep mountain valley, it was already past noon. Kogito's younger sister came to roust them out of bed, saying, "Mother's going out to work." When the two late risers wandered into the big dirt-floored room (the large door was open now, along with the smaller door they had squeezed in through the night before), Kogito's mother was sitting on the verandah, dressed in her gardening clothes and obviously waiting for them.

"Welcome!" she greeted Goro with high good humor, bowing from the waist. "We're very grateful for everything you've done for Kogito." (That was the customary pleasantry.)

"I'm sorry we made so much noise so late at night," Goro replied, equally formulaically. Wearing an exquisitely polite smile, he returned the bow with a grace and elegance that Kogito had never before witnessed in someone his own age.

Kogito's mother went out through the main gate with no further conversation, and as soon as she was out of sight Goro said, in a loud, excited voice, "She was wearing the turban!" At that moment they heard the horn of the little three-wheeled truck honking three times, just like the night before, and Kogito's little brother, Chu (who until then had been hiding timidly behind Asa, staring at Goro), turned and ran after their mother. Asa was in the tatami-matted room that was a step up from the dirt-floored entry hall, preparing breakfast for her older brother and his guest beside the sunken hearth that connected that room to the kitchen.

Led by Chu, who had evidently been sent back by his mother, the same taciturn young man from the training camp entered the house and remained standing in the dirt-floored room. He spoke to Goro and Kogito while they were digging into their late breakfast, and Kogito couldn't help thinking that the young man's grandparents probably would have behaved in the same deferential, class-conscious manner if they had come to talk to the head of the estate and his family (that is, to Kogito's grandparents) about some business or other. The young man's way of speaking, too, was a complicated mixture of reserve and supplication.

"Daio is really worried about how you two are going to get back to Matsuyama!" he said, addressing his remarks to Kogito. "He was saying that since today's Sunday, that's no problem, but if you guys miss school tomorrow your mother will surely be angry . . . and also, he figured she probably noticed that the friend you brought home was a trifle intoxicated. So that's why he sent me to pick you up. He was saying that if I take you back to our training camp, you can grab a ride back to Matsuyama with Peter, in that foreign car. Peter went back to his army base for a while, but he said he'd return in the evening. Daio also said that after Kogito's mother heard about last night, she might have ordered her son not to go back to the kind of place that serves alcohol to minors, but that your friend, Goro, doesn't answer to your mother and so she can't boss him around. And besides, we're living in a world of democracy now! That's what he was saying, anyway. It's none of my business, of course, but I couldn't help thinking that maybe the reason Kogito's mother went out to work in the fields on a Sunday—later than usual, but even so—is because she was angry with Kogito about last night."

Kogito knew, but didn't say, that his mother hadn't gone to work in the fields at all. She had set out for the overgrown remains of a botanical garden, featuring a collection of medicinal plants, that was between the basin of the valley, where they lived, and the other part of the village farther up the hill. According to local folklore, that garden had been created by the founder of the village. Nowadays it was just a plot of land covered with scrubby weeds and shrubs, rather than cultivated herbs and grasses, but Kogito's mother always managed to find some useful things amid the untamed vegetation. When she went on these horticultural treasure hunts she would sometimes come across a type of wild rhubarb called *daio*—known colloquially around these parts as *gishi-gishi*—and no doubt it had struck her that one of the young men who came to visit her husband during the war was named Daio. Hence (as Daio himself had explained earlier, under the Matsuyama cherry blossoms) the nickname, "Gishi-Gishi."

While the truck driver was making his pitch to Kogito, Goro sat quietly listening and devouring his breakfast. His body language made it clear that he wanted to go back to the training camp, and he seemed mystified by Kogito's momentary hesitation.

They arrived at Daio's training camp in the late afternoon, around 4 PM. Even now, Kogito still remembered the quizzical expression on Goro's face after they had crossed the rope suspension bridge and were trudging uphill through the grassy meadow. Kogito, too, was wondering whether the partying had started early. He couldn't identify any explicit sounds of festivity, but he had the definite impression that there was some sort of commotion taking place in the vicinity of the training hall.

The truck driver had told the boys that Daio was waiting for them in the main building. There was a tall step at the entrance (the structure reminded Kogito of the temple of the Tenrikyo sect of Buddhism that had been built in his village), and as Kogito and Goro entered the building they sensed immediately that their reception was going to be different from the hearty welcome they had received the day before. Indeed, when they first poked their heads into the office, they thought no one was there.

After a moment, they noticed Daio sitting on a couch against the wall, with his legs folded under him and bent to one side. There was a two-quart bottle of home-brewed sake on the floor beside him, and he was in the process of sloshing some into a teacup. Then, with no trace of the cheery expression he had worn at the previous night's banquet, he fixed them with a look that was so dark and doleful they were almost afraid to approach him. The words he spoke were still affable enough, but his face told a different story.

"Won't you join me for a drink, Goro?" he called out. "I know you're a man who can hold his liquor. I already got an angry letter from Kogito's mother, reading me the riot act for giving alcohol to minors, so I won't be pouring any for him, that's for sure."

"The sun's still a bit too high for that," Goro replied, refusing the offer in a sophisticated manner that sounded odd coming from someone so young.

Daio picked up the teacup full of *doburoku,* scooted down to one end of the couch, and set his bare feet on the floor. Goro sat down in the newly opened space, but there was no room for Kogito, so he grabbed a nearby wooden chair, turned it around, and plopped himself down. Daio observed this operation with an expression that was somehow arrogant and disdainful. Then, ignoring Kogito completely, he continued to address himself to Goro alone.

"I'm really happy you came back!" he exclaimed. "This morning, before Peter made a run to the army base—he'll be back later—I told him that you guys would probably be dropping by again this evening, as well. He's a sly one, that Peter. He came right out and said that if Goro wasn't here when he returned with the broken guns, he wouldn't be fooled again the way he was last night when you two sneaked off without telling anyone. He said that he would just turn around and go home, without even taking the weapons out of the car.

"When the young warriors heard that, they weren't too happy. They had started drinking toward the end, after you ran off, and the party last night ended up getting a little bit wild and out of control, so maybe they forgot their manners, or maybe it was just their youthful high spirits. They're kind of hot-blooded, and they don't always take the time to think things through. Anyway, they said to Peter, 'You may say that you won't give us the stuff you bring, but we won't let you get away with that.'

"And then Peter really showed his true colors. He said, 'That's a direct threat, and it would be my right as a soldier of the occupying army—more than a right: my *duty*—to shoot you to death just for saying that. I'll be keeping that in mind, and when I come back I won't just be bringing broken guns. I'll be bringing one that really works so I can defend myself!'

"But Peter's a young guy, too, so he really didn't need to say something like that, am I right? When the warriors heard that, instead of being concerned for their own safety, they were very excited at the prospect of getting their hands on a gun that they could actually use to shoot someone. He probably wouldn't bring a rifle, so if you have one man with a pistol, all you need is for five men to jump on him with the intention of knocking him down. They could easily restrain him—some of these young guys are demobilized soldiers, with experience in battle. No, Peter really blew it; he said something he never should have said. Even so, when he left he was wearing a very solemn expression. You'd have thought the young warriors would have been intimidated by what Peter said, but they let out a big, loud war whoop that I'm sure was audible even where he was, over by the Cadillac. I hope that when he heard the sudden roar of voices he realized how radically the circumstances had changed, because I think it would be just as well if he didn't come back . . .

"The young warriors held an emergency meeting, and they apparently worked out a strategy in case Peter did come back. If he returned with a working pistol, they were planning to take it from him right away, by force. But Peter's an officer in the military, so there's no way he's going to give up his pistol and bullets without a struggle! If he lost his gun, he would probably be punished in some way, and the Army of Occupation would come and root us out, and then our entire crew would end up doing hard labor in some Okinawan prison, isn't that right? For Peter, losing his gun here would be a very different story than if they just found out that he was doing the approximate equivalent of selling broken guns to black-market metal dealers, even if he did do that half in fun, as a sort of reckless game."

"Was the plan you told us about just a game, too?" Kogito couldn't stop himself from asking.

Daio's face returned to the dark, gloomy aspect it had worn before he noticed their arrival. The one-armed man drained the *doburoku* in his teacup and took a deep breath.

"Of course it wouldn't be just a game for us," he said, glaring at Kogito with seriously chilly eyes. "Your mother told us not to pass your father's ideas on to you, as if we were some kind of low-life vermin who would try to corrupt her precious son, but that isn't our aim at all. In any case, you have no business calling our carefully thought-out plan a game!

"I know I've talked about this before, but when this country was ignominiously occupied for the first time in its history, we made up our minds that it wouldn't do to let the peace treaty take effect without a single show of armed resistance from the Japanese people. But in this well-policed country, it simply isn't possible to put together a group of armed rebels. If it were possible, don't you think someone would have done so by now? That's why we came up with the next best thing: ten of us are going to storm the front gates of the army camp with automatic rifles at the ready—and it won't matter that they're broken, because no one will be able to tell just by looking at them. And then we'll be mowed down by a hail of bullets from the guns of the American soldiers.

"But the story doesn't end with us dying an honorable

death. After the word gets out that the attack was staged with
nonfunctional guns and the men who were shot to death were,
essentially, unarmed Japanese—and if the occupying army
doesn't make that information public, the survivors here at the
training camp will be handling PR and making sure the truth
gets out. Anyway, when that happens, the occupying army's
censorship will have come to an end! And don't you think that
there will be a nationwide outcry of anger and indignation? We
believe that outcry will determine the fate of this country after
the peace treaty takes effect, because these are the beliefs we've
acquired so far, and we're willing to die for them!

"And isn't this a natural extension of the philosophy of your
father, Choko Sensei, who stormed the bank—unarmed, as we
will be—and was shot to death in the process? I haven't been
teaching these young men that they should go out and kill
people. Rather, I've taught them that we should be willing to
give up our lives to restore the nationalistic ideology that's been
lost in this country. That's what I've been saying all along! So
what's the point of stealing a single pistol that's in working order?
On top of which, what if you're properly armed and you end up
killing your opponent on the spur of the moment? And what if,
among the soldiers of the occupying army, we killed a young
pro-Japanese, Japanese-speaking officer like Peter? What effect would that have? Would the peaceable-minded Japan of
today be sympathetic if we did something like that?

"But the young warriors end up getting carried away with
some reckless, half-baked plan, and they don't listen to what I
tell them! 'If you steal a pistol and end up killing your opponent in combat, especially before the peace treaty takes effect,
that's the same as annihilating one soldier of the occupying

army'—one idiot actually said that as if it was a good thing, and everybody clapped and cheered. Then there was the smart aleck who said, 'If the person whose pistol you stole is running away before your eyes, rather than letting him go and bring the Army of Occupation down on us, wouldn't it make more sense to kill him on the spot?' And another guy said that if you had one working pistol, you would feel more secure than if you were attacking with a bunch of broken rifles. In the end, the group didn't seem to understand a word I said. They really do behave like a bunch of brainless bumpkins sometimes."

After he had finished this tirade, Daio picked up his tea-cup and splashed another dose of *doburoku* into it, then lifted the cup to his mouth with a trembling hand and drained it dry in a single gulp. The area from his chin to his throat was wet with sake, and after a not entirely successful attempt to wipe it off with the back of his hand, he turned to Goro and began to speak in a tone that seemed to suggest that Goro owed him something or, at the very least, that Goro ought to appreciate Daio's noble efforts to remove the danger his volatile young followers might pose to Peter. Evidently he expected Goro to be grateful even if that effort turned out to be unsuccessful.

"If only Peter would sense that something weird is brewing and not come back, everything would be fine," Daio said. "But the thing is, Peter has his heart set on seeing Goro, so I'll bet he's behind the wheel of the Cadillac at this very moment, heading back this way . . ."

Daio had turned the back of his darkly sunburned neck toward Kogito and was plainly avoiding his gaze. But when he said that, Kogito blurted out, "From the beginning, you've been using Goro as bait to lure Peter here, and just a while ago you were saying that Peter would be happy that Goro had come back. So you're no different from the gang that's lying in wait to try to kill Peter! And what you're doing right now is creating an alibi for yourself, so that after Peter's been murdered, you can say, 'Oh, no, *I* was against it, but the young warriors just pushed me aside and ignored my warnings.' And you're trying to use us as witnesses for your self-serving alibi!"

Daio turned his head and looked at Kogito straight on, with a troubled expression. "No," he said, "I was truly glad that Goro decided to come back, and . . . just like the plan we made in the beginning, I hope that Peter won't have to take out his pistol and that he'll be able to enjoy his reunion with Goro. All I want is for him to leave ten broken rifles for us when he goes home.

"Just like yesterday, I've heated up the bath, and I'm having another feast prepared—today some of the young warriors butchered a cow, just for the occasion—and that's as far as it's gone. Beyond that, if Peter and Goro find themselves on the same wavelength and decide that they want to get together, we've already gotten a bedroom ready for the two of them, just in case.

"My plan is essentially a peaceful one. If everything goes well, we'll send Peter home with his desires satisfied. And if he leaves behind ten broken rifles for us, that's when we'll begin to set our plan in motion so we can go out in a blaze of glory, like true sons of Japan."

As Kogito was standing up he saw Daio glancing in his direction, and he suddenly kicked out wildly and hit the older man under the right eye. Daio tumbled from the sofa onto the floor with a loud crash, so easily that Kogito wondered whether he had fallen on purpose for dramatic effect. This impression was confirmed when Daio continued lying flat on the ground, fumbling around halfheartedly with his one remaining arm as he tried (though not very hard) to raise his torso to a sitting position.

Goro jumped to his feet. "Kogito," he scolded, "why do you always have to lose your temper? What's the point of doing something stupid like that?"

Evidently thinking that Kogito might aim another kick at the back of Daio's head or his side while the one-armed man was lying defenseless on the floor, Goro stood in "ready" position, clearly determined to stop his headstrong friend from doing any more damage. The truth was, seeing Daio in that pitiful state, feebly groping around—almost as if he was deliberately trying to exaggerate his own weakness and vulnerability— caused a new wave of anger to blaze up in Kogito. But Goro had put one arm around Kogito's shoulder and was propelling him toward the exit, and Kogito had no intention of defying his friend's wishes.

Kogito and Goro, who were both feeling as dispirited as if they had lost the confrontation with Daio (or, at least, as if they hadn't won), squatted down at the top of the tall steps at the entrance to the main building and put on their shoes. Then they set off walking toward the wide, sloping meadow, where the bright green grass was waving in the wind.

6

The sky was clear, and both the lush, grassy meadow and the deciduous forest on the other side of the valley (with a heavy cliff looming precariously above) were bathed in a diluted yellowish light, even though it wasn't yet dusk. The wind that was blowing up from the river was unseasonably chilly.

About halfway down the incline, some freshly cut timber from the periodic thinning of the forest (each log was about the diameter of a clenched fist) had been assembled into a sort of rack that resembled an oversized sawhorse. Goro and Kogito walked up to the odd-looking apparatus. Gingerly, the two of them clambered onto it—buttocks resting on the topmost crosspiece, feet supported by the lowest one—and gazed down the slope.

"Come on, Goro, let's just go home," Kogito pleaded.

"Why? Isn't this an exciting adventure?"

"I just think it's stupid to be curious about that sort of thing."

"Hmm," Goro said facetiously, pretending to address his remarks to an invisible third person. "Exactly what does Kogito mean by 'that sort of thing,' I wonder?"

"Well, then," Kogito shot back, "what *I* wonder is, why do you want to stay?"

"Because Peter's a friend, and he's risking his life by coming back here. He has absolutely nothing to gain from that, you know."

"It's only because he heard that you were going to come back today."

"In that case, it'll be even worse if I'm not here when he returns."

"Worse for whom?"

"For Peter, of course. But also for my self-respect. I don't like to play bait and switch."

"So you're going to offer yourself up as a sacrifice?"

"Don't worry, I won't do anything I don't want to do."

"What if you end up being forced at gunpoint?" As he said that, Kogito felt that he was being terribly childish and melodramatic.

"Even if there's a gun pointing at me, I still won't do it. Like I said, if I don't want to do something . . . ," Goro repeated.

"But there's no need to get yourself backed into a corner where you have to make that kind of choice, is there? 'Cause there's someone waiting to give us a ride back to Matsuyama in the three-wheeled truck, right now."

"Yeah, and they'll probably let you pass through to the place where the three-wheeled truck is parked—after all, this secret hideout was built by your father's followers. But do you really think they would let me cross the bridge so easily?"

Kogito's attention was suddenly drawn toward the lower right-hand corner of the slope, at the foot of the suspension bridge. There, a crowd of Daio's disciples—the young warriors,

as he liked to call them—was milling about. While Kogito and
Goro had been batting these short sentences back and forth, a
fair amount of time had elapsed. From a distance, it was impossible to read the expressions on the faces of the young men,
but it was clear that they were very busy doing something at
the bottom of the hill.

What bothered Kogito right away was the way the group
was moving. He could see a certain aggressive, overstated swag-
ger in their physical movements and gestures, which was typical of people from around here when they'd had too much to
drink. During the party the night before, as far as Kogito could
see, none of the young disciples had been partaking of the free-
flowing home-brewed sake. But according to Daio's account,
the party had gotten quite wild toward the end, after Kogito and
Goro had snuck off.

Whether the young warriors were making up for their previous abstemiousness or going the hair-of-the-dog route, they
must have started drinking well before dusk today (probably
right after their unpleasant confrontation with Daio), passing
around high-octane *doburoku* that had been decanted into giant-
sized beer bottles or something like that. And then there was
Daio, too, guzzling moonshine nonstop, all by himself. It seemed
likely that both sides were drinking as a distraction from everything that was weighing on their minds. What if everyone at
the training camp had decided to get rip-roaring drunk? That
prospect made Kogito feel distinctly uneasy.

At the bottom of the lower part of the slope, on the left
side, there was a thicket of leafy, luxuriant shrubbery covered
with reddish-brown buds. While Kogito watched, five or six
young disciples, who had apparently been engaged in some sort

of clandestine activity in the thicket, suddenly burst out of the bushes and began working in plain sight. First they would fill large, deep buckets with something, and then, as if setting out to walk down to the river, they would dump the contents of the buckets into the water, which wasn't visible from the top of the slope. There were also some large, bulky items, too big to fit into the buckets, which they carried to the edge of the cliff and flung into the river far below.

From the other side of the thicket, two black dogs sprang out in a frenzy of excitement. The dogs started eagerly jumping up on the young men, who were cleaning out the emptied buckets with wads of fresh-picked grass, but they were soon driven off. The hounds ran away at top speed along a road that couldn't be seen from the top of the slope, then dashed down the hill into the deep valley.

By and by Kogito noticed that several young disciples— the number seemed to have increased—were climbing up the slope, each lugging a bucket that had obviously been refilled with something. Behind them marched two strapping young men, carrying what looked like a messy, rolled-up carpet with jagged edges on their broad shoulders. As they drew closer, it gradually became evident that the men were extremely dirty— not only their upper torsos but their heads and faces, as well. It was also obvious from the way they lurched along that they were more than a little intoxicated.

The men were walking with exaggerated slowness, but soon enough they sidled up next to the sawhorse where Goro and Kogito were sitting, in the manner of innocent pedestrians who just happened to be passing by. Kogito realized then that the stuff in the buckets they were carrying was the flesh and internal organs of the slaughtered calf Daio had mentioned earlier in connection with the feast, and that the unwieldy ruglike object was that animal's pelt, although it was so massive that it looked more like the skin of a full-grown cow. The young men who were toting these gruesome burdens, whether by hand or on their shoulders, were grinning wordlessly and clearly feeling no pain. They looked like the grown-up versions of country children who have come to town for a festival parade, but Kogito had no idea what they were planning to do.

After a while one of the young acolytes, who seemed to be the most popular member of the group, put down the largest bucket as if it didn't weigh a thing and called out to Kogito and Goro, not addressing either one in particular: "Oh, that's the life! I guess it pays to be a pretty boy." After a moment's silence, Goro responded in a tranquil voice. "What are you talking about?" he asked mildly, but his response had an element of condescension, as if he wasn't taking the young men very seriously.

"This is what I'm talking about," the young warrior sneered. "Here we are, slaving away, doing menial labor and getting covered with all this disgusting blood and grease, and we aren't allowed to go to the bathhouse to get cleaned up. So after we deliver these heavy buckets to the old guy in the kitchen, we have to trudge back down to the valley, and then we have to wash ourselves off in the cold river, with the dogs right next to us, gobbling up the filthy offal. But it's a very different story for you two, isn't it? You have nothing to do but take refreshing hot-spring baths, and eat and drink till you're full. And after you've carefully washed everything, right down to your assholes, it's

'Wondafuu, sankyuu beriberi maachi,' am I right?" The next-to-last phrase was rendered, with maximum contempt, in phonetic English.

The young warriors, including the one who had just delivered this diatribe, burst out laughing, but there was something childish about their merriment. It seemed to have an edge of hostility, yet beneath the alcohol-fueled bravado there was a vestigial element of bashfulness, as well. The truculent remarks and derisive laughter gave Kogito a disheartening sense of the mean-spiritedness of his countrymen. He was shaking with anger and nervous tension, but Goro showed no signs of losing his cool. Finally, unable to control his temper, Kogito lashed out.

"Hey, if that's your lot in life, then just go ahead and wash off your dirt with the dogs! Why are you hanging around here, looking like you want something? You're just adding to your hardships by putting down those heavy loads and then picking them up again and loitering around where you aren't welcome."

At this, the young men erupted in uproarious laughter. Kogito had a feeling that they were laughing because in his excitement he had spoken to them in their own dialect, and that made him even angrier. What a bunch of mean-spirited jerks! He felt somehow ashamed of the young men—and, by extension, of himself, too, since they were all from the same place—and he felt embarrassed about subjecting Goro to such an unpleasant experience. The two men who were carrying the roughly rolled-up, raw calf pelt were laughing along with the others, but they appeared to be up to something else as well. They passed right by Kogito and Goro, then stopped, ominously.

"Yeah, it's a rough life, all right," one of them retorted. "But the main problem now is that the drying rack we need for our dirty work is being occupied by your pristine little asses!" And then in one quick movement the young warriors unfurled the large blood-soaked pelt they were carrying and dumped it right onto Kogito's and Goro's heads.

Teetering atop the high, rickety platform, the two boys were enveloped in a lukewarm, bloody-smelling, disorienting darkness as they struggled to keep their balance so they wouldn't go crashing to the ground. Their arms were pinned at their sides, and their attempts to kick the fetid calfskin off with their legs were woefully ineffectual. And as if from the other side of a thick wall, a great wave of laughter kept washing over them—now close, now far away. *A hard night! Dried blood smokes on my face, and nothing lies behind me but that repulsive little tree!*

Kogito had only a vague memory of what transpired immediately after he and Goro finally managed to extricate themselves from underneath the bloody calfskin, but that scene was set down with perfect clarity in the screenplay.

KOGITO: Come on, let's cross the bridge and get out of here.

GORO: But we're totally filthy. Even if we do decide to leave, I'm going to get cleaned up first.

In the gathering dusk, the two of them are surrounded by the young warriors, who are still laughing loudly about their prank.

GORO (*ignoring the young men*): Seriously, I need to go wash up. My shirt and trousers are dirty, too, so I need to rinse them out, as well. If I leave them like this, I won't be able to put them on again.

The young men are still falling down with laughter. They crane their necks, not wanting to miss a word of this exchange between their victims.

KOGITO (*more and more annoyed*): Well, I'm going home.

With that, he starts walking down the slope, but when he glances back, Goro isn't following. Kogito runs down the slope, gravity and momentum carrying him along so quickly that he stumbles from time to time. From the point of view of Goro, watching Kogito go, the camera traverses the gradually widening meadow, then takes in the entire scene as night begins to fall. Mist wells up from the bottom of the deep valley.

Encountering no resistance from the young warriors, Kogito makes his way across the unstable suspension bridge. In the opposite corner of the meadow the thick, dense tangle of shrubbery looms deep and black. Before long, in the depths of the picture plane, the three-wheeled truck can be seen intermittently through the trees as it starts to drive away from the elevated area where it was parked.

MUSIC: *Akari Choko's composition, "Sadness No. 2" (two minutes, ten seconds), can probably be used exactly as is.*

This has been mentioned before, but all the scenes that Goro incorporated into this screenplay were things he had actually experienced or observed. His scrupulous use of documentary technique was evident even in his first successful movie, *The Funeral*. If this screenplay had ended up actually being made into a film, then Goro's filmmaking career would have probably come full circle, ending as it began.

After the departure scene, of course, what happened to Kogito was out of Goro's line of sight. Kogito chose to re-create this part of the story—in other words, the part that Goro didn't write—using the novelist's techniques that had become second nature to him, rather than continuing in the screenplay format.

When Kogito crossed the suspension bridge and climbed up to the highway, the young man who was waiting next to the three-wheeled truck climbed into the saddle (that is, the motorcycle-style driver's seat) and started the engine without a moment's hesitation, as if he had known all along that Kogito was going to turn up alone. Kogito hopped into the empty cargo space and grabbed hold of the metal framework of the canopy that covered the driver's seat.

The film that Goro would have made, if he had been using the type of telescopic lens that can capture images even when there isn't much natural light, would probably have shown a pitiful-looking schoolboy standing on the platform of the three-wheeled truck, holding on with both hands while stoically enduring the pitching and rolling of the flimsy vehicle. One minute we see him through a gap in some sparsely leafed-out trees, the next minute he disappears, then we catch another glimpse, and so on . . .

After the three-wheeled truck carrying Kogito and the driver had been on the road for about twenty minutes, it came to a place about halfway to the three-road junction next to the tunnel. There, Kogito caught sight of the lights of a car descending from above. The three-wheeled truck pulled into a clearing where lumber from the forest was prepared for shipping, in order to let the oncoming car pass by on the narrow mountain road. But the vehicle that was advancing toward them turned out to be the big green Cadillac, with Peter at the wheel.

As the king-sized car approached, illuminating the road ahead with its powerful headlights, Kogito had the strange feeling that they were about to be stopped by the police and roughly frisked, just like in the movies. The Cadillac braked next to the three-wheeled truck, which had pulled over to the side of the road to avoid a collision. Kogito could tell that Peter was sticking his head out of the window, but it was already so dark that he couldn't make out the expression on the American's face. He imagined that Peter's eyes were probably searching both sides of the driver and the luggage platform behind the spot where Kogito was standing.

And then, sure enough: "What are you doing here?" Peter demanded. "Where's Goro?" Kogito raised his right arm and pointed with a grand, sweeping gesture toward some far-off place behind them. He had a feeling that he was imitating the unseemly American habit of gesticulating in a broad, exaggerated manner, but he didn't care. Peter got the message and promptly blasted off again in the Cadillac.

When the three-wheeled truck pulled back onto the road, the strong, sharp wind that had suddenly come up blew painfully into Kogito's eyes, and he began to cry. Although it was the stinging wind that had started the initial flow of tears, he went on weeping out of concern for Goro's welfare. And he had to admit, if only to himself, that the anger he felt at having been so rudely ignored by Peter was a factor as well.

After the truck had sputtered to a stop beside the trifurcated junction at the entrance to the near side of the tunnel, Kogito jumped off onto the edge of a field that was littered with clumps of straw and other detritus from the previous year's harvest. "This'll be fine, right here," Kogito called in the direction of the driver's cab. The young driver didn't reply, but after Kogito had clambered up what turned out to be a rather steep incline to the highest elevation of the tiered fields, he looked back and saw that the driver had parked the truck in a small space on the side of the road along the valley and had gone around behind and let down the tailgate of the luggage platform. He was perched there now, with the air of someone hunkering down for the duration.

Kogito, too, sat down on a ridge between two fields and gazed into the distance beyond the deep, dark valley. There was still some indigo light around the margins of the mountains that were stacked up on the horizon, but the sky was an intense, tawny yellow ocher. Even as he was gazing at that vista, the world abruptly went so completely dark that he actually found himself wondering whether the faint brightness of a moment before had been some sort of illusion.

And then, after nearly two hours had passed, Goro came marching briskly along, through a darkness so dense that the road was barely distinguishable from the trees that lined it on both sides. Kogito went rushing eagerly down the hill, slipping and sliding on the loose soil, but Goro barely glanced in his direction, and he didn't say a word to Kogito before heading for the three-wheeled truck, which was silhouetted against the dark hillside, suffused in the ambient light from the tunnel entrance.

"So where shall we go now?" Kogito called out. He was trying to emulate Goro's cool demeanor, but even to his own ears, his voice sounded angry, repressed, and immature.

"There's nowhere to go except back to Shindate, is there?" Goro said. (That was the section of Matsuyama where he and Chikashi rented lodgings in a temple compound.)

"Isn't Peter going to come after you?"

Silently, Goro turned his dark face toward Kogito, and— Kogito never forgot this—only the backlit rims of his ears were glowing gold.

When the three-wheeled truck finally pulled up beside the mud-brick wall that surrounded the temple grounds, it was already the middle of the night, but Goro called out at the entrance to the subtemple, loudly enough to awaken Chikashi. Goro and Kogito went around behind the building, stripped off their clothes, and washed themselves all over. Chikashi laid two bath towels and two sets of underwear out on the verandah, then disappeared.

When Kogito and Goro had finished dressing and had gone into the temple, Chikashi appeared to be already asleep, cocooned in a futon spread out in front of the household altar (which she had claimed as her own little domain), with the quilt pulled up over her head. On one side, in a wider space, she had laid out two futons, side by side. Shivering with cold and exhaustion, the two schoolboys lay down without exchanging a single word. They had passed the entire two-hour ride on the luggage platform of the three-wheeled truck in silence, as well.

As has already been pointed out, more than once, the films that Goro made arose directly out of his own experiences and observations, so it's a contradiction, by definition, to say that in this case Goro left behind two completely separate—and very different—versions of the most important scene in the entire screenplay: the ending. There was no way for Kogito to determine which was the true account of what actually happened, since he wasn't there. Simply put, the two scenes suggest what might have happened after Kogito left the training camp in the three-wheeled truck. The first version, rendered in screenplay form with storyboard illustrations attached, goes like this:

> *Goro is sitting on the dark stone staircase in front of the entrance to the outbuilding that's attached to the bathhouse. He is waiting for something. He has apparently been sitting there for quite some time, and he looks annoyed. The young disciples can be seen coming up the hill from the lower right-hand corner of the meadow, crowding around*

*Peter in an amicable way. They head toward the training
hall. Goro jumps to his feet with a decisive air and starts to
return to the road that leads to the main office. Suddenly
Daio appears before Goro, blocking his way. Daio is accompanied by two young girls and two boys. We have never seen
any of them before.*

DAIO: Good grief, Goro, you're really a mess! (*In stark contrast with the almost autistic blackness of his earlier
drunken mood, he has regained his usual good humor,
but for once it doesn't go too far, to the point of buffoonish rudeness.*)

*Meanwhile, the boys and girls are making no attempt to
conceal their forthright reactions to Goro's filthy, disheveled
appearance. The youngsters seem to be ignorant and unworldly, and they stare at Goro with undisguised contempt.
After pointing out the path to the bathhouse and telling the
four young visitors to go ahead, Daio offers Goro an ostensibly apologetic explanation, but he is clearly giving him the
brush-off.*

DAIO: Oh, I'll bet you came to get the bathhouse key yourself, because I didn't give it to you before. The thing is,
the situation has changed. We can't have you using the
bathing facilities in that state—that would be a major disaster. We may call it a hot-spring bath, but it's only designed to heat the hot water for a short time, and it's a
major undertaking to replace all the water in the tub if
any dirt or grease gets in. Let's leave it this way: if Peter
turns up and says that he wants to be with Goro, and no

one else will do, then we'll cross that bridge when we come to it. Till then, please wait in the office. Help yourself to *doburoku*, if you like.

Interior of a dark room. Goro is sitting on a wooden chair, seemingly lost in thought. (He probably hesitated to sit on the couch because he's still covered with blood and grease from the slaughtered calf.) Just then, Daio barges in unceremoniously, picks up the two-quart bottle from the floor, and fills a teacup with home-brewed sake. He quaffs the doburoku *in a single gulp. No traces remain of the stormy expression he wore earlier, but his high spirits have an edge of malice, and he comes across as a country trickster who can't be trusted for a minute.*

DAIO: Like the old proverb says, "The waiting is often the hardest part." As it turns out, Peter seems to be quite taken with both the boys and the girls. Just peeping from the ceiling overhead was more than I could bear, and I ended up going down to the bath to join the happy little group! Choko Sensei was truly a man of foresight, wasn't he!

Daio seems to be babbling incomprehensible nonsense. Goro is thrown into confusion and makes no attempt to reply.

DAIO (*dropping all pretense of politeness and not even bothering to address Goro by name*): Listen, why don't you just run along home? The only problem is, if you head down the hill now, you'll probably get roughed up pretty good by the young warriors. But if you go out the back of the office and follow the forestry road, you'll come upon a narrow mountain stream just before you go into the depths

depths of the forest. Go downhill along that stream, and you'll come to a river that runs parallel to the road. The dogs are probably still there, rooting around for the filthy remains of the dead beast. As long as you don't disturb them at their work, you should be able to climb up onto the road without getting mauled!

Goro climbs through the shady grove of trees as fast as his legs will carry him, then plunges toward the river in total darkness, looking extremely distressed.

Now, here's the second version of that scene in the screenplay, with storyboards attached.

Goro is in the washing area of the bathhouse, sitting on a stool with his already hand-laundered shirt and trousers in a soggy pile next to him. Thoroughly and meticulously, he's washing his hands and feet. He hears something going on outside. Goro stands up and peers out the window. His face is in profile, looking lonely and puzzled. We switch to another camera and see Peter running up the sloping meadow. The young disciples are racing after him; it almost looks as if they're playing a game of tag. Then Peter stops abruptly, turns, and aims his pistol at them. The young men throw themselves to the ground, facedown. Peter starts to run up the hill again. The young men get up and pursue him. Peter stops and points his gun at them. The same action is repeated over and over. By and by, instead of just pantomiming, Peter really does fire the pistol. There is an unexpectedly loud report, and the young warriors stay where they are, lying facedown in the grass. After a moment Peter appears in the bathroom, holding his pistol and looking triumphant.

GORO (*standing there naked but clearly unintimidated*): Are you planning to try to make me do something at gunpoint?

PETER (*gently, almost deferentially*): I would never do anything like that, dear Goro!

Goro is in the bathtub now, and Peter stands in front of him, his pale white body totally naked, no longer holding the pistol. There is the sound of the bathroom door being broken down. In a flash, a group of young disciples comes storming in, completely filling the room. They seize Peter and run down the sloping meadow, with the naked American held above their heads by a forest of arms, as if he were a sacred palanquin in a Shinto festival procession. One of the young men stumbles. This causes the mass of bodies to surge forward; Peter is thrown clear and lands on the ground. Peter, obviously weak with exhaustion, is once again hoisted over the heads of the young disciples; once again they begin to run, and once more the whole group collapses and Peter spills onto the ground. With each repetition, the game seems to be degenerating further, from rough horseplay into ever more barbaric violence. Finally, the entire group runs into the thicket and disappears from sight. After a brief moment, there's a hoarse, inarticulate scream that shades into an agonized wail. Goro has thrown on his soggy shirt and trousers, and he starts to walk down the slope, through the dark, silent, deserted meadow. There isn't another soul in sight.

When Kogito had finished reading the screenplay and the storyboards that went with it, and was putting everything back into the reddish-amber leather briefcase, Chikashi asked him a question that had evidently been germinating for quite some time.

"When you two were washing up behind the temple, I seem to remember that Goro was very dirty, too. Or is it possible that was just travel dust and sweat? Besides that, the thing that strikes me as strange is that from then on I never saw you and Goro together. Remember, my mother heard that you had gotten into Tokyo University, and she thought that you would have more free time now that your entrance exams were over, and so she asked you to look for some books for us at the used-book stores in Kanda? I wonder . . . up until that time, wasn't your friendship with Goro on a sort of hiatus?"

Chikashi's surmise was exactly right. But not long after THAT, when she had already moved to Ashiya (the fashionable suburb of Kyoto where their mother was living with her new husband), leaving Goro behind at the "Little Temple" lodgings, alone, Kogito did go again to visit him there just once, late at night.

It was the twenty-eighth of April of that year, the date of Daio's planned suicide attack on the American army base. For an entire hour, starting at 10:30 PM, Kogito and Goro sat silently in front of the radio, which was tuned to NHK. But there were no breaking stories, no news bulletins, no reports of anything out of the ordinary. After they had waited another hour, just in case, Goro concluded that nothing untoward had taken place after all. Then he suggested that he take a photograph of Kogito, as a memento, with his new Nikon camera—a gift from his equally new stepfather.

During the year Goro had spent giving Kogito French lessons, he had used bits of paper in lieu of a blackboard to write out and explain various texts, and he had a vast store of such scraps, as well as those on which Kogito had scribbled his own tentative translations of the passages in question. Goro got the idea of arranging some of the motley pages around a mirror, then taking a photograph of Kogito's profile, composed in such a way that his face was framed by sheaves of French translation and reflected in the mirror. By the time he finished, it was close to dawn.

When Kogito suggested that he take Goro's photo, in turn, Goro refused.

"I'll pass," he said. "I think I'm going to make my living with motion pictures, but since you'll probably end up working with a fountain pen instead of a camera, I'd rather have you immortalize me with words."

Outside Over There

1

While Chikashi was unpacking the large trunk that Kogito had used for his trip to Berlin, she came across two books that struck her as somewhat unusual. Whenever Kogito was in a foreign country—and especially when he was teaching at a university there—he always ended up buying a great many books. Because he didn't read German, he hadn't bought as many volumes as usual during his recent stay in Berlin, but even so, he had mailed home more than twenty boxes of books.

Whenever he returned from an overseas sojourn, Kogito's trunk usually contained notes for manuscripts, assorted suits and shirts, underwear, fountain pens, spare eyeglasses, and so on. As a rule, the only books packed among these quotidian necessities were several indispensable dictionaries. This time, though, Kogito had tucked two slim paperbacks between the suits in his trunk.

One was called *Outside Over There*. The author was Maurice Sendak, but this book had a very different feeling from the Sendak picture books Chikashi had read in the past. The

second stowaway was a privately published, not-for-sale booklet titled *Changelings,* whose cover was adorned in the familiar
Sendak style with minutely detailed portrayals of beguiling
monsters. That booklet was the record of a seminar that was held
at a research institute on the University of California's Berkeley
campus, and it bore the bylines of three prominent literary scholars and Maurice Sendak himself. Kogito was friendly with one
of those academics, who (Chikashi surmised) had probably
given her husband the booklet as a commemorative gift when
the two men happened to meet again at the Center for Advanced Research in Berlin. As she learned later, that was exactly what had happened.

Still only mildly curious, Chikashi opened the picture
book. When she saw the illustration on the opening spread, she
felt an uncanny jolt of recognition, and after taking a closer look
at the cover she found herself completely captivated. In this
state of enchantment, Chikashi read the picture book through
to the end, but when she had finished she felt oddly glum and
dispirited. After moping about in that state for a while, she had
an epiphany: "This girl in the book, this Ida—she's me!"

As she turned the pages again and again, Chikashi began
to realize what it was about the illustrations of the heroine,
before the narrative even commenced, that had excited her so
profoundly. It was the bare feet sticking out from under the hem
of the girl's long dress—they were the focal point of the entire
picture! The only parts of Ida's body that weren't covered by a
pale sky-colored dress were her head (long hair held back by a
matching blue headband), her neck (encircled by white frills),
her hands, and those extraordinary feet sticking out beneath
her long skirt's ruffled hem.

For one thing, they were of a size and a sturdiness not usually seen in the feet of a young girl, and the incongruous juxtaposition of the feet of a grown woman with the hem of that childish frock may have made them appear even larger and sturdier than they really were. The supple-looking calf muscles tapered down into the thick ankle bones that supported them, and the Achilles tendons looked particularly tough and strong. The toes were firmly planted on the ground, while the heels, their flesh as pale and elastic as *mochi* rice cakes, provided a stable foundation for the entire body.

When she tried comparing the feet of the girl, Ida, with those of the other characters in the book, Chikashi discovered that the mother was wearing small, flat-heeled shoes, like ballet slippers, and all that could be seen of her feet was a pale glimpse of her delicately modeled instep. The baby's feet were just that—typical infant feet—and even the fearsome goblins who snatched Ida's baby sister and fled through the open window had small, chubby, unformed-looking feet. (A goblin, Chikashi learned when she consulted a dictionary, is "a kind of small elf, in the shape of a miniature person, who derives pleasure from perpetrating cruel mischief on human beings.")

There was, Chikashi knew, a very clear-cut reason why she couldn't take her eyes off the preternaturally sturdy feet of the heroine of *Outside Over There*. She was just about to glance down at her own feet when something made her hesitate. Instead, she went into her bedroom and began rummaging through the piles of books and sketch pads that were stacked against one wall, looking for one thing in particular.

Before the war, there had been a period during which her filmmaker father had become consumed with a passion for still photography, after receiving a Leica as a gift from a German director with whom he'd collaborated on a movie project. When her father died, he had left behind two albums full of positive contact sheets, glued edge to edge on every page. Chikashi dug out the albums and found the snapshot she was looking for.

It showed her as a young girl, caught in the act of clambering up a big oak tree of some sort, possibly a Japanese emperor oak. In spite of the daredevil pose, the young Chikashi's face had a look of rather precocious maturity. Judging from the size of Goro, who was standing next to the tree, Chikashi deduced that she must have been five or six years old when the picture was taken. That seemed to provide a clue about the age of the girl in the picture book, who wore a similarly grown-up expression. But the important thing was that Chikashi's own bare feet, clearly visible as she hung upside down from the crotch of the tall tree with legs akimbo, looked exactly like the feet of the girl in the Sendak book.

2

From the very first page, it's clear that *Outside Over There* is going to tell the story of what happened while Papa was away at sea. Mama stands on the shore, dressed in a bonnet and a voluminous floor-length gown; it covers her so completely we can see only her left hand, which is fluttering languidly in the direction of a sailing ship that can be seen heading out to sea from an idyllic cove. Next to her stands Ida, holding a momentarily calm, well-behaved baby. Its distinctive little face is turned in our direction, eyes presciently angled toward the left-hand corner, where the goblins are lurking. Ida's powerful feet are planted firmly on a large boulder; clearly she, too, has come to see her father off on his voyage.

On the page across from this sweet family tableau, two ominous-looking characters are skulking in the left-hand corner, watching the ship's departure. Their heads and bodies are completely hidden by large, hooded brown cloaks, and they're sitting in a small rowboat that has been pulled up to the shore. Next to them, significantly, is a wooden ladder.

In the large illustration that dominates the following spread, Mama (as the text explains) has shed her bonnet and is sitting absentmindedly in the front garden in the shade of a lattice-work arbor with grapevines trailing over it. Later, Chikashi would hear from her husband that at the Berkeley seminar devoted to Sendak's work, the author himself revealed that the word *arbor* was forever linked in his mind with an important memory from childhood.

Ida is standing a short distance from where Mama sits ensconced in the arbor. She's still holding the baby, who is now bawling its eyes out. Ida's expression conveys a mixture of perplexity and resignation, and it is abundantly clear that she considers herself wholly responsible for the infant's care. Incidentally, while it is unmistakably a baby, Ida's sibling is startlingly large. Its head is nearly the same size as Ida's, and if it could stand up, it would probably be at least half as tall as its much older sister. Meanwhile, the pair of interlopers in their hooded cloaks can be seen cutting through the left-hand cor-ner of the scene, carrying the wooden ladder.

There was something in the very composition of that large double-truck illustration that seemed designed to arouse feel-ings of uneasiness, but the thing that Chikashi found especially strange was the large, realistically drawn German shepherd who sits in the middle of the scene. In her view, the dog didn't seem to have any relation to the story. Confused, Chikashi asked Kogito what he thought about this German shepherd, and that was when he first realized that she had more than a casual in-terest in the work of Maurice Sendak.

Kogito presumably had his own reasons for slipping those two books into his trunk, but he chose to overlook the fact that

Chikashi had carried them off to her bedroom and was now monopolizing them. What's more, he even found some additional books about Sendak among those that had been delivered to the house since his return, and took them down to the living room.

Apparently the Lindbergh kidnapping case had made a deep impression on Sendak's psyche when he was a child, and, as Kogito explained, this picture book was inspired by those memories. On the first page (where the dedication appears), the baby who's gazing toward us, as if to introduce itself, has the face of the Lindberghs' beloved child. The Lindbergh house was equipped with a splendid German shepherd watchdog, but even though the family was thus protected, their child was still stolen away. "What if some kidnapper decided to snatch a child of impoverished immigrants, like me?" the young Sendak thought. "There's no way I could escape!" That's the story the author told at the seminar.

But what bothered Chikashi was a technical detail. Why, she wondered, in such a fancifully illustrated book, was the German shepherd alone drawn in a superrealistic style? She simply couldn't figure it out. When she asked Kogito about this he went to his study and, returning with a recently published folio book of color and black-and-white photographs, showed her one of Sendak walking his German shepherd. Perhaps, Kogito theorized, the reason the dog looked so much more realistic than the other characters was because the artist had a real-life model close at hand.

There was another aspect of the picture book that had engraved itself on Chikashi's mind, but she didn't mention that one to Kogito. *No question about it,* she thought with absolute certainty. *The mama in this book is just like my mother!*

She was right: Chikashi's mother really was a person who often wore a vacant, abstracted expression—just like Ida's mama, sunk in a despondent reverie under the shade of a tree. The text of the picture book didn't explain why Papa's departure on a sea voyage had plunged Mama into such a deep abyss of dejection, but the beautiful illustrations made it amply clear that this woman was in seriously low spirits, with no relief in sight.

Ida has no way of knowing the cause of that condition (though an adult reader might be tempted to diagnose postpartum depression), but she seems resigned to the fact that her mother spends a good deal of time in a doleful daze beneath the trees, and that's just the way it is. Ida has taken over the baby's care, and even if some difficulty should arise, she wouldn't dream of turning to her obviously ineffectual mother for assistance. And then, something really *does* happen.

Back in the house, Ida is trying to mollify the fretful baby by playing her French horn. Before long she is so completely caught up in the music that she becomes oblivious to what's going on around her. Facing a window that frames a bevy of gigantic, blooming sunflowers, Ida plays her horn with tremendous verve, and the baby, too, seems enraptured by the music. Just then, two interlopers appear; all we can see of them is dark shadows in hooded coats, climbing up a ladder from a window in the background.

The goblins grab the baby, who is so surprised that no sound comes out when it tries to scream, and they spirit it off through the window. In the kidnapped infant's place they leave a substitute: a grotesque, grayish-white, bug-eyed replica made from ice. Poor Ida, not knowing what has happened, picks up the changeling—for that is the subject of Sendak's picture book, according to the discussion that took place at the Berkeley seminar—and holds it close. And then she murmurs, "Oh, how I do love you!" As she places her cheek on the floppy yellow cap the baby always wears, Ida is lost in her own reverie, and she doesn't realize that what she's holding in her arms is an expressionless little monster made of ice.

The sunflower-filled window through which the goblins made their escape changes into a sort of video screen that shows a scene from a distant place, and we see a sailing vessel pitching and rolling as it tries to navigate a suddenly storm-tossed sea. On this page, the sunflowers peeking in through the window (on whose sill Ida has left her horn) seem to be aggressively encroaching and increasing in both size and number, while their ever more fecund leaves run wild. This scene gave Chikashi an impression so intense that it was close to pain. She wasn't able to explain in words why the sunflowers seemed to be somehow synergistic with Ida's emotions, but she felt she understood it well enough from an artistic point of view.

There's Ida, down on her knees hugging the ice baby, with what might have been a look of remorse or regret on her face, even though she hasn't yet realized that the baby she is holding is a changeling. That's what Chikashi was thinking, anyway. Wasn't that because while she was playing her horn, she became completely free on a soul-deep level? Maybe losing herself in playing the horn was the equivalent, for Ida, of wishing that the baby had never been born or at least that it would go away and leave her in peace.

Chikashi had a visceral memory of having experienced exactly that sort of remorseful regret herself. As a baby and also as a young girl, she'd had a swarthy face, like the dark brown seed of a persimmon. Goro, on the other hand, had been such an angelically beautiful child that even his sister felt proud to be from the same family. But deep down, Chikashi would naturally have been feeling something more complicated than pride in her extraordinary sibling. Even though she didn't share Goro's intense interest in psychology, Chikashi knew there were children who wished that the baby who came after them (whether it was a brother or a sister) had never been born—or, once born, would just go away. But Chikashi always felt, strangely, that Goro wasn't really her younger brother, even though she was born before him. On the contrary, he seemed more like an older brother whose rights she was violating by appearing on the scene. She wasn't yet three when it really hit Chikashi that in relation to her charismatic younger brother, she was like someone who had tried to seize power from a rival and had totally botched the job.

Ida, though, realized very soon what had happened. The changeling was beginning to drip and melt, and all it did was stare at the floor. According to the narrative, when Ida figured out what the goblins had done she became terribly angry. While the hideous changeling was rapidly melting into a puddle on the floor, its head drooping ever lower, Ida showed her anger by shaking her fist at the window.

Meanwhile (the story continues), beyond that open window we see a stormy sea, and as lightning flashes, the white-sailed tall ship runs aground and its shattered mast slowly sinks beneath the waves. Galvanized by determination, Ida stands with her outsized feet planted firmly on the floor, while the eerily expressive crowd of sunflowers peers through the window like a throng of inquisitive faces. "They stole my sister away to be a nasty goblin's bride!" Ida cries, and the text on that page ends with "Now Ida in a hurry . . ."

Once again, Chikashi was startled. So the baby—which, until then, she had assumed was male—was a girl? But what a cruel and tragic fate, to be forced to marry a nasty goblin!

On the next page, the reason for Ida's haste becomes clear. She was in a hurry to go and fetch her mother's luminous, yellowish-gold rain cloak, which is evidently endowed with some sort of magical properties. After wrapping herself in the commodious rain cloak and shoving her horn into one large pocket, Ida makes what the text calls a "serious mistake."

She goes and jumps—or rather, falls—out of the window *backwards*! The illustration shows Ida wafting through the air faceup with her legs and arms extended in front of her, as if she were floating on her back in the ocean. And there she goes, bundled up in her mother's sunflower-yellow rain cloak, flying upside down against the backdrop of a sky that's just beginning to clear. (The moon is even visible, emerging from behind a charcoal-gray cloud.) In the distance, in the lower part of the scene, we see the goblins in their seaside hideout, along with a red ladder, a small boat, and the kidnapped, none-too-happy baby.

Kogito explained this scene and the next with obvious relish, analyzing them in terms of myth and folktale: "The secret of life and death isn't in the bright heavens above; it's hidden in the subterranean darkness. That's why it's a mistake to fly looking up. You have to fly looking down or else you won't be able to observe the chthonic secrets."

Eventually Ida hears her father singing a song. The lyrics explain, helpfully, that she needs to turn around and head in

the right direction, instead of flying "backwards in the rain."
After heeding this advice, Ida eventually manages to infiltrate
the grottolike den of the shape-shifting goblins. But everyone
there has more or less the same face and form as her kidnapped
baby sister, so how is she supposed to find the real human child
amid this crowd of tiny doppelgängers?

Putting her heart and soul into it, Ida starts to play her horn.
The babies begin to walk toward the water, dancing all the while,
but this is no simple, innocuous promenade. Soon, all the goblins begin to feel so unwell that they want desperately to lie down
and rest, but they can't stop moving—not as long as Ida keeps
playing "a frenzied jig, a hornpipe that makes sailors wild beneath
the ocean moon"! The dancing goblins are obviously suffering,
but Ida is fiercely determined. Striding forward with her large,
magnificent feet, she goes on relentlessly playing her horn.

On the next page, the goblin babies have strayed off into
the frothing water, presumably to drown, while Ida, having
accomplished her goal, stands on the shore looking calm and
poised, holding her horn in one hand as she checks for one last
time to make sure all the goblins are gone. And then, with a
rush of affection, Ida looks down at her little sister, who is sitting in the shell of a giant egg, stretching one chubby hand
toward her rescuer.

Now all they need to do is to find their way home. Carrying the baby, Ida is walking along a forest path that runs beside
a creek, while in a little summerhouse on the opposite shore,
who should be playing a pianoforte but Wolfgang Amadeus
Mozart, complete with powdered wig! As Chikashi gazes at this
scene, she shares Ida's evident sense of relief, but at the same
time an unresolved feeling is tugging at her heart.

There's probably nothing particularly strange, in a fantastic story like this, about having Mozart suddenly appear in a red-roofed house on the other side of the river, playing the piano. After all, Chikashi thought, here at home we, too, make Mozart's music part of our daily lives (just as Maurice Sendak does). But what was the meaning of the ominous-looking tree branches that seemed to be blocking the way as Ida headed for home with the baby in her arms—and what was the significance of the five creepy-looking butterflies that were flitting around?

Chikashi had a profound sense that this picture book was telling her a number of important things about her own life. She also realized that she needed to go on reading it over and over, concentrating on the details of the illustrations rather than on the text, in order to understand some crucial metaphors that were still unclear to her.

The more she read and reread this uncanny picture book, the more certain Chikashi felt that she was Ida, and Ida was herself. Chikashi had gone through a great many books since she first learned to read, but until now—and she was past fifty— she had never encountered a literary character with whom she identified so completely. Nevertheless, as she sat staring into space with the book on her lap after reading it for the umpteenth time, Chikashi couldn't help feeling that she must look very much like Ida's poor mama, who sat under the arbor for hours on end, lost in melancholy thought.

3

Chikashi's older brother was exceedingly good-looking, lavishly talented, and loved by many people—indeed, even when he was a child, people used to adore him with a sort of awestruck reverence. But from a certain time on, she felt that there was an unknowable part hidden inside of him, and he seemed to have turned into someone subtly different from the person he used to be. Even after that, he was still a brother Chikashi could be proud of, and she could always rely on him for kindness and moral support. But it had occurred to Chikashi more than once that this Goro wasn't the "real" Goro—and now, thanks to Sendak's book, she had learned a word that made it possible for her to accurately express for the first time what the other, different Goro was: a *changeling*.

After she and Kogito were married, while she was waiting for their first child to be born, Chikashi found herself thinking that this might be a chance to retrieve the real Goro. *In place of my own mother*, she thought, *I will try to give birth (or rebirth) to the beautiful child that was Goro. And then the Goro who dis-*

appeared will be brought into the world once again as a new baby.
And now, thanks to Sendak's picture book, she was finally able
to express this properly: If only she could have been as brave
and heroic as Ida and somehow brought Goro back . . .

Crazy as it sounded, Chikashi thought now that even if
she had never put it into those exact words, she had made up
her mind to do just that. But, she wondered, what role would
Kogito have played in her wild transubstantiation scheme?
Chikashi was unable to come up with an answer to that hypothetical question. She felt as if she were gazing at a mysterious
landscape that was forever enveloped in fog. Only, of course,
that perpetually misty landscape existed only in her mind. And
the mystery remained: *Why did I choose Kogito to be the father
of the child I wanted to bring into the world as a means of retriev-
ing the Goro who was taken away?*

When she thought back on it Chikashi realized that, for
her, Kogito had always been a person she could never fully
understand. In the beginning, she didn't perceive him as an
independent entity but just as one of Goro's sidekicks. After
she got the sense that Kogito was making an effort to do things
that would please Goro, Chikashi started to think of (and treat)
Kogito more warmly than any of Goro's other friends. *But then,*
Chikashi reflected, *when I began to talk about getting engaged
to Kogito, Goro was violently opposed. Ultimately, I did marry
Kogito, but I always felt that I didn't really understand what led
me to make that decision.*

But now, Chikashi thought, *an unexpected solution to that
mystery has floated to the surface, out of nowhere. When I tried
using the Sendak book as a clue, I realized that deep down in my
heart this is probably what I'd been feeling all along. Marrying*

this person, Kogito, was the same as flying out of the window at night in order to retrieve the real Goro. But maybe I made a mistake and jumped out the wrong way: faceup and backwards. The thing is, I had to fly out of the window at night in a hurry. And I couldn't afford to lose this person, this Kogito, because he was the last person who was with that beautiful Goro, before he was stolen away.

I remember that when Kogito was still a boy, he and Goro— who was about the same age—went to a place I'll call "Outside Over There," a place where something terrible happened, and after surviving that dreadful experience they came straggling back in the middle of the night. When I think about it now, even before that evening, Goro had definitely been changing, little by little. Even so, I think that was the night when Goro passed the point of no return.

After spending two days in a place I knew nothing about, Goro came home in the middle of the night. He must have stood in the front garden of the temple where we were lodging, calling out once or twice in a soft voice. If he hadn't kept his voice down, I would have been nervously worrying that a light might suddenly go on in the room of the head priest's eldest daughter, which was in a nearby part of the temple compound. Earlier that night, and all through the night before, I had been straining my ears, listening anxiously for any sign that Goro might have returned. When I slid open the wooden doors of the temple, being careful not to disturb the perfect stillness, the dim lamplight seeping out from behind me fell on two young boys who, even to my girlish eyes, looked extremely pathetic and bedraggled.

Even as a child, Chikashi was the type who didn't react emotionally to things, but she still found it difficult to look at that wretched, helpless-looking pair of boys for more than a few seconds. Beyond that, she had no distinct memories of how she felt at that moment, but she did remember how the boys behaved after they straggled in and what she did in response. They seemed to know what they needed to do—get cleaned up—but they were so exhausted that they were moving in slow motion, like zombies. Chikashi was perplexed rather than annoyed by this behavior, and she stood by on the sidelines, ready to be helpful.

The boys walked around to the back of the lodgings, and she followed the same route inside. She opened the shutters so the light would illuminate the outdoors, then closed the storm shutters that faced the front garden. She understood instinctively that Goro and Kogito were making every effort to avoid having anyone see them with their clothes off. At the base of a crape myrtle tree whose trunk resembled a naked animal, a stone basin had been placed to catch the water coursing down through a length of split bamboo. There was a verandah in front of the washbasin, and that was where Chikashi laid out two sets of Goro's clothing and two bath towels.

Big, plush towels were a rarity in those days, but their mother had presciently stocked up on them before commodities became scarce, as a treat for their father, who was recuperating from tuberculosis. Goro had gotten used to luxurious Western-style bath towels, and now he would get very cranky if he didn't have them instead of the narrow, flimsy Japanese versions, which tended to resemble an insubstantial dish towel or a length of cheesecloth.

Goro glanced around for just long enough to see what Chikashi was doing, but his friend was looking in the other direction, hanging his head. Chikashi was standing inside the shutters, and while she watched, Goro stripped naked to the waist and began to wash his body. (Although he was unusually tall and robust of build, on this night he looked oddly skinny and shrunken.) In due course his friend, who was standing next to him, followed suit. They were both roughly scrubbing their torsos with odd-shaped pieces of cloth, from their slender shoulders and narrow chests to their bent-over necks and abdomens, which resembled cylinders carved with furrows. The "washrags" they were using, Chikashi seemed to remember, were the boys' own white tank-style undershirts. Their other clothes lay in a heap on the ground at their feet.

Standing there together, Goro and Kogito looked like a couple of soot-colored, pointy-headed imps, about four feet tall. That was because they had stuck their heads into the stone washbasin to wet their longish hair, and the water had made it stand up in peaks. Goro nonchalantly shed his trousers, and his friend did the same; Chikashi thought they were probably too tired to feel embarrassed or shy. Her eyes had become accustomed to the dark, and she could make out their small, boyish buttocks, as well as their testicles (which reminded her of a baby's tightly clenched fist) and their penises, sticking out below their abdomens like misplaced fingers.

After Goro and his friend had dried themselves off with the bath towels and headed toward the verandah, with chilled-looking faces, to put on the clean, dry clothes Chikashi had left there, she quickly dived back into her futon in the shadow of the Buddhist altar. As she lay there with the quilt pulled over her head, listening to the sound of her own breathing, she could hear the two boys slowly, wearily making their way into the temple, and she was filled with pity once again.

4

During the five years before she married Kogito (there was a gap of time between the night she saw the pitiful youths at the temple in Matsuyama and the time when she and Kogito began corresponding after her mother had asked him to look for some books, including copies of *Winnie-the-Pooh* and *The House at Pooh Corner,* in the used-book store district of Tokyo), Chikashi respected him as "a person who reads books." She also thought in some vague way that Kogito would probably end up pursuing a line of work that was appropriate for "a person who reads books." She seemed to perceive a certain childlike simplicity, and a degree of disengagement from the real world, in Kogito's extreme bookishness. That was why, as their marriage plans proceeded, she had some remaining hesitation (quite apart from Goro's vociferous opposition). Yet the essence of the way she felt about Kogito didn't change after they were married, and even after Goro died, she felt keenly that her husband, as "a person who reads books," was still the same as he had been when he was young, with all that that implied.

When Kogito's mood had been buoyed by reading a new book, he would bring that excitement (and, sometimes, the book itself) to the dinner table and share it with his family. One night, he was talking about some new research into the Gospel according to Mark by a pioneering Japanese biblical scholar whom he held in great esteem. If someone had asked Chikashi whether or not her husband was a completely fair-minded human being when it came to living as a member of society, she would have had to admit to some reservations. However, when he talked about books, even if he disagreed with the content he never tried to oversimplify or second-guess what the author was saying.

There was an incident in which Professor Musumi (who had been Kogito's patron and mentor for most of his life and had even been the official go-between for his marriage to Chikashi) took his pupil to task over his critical methodology to such an extent that it was apparently painful even to remember. Kogito never spoke of the incident, but ever after that he had made a special effort to be scrupulously impartial.

On this night, Kogito began by reading aloud from a new, classically based, collaborative translation of the Bible by a Japanese research society whose leader was the author of the book that had made such an impression on Kogito. In this case, the passage was about how Mary Magdalene, Mary (mother of James), and Salomé tried to go anoint Jesus, after the Crucifixion. Chikashi, who as a rule didn't make hasty off-the-cuff comments, declared that in this translation, unlike in some earlier, stiffer versions, the women's behavior came across as so completely natural that she found herself identifying with them.

"Even if someone important to us was killed and buried in a cave, if we women needed to do something essential like going there to anoint him, we wouldn't think twice about it," she said. "I mean, I'm saying that even though I don't really know what's involved in anointing a dead body."

"I'm not an expert on that sort of thing, either," her husband said cheerfully.

"At any rate," Chikashi went on, "those three women summoned up their courage and set out, and on the way I think they would have been chatting about this and that. However, right after they had that frightening encounter with the supernatural being, the angel, all of them would probably just be walking quickly along, with downcast eyes, staring at the ground in silence, don't you think? And you know where it says in the Bible, 'They lifted their eyes and were amazed to see that the stone had been rolled away from the entrance'? That seems like a perfectly normal reaction, as well."

"That may be so," Kogito said, "but I really don't think these were ordinary women. Although of course you aren't an ordinary woman, either—maybe that's why you understand them so well. Now that I think about it, there's a similar scene in one of my novels when the older brother, Gii, drowns, and his sister, Asa (who's named after my own sister, of course), single-handedly recovers the corpse and then stands guard until the police arrive, to make sure the curiosity seekers don't come too close . . ."

"Being able to rely on women like Asa and me—'not ordinary women,' as you put it—must have been convenient for you and Goro, too," Chikashi remarked.

Unfazed by that response, which seemed to be tinged with sarcasm, Kogito began to read aloud the next passage, in which the messenger angel is waiting for the women in the tomb.

When he had finished, he recapped the author's questions about what happened when Jesus rose from the dead: "Why were the women so frightened that they didn't say anything to anyone, in spite of having been ordered by the angels to 'go, tell his disciples and Peter'—sometimes called Simon Peter—'that he is going before you to Galilee; there you will see him, as he told you.' And why did Mark end so abruptly, at that point?"

Kogito was particularly intrigued by the writers—the authors of the Bible—whose work seemed to parallel his own, and although he didn't think his own novelist's opinions had any bearing on the interpretation of the Gospel, he felt, personally, that the original author's ambiguous way of ending this particular tale was an effective literary technique. However, while they disagreed on that point, he gave the Bible scholar's treatise high marks for the way (unusual in Japan) that he presented the research, first setting out all the little differences in interpretive methodology and then proceeding to examine, one by one, the pros and cons of various theories and opinions—his own and those of others.

As Kogito rambled on in that vein Chikashi was only half listening, in a vague, abstracted way, for she was caught up in a daydream of her own. These women, she was thinking, had been followers of Jesus from the early stages of his community-organizing activity, and they themselves had been seriously tested. They were so resolute that when Jesus was nailed to the cross, they stayed there and watched over him from a distance, even after all the male disciples had fled. Surely there was some significance in the fact that these same brave, stalwart women had later been so frightened that they had run away in silence.

Was it enough simply to accept that that's the way the Gospel ends, with the seemingly negative information that the angel's words had not been relayed to the disciples—just as was written at the end of the Gospel?

But suppose the angel had asked the women to spread the word that Jesus had risen, and suppose that Jesus hadn't happened to meet up with the disciples in Galilee, after the Resurrection. If that had been due to the women's failure to relay the angel's message, and if their fearful silence had been recorded in the Gospel, they would probably have been blamed for eons to come. But all's well that ends well, and didn't Jesus rise up and appear in front of his disciples, restored to life, even though the women never relayed the angel's message?

Continuing along those lines, Chikashi thought: *On that dark night when my brother hadn't come home for two days, I was waiting for him, and I was afraid. And after my brother and his friend finally came back, when I saw how pathetic they looked I trembled violently and almost ended up passing out, just like those biblical women. And they said nothing to anyone, for they were afraid . . .*

I never told anyone about that night, either, because I was filled with fear. That's all there was to it. But what does it mean that the terror I felt, as I lay awake in the total darkness just before daybreak, is still resonating inside me? Even if there is some special significance, it doesn't help my dead brother or my living husband or me as I am now. But still, I can't help wondering—if the events of that dark night had never happened, would things have ended up as they did?

Chikashi imagined the scene that had taken place two thousand years before, when the terrified women ran away and hid in their homes without telling anyone what had happened, at the same time that the resurrected Jesus was trying to meet with his disciples in Galilee. While the women were keeping their frightened silence, the disciples—who, as related in the Gospel according to Luke, had heard what had befallen the women—were walking toward the village of Emmaus, and their hearts had been "set ablaze" by the story they heard from the mysterious stranger who appeared along the way. Not realizing that their new companion was actually Jesus, they listened to his words, and "their hearts burned within them." When Chikashi thought about the disciples and the women who were frightened into silence, she found a certain measure of comfort in the realization that she felt a common bond with those scared, silent women.

And then Chikashi thought once again about the picture book Kogito had brought back from Berlin and how it had shaken her to the core. Ida's mother, who did nothing but mope around, appeared to be a weak, helpless female, but Sendak drew her as if she were one of those biblical women in the Gospel according to Mark, frightened into silence. The first time she read *Outside Over There*, Chikashi had felt an overwhelming rush of fond recognition and sympathy for that sad-faced mother under the trees . . .

For myself, Chikashi thought, *I can pinpoint the precise time when I had the feeling of silently fleeing from an unbearably frightening experience. It was when I gave birth to an abnormal baby. Somewhere beyond my two naked, elevated legs, I heard the nurse who had just caught the newborn baby exclaim, "Oh, my God!" And ever after that, in the darkest depths of my heart, that nurse's voice has been echoing endlessly. I've even gone* so far as to think that her horrified exclamation might have been the same scream I stifled in my own throat when I saw Goro and his friend standing outside the temple at midnight in such a terrible state.

And when I regained consciousness after having passed out from shock, that day in the maternity ward, for a moment I couldn't tell whether I was waking up in a private room in a hospital in Tokyo or in that dark, cold temple in Matsuyama.

5

There was a long stretch of time during which Goro never came to the house in Seijo Gakuen for the express purpose of seeing Kogito. He did, however, drop by the Choko household occasionally—for example, when he was filming at a former major movie soundstage in nearby Tamagawa that had been turned into a rental facility since the slump in the filmmaking business.

One of the things about Kogito that Chikashi had come to find interesting was that although he didn't like to have outsiders handle the books in his personal library, he made an exception for Goro and no one else. Not only did he allow Goro free access to his precious books, but he didn't even make a fuss when Goro ran off with a book that Kogito hadn't yet gotten around to reading. But once Goro had taken a volume home with him, it was his custom to read that book intensively until he had fully understood it, so Kogito knew better than to hold his breath waiting for a given book to be safely returned.

On the day in question, a book had arrived in a hard-paper case that Chikashi found very attractive. It was an English translation of the revised edition of *The Man Without Qualities,* by the Austrian writer Robert Musil, and Kogito explained that the difference between this edition and earlier compilations was that this time the editors had tried a different way of organizing the unfinished portions of the manuscript. He also said that when he read the original translation, it was the less-polished early notes, memos, and scribblings that he had found inspiring, rather than the more advanced drafts. He had even gotten the idea of writing a novel of his own made up entirely of that sort of ephemera.

Goro didn't have time to read novels in English, so after checking out the cover design, which featured an interesting variation on the usual treatment of an author photo, his eyes wandered to the window and he began gazing dreamily out at the flowering dogwood, which was showing the first flush of fall colors, and the deep red petals of the autumn-blooming rosebush. Chikashi remembered now that the rosebush in question had the rather overblown name of "William Shakespeare," and she remembered, too, that Goro's hair had still been jet-black. Although Umeko had once whispered to her that some of that youthful darkness came from dye . . .

After a while, Goro said to Kogito, "When you were first reading *An Ordinary Man,* it was right around the time that Akari was born, wasn't it? I remember your saying, 'If I used this collage-like style of writing, I would probably be able to write about things that I haven't tackled before.' But you never did it."

Chikashi didn't detect any trace of sarcasm in Goro's voice, but Kogito, apparently feeling that he was being chided, shot back, "All right, I'll try giving a careful reading to the notes-and-memos section of this edition one more time, and I'll try to figure out what made me think that would be a workable format. After all, it's been twenty years since I first read this book, and I've been learning my craft as a novelist all that time, so maybe now I'll be able to do what I only talked about then."

In response, Goro did something that struck Chikashi as unusual for him: he made an effort to smooth Kogito's ruffled feathers by being deliberately conciliatory. "I truly hope that you'll be able to take that expressive style and make it your own," he said. "Because in the long run, I think we share a common artistic goal, and that approach might actually work well for both of us . . ."

At this point Chikashi impulsively jumped into the conversation, unable to tolerate what she saw as Goro's capitulation—throwing the match, in sumo terms. At least, that's how she analyzed it later. "But when you talk about your own artistic expression, Goro, don't you mean in films?"

"No, no. It's not that simple," Goro responded cryptically, still staring out at the garden, where the fall-blooming roses were slowly trembling on their singularly long stems.

Much later (this was after Goro had died), when Chikashi's uncanny attraction to the Maurice Sendak picture book Kogito had brought back from Berlin became a catalyst for rethinking some of the things that were always lurking in the recesses of her mind, Kogito broached a subject that must have been directly connected to the conversation they'd had with Goro on that autumn evening, while the William Shakespeare roses were blooming in the garden. By then Chikashi had already asked Kogito to write about what happened on that fateful night, when he and Goro were teenagers.

"Haven't you, too, found a style to express the things that you've been thinking about forever?" Kogito asked. "Of course, in a totally different genre than the ways of expressing ourselves that Goro and I found. But I really think that Goro would be . . . I mean, would have been delighted if you wrote a picture book."

Chikashi didn't reply. She had been aware since earliest childhood of the difference in temperament and talents between her dazzling older brother and herself; there had even been times when she became convinced that there wasn't a single point of similarity. Many friends of the family had pointed out that she and Goro shared an aptitude for drawing pictures, but to Chikashi herself, the pictures she drew and the pictures Goro drew were radically different entities. She had been rather surprised when, toward the end of his life, Goro began to praise the style of her drawings, but she still couldn't imagine that she would ever be able to create a picture book about the sort of thing that was important to Goro and Kogito.

This is a bit of a detour, but one of the things Chikashi had discovered since getting married was that her husband was the type of person who couldn't remain silent if someone asked him a question. She and Goro, on the other hand, always felt that it was more natural to remain silent than to argue a point with a torrent of words; this was one of the few traits they shared. In the course of a typical day, Chikashi would frequently let any number of her husband's questions go unanswered.

From the outset—that is, from the time they first began going out until after they'd been married for quite a while— there were numerous occasions when Chikashi didn't really understand what her husband was talking about. And when Kogito was chatting with Goro, she noticed that her brother often responded to her husband's questions with silence. There were times when Kogito appeared to be nettled by this behavior of Goro's (though not every single time it happened, by any means), but Chikashi decided that there was no point in letting it bother her, since there was nothing she could do.

After Chikashi came across *Outside Over There* (a book that had awakened and inspired her in a powerful, all-encompassing way because it felt so eerily close to her own life), she began to think about what had happened to Goro and Kogito during that lost weekend more deeply than ever before. It hadn't occurred to her until now that she might be able to turn those thoughts into a picture book and then show it to Kogito. And wouldn't Goro have been likely to say the same thing regarding that unmade, extralong film he had started to work on, without mentioning it to Kogito?

Yes, Chikashi thought ruefully, *Goro and I did have something in common, after all, unusual as that might seem. We both gave Kogito the silent treatment on a regular basis—and we both kept our little secrets from him, as well.*

6

It was the middle of the night when Chikashi got the call from Umeko, telling her that Goro had leapt to his death from the roof of a building. The actual incident had taken place earlier that evening, and now that the body had finally been identified, Umeko needed to report to the police station right away. After hanging up the telephone, Chikashi immediately went into Kogito's sleeping room—that is, his library, where he had installed an army cot. This was only the second time during their marriage that Chikashi had gone into Kogito's sleeping room with the explicit intention of waking him up. The first time, it had already been morning, albeit extremely early, when Chikashi rushed into the library to announce to her sleeping husband: "President Kennedy has been assassinated!"

On that November morning, Chikashi had heard the breaking news about the Kennedy assassination as soon as she got out of bed, and she was very upset. How was it possible that a man who had everything—good looks, superior character, phenomenal talents, the love of an admiring public—could be wiped out in one fatal moment by some scruffy-looking lowlife? She saw, with sudden clarity, the ubiquity of that dark, world-destroying power, and she felt as if there was some sort of parallel with what had happened to Goro as a youth. (She could almost hear Goro saying, with a grim little smile, "Oh, now you're comparing me to *Kennedy?*")

And when Chikashi first came across that picture book by Maurice Sendak, she felt as if everything written in there was something she already knew. People said that the kidnapping of the Lindberghs' beloved child was Sendak's inspiration for *Outside Over There*, and wasn't the Kennedy assassination, too, a similarly tragic showdown between the forces of darkness and light? It was on the morning when she learned Kennedy had been shot, Chikashi thought, that the essential core of everything she now believed had first begun to crystallize.

The previous night, her husband, as was his habit in those days, had read until late while nursing a half cup of whiskey and then had gone to sleep. When she woke him up with the news of the assassination, he poked his bleak-looking head out from under the blanket and listened to the details with an increasingly desolate expression on his face. Then, without saying a word, he dived back under the blanket and pulled it up over his head. Chikashi had actually been expecting him to say something like: "Oh, right, that type always ends up getting the worst of it."

Of course, this was all surmise on top of speculation, but if Kogito had said something like that back in 1963, then when Chikashi went to tell him that her brother had taken a fatal plunge off the roof of a building, suppose she had made some reference to what he had said (but didn't) when he heard the news of Kennedy's death? If she had put that into words, her husband probably would have replied with something similar to what he might have said (but didn't) that time about Kennedy, something like "I always thought Goro was the kind of person who would end up this way." (A tendency to indulge in convoluted conjecture was one trait, at least, that Chikashi and Kogito shared.)

A week or so after the day Kogito gave his dinner-table dissertation on the newly published research into the Gospel according to Mark, Chikashi happened to see her husband looking alarmingly somber—the polar opposite of the cheerful, upbeat person who had held forth about the adventures of Mary Magdalene, the other Mary, and Salomé. He was staring out the sitting-room window into the garden with his head, which no longer had a single section unthreaded with white hair, pressed against the glass.

After observing his unusual posture from behind, Chikashi went back to her own room without saying a word. But when she reemerged nearly an hour later, Kogito was still in the same position. It didn't seem like the way a man who was well on his way to old age would behave, as a rule. Chikashi felt a wave of pity, thinking that now that Kogito was getting on in years he must be reflecting on the details of his life and regretting all the mistakes he had made. But there was no way for anyone to stick a finger into his salt-and-pepper-colored head (in Kogito's case, now mostly salt) and erase all the painful memories.

But wasn't that exactly what Goro had tried to do for himself? If Goro, like everyone else on the planet, was running a continual-loop mental slide show of regrettable scenes from his life, how difficult that must have been for him—especially since

he was known for his extraordinary ability to remember the
details of things he'd experienced (a facility he used in his films,
to marvelous effect). Goro had often remarked on Kogito's phenomenal memory, but Kogito was the type of person who remembers words, while Goro had a remarkable capacity for
recalling and reconstructing visual scenes. But if a human
being decided to obliterate all those intricately detailed memories by violent, self-destructive means, that was rather easily
done . . .

Chikashi sat down behind Kogito, who had been standing by the window in the same unnatural pose for nearly two
hours. It seemed almost cruel to even look at him in that state.
Kogito had never been a sportsman type, but he had always been
active, and if he wasn't reading or writing it was unusual to see
him sitting still for very long. How, she wondered, had he suddenly fallen into this vegetative state? Then she noticed that
Akari was standing next to her.

After determining that this peculiar behavior was not restricted to his father but had apparently spread, like a virus, to
his mother as well, Akari addressed his words to both parents,
subtly swiveling his head back and forth between them. "People!"
he exclaimed. "What on earth is going on?"

Just as Chikashi hadn't been able to do anything to prevent Goro from destroying himself, now—even compared with
Akari's small gesture—she was unable to do anything to prevent the same sort of behavior in Kogito, and she felt deeply,
profoundly sad. (Ida had at least been able to "straighten up
and fly right" after hearing Papa's song.)

Toward the end of that strange day, after Akari had
trundled off to his bedroom, Chikashi sat down on the sofa

next to the armchair where Kogito was working with his back to the garden. He was writing away, with a drawing board— black hardboard bordered with persimmon-colored wood— balanced on his knee. It was the only thing he had brought back from Berlin for himself, apart from books. After a while he lifted his stubbly, unshaven face (for some reason, ever since his whiskers had turned noticeably white, they had started to grow much more rapidly) and looked at Chikashi with a quizzical expression. At times like this Kogito would usually launch into an account of what he had read that day, as if he had been waiting for the opportunity, and the fact that he didn't do so on this day seemed to confirm the severity of his depression.

"I wanted to ask you about earlier today," Chikashi ventured. "Until now I don't think there's ever been a time when you just stood and stared into the garden, has there?"

"I did notice that you were watching me," Kogito replied. "But it just seemed like too much of an effort to turn around and look at you."

"What's the matter?"

"There was a guy called Arimatsu, remember? The one who seemed to be one of Goro's hangers-on, but then again, maybe he wasn't; it was hard to tell. Anyway, today after you and Akari had left to go to the hospital to pick up Akari's medicine, I got a letter from Arimatsu, sent by express registered mail—what do they call it now, 'simplified registered mail'? I guess it's a quick and easy variation on the certified delivery that big-shot journalist always used to use when he sent me poison-pen letters. It's just a kind of precautionary device for the journalist, so he can insert a postscript to his defamatory article stating that he had sent a certain letter that way, and therefore he was confident it had been delivered.

"It's the same old technique; the journalistic weasels of today learn their tricks by emulating the weasels of yesteryear. In any case, I knew from the start that it would have been pointless for me to rise to the bait. He knew that too, of course, but he'll still lead off his article by proclaiming that I willfully disregarded his so-called 'polite letter.' Arimatsu's letter was honest on one point, at least: it didn't hide the fact that it was a copy of an original written on graph-style manuscript paper, the kind that holds two hundred characters per page."

"Was it something to do with Goro?"

Kogito nodded. "It wasn't clear which weekly tabloid magazine he was talking about, but anyway the letter said that the woman who was mentioned in some article about the 'scandal' had been hiding out abroad, but she got tired of being in exile, so now she's back in Japan, and didn't I feel that it was my duty to meet with this woman and hear her story? The letter also said that he had heard from a number of journalists that while I tended to be very overprotective of my family, especially Akari, when it came to helping out some unnamed underdog, I would flatly refuse."

"I don't think you have any sort of obligation at all in this case, and besides, what good could possibly come of your meeting with that woman?"

"That's exactly why Arimatsu is probably planning to make up a scurrilous story based on the premise that I ignored his proposition. It's all rather unclear, but even if a woman like that does exist, I would be surprised if she had hired him to play a part in some sleazy scheme."

"And that's what you've been brooding about all day?" Chikashi asked.

There didn't seem to be any sort of hidden agenda behind her question, but Kogito's snowy-stubbled face showed a disproportionate degree of consternation as he replied, "All I can think of is that there was a girl Goro met three years ago at the Berlin Film Festival—remember, he told us about her?—and maybe she has somehow fallen on hard times to the point where a cad like Arimatsu would call her a 'wretched woman.' But that's pure speculation on my part; it could be someone else entirely."

"Speculation or not, surely he wouldn't venture a theory like that without some basis in fact. Did you hear anything about such a woman while you were in Berlin?" Chikashi asked.

"To be sure, I did hear some confusing rumors about a vengeful girl Friday or some such," Kogito replied. "But I have a feeling that particular gossip isn't related to the case Arimatsu's talking about. There's something else that keeps running through my head, though. There *was* a girl in Berlin the last time Goro was there; he spoke about her at great length on some of the cassette tapes he made for me. And that drawing he sent of Berlin in wintertime—you were saying that he drew it with someone standing next to him, and I can't help thinking it might have been the same young woman. From what I heard, those tapes seem like an unusually joyful memento that Goro left behind for the world on this side. When I realize that he made this sort of happy human connection toward the end of his life, I feel as if we, too, can take positive encouragement from that. But now even those good feelings seem to have been polluted by Arimatsu's toxic letter."

"This is hard to say, especially since I'm the one who asked you to stop your midnight, um . . . interactions with Goro's recordings, but I would really like to listen to those tapes," Chikashi said slowly. "Though since you've never mentioned this before, I imagine the monologue in question might have been meant for your ears only. But if it truly is a memento of something joyful that Goro experienced toward the end of his life, I'd like to hear that, too."

When Chikashi said this, Kogito—unusual, for him—didn't reply right away. But when she went into the kitchen the next morning, there they were on the table: a small stack of cassette tapes, in consecutive order, each labeled with its sequential number and a brief summary of the contents. Next to the tapes was the Tagame apparatus: batteries inserted, ready to go. *Cooking breakfast can wait,* Chikashi thought as she returned to her bedroom. There were three tapes, with the pertinent passages of each one clearly marked. She pressed PLAY, and her late brother's voice filled the room.

> *You know something about my checkered past, of course, but here I am, at this rather advanced age, learning amazing new things about the realm of sex from a mere slip of a girl. You might even say that I've been allowed to see sexuality in a completely new light. I can just picture the complicated expression on your face when you hear me saying this sort of thing, but believe me, it has nothing to do with any unseemly dirty-old-man perversions. It's just the carefree, open, wholesome world of sexual delight, that's all. So anyway, this is what happened, and I hereby swear that everything I'm about to tell you is the whole truth and noth-*

ing but the truth, from my own strange and wonderful experience!

The first thing (and for that matter the last, as well, and everything in between) is the kiss. To put it simply: we kiss. In the beginning, I thought this young girl—she was only seventeen when we first met—had probably never kissed anyone except in the way a child kisses its mother. That was the way she kissed me at first, innocently, and that was the way she returned my early kisses, too. However, things progressed rather rapidly from there; I suppose that's not too surprising, since we spent half a day doing nothing but kissing. She was a natural-born master of the art of passionate kissing, and she was incredibly innovative and creative, as well. Every part of the lips, every trick of the tongue, every nook and cranny of the mouth—those were her instruments, and each variation and every repetition would bring some thrilling new revelation. (The way she used her teeth!) Before long I, too, had mastered the art of creating the most epic, ardent kisses of all time. I even invented some new variations myself! That's right, me: the battle-scarred veteran of the sexual wars. For an entire hour, sometimes two, we would do nothing but kiss, until my entire mind and body were aflame with desire. To put it in your terms, for the first time in a long while my sex life was radically transmogrified.

So there we are, lying on the bed in my hotel room in Berlin, and I'm putting my finger into the left side of her half-opened mouth. Her teeth, wet and glistening with saliva, are nibbling gently on my finger. All the while, she's kissing me with the right side of her mouth. My mouth is partly open, too, and my tongue is in constant motion. The girl's face is as flushed as if she'd just finished a strenuous workout. Suddenly, she throws back her head and says with a laugh, "I can't handle this—you have too much sex appeal."

Now, the phrase "sex appeal" may have been in her vocabulary for a while, but I'm pretty sure this is the first time she's ever used it in this context. That's what I thought, anyway. There was something endearing about her unconventional use of that term (after all, people usually talk about sex appeal as part of early-stage courtship, not in bed, right?), but it struck me as a perfectly vivid remark—just amazingly cool and chic and candid. It seemed like the brash, straightforward sort of thing a man might say, but not a young girl. It really was the epitome of Professor Musumi's definition of "chic," in its original meaning.

Anyway, while we're kissing I slide both my hands under her casual slacks—she's astride me, sitting on my lap—and I start to stroke her smooth, satiny skin, from the loins all the way around to her rear end. I can't get over the shapeliness of her small, perfect buttocks: tight and sleek, without an ounce of extra fat. She's fresh and unsullied, and the eroticism we're sharing is utterly pellucid and pure. Before long, my right hand steals up to explore her flat abdomen. The reconnaissance progresses very slowly, over several days, but eventually my fingers wend their way into the uncharted territory below her waist. Tentatively, I caress the outer edges of her pubic hair, and she doesn't seem to mind. From then on, touching that secret meadow becomes routine. It's like a military campaign: once I gain a victory in a strategic location, that site is mine, and it can't be taken back. However, she absolutely refuses to let my fingers de-

scend any lower. She vetoes any such attempts clearly but not unkindly, being careful not to hurt my feelings. And thus it's settled: she places certain limits on my ongoing survey of her terrain, and I must abide by those rules.

Clinging tightly to each other, we tumble onto the sofa in my hotel room. The hand that has slipped under her slacks doesn't run along the periphery of her panties; rather, following the imaginary line of a high-cut bikini bottom, it traces a long, slow arc from the lower reaches of her pelvic bone down to her groin. I know that if I touch her private parts, even by accident, I'll be firmly pushed away and may never get a chance to try again. Very carefully, my hands continue their delicate infiltration of the upper reaches of her thighs, almost as if there were a counterweight keeping them within bounds at all times. But instead of wanting to hurry things along, I'm savoring the exquisite eroticism of my hand's slow progress. The only way I can express my male sexual power is by rubbing my tumescent member against her thighs, through my trousers, and my epic desire can only find release in a kiss. And so we go on like that, kissing till the end of time.

It's her eighteenth birthday, the day I gave her a soft, cream-colored dress to wear to our celebratory dinner (I remember the understated elegance of that Berlin department store and the dedication of the employees who helped us choose the perfect frock). The girl—still wearing that dress, and a trifle tipsy on half a glass of Sauternes—is abandoning herself to our kissing, heart and soul. We're lying intertwined on the sofa, and she doesn't seem to care if her new dress gets covered with wrinkles. Before I know it my *finger, following the line of her groin, ends up losing its way along the rim of her underwear. While our legs have been chafing violently against each other, the girl has probably gotten her stylish, gossamer-thin knickers into a twist, quite literally. Hesitating a bit, I try to return to the previously approved course, and somehow the tip of my index finger wanders into a thick, fleshy place. I feel the dampness around the edges. The bulb of my finger, which had been touching the soft, downy fuzz on the outer margins, now enters the jungle of thick, tightly curled hair. The girl decisively torques her abdomen, driving away not just the renegade finger but my entire palm, and my hand ends up back in the safe zone on the outside of her thighs.*

"We had a deal, remember? You mustn't break the rules," she says in a brave voice. Now her private parts are wet to the point of overflowing the outer periphery, and the joy of discovery beats wildly in my heart like a second pulse. The eros of only kissing is being transformed into something strong and systemic: a kind of pansomatic desire.

How can merely kissing feel so rich, so complex, so— I really don't want to use this old cliché, but here goes: so profound? I ask that question almost rhetorically, half talking to myself, but the girl surprises me by answering. "Because," she whispers, "you're about to be taken as far as you can go, just by kissing." She says this as if she'd given the matter a lot of thought. "Do you remember the time I stopped in the middle of a kiss and said, 'You have too much sex appeal,' and you kindly told me that I was using that term improperly and set me straight? I actually said that out of embarrassment because I was on the verge of crossing a 'cer-

tain line,' as they say, and I thought I was the only one who was starting to have those feelings. But after that you said, 'If we go on like this, I'm afraid I'm going to end up coming.' And I was so happy that I shouted, 'Go ahead and come!'" And then the girl said earnestly, trying to steer the conversation back to the original topic, "It's because I know I can't have sex with you, that's why a kiss can take me all the way, as high as I can go."

As the day approached for my return to Tokyo, she consented to take off her slacks, just once. We were lying on the bed at the time, and somehow, purely by accident, her panties ending up coming off, as well. I couldn't see her private parts, but I did get a glimpse of the pale, circular mound of fat around her navel, like a rice cake, and (echoing that shape) the perfectly round halo of pubic hair below.

"Let's try lying on top of each other," the girl says. "And since that big, thick thing looks kind of cramped in your pants—it seems to be especially big and thick today, for some reason—you can put it between my thighs, just this once." Like someone who has done this sort of thing before (or maybe it was because she had never done it), the girl even elevates her knees, but by mutual agreement we don't allow my penis to follow its natural inclinations. She does let me ejaculate into her hand, but as she put it at the time, what she experienced with me was beyond sex, even though technically, by her definition, it wasn't "real sex." Afterward she said, "This is the best feeling I've ever had in my life, but even so, I didn't come." As for me, I'm certain that I'll always remember this, in its tantalizing totality, as one of the top one or two erotic experiences of my life.

So why didn't I have "real sex" with this lovely and passionate young girl? Well, apart from the matter of her chastity boundaries, it was because I couldn't help seeing in her an uncanny resemblance to myself—that is, to the way I looked when I was young. (I realize not everyone would agree, but it was very obvious to me.) Chikashi and I look a lot alike, but even more clearly than my younger sister, this girl is really the spitting image of me during the time when I was very young and it was hard to tell whether I was a girl or a boy. Even if she had been willing, there's no way I could have had sexual intercourse with a girl who seemed to have my own face from childhood. That would be exceedingly dangerous, and weird, too, if you know what I mean. And besides, our erotic experiences had already accumulated to the point where it was almost starting to feel like too much of a good thing . . .

At this point, Chikashi stopped the tape, cutting off her brother's narrative. Akari had crawled out of bed and was now in the living room, listening to Hidetomo Yoshida's classical-music program on the radio with the volume turned down low. He had been listening to that show every week for the past twenty years, and he had never missed a single broadcast. It had become a family touchstone; if Akari's radio program was on, it must be Sunday.

Chikashi had been deeply moved by the sound of Goro's exuberant voice, but now it was time to pull herself together and make breakfast for her family. She decided to keep the "Berlin tapes" for herself, rather than returning them to her husband. For the first time in a very long while, mixed in with a complex stew of other emotions, she even felt a faint stirring of sexuality.

And based on what she'd gleaned from Goro's recorded narrative, Chikashi felt absolutely certain that the girl in question would never turn into the type of person who could be called a "wretched woman" by some third-rate tabloid journalist.

7

Three months went by, or thereabouts. And then, out of the blue, who should appear in Chikashi's life but the young woman Goro had talked about with so much passion? First, there was a phone call from the girl, which was an unexpectedly pleasant experience in itself.

After Goro's death, there had been a sudden increase in phone calls from complete strangers, and as a result Chikashi had developed a not entirely irrational feeling of dread and aversion toward the telephone itself. In one sense, those calls had been harder to deal with than the complaints about Kogito's always-controversial work that had flooded in on numerous occasions in the past, from both ends of the political spectrum. But when the call came from the girl, and even before Chikashi had any idea who the caller was or what her business might be, she somehow got the feeling, just from the young woman's voice and way of talking, that maybe the telephone wasn't such a bad thing, after all. This quasi-magical system that could link two human beings together by way of a feeble electrical current flowing over a telephone line: why had she forgotten how comforting that connection could be? And that very phenomenon—two strangers on either end of a telephone line—turned out to have the power to rescue Chikashi from the submerged feelings of isolation and helplessness that had been haunting her for so long she wasn't really conscious of them anymore.

"Three years ago, in Berlin, I was working for Goro Hanawa, and he gave me this number," the girl began. "Is this Chikashi, by any chance? If you don't mind, I'd like to talk to you for a minute. My name is Ura Shima."

The voice on the telephone had the affectless quality so often heard in the voices of young women these days, a sort of unobtrusive monotone from which any tinge of emotion had been erased, but even so, it gave Chikashi a good feeling. It was as if the initial surprise at hearing that the voice belonged to the girl who was with Goro in Berlin had been quickly subsumed in a sensation of warmth and consolation.

"I'll be happy to talk to you," Chikashi said with complete sincerity.

"Thank you very much. I'll get right to the point, then. I know this is rather sudden, but I have a favor to ask. Three years ago, at the time of the Berlin Film Festival, Goro sent you a watercolor painting. What I'm wondering is, would it be possible to get a color copy? When Goro was painting it, I was working as his interpreter/attendant, and I was at his side the entire time. I'm just back in Japan for a short time, and I've set my mind on taking a color copy of that painting with me when I return to Germany, no matter what. So I'm asking you to help me make that happen."

"You call it a watercolor," Chikashi responded, "but it's actually a picture that was drawn with colored pencils, then liquefied with a wet paintbrush, isn't that right? A picture of trees in winter, in Berlin?"

"That's right, Goro was in Ku'damm—that's Berlin's equivalent of the Ginza, more or less—anyway, he was walking around in Ku'damm and that colored-pencil set caught his eye. He said that it would be good for making sketches when he was out scouting locations, and so he ran in and bought it."

Chikashi could picture her brother, the quintessential sophisticated shopper, caught up in that spontaneous, high-spirited moment. "That painting is in my room right now," she said. "I'll be glad to take it to the local stationery store and make a color copy."

"Oh, thank you so much. When would it be convenient for me to come pick it up?"

"Either the end of this week or the beginning of next—anytime around then would be fine. On Wednesdays I go to visit our mother at the hospital, but I'll be back in the late afternoon."

"Well, then, if you're really sure it's all right, I'd like to stop by the day after tomorrow—Saturday—at around two o'clock. If you could spare the time to talk to me for an hour or so, that would really make me happy. But if a visit would interfere with your husband's work, I don't need to go beyond the front door."

"On Saturday afternoon he'll be at the pool with our son, so there's no need to worry."

As soon as Chikashi had hung up the phone, she went to her bedroom to get the painting. The technique was as she had described it to Ura Shima; she hadn't tried it herself, but she thought it might be more difficult than it looked. Just before Kogito went to Berlin, the conversation had turned to Goro, and they had looked at this picture together. She took the painting out of the frame that Kogito had put it in, that night, and then she looked again at the writing in the lower right-hand corner, next to the date. It wasn't entirely legible because the colored-pencil letters had blurred when they were accidentally painted over with a wet brush, but she could tell that it wasn't Goro's signature. Rather, it read: "With Urashima Taro, on Wallotstrasse."

If a Japanese person who would be known in her native country as Shima Ura (Shima being her surname) was working as an interpreter/attendant in Berlin, it would be customary to introduce herself the Western way, last name last, as Ura Shima. From that, it would be a short leap for Goro to give her the nickname "Urashima Taro," after the old man in the famous folktale—the approximate Japanese analogue of Rip Van Winkle, transplanted to the bottom of the sea. Goro had always enjoyed that sort of wordplay, from the time he was very young.

Chikashi stuck the watercolor between the pages of one of her own sketchbooks, and then, intending to combine the color-copying errand with shopping for the evening meal, she pedaled her bicycle toward the shopping area in front of the station in a state of ebullient excitement. Now that she thought about it, she seemed to remember having heard from Goro that Ura Shima had been given the name "Ura," written with archaic *kanji,* as a Japanese equivalent of the German name "Ulla." (There is, of course, no *l* in Japanese.)

The following Saturday, Ura Shima arrived a few moments after the time she and Chikashi had agreed upon. While she

was waiting—after having sent Kogito and Akari off to the
Nakano pool—Chikashi busied herself with tidying up the pots
of rosebushes in the garden, most of which had already finished
blooming. It was the rainy season, but during this rare interval
of clear weather the weak sunlight was shining through the thin
clouds. Counting the bushes in the ground and the potted
plants, Chikashi was raising as many as 120 varieties of English
roses in the narrow garden. While she was moving the pots of
tall, lush-leafed rosebushes, it occurred to her that after Goro
had suddenly vanished from her life she had thrown herself into
caring for the rapidly multiplying potted roses as a temporary
substitute for some more serious passion (such as making art)
that she longed for but, at that time, hadn't yet found.

Before long, she noticed a sedate-looking green car being
adroitly maneuvered into a parking place on the other side of
a tall, dense hedge where flowering dogwood grew in profusion and the dark green leaves of camellia bushes glowed with
a deep luster. Chikashi hurried down the narrow path to the
gate. A tall, well-built young woman wearing a dress of soft,
cream-colored fabric (Goro's trademark taste, Chikashi
thought) was approaching the gate with a poised, graceful gait.
Her hair, which appeared to be a dark chestnut color, was
bound in a knot at the nape of her neck, and she was looking
down at the path.

"Oh, you came by car?" Chikashi called out. "If I'd known
I could have faxed you a map, instead of telling you how to walk
here from the station. Did you have a hard time finding it?"

"No, it was easy. I'm Ura Shima," the young woman said,
lifting her head and fixing her large eyes on Chikashi. Ura Shima
was nearly four inches taller than Chikashi. Of course, if she

had been wearing pumps instead of casual canvas sneakers, the difference would have been even more noticeable. About the time Chikashi had first started going out with Kogito, while Goro was still in good spirits (that is, before he decided to oppose their marriage), he had teased, "Since you two are about the same height, I guess Chikashi won't be able to wear high heels any more!" The fact was, Goro had always been attracted to tall women.

Looking around at the pots of bloomed-out rosebushes that were piled high, one on top of another, in the narrow space, Ura sheepishly held out a large, bulky bouquet wrapped in sturdy brown paper.

"These roses were sent to my house as a gift, and I wanted to share them," she said. "But since you're growing them yourself, I guess it's a bit like carrying coals to Newcastle!"

Chikashi accepted the bouquet. "As you can see, most of my flowers have finished blooming, so these will be lovely," she called over her shoulder as she went to get a vase for the deep-pink roses, which were charmingly striped in a darker pink, like peppermint candy. She thought they were called 'Vick's Caprice.'

When Chikashi returned to the living room, she found Ura staring at a framed drawing that hung on the wall. It was the work of an artist, a family friend who had also been Chikashi and Goro's art teacher when they were in high school; they had posed for this portrait when they were children, and Kogito had bought it some time ago from the artist, who was now an established painter. Ura seemed transfixed by the image of Goro, who was wearing a beret and cupping his cheek in the palm of one large hand.

"You and Goro look a lot alike, don't you?" Ura said, turning her gaze back to Chikashi. Her eyes, like her dress and her height, were exactly to Goro's taste: so widely placed on either side of the well-defined bridge of her nose that they seemed to walk an aesthetic tightrope between beauty and caricature.

"That wasn't really true when we were children," Chikashi replied. "But Goro always used to say that when we got to a certain, more advanced age, we would end up resembling each other the way old couples do."

Ura didn't reply, so Chikashi added, "I made the color copy of Goro's watercolor—it's there on the table, so please take a look. I'll be back in a jiffy with some tea."

That was how Ura and Chikashi began their conversation. Then they moved on to Goro's watercolor painting: *What were those leafless trees in the foreground? It would be hard to tell during winter, but now that they're covered with green leaves it should be possible to identify them. And that building in the painting, the one that's visible on the opposite shore of the lake through the gaps between the bare-branched trees? You probably can't see it from that window anymore, now that the trees have leafed out.* That was the kind of small talk they made.

After a while Ura sat up straighter on the couch, with an air of determination. Then, plainly nervous, she embarked on a different conversational tack with Chikashi, who was feeling rather tense herself.

"When I was assigned to work with Goro, it was the winter of the year I turned eighteen. I had met the requirements for admission to the University of Hamburg, but first I wanted to get some experience in the wider world for a year or two. Then, right after I started working part-time for the Japan-Germany

Center in Berlin, I had the incredible good fortune to be chosen to be the assistant to Goro, who was there for the film festival. 'Interpreter/attendant' was the job title, though I don't know whether I was much use as an interpreter . . . For me, the time I spent with Goro was the first time I'd ever felt the joy of being a fresh, desirable young woman instead of just an awkward, clumsy, ill-favored girl with big feet."

"I think it was a very happy time for Goro, as well," Chikashi said. "You were there with him while he was painting this picture, weren't you? I can tell that he was enjoying himself, and I think that must be why—even though it portrays a bleak, wintry landscape—this painting ended up having such a bright feeling to it."

Ura flushed deeply all the way up to the firm skin under her eyes, as if her cheeks were being heated from inside. "'An awkward, clumsy, ill-favored girl with big feet': that was what my parents always used to say about me, until it got to be a sort of mantra. I guess it was their way of trying to motivate me to make the most of my academic strengths. But thanks to all their negative reinforcement, I was pretty much resigned to a future devoid of romance. And then Goro came along, and he told me that my face and figure were still sorting themselves out and assured me that one of these days I would suddenly become so startlingly beautiful that people who had known me before would laugh out loud in disbelief. He explained that the fable of the Ugly Duckling probably came from observing late-blooming girls like me, rather than being rooted in psychology. He even said that my transformation had already begun and that he thought I was really beautiful already." As she said this, Ura once again blushed all the way up to her eyes.

"Goro talked to me about that," Chikashi said. She didn't feel as if she was telling a lie, but even so, she felt the need to backtrack: "Well, he didn't actually talk to me directly, only through a cassette tape, but he said other things about you, too—like that if you were a feminist, you might say that even looking at women in 'Ugly Duckling' terms was the very essence of sexist discrimination. He was actually talking very seriously, for him."

"I know, because I was with him when he made the tape," Ura said. "I was listening to him and thinking about what an extraordinary education he had given me."

Ura said this bashfully, with downcast eyes, and as Chikashi looked at the young woman's face she could see how the border-line-comical irregularities in her features had settled into an unusual but indisputable sort of beauty—a beauty that, at certain angles, did remind her a bit of Goro's angelic face as a child. They both fell silent, and Chikashi found herself remembering one particularly explicit passage on the cassette tape—though not with any feelings of prurience or indiscretion.

> Compared with the sexual landscape of a mature woman, there was something wild and untamed about her topography. It was like a vast, abundant wetland, still not fully formed. Based on my prior experience with the female anatomy, I really couldn't say definitively, 'Okay, this is this,' or 'Yes, I recognize that.' I just had fragmented impressions: featurelessly wide . . . opulently wet . . . a healthy sexual appetite somehow managing to coexist with a stubborn attachment to virginity. Yet her outpouring of sexual self-expression

(and the way she moved) seemed to have its own natural power, and her responses didn't feel like mere preliminaries that would normally have led (but didn't) to sexual intercourse. No, everything we did together felt like the real thing, perfectly whole and complete just the way it was.

Slowly, Chikashi and Ura resumed their conversation. Mostly, Ura shared stories about Goro. Like the time he told her about a book that shows a series of pictures demonstrating how the faces (and physiognomy) of human beings have evolved, step by step, from the ape stage. When Ura rushed off to an antique-book store to find that book, Goro went along. Later, while looking at snapshots of Ura taken when she was a child—they were mostly taken by her father, which seemed to prove, Goro pointed out, that even if she was an awkward, ungainly girl, she wasn't unloved at home, and she found that reassuring—anyway, Goro sketched the evolution, by stages, of a funny-faced little girl, showing how he envisioned Ugly Duckling Ura evolving into an ever more beautiful swan. Chronic low self-esteem dies hard, and in spite of Goro's compliments she couldn't help thinking how wonderful it would be if he was right and that fairy-tale transformation really was under way.

After a time, certain small fluctuations in Ura's expression seemed to indicate that something was amiss. It wasn't a reflection of her changing emotions but rather something more directly physical. Suddenly she stood up and said, "I wonder whether I might use your restroom? I know it's a rude thing to ask the first time you visit someone's house, but I'm not feeling well at all."

Chikashi led the way to the guest bathroom just off the entry hall, then Ura knelt down in front of the toilet, just like that, and began to throw up. Chikashi couldn't bear to stand there and watch the girl's broad, muscular shoulders heaving with every spasm, so she quickly stepped back and closed the door.

8

Although she had been expecting something of the sort, Chikashi was still shocked when Ura returned from her emergency visit to the lavatory with all the color drained from her face. Her skin was so pale that she looked as if she were wearing a fencing mask.

"I know this is none of my business," Chikashi said, "but are you pregnant, by any chance?"

"I'm four months along," Ura replied frankly, looking as if she might be about to burst into tears.

"So you came back to Japan to have the baby at your parents' house?"

"No, actually, I came back to have an abortion. The guy told me it would be easy to do in Japan . . ."

Once again, Chikashi was shocked. The girl's use of the slangy, impersonal term "the guy" to describe the father of her unborn child hit her like a punch in the solar plexus, but Ura wore the defiant expression of an awkward little girl who has grown up but not matured.

"That's no way to talk!" Chikashi scolded.

Ura continued, unfazed. "He said he didn't want to continue our relationship, but when I told him I was pregnant he offered to take responsibility. I really don't care for the man at all anymore; to be honest, I think I only got involved with him because he looked like Goro. It wasn't much of a relationship anyway—it had gotten to the point where whenever we got together all we did was have sex."

"And are you still planning to have an abortion?"

"No, as a matter of fact, I'm not. While I was on my way back here on a cheap flight, by way of Hamburg, I happened to read an article by your husband in a south German newspaper. It was the Sunday magazine of the *Süddeutsche Zeitung*. Anyway, after that, I changed my mind and decided to go ahead and have the baby, somehow."

"Now that you mention it, he did tell me that he wrote an article while he was in Berlin, and it was translated into German," Chikashi said. "I believe he wrote it in English, so it would be easier for them to find a translator? If there were a Japanese version, I think he would have shown it to me . . ."

Ura reached out and grabbed her big, bulky designer handbag—it was one of those sturdy all-purpose totes they sell at airport duty-free shops, advertised as "Ideal for the Busy Executive." She pulled out a sheaf of thin newsprint-type paper. "Would you like to read it?" she asked.

"The thing is, I don't read German . . ."

"If I translate, will you listen? It's a wonderfully strange little story. It's written in the form of a reply to the question 'Why do we have to send our children to school?' It talks about Mr. Choko's childhood experiences and about Akari's education at the school for handicapped children, up to graduation.

The first half is especially beguiling. It begins right after the war ended, when Mr. Choko used to go into the forest every day with an illustrated book about botany and study the trees, instead of going to school."

Ura Shima began to read Kogito's essay, translating from the German with impressive facility as she went along:

> One day in the middle of fall, even though it was pouring rain, I went into the woods as usual. As it continued to rain even harder, torrents of rushing water suddenly appeared here and there in the forest, and the road collapsed. By the time night fell, I was unable to get out of the valley. On top of that, I had fallen ill with a fever, and I spent the next two days more or less comatose in the hollow trunk of a large horse chestnut tree, until I was finally rescued by the local firefighting brigade.
>
> Even after I returned home, my high fever refused to subside. The doctor who came from a neighboring town to examine me announced that there was no medicine—or any other means of treatment—that could make me better, and took his leave. (I was listening to this dire conversation as if to something in a dream.) Only my mother was unwilling to give up hope, and she continued to do everything she could to nurse me back to health.
>
> Then, late one night, while I was still weak and feverish, I suddenly awakened from the nightmare world where I'd been living, perpetually engulfed in a hot, fiery wind, and I noticed that my mind had become clear again.
>
> You no longer see this arrangement very much these days, even in the country, now that Western-style beds have

become so popular, but in keeping with the way it used to be done in Japanese homes, I was lying on a futon spread directly on top of the tatami-matted floor. My mother, who probably hadn't slept in days, was sitting by my bedside watching over me. In a slow, small voice that sounded strange even to me, I asked:

—Mommy, am I going to die?

—I don't think you're going to die. I'm praying that you won't.

—But the doctor said, "This child is probably going to die. There's nothing more we can do." I heard him. That's why I think I'm going to die.

My mother was silent for a moment. Then she said:

—Even if you die, I'll give birth to you again, so don't worry.

—But wouldn't that child be different from the me who died?

My mother shook her head.

—No, it would be the same. After I gave birth to you again, I would tell the new you about all the things you've seen and heard and all the things you've read and all the things you've done up till now. And the new you would learn to speak all the words that you know now, so the two children would end up being exactly the same.

I didn't really understand what my mother was talking about, but after that conversation I was able to fall asleep with a truly tranquil heart. The next morning, I began to get better. It was a very slow process, and it wasn't until the beginning of winter that I was finally ready—and more than willing—to return to school.

*When I was studying in the classroom or playing base-
ball on the field (baseball had become a popular sport after
the war, though most people here believed it was a Japanese invention), before I knew it I would fall into a reverie
and be lost in a world of my own. Wasn't it possible, I mused,
that the person who was here right now wasn't the original
me, but was, rather, a new child that my mother had given
birth to after the death of her first son, who hadn't survived
that terrible fever? And wasn't it possible that she had told
this new child about everything that the original child had
ever seen and heard and read and done, and now I (the new
child) felt as though all those memories had been mine from
the start? And even now, wasn't it possible that I was thinking and talking with the vocabulary I had inherited from
the child who died, who used to use the very same words?*

*And all the other children who were in the classroom
and on the playing fields—wasn't it possible that they, too,
were children who had been born to take the places of the
dead children who would never grow to adulthood, and that
(like me) they had been told, secondhand, about everything
those dead children had ever seen and heard and read and
done? The proof of that, I thought, was that all of us were
using the same inherited language when we talked.*

*And the reason all of us had to go to school was to
make those inherited words our very own! Not just Japanese language, but science, math, even physical education;
we needed them all in order to inherit the language—and
by extension, the knowledge, culture, and social traditions—
of the children who had died. I realized that I couldn't become a new child to replicate and take the place of the child*

I thought had died of fever, just by going deep into the forest and comparing the trees and shrubs I saw before me to the illustrations in my botany book. That's why we were coming to school like this and studying and playing together every day . . .

I imagine that anyone who is reading this might think that the story I've just related is very strange indeed. And even while I've been recalling something that happened to me a very long time ago, at the beginning of that winter when I was finally over my illness and was able to return to school with quiet joy, I have a feeling, now that I'm an adult, that there are things I used to understand very clearly that now make no sense to me at all. On the other hand, I've talked here about a memory that I have never written about before in the hopes that those of you who are children (or "new" children) right now will understand this perfectly well.

"That's the gist of it, though I've only covered the first third of the essay or so," Ura said. "Of course, this is my impromptu translation from the German version, which was translated from English, so if it had been written in Mr. Choko's usual Japanese style I imagine it would probably be very different."

"I don't think so at all," Chikashi protested earnestly. "If he was writing with the intention of having it sound as if he were talking to children, I think Kogito would use exactly that sort of style. The one minor thing I would change in your translation is that my late mother-in-law would probably have been speaking to my husband in the local mountain dialect. But still—why did reading this essay make you decide to have your baby? The truth is, I think I understand your feelings, but I'd like to hear the explanation directly from you."

While Ura was reading the pages she'd torn from a magazine, she had been wearing a pair of square, thick-framed, rather mannish-looking reading glasses. Without taking them off, she looked back at Chikashi with a face that was full of intelligence and showed no sign of being on the verge of tears. She appeared to be blushing again, from the depths of her transparent, radiantly alive skin, but this time the stimulus was positive: excitement, rather than embarrassment.

"I was thinking that I could be the kind of mother who gave birth to a new child for the sake of the child who had died, and I could tell that new child about everything the dead child ever saw or read or did, and I could teach him all the words that the dead child used to know."

"So you're saying that you're going to give birth to a child to take the place of Goro . . ."

"You're probably thinking that's a pretty presumptuous plan, for someone who was still playing with dolls not so long ago."

"No," Chikashi responded, straight from the heart. "I wasn't thinking anything of the sort. It's just that our mother, and Umeko, and I—none of us can give Goro another chance at life. We're all past that age."

Ura looked at Chikashi with great intensity, and it was hard to tell whether her eyes held a plea for help or a declaration of defiance. "Earlier this year, you didn't accompany your husband when he went to Harvard to accept an honorary doctorate," she said. "I thought at the time that it was because you were in mourning for Goro. And that's how I knew that you were someone I could rely on and trust." So saying, Ura began to sob loudly without making any effort to cover her face, which had already turned bright red.

No matter who it was, when Chikashi was with someone who was crying—even watching brave Umeko, who had wept while she was talking into the television cameras after Goro's death—she couldn't help feeling ill at ease. In spite of that, Chikashi's heart was at peace at that moment (even though she didn't quite understand why her decision not to go on the Harvard trip held so much significance for Ura). She felt sympathetic toward the young woman who was crying her eyes out in front of her, shedding what seemed to be the heartfelt emotional tears of an adult rather than the self-indulgent tears of a child.

To echo something Goro had said in a different context, Chikashi could sense a healthy, natural harmony between the weeping Ura's outpouring of emotion and her voluntary restraint. *If this person is determined to keep her child and see things through to the end despite the difficulties her pregnancy has caused for her,* Chikashi was thinking, *then if I can help her out somehow, that's what I'm going to do.*

Ura got her tear ducts under control and regained her composure, and then she began to speak. The story she told to Chikashi, who was listening with total concentration, went like this:

At the beginning, when Ura called her parents from Berlin and told them the situation she was in, both her father and mother were very magnanimous about their daughter's "indiscretion," as they called it. They agreed that the only thing to do was to come home to Tokyo and have an abortion, and they offered to pay for everything. "What's done is done," they said, and after Ura had sensibly disposed of the accidental fruit of her indiscretion, she could once again settle down with new resolve and continue the academic journey she'd begun as an undergraduate at Berlin Free University, going on to a master's-degree course that would enable her to become a professional person. Moreover, after that, they wanted her to press ahead and get her PhD.

"Oh, you're a student at the Berlin Free University? Did you know that Kogito was teaching there during this past winter semester?"

When Chikashi interrupted the narrative with this question, Ura explained a trifle apologetically, "I was actually taking some prerequisite courses so that I could eventually go on to the Department of Economic Anthropology. The buildings are far apart, too, so I never even saw your husband from a distance. The guy—I'm sorry, the father of my child—was enrolled in the Japanese curriculum, so he registered for Kogito's lectures. Apparently he thought the classes were going to be in Japanese. But that wasn't the case, and he said that he found Mr. Choko's English difficult to understand, so he wasn't very conscientious about attending. However, he still wanted to get credit for the course, so he went to see Mr. Choko during office hours and asked whether it would be all right to write his report in Japanese. He was complaining afterward that your husband told him Japanese students had to write their reports in something other than Japanese—presumably German or English. We broke up shortly after that, so I don't know how it turned out . . ."

Ura's parents had met when they were classmates in college, and they both had their hearts set on careers as researchers

or scholars. But because they had married young, they needed
to find a way to make a living right away, and somehow they both
ended up doing something unrelated to academia. Her father was
a top executive in a trading company, and in the eyes of the world
he was probably considered a very successful person, but her
mother was obsessed with the idea that Ura should become a
college professor, as compensation for her parents' unrealized
dreams. That was why they thought Ura should go through the
ordeal of an abortion rather than getting married right out of
school, as her parents had done—not that marriage was a realistic option in this case. *Look at it this way,* they seemed to be saying. *If you learn a lesson you'll never forget, then something positive
will have come out of this mess you've gotten yourself into.* Ura was
aware that her parents' apparent magnanimity arose from that
kind of calculation.

If you put yourself in their shoes, that may seem like a
natural reaction, but when Ura announced that she had decided
to keep the baby and take it with her back to Germany, her
parents' attitude underwent a radical change. "There's no way
you could live alone in a foreign country, raising a child, and
still outshine your academic peers," they argued. They wouldn't
even consider her "self-indulgent" idea of giving birth to the baby
at home in Tokyo, nor would they approve her backup plan,
conceived in desperation, of going back to Germany and delivering the child there. They cut off her allowance and announced
that the place where she'd been living, an apartment that was
owned by her father, had already been sold to the company he
worked for and would henceforward be used as lodgings for their
representatives in Berlin. It was clear that her parents' game
plan was to drive Ura into a corner so that she would have no

choice but to terminate the pregnancy as quickly as possible. They wouldn't even buy her an airline ticket for the trip back to Berlin.

After three hours of intense conversation with Chikashi, Ura started to make noises about going home. Earlier, Chikashi had given Ura the color copy of Goro's drawing she had requested, but now she impulsively took it back and substituted the original drawing, which she quickly remounted in its frame. Chikashi asked her young visitor to return a week from then, at the same time. Until then, she urged Ura not to give in to her parents' pressure or threats.

Once Chikashi was alone, before Kogito and Akari came back from the swimming pool, she opened Sendak's *Outside Over There* and spent a long time looking at the illustration of the scene where Ida sets out to look for her baby sister by flying through the window into the night beyond but makes a tactical error by falling out backwards, like a scuba diver going over the side of a boat. Chikashi knew that in the present situation, she, too, needed to be very careful to conduct herself properly and to make sure she was always flying right side up.

9

The idea that she was Ida, and vice versa, was at the heart of Chikashi's powerful emotional response to Maurice Sendak's picture book. While she was rereading the book over and over, to the point where she knew it by heart, Chikashi made an English-Japanese translation for her own private use.

When she showed it to Kogito, he gave it back to her all marked up with a thin red pencil, because he was the sort of person who couldn't look at the original text of anything without wanting to mark it up and make corrections. Evidently realizing that his wife's interest in Sendak was not just a passing fancy, he gave Chikashi, for her own library, the pamphlet from the symposium at Berkeley along with a big book called *Angels and Wild Things: The Archetypal Poetics of Maurice Sendak,* in which he had already pointed out the photograph of Sendak taking a stroll with his German shepherd. Chikashi deduced that it would be all right for her to read those books and annotate them with her own red pencil.

Little by little, as if she were remembering the story of her own life, Chikashi worked her way through the Sendak picture book and the books about his work. As the days went by, she became aware that although her own "tale" and the story of Ida in the picture book converged in a profound way, there were also some clear points of disparity. It wasn't that the stories strayed apart and by chance ended up turning into a different thing; on the contrary, it was because of the divergences that the significance linking the two seemed to become even deeper.

Kogito had touched on this topic in his book *The Technique of the Novel,* and had revisited it in a revised paperback edition, as well as during a series of programs on educational television. Chikashi was very interested in Kogito's theory of reiterative divergence: that is, a difference that is developed slowly, rather like the method used to create the illusion of motion in a cartoon or anime, by means of tiny accretional changes from one advancing image to the next. According to Kogito's analysis, "divergence" takes on a special meaning when the progression of time is layered with the unfolding of the novel's narrative; in other words, meaning emerges from the progression of slight variations.

Chikashi felt that she was seeing that same principle of reiterative divergence at work in Sendak's book and in her own life story (which she just kept remembering over and over but never set down in words). Hoping to attain a more complete understanding, Chikashi tried sorting the respective elements into a list of specific topics. In a little sketchbook that she used for watercolors, she wrote down the similarities and differences between the concept of the "changeling," as Sendak explained it in his essay for the seminar, and her own thoughts about Goro and Akari as changelings of a sort.

1. The goblins came to steal Ida's baby sister, and a baby made of ice was left in its place. (But why wasn't Ida herself taken away? I knew that I didn't need to think about that, because I myself had never been stolen by goblins, metaphorical or otherwise.) Ida felt completely responsible, and her anguish was profound. She immediately set out to rescue her sister, but she made a blunder right at the start. Wrapped up in her mother's yellowish-gold rain cloak, she took off into the space beyond the window full of night, but she went out the window backwards and found herself flying faceup. How perfectly the text and the illustration portrayed Ida's adventures and her predicament!

2. When I gave Kogito the red leather briefcase containing the screenplay and storyboards that Goro left behind, Kogito immediately compared them with his collection of Tagame tapes, then sorted out the various scenes in the order that they were likely to be filmed, and returned them to me. After I had read the screenplay and storyboards once more, I asked Kogito which of the two versions of the last scene he thought Goro would have been likely to film. The reason I didn't ask Kogito which depiction was true to what really happened that night was because it was clear that he wasn't present, so I knew he wouldn't be able to answer that question.

"Since Goro wrote such a meticulously detailed screenplay and drew such complete storyboards, I think he must have been planning to film both versions," Kogito replied.

I was hoping for a more definitive answer. But instead of pursuing the matter, I asked Kogito what he actually knew for sure about the events depicted in these scenes, and that was when I realized that my husband, even now, didn't have the details of everything that had happened to Goro during that time.

Kogito believed that during the week after he introduced Goro to Peter, he was with them in the role of intermediary at all times; in other words, he didn't think Goro had ever met up with Peter when Kogito wasn't present as well. But I remembered that a few days before they went missing over that weekend, Goro cut all his classes at the high school, from morning, and took the streetcar to the CIE. He went to Peter's office, and the American showed him all his movie-related materials—books, magazines, clippings. Peter was exhorting Goro to attend his own alma mater, UCLA, as a foreign student, saying that Goro ought to major in filmmaking and follow in his father's footsteps by becoming a film director. When Goro came home that afternoon, he told me about this rather far-fetched idea with a kind of euphoric enthusiasm that struck me as terribly innocent and naïve. Given the national climate of postwar recovery, very few students had the opportunity to study abroad in those days so it wasn't likely to happen, but even so I felt exceedingly uneasy about the talk of Goro's going to UCLA. Wouldn't that be just the same as if he were abducted and spirited away to America?

The next day, or perhaps it was the day after that, Goro told me that he was going to go for a drive with Peter. I felt the same sense of foreboding and unease, especially when he told me that their destination was the depths of the mountains, where his friend Kogito had been born and raised. Goro was saying lightheartedly, as if it was all a big joke, that in that part of the country there were still a lot of odd people and curious beliefs.

When Goro left home to go on that "Saturday drive" and didn't return for two whole days, I was truly frightened, and my imagination ran wild. What if he was being held captive in some hidden fortress in a village deep in the mountains—or what if he had been forced aboard an American warship and carried off to the United States against his will? And then on the third day, close to dawn, when Goro finally returned in that strange, wretched state, with his equally disheveled friend in tow, it didn't exactly put my heart at ease.

3. What happened at the hidden fortress that last night, after Kogito and Goro left? I wasn't able to figure that out from the two versions of Goro's scenario-*cum*-storyboards, and the same doubt appeared to still be lurking in Kogito's and Goro's minds, many years later.

After Goro became a film director, and especially when *Dandelion* was such a huge hit in America, he often traveled to the United States, even going so far as to set up a branch office of his production company in Los Angeles. Even if the bloody incident described in the second scenario didn't really take place, Peter would probably have ended up being sent home for the offense of removing military equipment from the army base, even though the guns in question weren't operational— that is, assuming he got caught and that he was still alive. After he had been court-martialed and had served his prison term (or whatever his punishment turned out to be) and returned to civilian life, Peter would surely have stayed abreast of what was going on in the world of Japanese cinema, and one day— perhaps at some film festival or awards ceremony—he would have turned up to greet Goro, who had become an internationally acclaimed director.

Wasn't Goro dreaming of that sort of happy ending? But behind the façade of that rosy fantasy, Goro must have been horribly tormented, all his life, by the ominous shadow of those nightmarish memories—whether THAT had actually concluded with Scenario A or Scenario B. On the other hand, I couldn't help wondering why Peter's fate was such a mystery. It would have been a simple matter for Kogito or Goro to stop by the CIE and ask whether Peter had returned safely, but perhaps they couldn't bring themselves to go back there after all that had transpired that weekend.

4. From the way Goro behaved after that two-night absence, I gradually came to feel, ever more strongly, that my brother had changed in some fundamental way. Finally, and completely by accident, I ended up figuring out what it was. When I first saw the title page of Sendak's *Outside Over There,* I felt as if that book was speaking directly to me, and as I read it again and again, my eyes were opened to a number of new insights.

That late night when Goro came straggling in close to dawn I was, of course, happy that he had come home safely, but the reason I still felt anxious was because I had a strange sense that the person who had returned to our temple lodgings was a changeling who had somehow been substituted for the real Goro. I was certain that the Goro I knew from then on really was my brother—that was the point where my story deviated from the Sendak book. But even so (to put what I was feeling at that time into Sendak's words), the Goro who came home that night seemed to carry a subtle redolence of "Outside

Over There." And forever after THAT, wherever Goro was, I always detected a faint whiff of "Outside Over There," as well.

In Sendak's picture book, Ida and her baby sister (newly rescued from the goblins) are walking along a forest road. Ahead of them is a tree with a low-hanging branch that looks like a sinister arm, stretched across the path to block their way. In the shadow of the tree, five rather creepy-looking butterflies are flitting about, which does nothing to relieve Ida's continuing tension. In the discussion at the Berkeley seminar, Sendak himself talked about the darkly prophetic nature of this scene· "It's showing that Ida's hard-earned hour of peace and quiet is just a momentary thing. Every part of that picture is filled with signs that danger lies ahead. Her interlude of tranquillity, we gather, is going to be very short-lived."

"Is that so?" asked one of his colleagues at the seminar in a skeptical tone, whereupon Sendak offered a more detailed explanation.

"Yes, even now the tree looks as if it's about to reach out and grab her. And the five butterflies dancing around tell us that there are still the same number of goblins in the vicinity."

When Goro was attacked by the yakuza who were lying in wait when he pulled into his garage in his Bentley, the thing that frightened me more than anything was that I felt he had been stabbed by people who had come from "Outside Over There"—although of course at the time I hadn't yet heard that phrase. That reminds me: when Kogito had the joint of the big toe of his left foot crushed by some unidentified strangers armed with a rusty miniature cannonball, I went with him to the hospital. And when the incredulous doctor took me aside and asked politely whether my husband was by any chance a pathological liar, didn't I have an intuition that the violence that crushed Kogito's foot had originated in "Outside Over There"? That sort of attack happened more than once, and I always had a feeling that he wasn't sharing all the details.

5. For me, from the very beginning, there was always a part of Kogito that I couldn't understand. But I think the reason I married him in spite of that—granted, there were other factors as well—was because he was the one human being on earth who went along, as Goro's traveling companion, when Goro was taken to "Outside Over There."

When Kogito was still a young man, the Nigerian playwright and 1986 Nobel laureate, Wole Soyinka (whom Kogito had met at a conference at the University of Hawai'i), came to Japan, and I went along to hear the two of them take part in a public panel discussion. I was interested because I had heard from Kogito that Soyinka's play, *Death and the King's Horseman*, was a story about a guide who is supposed to escort a dead king to the world of the ancestors, in accordance with ancient Yoruba tradition, by ritually willing himself to die on the night of the king's burial. The thing is, I always had a feeling that Kogito was the guide who led Goro to "Outside Over There." I always wondered, too, whether Goro's vociferous opposition to my marriage to Kogito might have been due to the fact that he didn't want his sister's life to be intertwined with someone who had a connection with that dark, mysterious realm.

6. When Akari was born, there was a swelling on the back of his head that was like another little head. Maybe it was the result of passing through the birth canal with that thing attached, but his face was strangely narrow and covered with wrinkles. When Goro came to visit me in the maternity ward, I

was hurt and indignant when he took one look at his new nephew and said, "Yikes! He looks like a little old woman!" That comment was doubly wounding because I had hoped to give birth to a child who was as beautiful as Goro had been when he was small, and somewhere deep in my unconscious I must have wanted to exchange my flawed child for the lost Goro, in all his purity and innocence.

Knowing that my curiosity had been piqued by the idea of changelings, Kogito went out and bought a number of encyclopedia-type books about spirits of the dead, ghosts, elves, fairies, sprites, and the like. And in all the illustrations in those books, every one of the changelings was a baby with the face of a sly, cunning old trickster.

When the child I gave birth to grew up and, in spite of having to deal with cognitive difficulties and other impediments, began to create musical compositions, I felt that through the medium of music Akari had been able to recapture his own perfectly beautiful self. Sendak explains why he drew Mozart sitting at a pianoforte (and, I imagined, playing *The Magic Flute*) in a little house across the river that resembled an opera set, as Ida was passing through the frightening forest on her way home. Music always inspires Ida and lifts her spirits—and Sendak has often spoken about his personal affinity for Mozart.

7. When Goro made the film version of Kogito's novel, *A Quiet Life*, I was happy to hear the prolonged applause resounding in the darkened theater where we saw the preview, because I felt that by making this movie Goro, too, had regained his original self, in all its purity. But then, almost without stopping to take a breath, Goro had gone and jumped off the roof of a

building. What a terrible, wrongheaded way of leaving this world and going to "Outside Over There"!

Akari mourned the loss of his uncle by writing a composition for cello and piano titled, simply, "Goro." I believe that by creating that music Akari managed to recover from the feelings of sadness and terror that he himself didn't fully understand. Goro's death caused my husband a great deal of pain, and it was also the reason he became addicted to the Tagame tapes. But before too long won't Kogito, too, reach a point where he will be able to write a completely truthful account of THAT—which is to say, what happened "Outside Over There"? Maybe that process will reveal to him the true meaning of approaching death as a novelist—writing his way to the grave, so to speak.

I know that I have never once said to Kogito, in so many words, "I love you." That's just the way I am, and besides, I truly do believe that actions speak louder than words. When I see him with his hoary head pressed against the window glass for hours on end it makes my heart ache, but I would never mope around like that, and I know that no matter how long we go on living together we're never going to come to resemble each other, the way some couples do. All I can do is watch over him while he does his last work with complete freedom. But what's going to become of me? How shall I prepare for what lies ahead? What would Ida do, in my place? That's what Chikashi was thinking. And yet she also knew that asking herself those questions was just a way of summoning up the courage to deal with the answers she had already found.

After their first encounter amid the waning roses, Chikashi met and talked with Ura Shima any number of times, and when Chikashi laid out the plan she'd come up with, Ura was in complete agreement. That is, Chikashi would take the royalty payments she had received for the illustrations she'd drawn for two volumes of essays (mostly revolving around Akari) that Kogito had written, and she would use that small nest egg to cover Ura's expenses in finding and renting an apartment in Berlin. And when Chikashi bought a ticket for Ura to return to Germany, she also booked a ticket of her own so she could follow later on and help with Ura's postnatal care.

If Kogito asked about her reasons for doing all this, Chikashi thought she would answer that she didn't want to let any goblins (whatever deceptive form they might take) get close enough to kidnap Ura's baby. Moreover, she also intended to say that her thoughts on this matter were perfectly expressed in the concluding lines of *Death and the King's Horseman,* which Kogito had spot-translated and then quoted at the public discussion.

In Soyinka's play, the tragedy swells to a violent crescendo after the king's horseman has hastily gotten married and impregnated his very young bride, as one last fling for his mortal flesh. He is arrested and finally manages to kill himself in jail, as he is duty-bound to do.

Meanwhile, outside the jail, the women of the marketplace are swaying back and forth and singing a dirge, as the "mother of the marketplace," Iyaloja, chants these words:

Now forget the dead, forget even the living. Turn your mind only to the unborn.

THE END